D0048961

MACHADO DE ASSIS

MACHADO DE ASSIS

26 STORIES

Joaquim Maria Machado de Assis

Translated by

MARGARET JULL COSTA

AND

ROBIN PATTERSON

LIVERIGHT PUBLISHING CORPORATION

A division of W. W. Norton & Company

Independent Publishers Since 1923

NEW YORK | LONDON

Copyright © 2018 by Margaret Jull Costa and Robin Patterson
Foreword copyright © 2018 by Liveright Publishing Corporation

All rights reserved
Printed in the United States of America
First published as a Liveright paperback 2019

For information about permission to reproduce selections from this book,
write to Permissions, Liveright Publishing Corporation, a division of
W. W. Norton & Company, Inc., 500 Fifth Avenue, New York, NY 10110

For information about special discounts for bulk purchases, please contact
W. W. Norton Special Sales at specialsales@wwnorton.com or 800-233-4830

Manufacturing by LSC Communcations, Harrisonburg
Book design by Ellen Cipriano
Production manager: Anna Oler

ISBN 978-1-63149-598-4 pbk.

Liveright Publishing Corporation, 500 Fifth Avenue, New York, N.Y. 10110
www.wwnorton.com

W. W. Norton & Company Ltd., 15 Carlisle Street, London W1D 3BS

1 2 3 4 5 6 7 8 9 0

CONTENTS

FOREWORD

JOAQUIM MARIA MACHADO DE ASSIS wrote short stories throughout his career, publishing seven collections between 1870 and 1906, interspersed with his nine novels. Critics like to divide the novels into two sets, seeing the first four as slender and "romantic" (the author's own term) and the last five as complex, ironic masterpieces. We can't do anything like this with these stories, although we may say that with the years the continuing lightness of touch is applied to darker subjects. We move from young love and shallow social ambition to suicide and slavery, from portraits of manners to deep philosophical questions. But even this impression calls out for some correction. There are dark early stories too, and light late ones. So perhaps the firmer truth is that if we read the stories in sequence we get better at registering the darkness, at seeing through the light, so to speak.

Machado's short stories resemble those of Chekhov in their talent for saying too little (that is, just enough), but his closest literary companion, if we are looking for comparisons, is his almost exact contemporary Henry James, and especially in his longer pieces, where he appears as a great master of the form that James called "our ideal, the beautiful and blest nouvelle."

But more than either of these writers, Machado constantly engages in an open playfulness with the reader. In the stories as in the novels, his style of wit belongs with that of Henry Fielding or Laurence Sterne, whose work he knew well. We could also cite the excellent company he could not know he would come to keep, that of Vladimir Nabokov and Italo Calvino.

Machado has generally been well served by translators, although many of his stories have not until now appeared in English versions. But no one has caught the ease and grace of his prose as Margaret Jull Costa and Robin Patterson have. This achievement is important not only because it allows us

actually to see a style traveling from one language to another but because
the apparently casual movement of Machado's writing, so well rendered
here, allows all kinds of implications to arise as if of their own accord.

In one story, a single narrator tells us both that "there are no mysteries
for an author who can scrutinize every nook and cranny of the human heart"
and that one of his characters "had a series of thoughts that remained hidden from the author of this story." In others we meet imagined readers who
are "less canny," "less demanding," or "more experienced."

Machado teases his readers, but he also relies on them to be his accom-
plices; and sometimes he makes our complicity distinctly uncomfortable.
In the last story in this volume, "The Tale of the Cabriolet" (1906), a slave
arrives at the church of São José in Rio de Janeiro and asks the priest to
perform the last rites at a nearby house. The man seems "quite distraught"
about the news he is carrying, and the narrator comments:

> Anyone reading this with a darkly skeptical soul will inevitably ask
> if the slave was genuinely upset, or if he simply wanted to pique the
> curiosity of the priest and the sacristan. I'm of the view that any-
> thing is possible in this world and the next. I believe he was genu-
> inely upset, but then again I don't *not* believe that he was also eager
> to tell some terrible tale.

The sacristan in fact spends the rest of the story sniffing out the tale for
himself, not because he is a gossip or a meddler but because he loves tales.
"With him it was a case of art for art's sake." And with us? With Machado himself? Aren't we looking for tales, terrible or not? How far are we from being
upset?

The wit and grace of Machado's writing never diminish in these stories,
and the scene is almost always the same. We are watching the bourgeoisie
of Rio Janeiro at play, and occasionally trying to be serious. They misun-
derstand each other, they get married, they worry about dying, there is the
occasional violent murder. Money and the business of keeping up appearances are large questions. The characters read Hugo and Feydeau, Dumas
père and Dumas *fils*, and indeed the general tone is that of nineteenth-
century Paris as reconstructed in so many Latin American locations of that
time. Machado is gently mocking this class that believes only in borrowed
culture, or in what the Brazilian critic Roberto Schwarz calls "misplaced
ideas," but he is not advocating any kind of nativism.

When the chief character of "The Alienist," refusing distinguished positions offered to him by the king of Portugal, refers to the Brazilian city of Itaguaí as "my universe," we laugh because he seems to have made his world so small. But then we may also feel that his grandiose claim for his hometown and the exclusive fascination of others with the culture of Europe are simply rival forms of provincialism. There is a third way. We can take all culture, local and international, as our own, and this is the practice suggested by Machado's own allusions, as it is by those of Jorge Luis Borges, writing a little later in a neighboring Latin American country. "We cannot confine ourselves to what is Argentine in order to be Argentine," Borges says, and Machado might add that we don't have to believe that Paris is the capital of the world in order to read French literature.

In "Father Against Mother," first published in 1905, near the end of Machado's life, the stage belongs not to the bourgeoisie but to a lower social sector, that of a man who has been a clerk in a store, a bookkeeper to a notary, an office boy, and a postman, and is now a slave catcher. This was "one of the trades of the time," the narrator says, and of course "not . . . a very noble profession." This understatement has considerable force because the story has already informed us in some detail about "certain . . . implements" of slavery:

There was the neck iron, the leg iron, and the iron muzzle. The muzzle covered the mouth as a way of putting a stop to the vice of drunkenness among slaves. It had only three holes, two to see through and one to breathe through, and was fastened at the back of the head with a padlock.

Nothing very noble here, just ingenious mechanical cruelty. The idea of putting a stop to vice must be rank hypocrisy, but Machado continues to imitate the voice of moral piety:

[T]he muzzle also did away with the temptation to steal, because slaves tended to steal their master's money in order to slake their thirst, and thus two grave sins were abolished, and sobriety and honesty saved. The muzzle was a grotesque thing, but then human and social order cannot always be achieved without the grotesque, or, indeed, without occasional acts of cruelty.

The same tone is present when the narrator remarks that slave catchers

are "helping the forces who defend the law and private property," and that
their trade therefore may be said to have "a different sort of nobility, the
kind implicit in retrieving what is lost."

Slavery was finally abolished in Brazil in 1888, by which time Machado
had published four of his seven volumes of stories. The slave trade itself had
ended in 1850. Slaves are everywhere in these works, a fact of life, and not
often commented on. We can be sure Machado has little sympathy for the
woman who complains of her "feckless slaves," or the man who alternately
smashes plates over his slaves' heads and calls them by "the sweetest, most
endearing names." There is a slave who is "more brother than slave as regards
devotion and affection." But generally the slaves are just slaves, part of a sub-
jugated work force taken for granted. Is Machado endorsing the institution
of slavery? No, he is evoking a world and leaving the judgment of that world
to the reader's conscience. And in "Father Against Mother" he is slyly hoping
we will *not* share the opinions offered.

But then after evoking the horrible instruments and the fragile justifications for their use, he invites us to think of both the slave catcher and a caught
slave as human beings capable of love and distress. The slave catcher and his
wife are very much in love and desperately want to have a child. At last they
have a son, but then they have no money—the trade is not going well. They
are evicted from their house, and the man is about to leave his son at the
foundling hospital, when he sees and arrests a runaway female slave. He is the
father named in the title, and she is the mother. I won't reveal the plot further,
since the point is to signal the incredible poise and moral reach of Machado's
narrator. We don't exactly feel sympathy for the man, but we are tempted to
something like it, even if our minds are still full of the thought of those horrible implements described at the story's start. Of course the system doesn't
excuse him, but he didn't invent the self-serving regime of "human and social
order" that everyone is so happy to take as a norm.

Roberto Schwarz calls the story "How to Be a Bigwig," first published
in 1881, "the key to [Machado's] mature satirical style." This story has no
apparent darkness, and the reader's role is essential. The work is pure dialogue, so we don't even have Machado's narrator as an unreliable playmate
or misinformant. A father decides to have a chat with his son, who has just
turned twenty-one. The boy has "a private income and a college degree,"
he could do almost anything. "[P]olitics, the law, journalism, farming,
industry, commerce, literature, or the arts" all await him if he wants them.

Whichever he chooses, the father says, he will need a very particular second career, "just in case the others fail entirely, or do not quite meet [your] ambitions." This career is that of a bigwig. The boy doesn't understand, and the father explains. The bigwig is a man of "measure and reason," who fits the role so perfectly because he has nothing in his mind that might compete with the steady, empty gravity of his comportment. There are people who have ideas and conceal them, but it is far better, the father says, to have no ideas at all, and he finds in his son "the perfect degree of mental vacuity required by such a noble profession." It is important to waste a lot of time in the company of others, because "solitude is the workshop of ideas." A good habit is to go into bookstores to chat, rather than to read or buy anything, and a proper mastery of clichés is invaluable. "Publicity" is to be wooed, the young man's future speeches are to be packed with ready-made phrases, and above all, the father says, "whatever you do, never go beyond the boundaries of enviable triteness." He adds, "I forbid you to arrive at any conclusions that have not already been reached by others." The son thinks this is all going to be quite difficult, and the father agrees. The father, very pleased with himself, compares the advice he has just given to his son with Machiavelli's instructions in *The Prince*.

Clearly Machado's mature style involves a mockery of this complacent, cynical advisor and his passive, all too obedient client. But then we think perhaps the father is a satirist himself, mocking the world he lives in, and trying to provoke his son into the very thinking he says he should avoid. Does he really need to compliment him on his mental vacuity? And what about the son? Could he be playing a waiting game, aghast at his father's nonsense but not sure what to do? What if all three of these interpretative possibilities are in play? I doubt whether many of us can juggle them all at once, but there is nothing in the story that will allow us finally to choose among them. And the readings I have just suggested do not even include the one that is hiding in plain sight: the father may be sincere and also quite right. His views and the world he evokes are regrettable affairs, but since when did regret do away with the truth?

Machado's stories—delicate, funny, elusive, never bitter, often near to unacknowledged horrors—teach us how to read: how to read the stories themselves and how to read their often too complacent world, perhaps even more subtly than his novels teach their related lessons. We might think, in conclusion, of the masterpiece called "Midnight Mass" (1894), which begins with the voice of a man saying, "I've never quite understood a conversation I had with a lady many years ago, when I was seventeen and she was thirty." We think we already know this story, simply by learning the sexes and ages in question. In one sense we do. It is all about mutual desire and embarrassment and missed implications. But then we remember that the narrator is saying he doesn't understand it even now, and we wonder if we really are wiser than he is. What does it mean when nothing happens, and that same nothing lingers unforgettably in your life?

Michael Wood

INTRODUCTION

MUCH HAS BEEN MADE OF Joaquim Maria Machado de Assis's humble beginnings, and yet he, apparently, thought his own life to be of little interest and insisted that what counted was his work. Of course, in general terms, he's right, but, given his evolution from a poorly educated child of impoverished parents to Brazil's greatest writer and pillar of the establishment, a brief biographical note would not seem out of place. His paternal grandparents were mulattos and freed slaves. His father, also a mulatto, was a painter and decorator, his mother a washerwoman, a white Portuguese immigrant from the Azores. Both parents, however, could read and write, which was not common among working-class people at the time.

Machado was born in 1839 and brought up for the first ten years of his life on a country estate on the outskirts of Rio owned by the widow of a senator, Maria José de Mendonça Barroso Pereira, who became his godmother. Machado also had a sister, but she died when only four years old. Although he did go to school, he was far from being a star pupil. It seems, however, that Machado helped during mass at the estate's chapel, and was befriended by the priest, Father Silveira Sarmento, who may also have taught him Latin. Machado's mother died of tuberculosis when Machado was only ten. He then moved with his father to another part of Rio, and his father remarried. Some biographers say that his stepmother, Maria Inês da Silva, looked after him, and that Machado attended classes in the girls' school where she worked as a cook. Some say that he learned French in the evenings from a French immigrant baker. Others describe Machado as showing a precocious interest in books and languages. What is certain is that he published his first sonnet in 1854, when he was fifteen, in the *Periódico dos Pobres* (the *News-*

paper of the Poor). A year later, he became a regular visitor to a rather eccentric bookshop in central Rio owned by journalist and typographer Francisco de Paula Brito, which was a meeting place for all kinds of people, including artists and writers.

At seventeen, Machado was taken on as an apprentice typographer and proofreader at the Imprensa Nacional, where the writer Manuel Antônio de Almeida encouraged him to pursue a career in literature. Only two years later, the poet Francisco Otaviano invited him to work as writer and editor on the *Correio Mercantil*, an important newspaper of its day and one that is often mentioned in these stories. He wrote two operas and several plays, none of which met with great success, but he loved the theater and became involved in Rio's theater world from a very young age. Indeed, by the time he was twenty-one, he was already a well-known figure in intellectual circles. He worked as a journalist on other newspapers and founded a literary circle called Arcádia Fluminense. During all this time he read voraciously in numerous languages—it is said that, as well as modern literature, he set himself the lifetime goal of reading all of the universal classics in their original language, including ancient Greek. He built up an extensive library, bequeathed to the Brazilian Academy of Letters (of which he was cofounder and first president). Between the ages of fifteen and thirty, he wrote prolifically: poetry, plays, librettos, short stories, and newspaper columns, as well as translations from French and Spanish and all or most of Dickens's *Oliver Twist*. It would appear that his reported ill health, notably the epilepsy described by several of his biographers, did not in any way hold him back.

In 1867 he was decorated by the emperor with the Order of the Rose, and subsequently appointed to a position in the Ministry of Agriculture, Commerce, and Public Works. He went on to become head of a department, serving in that same ministry for over thirty years, until just three months before his death. The job, although demanding, left him ample time to write, and write he did: nine novels, nine plays, more than two hundred stories, five collections of poems, and more than six hundred *crônicas*, or newspaper columns. He also found time to marry, his wife proving crucial both to his happiness and to the expansion of his literary knowledge. Carolina Augusta Xavier de Novais, the sister of a close friend, was five years older than Machado; they fell in love almost instantly and were soon married, despite her family disapproving of her marrying a mulatto. Carolina was extremely well educated and introduced him to the work of

many English-language writers. They remained happily married for thirty-
five years, and when she died in 1904, at the age of seventy, Machado fell
into a deep depression. He wrote only one novel after her death, *Memorial
de Aires* (1908), and his last collection of stories, *Relíquias de Casa Velha*
(*Relics from an Old House*), published in 1906, is prefaced by a very tender
sonnet dedicated to her. On his death in 1908, he was given a state funeral.
And yet his occupation on his death certificate was given as "Civil servant,"
and when his final work, *Memorial de Aires*, was published later that year, it
went almost unnoticed.

That, very briefly, was his life, but, as Machado so rightly said, his writing *was* his life. He is probably best known to the English-language reader
for three novels: *Memórias Póstumas de Brás Cubas* (1881; published in
English as *The Posthumous Memoirs of Brás Cubas* or *Epitaph of a Small
Winner*), *Quincas Borba* (1891; published in English as *Philosopher or Dog?*),
and *Dom Casmurro* (1899). During his lifetime Machado published seven
collections containing six short stories. He wrote at least another 129 stories that remained unpublished in book form until after his death. Most
of the stories were originally published in daily newspapers—principally
Gazeta de Notícias—or in magazines—*Jornal das Famílias, A Estação*, and
Almanaque Brasileiro Garnier—with longer stories being published in serial
form, chapter by chapter. Our translation of those seven collections was
published by Liveright Publishing Corporation in 2018 as *The Collected Stories of Machado de Assis*—the first time all of those seventy-six stories had
been translated into English in their entirety. In condensing that number
to twenty-six stories for the purposes of this paperback edition, we have
endeavored to choose the most important and the most original, while
retaining a sense of the overall range and development of Machado's story-
writing. We have also unashamedly chosen our own favorites. The stories
appear here in the same order in which Machado arranged them in the
original seven collections.

The stories are predominantly set in Rio de Janeiro, then the capital of
the Brazilian Empire. (Dom Pedro I had been proclaimed emperor of Brazil
following independence from Portugal in 1822.) There are the occasional
sorties to places a day or two's journey from the city, such as Petrópolis, the
fashionable summer capital in the mountains just north of the city. Other
Brazilian towns, cities, and provinces get an occasional mention, but usually only as places that characters disappear to or return from, and vague

references to "the North," "the South," and "the interior" abound. Machado himself scarcely traveled beyond the immediate environs of the city, and while his characters do travel widely, including to Europe, we, the readers, bid farewell to them on the quayside and only hear about their distant exploits secondhand.

The city itself is often simply a stage set, almost an outdoor drawing room for his characters—although street names and landmarks are mentioned frequently, there is almost nothing in terms of physical description, and only the most fleeting references to its tropical climate. Machado is, of course, describing the city to its own inhabitants, and so the street names he mentions are signposts indicating social status, and the landmarks are the places familiar to the city's upper classes: the Passeio Público, which were elegant gardens on the shoreline of the bay between the city center and the well-to-do suburb of Catete; the Jardim Botânico, the magnificent botanical gardens a short ride out of the city on the other side of Corcovado mountain; and, most frequently of all, Rua do Ouvidor, the long, narrow street of fashionable shops, theaters, and cafés, "the Via Dolorosa of long-suffering husbands," as Machado described. Occasional references are made to the city's less salubrious quarters—the port area of Gamboa, and the former Valongo slave market.

In some cases, Machado is describing a city that no longer existed, for Rio, with its burgeoning population, was in the midst of an intense transformation from colonial backwater to imperial metropolis, and many of the stories are set several decades earlier. Events are often given a specific date, and geographical signposts are also in some cases historical ones. To a contemporary reader, of course, all of this would have been much clearer than it is to us; reading the stories today, we should simply bear in mind that the Rio the narrator presents as such a concrete and real world is often nothing of the sort.

Political considerations as well as artistic license may have encouraged Machado to place his stories at a discreet distance in time. During most of Machado's lifetime, Brazil was ruled by a constitutional, although often authoritarian, monarchy that was prone to factionalism and abrupt shifts in political favor. The last of these shifts led to the overthrow of the monarchy itself in 1889, precipitated by the abolition of slavery the previous year. The importation of slaves had been banned, at least in theory, in 1850, and, in 1871, a year after the publication of the first collection of these stories, the

"Law of the Free Womb" (or "Law of September 28," as Machado more discreetly refers to it) granted freedom to all children born to slaves after that date, thus making the eventual abolition of slavery inevitable, even if it took another seventeen years to come about. Machado rarely confronts the issue head-on. ("The Cane" and "Father Against Mother," both written after abolition, are notable exceptions.) Casual references to slaves abound; sometimes these are fond, sometimes cruel, but most often (and shockingly, to a modern reader) they simply pass without comment as a feature of everyday life. Machado was criticized by some of his contemporaries for not writing more openly about the evils of slavery. And yet, for the grandson of freed slaves writing for a predominantly slave-owning elite, we are left in little doubt about what a controversial and sensitive subject it was for Machado, or where his sympathies lay.

Other historical events and controversies are also noticeable by their near absence. Machado published his first collection of stories in the immediate aftermath of the War of the Triple Alliance (1864–70), a long and bloody conflict between Paraguay on one side, and Brazil, Argentina, and Uruguay on the other. And yet, perhaps precisely because memories of it were so raw, Machado refers to it only in passing in a handful of stories. Much later, however, "Maria Cora," first published in 1898, deals more explicitly with the then recent, and bloody, civil war of 1893–95 between the new republic and federalist rebels based in the southern state of Rio Grande do Sul. Machado, characteristically, dwells on the absurdity of the dispute.

To return to the stories themselves, some critics, perhaps somewhat dismissively, describe the early stories as belonging to Machado's "romantic phase," and while some of the plots could be viewed as such, the coolly ironic voice in which they are told already seems strikingly modern. In fact, that voice may have had its origins in two books that seem to have been a major influence on Machado's own writing: Laurence Sterne's *Tristram Shandy* and Xavier de Maistre's *Voyage Around My Room*. As readers, we are both fully aware that these stories are fiction and simultaneously drawn in as gullible readers. Our narrator is often unromantically unreliable, too, claiming that he can't tell us a character's name or doesn't know it or has forgotten, or declaring that what happened next was quite simply indescribable and then going on to describe it in detail. The first-person narrators are no better in this respect and, like us, have faulty memories and cannot necessarily be trusted.

Machado was passionately interested in chess and was himself a brilliant player. In his stories, too, he is very much the grand master, placing his pieces on the board and then seeing what happens, how those pieces react and interact.

One of Machado's main themes is obsession, and it is a strong presence from the earliest stories to the last. Some characters are merely obsessed with themselves, with losing their looks or their money; others are obsessed with the past or with rereading the same books over and over, or accumulating as much money as possible, or, in the marvelous Swiftian short story–cum–novella "The Alienist," with imposing a particular psychological theory on society as a whole, and here obsession veers into outright madness. Jealousy, too—another form of obsession—raises its ugly head in many stories; in some cases the characters land safely on the other side of a bout of jealousy, while others are left standing amid the debris of a marriage.

The repeated, seemingly erudite, references—Dante, Rabelais, Homer, Socrates, Pascal, Molière, Milton, Hegel, to name but a few—are part of that thread of sly humor running through his work. Is the assumption that we, the readers, are equally erudite or is he just playing with us, as he appears to be with the often slightly inaccurate quotations with which he sprinkles the stories?

More erudition, serious or otherwise, is on display in the stories that seem to spring straight from Machado's fertile imagination, spurred on by his own extensive reading. These take us to an ethereally exotic Thailand ("The Academies of Siam"), and even to the end of time itself, for an imagined encounter between Prometheus and Ahasuerus ("Life!"). The world of books and his imagination were for Machado a very real complement to that of the city and people around him, and they frequently collided, perhaps most vividly in "A Visit from Alcibiades," where our unnamed narrator sits down after dinner to read a chapter of Plutarch and accidentally summons up the physical presence of the ancient Greek statesman himself, leading to an incident requiring the attention of the Rio chief of police.

Often there are references to the process of writing itself. Nouns and adjectives chase each other around the clergyman's head in "The Canon, or the Metaphysics of Style"; verbosity and literary theory are lampooned in "How to be a Bigwig," and, in "Fame," a composer despairs at his loss of creative inspiration. Machado doesn't just tell us his stories—he pulls back the curtain and invites us to watch his own process of invention.

The overall tone of the stories is one of ironic distance, an assumption that we share the author's bemused fascination with the foibles and fates of these strange creatures, real or imagined. And while Machado gives us many male characters in all their flawed variety, there are possibly even more notable female characters: some faithful unto death and utterly decent, some infinitely vain, some maligned or scheming or flirtatious or indolent. Many of the stories appear to be filled with a kind of nostalgia for the past, as if the present were unsatisfactory or too shallow and transient, and yet the past is seen as something both irretrievable and inscrutable. One of Machado's most famous stories, "Midnight Mass," begins: "I've never quite understood a conversation I had with a lady many years ago, when I was seventeen and she was thirty." Machado's characters are often still puzzling over some past event, or hoping to set the record straight or to revive long-lost feelings. There are a few happy endings and happy marriages, but the stories abound in thwarted ambitions or loves unspoken or unrequited, even, in one story ("The Mirror"), a loss of all sense of identity, which can only be retrieved by the narrator standing in front of a mirror in his lieutenant's uniform to remind himself that he does exist.

Machado is also a brilliant stylist, but not in any flamboyant way. He writes in a Portuguese that is deceptively simple and straightforward, but he chooses his words with great precision, and has a superb ear for how people speak, whether it be a jaded old man, a frivolous young woman or a child. Machado's translator needs to remain very alert if he or she is to capture every nuance.

Machado sprang from the romantic-realist school of literature in Brazil, and his early stories were clearly written for the largely female readership of magazines and newspapers. The turning point came in 1881 with the publication of his novel *The Posthumous Memoirs of Brás Cubas*, almost immediately followed by *Miscellaneous Papers*, the collection of stories that included "The Alienist" and the six stories that follow it in this selection. For whatever reason, from that point on, his writing took a radically different path from that of his contemporaries. In the case of his short stories, we see a greater inventiveness in form and subject matter, frequently delving into the wilder reaches of his imagination in a way that is often thought to prefigure magical realism—"The Most Serene Republic," "The Canon, or the Metaphysics of Style," and "Canary Thoughts" being but three examples. Other stories, particularly the later stories such as "Father Against Mother,"

"Maria Cora," and the "The Tale of the Cabriolet" have their feet more firmly rooted in reality, with a mature and almost elegiac tone. This is not to denigrate the earlier stories, such as "August'a Secret" and "Luis Duarte's Wedding," which, if more conventional, are, by turns, touching and funny and satirical, and always hold the reader's attention, perhaps because of that alluring, coaxing, and often unreliable narrator.

It is difficult fully to measure the influence of Machado de Assis in other Latin American countries, or indeed elsewhere, but the first English translation of three of his short stories did not appear until 1921, and it was another thirty years before English translations of *The Posthumous Memoirs of Brás Cubas* (under the title *Epitaph of a Small Winner*) and *Dom Casmurro* were published. Other translations followed, including somewhat wider selections of his short stories (but never the complete collections), and it was not until the 1990s that eminent American and British writers began to take notice, notably Susan Sontag, Philip Roth, Harold Bloom, and Salman Rushdie. One could put this belated recognition down to a certain parochialism among British and American publishers and readers, or to a twentieth-century disdain for so much that was handed down from the nineteenth (ironical in Machado's case, given that he prefigured so much of what we think of as quintessentially "twentieth" century), but whatever the reason, we can at least take comfort that his precocious genius is being recognized now.

One reason for this may be that his stories bear witness to a desire to map the human psyche in all its endless variety. Is there perhaps a self-portrait in "The Tale of the Cabriolet," the last story in the last collection, published two years before his death? Machado introduces us to a sacristan who is obsessed (yet another one) with hearing and collecting other people's stories, not in order to approve or disapprove or to gossip about them, but for the sheer pleasure of the story itself, however mundane, bizarre, or terrible. This sounds very much like Machado himself, an avid and, yes, obsessive collector of other people's lives.

Margaret Jull Costa and Robin Patterson

MACHADO DE ASSIS

AUGUSTA'S SECRET

———

I

IT'S ELEVEN O'CLOCK in the morning.

Dona Augusta Vasconcelos is reclining on a sofa with a book in her hand. Adelaide, her daughter, is tinkering at the piano.

"Is Papa up yet?" Adelaide asked her mother.

"No," Dona Augusta said, without glancing up from her book.

Adelaide left the piano and went over to her mother.

"But it's so late, Mama," she said. "It's eleven o'clock. Papa does sleep a lot."

Augusta put the book down on her lap and, looking at Adelaide, said:

"That's because he came home very late."

"I've noticed that now Papa's never here to kiss me good night when I go to bed. He's always out somewhere."

Augusta smiled.

"You're still such a country bumpkin," she said. "You go to bed at the same time as the chickens. Things are different here. Your father has things to do at night."

"Is it to do with politics, Mama?" asked Adelaide.

"I don't know," said Augusta.

I began by saying that Adelaide was Augusta's daughter, and this information, so necessary to the story, was no less necessary in reality, because, at first sight, no one would ever have thought they were mother and daughter; Vasconcelos's wife was so young that mother and daughter looked more like sisters.

Augusta was thirty and Adelaide fifteen, but, comparatively speaking, the mother looked even younger than the daughter. She still had all the freshness of a fifteen-year-old, as well as something that Adelaide lacked: an awareness of her own beauty and youth, an awareness that would have been praiseworthy were it not combined with a vanity that was as immense as it was deep. She was of only average height, but nevertheless cut an imposing figure. Her skin was, at once, very pale and very rosy. She had brown hair and green eyes. Her long, shapely hands seemed made for loving caresses. Augusta, however, put her hands to better use, covering them in soft kid gloves.

All of Augusta's graces were there in Adelaide, but in embryonic form. You could tell that, by the time Adelaide was twenty, she would rival Augusta; meanwhile, she still retained certain childish qualities that somewhat masked those natural gifts.

And yet a man could easily have fallen in love with her, especially if he was a poet with a liking for fifteen-year-old virgins, perhaps because she was rather pale, and poets down the ages have always had a weakness for pale women.

Augusta dressed with supreme elegance, and while she did spend a lot of money on clothes, she made the most of those enormous expenditures, if one could describe it as "making the most" of them. To be fair, though, Augusta never haggled, she always paid the asking price for everything. She was proud of this, and felt that to behave otherwise was ridiculous and low-class.

In this, Augusta both shared the sentiments and served the interests of certain traders, who agreed that it would be dishonorable to beat them down on the price of their merchandise.

Whenever they spoke of this, Augusta's draper would tell her:

"Asking one price and then selling the product for a lower price is tantamount to confessing that you intended to swindle your customer."

The draper preferred to do so without confessing to anything.

And again to be fair to Augusta, we must acknowledge that she spared no expense in ensuring that Adelaide was always dressed as elegantly as she herself was.

And this was no small task.

From the age of five, Adelaide had been brought up in the country by some of Augusta's relatives, who were more interested in growing coffee than in spending money on clothes, and Adelaide grew up with those habits and those ideas. This is why arriving in Rio to rejoin her family proved to be a real transformation. She passed from one civilization to another; she lived through several years in the space of one hour. Fortunately for her, she had an excellent teacher in her mother. Adelaide changed, and on the day this story begins, she was already quite different, although still a long way behind her mother.

As Augusta was answering her daughter's curious question about what Vasconcelos actually did at night, a carriage drew up at the front door.

Adelaide ran to the window.

"It's Dona Carlota, Mama," she said.

A few minutes later, Dona Carlota entered the room. To introduce readers to this new character, I need say only that she was like a volume two of Augusta: beautiful, like her; elegant, like her; vain, like her, which is to say that they were the very best of enemies.

Carlota had come to ask Augusta to sing at a concert she was planning to give at home, a concert dreamed up purely as an opportunity to show off her magnificent new dress.

Augusta gladly accepted.

"How's your husband?" she asked Carlota.

"He's gone into town. And yours?"

"He's sleeping."

"The sleep of the just?" asked Carlota with a mischievous smile.

"Apparently," said Augusta.

At this point, Adelaide, who, at Carlota's request, had gone over to the piano to play a nocturne, rejoined them.

Augusta's friend said to her:

"I bet you've already got a sweetheart in your sights."

Greatly embarrassed, Adelaide blushed deeply and said:

"Don't say such things."

"I'm sure you do; either that or you're getting to the age when you certainly will have a sweetheart, and I'm telling you now that he'll be very handsome."

"It's still too early for that," said Augusta.

"Early!"

"Yes, she's only a child. She'll get married when she's ready, but that won't be for a while yet."

"I see," said Carlota, laughing, "you want to prepare her. And I entirely approve, but in that case, don't take her dolls away from her."

"Oh, she's given up dolls already."

"Then it will be very hard to fend off any sweethearts. One thing replaces the other."

Augusta smiled, and Carlota got up to leave.

"Are you going already?" said Augusta.

"Yes, I must. Bye-bye."

"'Bye!"

They exchanged kisses, and Carlota left.

Immediately afterward, two delivery boys arrived: one bearing some dresses and the other a novel, all of which had been ordered the day before. The dresses had cost a fortune, and the book was Ernest-Aimé Feydeau's novel *Fanny*, a satire on society manners.

II

At about one in the afternoon that same day, Vasconcelos rose from his bed.

He was about forty, good-looking, and endowed with a magnificent pair of graying side-whiskers, which gave him the air of a diplomat, something that he was a million miles from being. He had a smiling, expansive face, and positively oozed robust health.

He possessed a decent fortune and did not work, or, rather, he worked very hard at squandering said fortune, with his wife as enthusiastic collaborator.

Adelaide had been quite right about her father; he went to bed late, always woke up after midday, and left again in the evening, only to return the following morning in the early hours, which is to say that he made regular brief visits to the family home.

Only one person had the right to demand that Vasconcelos become a more assiduous visitor, and that was Augusta; but she said nothing. They got on well enough, though, because the husband, as a reward for his wife's tolerant behavior, denied her nothing and every whim of hers was quickly granted.

If Vasconcelos could not accompany her to every outing and every ball, a brother of his stood in for him; Lourenço was a commander of two different orders, an opposition politician, an excellent player of ombre, and, in his few moments of leisure, a most amiable fellow. He was what might be described as "an awkward so-and-so," at least as regards his brother, for while he obeyed his sister-in-law's every order, he would address the occasional admonitory sermon to his brother. Good seed that fell on stony ground.

Anyway, Vasconcelos had eventually woken up, and he woke in a good mood. His daughter was very pleased to see him; he spoke to his wife most affably, and she responded in kind.

"Why do you always wake up so late?" asked Adelaide, stroking his side-whiskers.

"Because I go to bed late."

"But why do you go to bed late?"

"What a lot of questions!" said Vasconcelos, smiling.

Then he went on:

"I go to bed late because my political duties require it. You don't know what politics is: it's something very ugly, but very necessary."

"I *do* know what politics is!" said Adelaide.

"All right, then, tell me."

"In the country, whenever they were beating up the magistrate, they always used to say that the motive was political, which I thought was really odd, because politically speaking, not beating him up would have made much more sense . . ."

Vasconcelos laughed out loud at his daughter's remark, and was just going off to have his breakfast when in came his brother, who could not resist saying:

"A fine time to be having breakfast!"

"Don't you start. I have my breakfast whenever I feel like it. Don't try and pin me down to certain hours and certain meanings. Call it breakfast or lunch, I don't mind, but whatever it is, I'm going to eat it."

Lourenço responded by pulling a face.

When breakfast was over, Senhor Batista arrived. Vasconcelos received him in his private study.

Batista was twenty-five and the typical man-about-town; excellent company at a supper attended by rather dubious guests, but absolutely useless in respectable company. He was witty and quite intelligent, but he had to be in the right situation for these qualities to be revealed. Otherwise, he was handsome, sported a fine mustache, wore expensive shoes, and dressed impeccably; he also smoked like a trooper, but smoked only the finest cigars.

"Only just woken up, have you?" Batista asked as he went into Vasconcelos's study.

"Yes, about three-quarters of an hour ago. I've just finished breakfast. Have a cigar."

Batista took one and sat down in a chair, while Vasconcelos struck a match.

"Have you seen Gomes?" asked Vasconcelos.

"Yes, I saw him yesterday. The big news is that he's given up society life."

"Really?"

"When I asked him why he hadn't been seen for over a month, he told me he was undergoing a transformation, and that the Gomes he was will live on only as a memory. Incredible though it may seem, he appeared to mean it."

"I don't believe him. He's having a joke at our expense. Any other news?"

"None, not unless you've heard any."

"Not a peep."

"Come on! Didn't you go to the Jardim yesterday?"

"Yes, there was a supper on there . . ."

"A family do, eh? I was at the Alcazar. What time did that 'family supper' end?"

"At four in the morning."

Vasconcelos lay down in a hammock, and the conversation continued along the same lines, until a houseboy came to tell Vasconcelos that Senhor Gomes was in the parlor.

"Ah, the man himself!" said Batista.

"Tell him to come up," ordered Vasconcelos.

The houseboy went back downstairs, but Gomes only joined them a quarter of an hour later, having spent some time chatting with Augusta and Adelaide.

"Well, long time no see," said Vasconcelos when Gomes finally entered the room.

"You haven't exactly searched me out," Gomes retorted.

"Excuse me, but I've been to your house twice, and twice they told me you were out."

"That was pure bad luck, because I hardly ever go out now."

"So you've become a hermit, have you?"

"I'm a chrysalis at the moment, and will reemerge as a butterfly," said Gomes, sitting down.

"Poetry, eh? Watch out, Vasconcelos."

This new character, the longed-for, long-lost Gomes, appeared to be about thirty. He, Vasconcelos, and Batista were a trinity of pleasure and dissipation, bound together by an indissoluble friendship. When, about a month before, Gomes stopped appearing in the usual circles, everyone noticed, but only Vasconcelos and Batista really felt his absence. However, they did not try too hard to drag Gomes out of his solitude, in case there was some ulterior motive on his part.

Nevertheless, they greeted Gomes like the prodigal son.

"Where have you been hiding? What's all this business about chrysalises and butterflies? Who do you think you're fooling?"

"No, really, my friends. I'm growing wings."

"Wings!" said Batista, trying not to laugh.

"Only if they're the wings of a sparrow-hawk ready to pounce on its prey . . ."

"No, I'm serious."

And Gomes seemed absolutely genuine.

Vasconcelos and Batista exchanged a sideways glance.

"Well, if it's true, tell us about these wings of yours and where exactly you want to fly," said Vasconcelos, and Batista added:

"Yes, you owe us an explanation, and if we, your family council, think it a good explanation, we will give our approval. If not, there'll be no wings for you, and you'll go back to being what you've always been."

"I second that," said Vasconcelos.

"It's quite simple. I'm growing angel's wings so that I can fly up into the heaven of love."

"Love!" exclaimed his two friends.

"Yes, love," said Gomes. "What have I been up until now? A complete wastrel, a total debauchee, squandering both my fortune and my heart. But is that enough to fill a life? I don't think so."

"I agree, it isn't enough, there needs to be something else, but the difference lies in how . . ."

"Exactly," said Vasconcelos, "exactly. It's only natural that the two of you will think otherwise, but I believe I'm right in saying that without a chaste, pure love, life is a mere desert."

Batista gave a start.

Vasconcelos fixed his eyes on Gomes.

"You're thinking of getting married, aren't you?" he said.

"I don't know about marriage, I only know that I'm in love and hope one day to marry the woman I love."

"Marry!" cried Batista.

And he let out a loud guffaw.

Gomes was so serious, though, and insisted so gravely on his plans for his own regeneration, that the two friends ended up listening with equal seriousness.

Gomes was speaking a strange language, entirely new on the lips of a man who, at any dionysian or aphrodisiac feast, was always the wildest and rowdiest of guests.

"So, you're leaving us, then?" said Vasconcelos.

"Me? Yes and no. You will find me in certain salons, but never again will we meet in theaters or in houses of ill repute."

"*De profundis* . . ." sang Batista.

"May we at least know where and who your Marion is?" asked Vasconcelos.

"She's not a Marion, she's a Virginie. At first I merely felt fond of her, then fondness became love and is now out-and-out passion. I fought it for as long as I could, but lay down my arms in the face of a far more potent force. My great fear was that I would not have a soul worthy to be offered to this gentle creature, but I do, a soul as fiery and pure as it was when I was eighteen. Only the chaste eyes of a virgin could have discovered the divine pearl beneath the mud in my soul. I am being reborn a far better man than I was."

"The boy's clearly insane, Vasconcelos. We should pack him off to the lunatic asylum this minute, and just in case he should suffer some new attack of madness, I'll leave right now."

"Where are you going?" asked Gomes.

"I have things to do, but I'll come and see you shortly. I want to find out if there's still time to haul you out of the abyss."

And with that he left.

III

Once they were alone, Vasconcelos asked:

"So you really are in love?"

"Yes, I am. I knew you'd find that hard to believe; I myself don't quite believe it, and yet it's true. I'm ending up where you began. For better or worse? For better, I think."

"Do you intend to conceal the person's name?"

"I'll conceal it from everyone but you."

"You clearly trust me, then . . ."

Gomes smiled.

"No," he said, "it's a necessary condition. You, above all men, should know the name of my heart's chosen one, for she's your daughter."

"Adelaide?" asked Vasconcelos in astonishment.

"Yes, your daughter."

This revelation was a real bombshell. Vasconcelos had never suspected such a thing.

"Do you approve?" asked Gomes.

Vasconcelos was thinking, and, after a few moments of silence, he said:

"My heart approves of your choice; you're my friend, you're in love, and as long as she loves you . . ."

Gomes was about to speak, but, smiling, Vasconcelos went on:

"But what about society?"

"What society?"

"The society that believes both you and me to be libertines; they're hardly going to approve."

"So that's a no, is it?" said Gomes sadly.

"No, it's not, you fool! It's an objection you could rebut by declaring that society is a great slanderer and famously indiscreet. My daughter is yours, on one condition."

"Which is?"

"Reciprocity. Does she love you?"

"I don't know."

"So you're not sure . . ."

"I really don't know, I only know that I love her and would give my life for her, but I have no idea if my feelings are requited."

"They will be. I'll test the waters. In two days' time, I'll give you my answer. To think you could be my son-in-law . . ."

Gomes's response was to fall into his friend's arms. The scene was verging on the comic when three o'clock struck. Gomes remembered that he'd arranged to meet another friend. Vasconcelos remembered that he had to write some letters.

Gomes left without speaking to the two ladies.

At about four o'clock, Vasconcelos was preparing to go out, when he was told that Senhor José Brito had come to see him.

When he heard this name, the normally jovial Vasconcelos frowned.

Shortly afterward, Senhor José Brito entered his study.

Senhor José Brito was, as far as Vasconcelos was concerned, a specter, an echo from the abyss, the voice of reality—a creditor.

"I wasn't expecting to see you today," said Vasconcelos.

"I'm surprised," answered Senhor José Brito with a kind of piercing calm, "because today is the twenty-first."

"I thought it was the nineteenth," stammered Vasconcelos.

"The day before yesterday it was, but today is the twenty-first. Look," said the creditor, picking up the *Jornal do Commercio* lying on a chair, "Thursday the twenty-first."

"Have you come for the money?"

"Here's the bill of exchange," said Senhor José Brito, taking his wallet out of his pocket and a piece of paper out of the wallet.

"Why didn't you come earlier?" asked Vasconcelos, trying to put off the evil hour.

"I came at eight o'clock this morning," replied the creditor, "and you were asleep; I came at nine, *idem*; I came at ten, *idem*; I came at eleven, *idem*; I came at noon, *idem*. I could have come at one o'clock, but I had to send a man to prison and I couldn't get away any earlier. At three, I had my dinner, and here I am at four o'clock."

Vasconcelos took a puff on his cigar to see if he could come up with some clever way of avoiding making a payment he had not been expecting.

Nothing occurred to him, but then the creditor himself gave him an opening.

"Besides," he said, "the time hardly matters, since I was sure you would pay me."

"Ah," said Vasconcelos, "that explains it. I wasn't expecting you today, you see, and so I don't have the money with me."

"What's to be done, then?" asked the creditor innocently.

Vasconcelos felt a glimmer of hope.

"You could wait until tomorrow."

"Ah, tomorrow I'm hoping to be present at the confiscation of assets from an individual I took to court for a very large debt, so I'm afraid I can't . . ."

"I see, well, in that case, I'll bring the money to your house."

"That would be fine if business worked like that. If we were friends, then obviously I would accept your promise and it would all be settled tomorrow, but I'm your creditor, and my one aim is to protect my own interests. Therefore, I think it would be best if you paid me today."

Vasconcelos smoothed his hair with one hand.

"But I don't have the money!" he said.

"Yes, that must be very awkward for you, but it doesn't upset me in the least; that is, it ought to upset me a little, because you clearly find yourself in a very precarious situation."

"Do I?"

"Indeed. Your properties in Rua da Imperatriz are mortgaged up to the hilt; the house in Rua de São Pedro was sold, and the money from the sale long since spent; your slaves have all left one by one, without you even noticing, and you recently spent a vast amount on setting up house for a certain lady of dubious reputation. You see, I know it all. More than you do yourself."

Vasconcelos was visibly terrified.

The creditor was telling the truth.

"But," said Vasconcelos, "what are we to do?"

"That's easy enough, we double the debt, and you give me a deposit right now."

"Double the debt, but that's—"

"Throwing you a lifeline. I'm really being very reasonable. Come on, say yes. Write me a note for the deposit now and we'll tear up the bill of exchange."

Vasconcelos tried to object, but it was impossible to convince Senhor José Brito.

He signed a note for eighteen *contos*.

When his creditor left, Vasconcelos began thinking seriously about his life.

Up until then, he had spent so wildly and so blindly that he hadn't noticed the abyss he himself had dug beneath his feet.

It had taken the voice of one of his executioners to alert him to this.

Vasconcelos pondered, calculated, and went through all his expenses and his obligations, and saw that he had less than a quarter of his fortune left—a mere pittance if he were to continue living as he had until now.

What to do?

Vasconcelos picked up his hat and went out.

It was growing dark.

After walking for some time, deep in thought, he went into the Alcazar.

It was a way of distracting himself.

There he found the usual people.

Batista came to greet his friend.

"Why the glum face?" he asked.

And for want of a better answer, Vasconcelos replied: "Oh, it's nothing. Someone just stepped on a corn."

However, a chiropodist standing nearby heard this remark and thereafter did not take his eyes off poor Vasconcelos, who was in a particularly sensitive mood that night. In the end, he found the chiropodist's insistent gaze so troubling that he left.

He went to the Hotel de Milão to have supper. However preoccupied he might be, his stomach was still making its usual demands.

In the middle of eating, he suddenly remembered the one thing he should never have forgotten: Gomes's proposal of marriage to his daughter.

It was like a ray of sunshine.

"Gomes is rich," thought Vasconcelos. "That's the best way out of all these problems. Gomes can marry Adelaide, and, since he's my friend, he couldn't possibly deny me what I need. For my part, I will try to get back what I've lost. What a stroke of luck!"

Vasconcelos continued his meal in the best of moods, then returned to

the Alcazar, where a few other lads and some members of the female sex
helped him to forget his troubles completely.

He returned peacefully home at his regular time of three o'clock in the
morning.

IV

The following day, Vasconcelos's first priority was to sound out Adelaide.
He wanted to do so, though, when Augusta was not there. Fortunately, she
needed to go to Rua da Quitanda to view some new fabrics, and she set off
with her brother-in-law, leaving Vasconcelos entirely free.

As readers will already know, Adelaide loved her father deeply, and
would do anything for him. She was, moreover, the soul of kindness. Vasconcelos was counting on those two qualities.

"Come here, Adelaide," he said, going into the living room. "How old
are you now?"

"Fifteen."

"Do you know how old your mother is?"

"She's twenty-seven, isn't she?"

"No, she's thirty, which means that your mother married when she was
just fifteen."

Vasconcelos paused to gauge the effect of these words, but in vain. Adelaide had no idea what he was getting at.

Her father went on:

"Have you considered marriage?"

She blushed deeply and said nothing, but when her father insisted, she
answered:

"Oh, Papa, I don't want to marry."

"You don't want to marry? Whyever not?"

"Because I don't want to. I'm happy living here."

"You could marry and still live here."

"Yes, but I don't want to."

"Come on, you're in love with someone, aren't you? Admit it."

"Don't ask me such things, Papa. I'm not in love with anyone."

Adelaide sounded so genuine that Vasconcelos could not doubt her sincerity.

"She's telling the truth," he thought. "I need to try another tack."

Adelaide sat down next to him and said:

"So can we just not talk about this anymore, Papa?"

"We must talk, my dear. You're still a child and can't yet look to the future. Imagine if I and your mother were to die tomorrow. Who would look after you? Only a husband."

"But there's no one I like."

"Not at the moment, but if your fiancé were a handsome lad with a good heart, you would come to like him. I've already chosen someone who loves you deeply, and you'll come to love him too."

Adelaide shuddered.

"I will?" she said. "But who is it?"

"Gomes."

"But I don't love him, Papa."

"Not now, I'm sure, but you can't deny that he's worthy of being loved. In a couple of months you'll be madly in love with him."

Adelaide said not a word. She bowed her head and started playing with one of her thick, dark plaits. She was breathing hard and staring down at the carpet.

"So that's agreed, is it?" asked Vasconcelos.

"But, Papa, what if I was unhappy?"

"That's impossible, my dear. You will be happy and you'll adore your husband."

"Oh, Papa," said Adelaide, her eyes brimming with tears, "please don't make me marry yet."

"Adelaide, a daughter's first duty is to obey her father, and I'm your father. I want you to marry Gomes and you will marry him."

To have their full effect, these words needed to be followed by a quick exit. Vasconcelos knew this and immediately departed, leaving Adelaide in deep despair.

She didn't love anyone. No other love object lay behind her refusal, nor did she feel any particular aversion for her would-be suitor. She merely felt complete indifference.

In the circumstances, marriage could only be a hateful imposition.

But what could Adelaide do? Who could she turn to?

She had only her tears.

As for Vasconcelos, he went up to his study and wrote the following lines to his future son-in-law:

Everything is going well. I give you permission to come and pay court to my daughter, and hope to see you married in a couple of months.

He sealed the letter and sent it off.

Shortly afterward, Augusta and Lourenço returned.

While Augusta disappeared up to her boudoir to change her clothes, Lourenço went looking for Adelaide, who was out in the garden.

Noticing that her eyes were red, he asked her why, but she denied she had been crying.

Lourenço didn't believe his niece and urged her to tell him what was wrong.

Adelaide trusted her uncle, almost because he *was* so direct and gruff. After a few minutes, Adelaide told Lourenço all about the scene with her father.

"So that's why you're crying, little one."

"Yes. How can I avoid getting married?"

"Don't worry, you won't have to. I promise."

Adelaide felt a shiver of joy.

"Do you promise, Uncle, to persuade Papa?"

"Well, persuade or prevail, one or the other, but you won't have to get married. Your father is a fool."

Lourenço went up to see Vasconcelos at precisely the moment when the latter was about to leave.

"Are you going out?" asked Lourenço.

"I am."

"I need to talk to you."

Lourenço sat down, and Vasconcelos, who already had his hat on, stood waiting for him to speak.

"Sit down," said Lourenço.

Vasconcelos sat down.

"Sixteen years ago—"

"You're going an awfully long way back. If you don't shave off half a dozen years, I can't promise to hear you out."

"Sixteen years ago," Lourenço went on, "you got married, but the difference between that first day and today is enormous."

"Of course," said Vasconcelos. *"Tempora mutantur, nos et—"*

"At the time," Lourenço went on, "you said you'd found paradise, a true paradise, and for two or three years you were a model husband. Then you changed completely, and paradise would have become a real hell if your wife were not the cold, indifferent creature she is, thus avoiding some truly terrible domestic scenes."

"But what has this got to do with you, Lourenço?"

"Nothing, and that isn't what I wanted to talk to you about. What I want to do is to stop you sacrificing your daughter on a whim, handing her over to one of your fellow dissolutes."

Vasconcelos sprang to his feet:

"You must be insane," he said.

"No, I'm perfectly sane and prudently advising you not to sacrifice your daughter to a libertine."

"Gomes isn't a libertine. True, he's led the life of many a young man, but he loves Adelaide and is a reformed character. It's a good marriage, and that's why I think we must all accept it. That's what I want, and I'm the one who gives the orders around here."

Lourenço was about to say more, but Vasconcelos had left.

"What can I do?" thought Lourenço.

V

Vasconcelos was not greatly bothered by Lourenço's opposition to his plans. He could, it's true, sow the seeds of resistance in his niece's mind, but Adelaide was easily persuaded and would agree with whoever she happened to be speaking to, and the advice she received one day would easily be overthrown by any contrary advice she was given the following day.

Still, it would be wise to get Augusta's support. Vasconcelos decided to do this as soon as possible.

Meanwhile, he needed to organize his own affairs, and so he found a lawyer, to whom he gave all the necessary documents and information, charging him with providing the necessary guidance and advising him on what measures he could take to oppose any claims made against him because of his debts or his mortgages.

None of this should make you think that Vasconcelos was about to change his ways. He was simply preparing himself to continue life as before.

Two days after his conversation with his brother, Vasconcelos went in search of Augusta, in order to speak frankly with her about Adelaide's marriage.

During that time, the future bridegroom, taking Vasconcelos's advice, was already paying court to Adelaide. If the marriage was not forced on her, it was just possible that she might end up liking the lad. Besides, Gomes was a handsome, elegant fellow and knew how to impress a woman.

Would Augusta have noticed his unusually assiduous presence in the house? That was the question Vasconcelos was asking himself as he went into his wife's boudoir.

"Are you going out?" he asked her.

"No, I'm expecting a visitor."

"Oh, who?"

"Seabra's wife," she said.

Vasconcelos sat down and tried to find a way of beginning the special conversation that had brought him there.

"You're looking very pretty today!"

"Really?" she said, smiling. "Well, I'm no different today than on any other day, and it's odd that you should pick today to say so."

"No, I mean it, you're even prettier than usual, so much so, that I could almost feel jealous."

"Come, now!" said Augusta with an ironic smile.

Vasconcelos scratched his head, took out his watch, wound it up, tugged at his beard, picked up a newspaper, read a couple of advertisements, then threw the paper down on the floor; finally, after a rather long silence, he thought it best to make a frontal assault on the citadel.

"I've been thinking about Adelaide," he said.

"Why's that?"

"She's a young woman—"

"A young woman!" exclaimed Augusta. "She's still a child."

"She's older than you were when you got married."

Augusta frowned slightly.

"What are you getting at?" she asked.

"What I'm getting at is that I want to make her happy by seeing her happily married. Some days ago, a very worthy young man asked me for her hand and I said yes. When I tell you the young man's name, I'm sure you'll approve. It's Gomes. They should marry, don't you think?"

"Certainly not!" retorted Augusta.

"Why not?"

"Adelaide's just a child. She's not old enough or sensible enough yet. She'll marry when the time is right."

"When the time is right? Are you sure the young man will wait that long?"

"Patience," said Augusta.

"Do you have something against Gomes?"

"No. He's a distinguished enough young fellow, but he's not right for Adelaide."

Vasconcelos hesitated before continuing; it seemed to him there was no point in going on. However, the thought of Gomes's fortune gave him courage, and he asked:

"Why isn't he?"

"Are you so very sure he's right for Adelaide?" said Augusta, avoiding her husband's question.

"Yes, I am."

"Well, whether he's right or not, she shouldn't get married now."

"What if she were in love?"

"What does that matter? She'll wait!"

"I have to tell you, Augusta, that we can't let this marriage pass us by. It's an absolute necessity."

"An absolute necessity? I don't understand."

"Let me explain. Gomes has a large fortune."

"So do we."

"That's where you're wrong," said Vasconcelos, interrupting her.

"How so?"

Vasconcelos went on:

"You'd have to find out sooner or later, and I think this is the moment to tell you the truth, and the truth is that we're poor, ruined."

Augusta heard these words, her eyes wide with horror.

"It's not possible!"

"Unfortunately, it is."

A silence fell.

"There, I've got her," thought Vasconcelos.

Augusta broke the silence.

"But if our fortune has gone, I'd have thought you would have something better to do than sit around talking about it; you need to rebuild that fortune."

Vasconcelos gave her a look of utter astonishment, and as if this look were a question, Augusta quickly added:

"Don't look so surprised. I think it's your duty to rebuild our fortune."

"That isn't what surprises me, what I find surprising is that you should put it like that. Anyone would think I was to blame."

"Oh," said Augusta, "I suppose you're going to say that I am."

"If blame there is, then we're both to blame."

"What, me too?"

"Yes, you too. Your wildly extravagant spending sprees have been a major contributor to our downfall; and since I've denied you nothing and still deny you nothing, I take full responsibility. And if that's what you're throwing in my face, then I agree."

Augusta gave an angry shrug and shot Vasconcelos a look of such scorn that it would have been valid grounds for divorce.

Vasconcelos saw the shrug and the look.

"A love of luxury and excess," he said, "will always have the same consequences, which are terrible, but perfectly understandable. The only way of avoiding them is to live more moderately, but that never even occurred to you. After six months of married life, you plunged into the whirlwind of fashion, and your little stream of expenditures became a vast river of profligacy. Do you know what my brother said to me once? He said that the reason you sent Adelaide off to the country was so that you would be free to live with no obligations of any kind."

Augusta had stood up and taken a few steps across the room; she was pale and trembling.

Vasconcelos was continuing this litany of recriminations, when his wife interrupted him, saying:

"And why did you not put a stop to my extravagance?"

"For the sake of domestic harmony."

"Lies!" she cried. "You wanted to live a free and independent life. Seeing me embarking on that life of excess, you thought you could buy my tolerance of your behavior by tolerating mine. That was the only reason. The way you live may be different from mine, but it's far worse. I may have squandered money at home, but you did the same out in the street. There's no point denying it, because I know everything; I know all the names of the succession of rivals you've given me, and I never said a word, and I'm not censuring you now, that would be pointless and too late."

The situation had changed. Vasconcelos had begun as judge and ended up as codefendant. It was impossible to deny, and arguing was risky and futile. He preferred to appear reasonable, even cajoling.

"Given the facts (and I accept that you're right), we are clearly both to blame, and I see no reason to lay all the blame on me. I should rebuild our fortune, I agree. And one way of doing that is to marry Adelaide off to Gomes."

"No," said Augusta.

"Fine, then, we'll be poor and even worse off than we are now; we'll sell everything . . ."

"Forgive me," said Augusta, "but I don't understand why you, a strong young man, who clearly played the larger role in bringing about this disaster, cannot throw yourself into rebuilding our squandered fortune."

"It would take a very long time, and meanwhile life goes on and we keep spending. As I've said, the best way out of this is to marry Adelaide off to Gomes."

"No, I don't want that," said Augusta, "I won't consent to such a marriage."

Vasconcelos was about to respond, but Augusta, having uttered these words, had flounced out of the room.

Vasconcelos followed a few minutes later.

VI

Lourenço knew nothing about this scene between his brother and sister-in-law, and, given Vasconcelos's stubbornness, he had decided to say nothing more; however, since he was very fond of his niece and did not want to see her handed over to a man of whose habits he disapproved, he decided to wait until the situation took a more decisive turn and only then play a more active role.

In order not to waste time, though, and possibly to gain the use of some potentially powerful weapon, Lourenço began an investigation intended to gather detailed information on Gomes.

Gomes, for his part, believed the marriage to be a certainty, and did not waste a moment in his conquest of Adelaide.

He could not fail to notice, however, that for no reason he could ascertain, her mother Augusta was becoming increasingly cold and indifferent, and it occurred to him that she was possibly the source of some opposition.

As for Vasconcelos, discouraged by the discussion in his wife's boudoir, he was hoping for better days and depending, above all, on the sheer force of necessity.

One day, however, exactly forty-eight hours after his argument with Augusta, he asked himself this question:

"Why is Augusta refusing to give Adelaide to Gomes in marriage?"

One question led to another, one deduction led to another, and a painful suspicion took root in Vasconcelos's mind.

"Does she perhaps love him?" he wondered.

Then, as if one abyss attracted another abyss, and one suspicion called to another suspicion, Vasconcelos thought:

"Were they once lovers?"

For the first time, Vasconcelos felt the serpent of jealousy biting his heart.

I say "jealousy" for want of a better word, because I don't know if what he was feeling was jealousy or merely wounded pride.

Could Vasconcelos's suspicions have any basis in fact?

To be honest, no. However vain Augusta might be, she remained faithful to her unfaithful husband, and for two reasons: her conscience and her temperament. Even if she hadn't been convinced of her duty as a wife, she would never break her wedding vows. She was not made for passions, apart from the ridiculous passions aroused by vanity. She loved her own beauty above all things, and her best friend was whoever would tell her she was the most beautiful of women; and yet, while she would give away her friendship, she would never give away her heart, and this is what saved her.

And there you have the truth: But who would tell Vasconcelos? Once he began to suspect that his honor was at risk, Vasconcelos started to review his whole life. Gomes had been a visitor to his house for six years and was

free to come and go as he liked. An act of betrayal would be easy enough.
Vasconcelos recalled words, gestures, glances, none of which had been of
any significance before, but which, now, began to look suspicious.

For two days, Vasconcelos was consumed by these thoughts. He did not
leave the house, and whenever Gomes arrived, he would observe his wife
with unusual interest; even the coldness with which she received Gomes
was, in her husband's eyes, proof of the crime.

Then, on the morning of the third day (Vasconcelos now rose early), his
brother came into his study, looking his usual disapproving self.

Lourenço's presence prompted Vasconcelos to reveal everything to him.

Lourenço was a man of good sense and, when necessary, could be sup-
portive too.

He listened to Vasconcelos, and when the latter had finished, he broke
his silence with these words:

"This is pure nonsense. If your wife is against the marriage, then it's for
some other reason."

"But it's the marriage to Gomes she's objecting to."

"Yes, because you presented Gomes to her as the suitor, but she might
well have reacted in the same way if you had suggested someone else. There
must be another reason; perhaps Adelaide has spoken to her and asked her
to oppose the marriage, because your daughter doesn't love Gomes and
can't marry him."

"But she will."

"That's not the only reason she can't marry him, though . . ."

"Go on."

"There's also the fact that the marriage is pure speculation on Gomes's
part."

"Speculation?" asked Vasconcelos.

"Just as it is for you," said Lourenço. "You're giving him your daughter
because you have your eyes on his fortune; and he will take her because he
has his eyes on yours . . ."

"But he—"

"He has nothing. He's ruined like you. I did a little investigating and
learned the truth. Naturally, he wants to continue the same dissolute life he
has led up until now, and your fortune is a way to do that."

"Are you sure of this?"

"Absolutely."

Vasconcelos was terrified. In the midst of all his suspicions, he had still clung to the hope that his honor would be saved and that the marriage would set him up financially.

Lourenço's revelation put paid to that hope.

"If you want proof, send for him and tell him you're penniless and, for that reason, cannot allow him to marry your daughter. Observe him closely and see what effect your words have on him."

There was no need to summon the suitor. An hour later, he called at the house.

Vasconcelos told him to come straight up to his study.

VII

After an initial exchange of courtesies, Vasconcelos said:

"I was just about to write and ask you to come."

"Why's that?" asked Gomes.

"So that we could talk about . . . about the marriage."

"Ah, is there a problem?"

"I'll explain."

Gomes grew more serious, foreseeing some grave difficulty.

Vasconcelos spoke first.

"There are certain circumstances," he said, "that need to be set out very clearly, so that there can be no room for misunderstanding . . ."

"I agree entirely."

"Do you love my daughter?"

"How often do I have to tell you? Yes, I do."

"And you will love her whatever the circumstances?"

"Yes, unless those circumstances might affect her happiness."

"Let's be frank, then, since, as well as the friend you have always been, you are now almost my son. For us to be discreet would be decidedly indiscreet."

"Indeed," said Gomes.

"I've just found out that my financial affairs are in a parlous state. I have overspent and am basically ruined, and it would be no exaggeration to say that I am now poor."

Gomes did his best not to look shocked.

"Adelaide," Vasconcelos went on, "has no fortune, not even a dowry. All I am giving you is a young woman, although I can promise you that she's a real angel and will make an excellent wife."

Vasconcelos fell silent, his eyes fixed on Gomes, as if, by scrutinizing his face he might discover what was going on in his heart.

Gomes should have responded at once, but, for a few minutes, a deep silence reigned.

Finally, he spoke.

"I appreciate your frankness and I will be equally frank."

"I would expect no less."

"It was certainly not money that prompted my love for your daughter; I trust you will do me the justice of believing that I am above such base considerations. Besides, on the day when I asked you for the hand of my beloved, I believed myself to be rich."

"Believed?"

"Yes, only yesterday, my lawyer told me the true state of my financial affairs."

"Not good, eh?"

"Oh, if only it were as simple as that. But it seems that for the last six months I have been existing thanks entirely to my lawyer's extraordinary efforts to scrape together some money, because he couldn't bring himself to tell me the truth. And I only found out yesterday!"

"I see."

"Imagine the despair of a man who believes himself to be wealthy and, one day, discovers he has nothing!"

"I don't need to imagine it!"

"I came here today feeling happy, because any happiness I still have resides in this house; but the truth is that I'm poised on the edge of an abyss. Fate has chosen to punish us both at the same moment."

After this explanation, to which Vasconcelos listened unblinking, Gomes tackled the thorniest part of the matter.

"As I say, I appreciate your frankness and I accept your daughter even without a fortune. I have no fortune, either, but I am still strong enough to work."

"You accept her, then?"

"Listen, I accept Dona Adelaide on one condition: that she wait awhile

for me to begin my new life. I intend going to the government and asking for
a post there, if I can still remember what I learned at school. As soon as I'm
properly established, I will come back for her. Do you agree?"

"If she's happy with that," said Vasconcelos, grasping at this one last
hope, "then it's decided."

Gomes went on:

"Good, speak to her about this tomorrow, and send me her response.
Ah, if only I still had my fortune, then I could prove to you how much I
love her."

"Fine, we'll leave it at that."

"I await your response."

And with that they said goodbye.

Vasconcelos was left with this thought:

"The only credible part of what he said is that he now has nothing. But
there's no point in waiting: hard on hard never made a brick wall."

As Gomes was going down the stairs, he was saying to himself:

"What I find odd is that he should tell me that he's poor at precisely the
moment when I've just discovered my own ruin. But he'll wait in vain: in
this case, two halves don't make a whole."

Vasconcelos went downstairs.

His intention was to tell Augusta the result of his conversation with
Adelaide's suitor. One thing, however, was still bothering him: Augusta's
refusal to agree to Adelaide's marriage without giving any reason.

He was still thinking about this when, as he walked through the hall, he
heard voices in the parlor.

It was Augusta talking to Carlota.

He was about to go in when these words reached his ears:

"But Adelaide's still such a child."

It was Augusta's voice.

"A child!" said Carlota.

"Yes. She's not old enough to marry."

"If I were you, I wouldn't stop this marriage, even if it does take place in
a few months' time, because Gomes really doesn't seem such a bad fellow."

"Oh, he isn't, but I just don't want Adelaide to marry."

Vasconcelos pressed his ear to the keyhole, anxious not to miss a single
word of this dialogue.

"What I don't understand," said Carlota, "is your insistence on her not marrying at all. Sooner or later, she'll have to."

"Yes, but as late as possible," said Augusta.

A silence fell.

Vasconcelos was growing impatient.

"Oh," Augusta went on, "if you knew how I dread Adelaide getting married."

"But why?"

"Why? You seem to have forgotten something, Carlota. What I dread are the children she'll have—my grandchildren! The idea of being a grandmother, Carlota, is just too awful!"

Vasconcelos breathed a sigh of relief and opened the door.

"Oh!" cried Augusta.

Vasconcelos bowed to Carlota, and, as soon as she left, he turned to his wife and said:

"I overheard your conversation with that woman."

"Well, it wasn't a secret conversation, but what exactly did you hear?"

Vasconcelos smiled and said:

"I heard the reason why you're afraid. I never realized that love of one's own beauty could lead to such egotism. The marriage to Gomes won't now happen, but if Adelaide ever does love someone, I really don't see how we can withhold our consent."

"We'll see," answered Augusta.

The conversation stopped there, because these two consorts were drifting ever further apart; one was thinking about all the noisy pleasures of youth, while the other was thinking exclusively about herself.

The following day, Gomes received a letter from Vasconcelos:

Dear Gomes,
Something unexpected has happened. Adelaide does not wish to marry. I tried to reason with her, but could not convince her.
Yours, Vasconcelos

Gomes folded up the letter and used it to light a cigar, then began thinking this deep thought:

"Where am I going to find an heiress who'll want me as a husband?"

If anyone knows of one, do tell him.

Vasconcelos and Gomes still sometimes meet in the street or at the Alcazar; they talk and smoke and take each other's arm, exactly like the friends they never were or like the rogues they are.

LUÍS DUARTE'S WEDDING

O<small>N</small> A<small>PRIL</small> 25, a Saturday morning, José Lemos's house was in total uproar. The dinner service that was only used on special occasions was being brought out, stairs and hallways were being scrubbed, and suckling pigs and turkeys were being stuffed ready to be roasted in the baker's oven across the road; there was no rest for anyone; something of great importance was about to happen.

José Lemos was in charge of sorting out the parlor. Perched on a bench, the worthy master of the house was attempting to hang the two engravings he had bought the day before from Bernasconi's; one depicted *The Death of Sardanapalus*, the other *The Execution of Mary Stuart*. He and his wife were having a bit of a battle about where to hang the first engraving. Dona Beatriz thought it indecent, all those men embracing a lot of naked women. Besides, such gloomy subjects were hardly suitable for a celebration. José Lemos had been a member of a literary society in his youth, and replied loftily that these were historical paintings, and that history had a place in every family. He might have added that not every family had a place in history, but that little joke was in even poorer taste than the engravings.

Keys in hand, but not quite as disheveled as the lady in Tolentino's famous satirical sonnet, Dona Beatriz was bustling back and forth between parlor and kitchen, issuing orders, chivying the slaves, gathering up clean tablecloths and napkins, and dictating shopping lists; in short, dealing with the thousand and one things that every mistress of the house has to deal with, especially on such an important day.

Now and then, Dona Beatriz would go to the foot of the stairs and shout:

"Girls, come down and have your breakfast!"

It seems, though, that the girls were in no hurry, because they only obeyed their mother's summons when it was past nine o'clock, and she had already called up to them eight times and was even about to climb the stairs to their bedroom—quite a sacrifice for such a plump lady.

The Lemos girls were two dark-haired beauties. One was about twenty, the other seventeen; both were tall and slightly overdressed. The older girl looked somewhat pale, while the other, pink-cheeked and cheerful, came down the stairs singing a popular ballad of the time. Of the two, it would seem that she was the happier one, but this was not the case; the happier sister was the older girl, who, that very day, was to tie the knot with young Luís Duarte, after a long and persistent courtship. She was pale because she had barely slept, even though she had never before suffered from insomnia, but then some illnesses do just come and go.

The two girls came downstairs, received their mother's blessing as well as a brief telling-off, then went into the parlor to talk to their father. José Lemos, who had just changed the position of the pictures for the seventh time, asked his daughters whether the engraving of Mary Stuart would be better on this side of the sofa or on the other. The girls said it would be best left where it was, and this verdict put an end to all José Lemos's doubts, and, deeming his work to be done, he went off to have his breakfast.

Also seated at the breakfast table, along with José Lemos, Dona Beatriz, Carlota (the bride), and Luísa, were Rodrigo Lemos and little Antonico, the Lemoses' two sons. Rodrigo was eighteen and Antonico six; Antonico was a miniature version of Rodrigo, with whom he shared another brotherly trait, that of extreme idleness. From eight o'clock in the morning on, Rodrigo was to be found doing one of two things: either reading the advertisements in the newspaper or going into the kitchen to find out when breakfast would be served. As for Antonico, he, as usual, had eaten a large plate of porridge at six o'clock, and then slept peacefully until the nursemaid called him.

Breakfast passed without incident. José Lemos preferred not to talk while he was eating; Rodrigo recounted the plot of the play he had seen the previous night at the Ginásio; and that was the sole topic of conversation. When breakfast was over, Rodrigo got up to smoke a cigarette, and José Lemos leaned his elbows on the table, peered out at the rather ominous sky over toward Tijuca, and asked if it looked as if rain were likely.

Antonico was just about to leave the table, having first asked permission, when his mother issued this warning:

"Now, Antonico, at supper, I don't want you to do what you always do when there are strangers here."

"What's that?" asked José Lemos.

"He gets all embarrassed and sticks his finger up his nose. Only silly boys do that, and I don't like it."

Deeply humiliated, Antonico ran into the parlor in floods of tears, Dona Beatriz hurried after her youngest child to comfort him, and everyone else left the table.

José Lemos checked with his wife that no one had been omitted from the guest list, and, having established that everyone who should have been invited was there, he prepared to go out. He was immediately given various errands: to ask the hairdresser to come early, to buy gloves for his wife and his daughters, to make sure the carriages were ready, to order ice cream and wines, and certain other tasks in which he could have been helped by young Rodrigo, had that namesake of El Cid not gone upstairs to sleep off breakfast.

No sooner had the soles of José Lemos's shoes touched the cobbled street outside than Dona Beatriz instructed her daughter Carlota to follow her into the parlor, where she immediately addressed her as follows:

"Today, my dear, your life as a single woman will end, and tomorrow, married life will begin. Having undergone the same transformation myself, I know from personal experience that being married brings with it many heavy responsibilities. Obviously, every woman must learn for herself, but I am following the example of your grandmother, who, on the eve of my marriage to your father, set out in clear and simple language what it means to be married and the great responsibility involved in this new role . . ."

Dona Beatriz stopped speaking, and Carlota, attributing her mother's silence to a desire for some response, said nothing, but planted a fond, filial kiss on her mother's cheek.

Had Luís Duarte's bride peered through the keyhole of her father's study only three days before, she would have realized that Dona Beatriz was reciting a speech composed by José Lemos, and that her silence was merely a temporary memory lapse.

It would have been far better had Dona Beatriz, like other mothers, offered advice drawn from her own heart and experience. Maternal love is the best rhetoric in the world, but Senhor José Lemos, who, ever since he was a young man, had preserved a certain literary bent, felt that, on such a solemn occasion, it would be wrong to run the risk of his better half making any grammatical errors.

Dona Beatriz resumed her speech, which was not that long, and concluded by asking if Carlota really did love her fiancé and was not, as did occasionally happen, getting married out of pique. Carlota replied that she loved her fiancé as dearly as she loved her parents, and the mother then kissed her daughter with a tenderness not provided for in José Lemos's prose.

At about two o'clock in the afternoon, José Lemos returned, dripping with sweat, but feeling very pleased with himself, because, as well as carrying out all his wife's errands as regards carriages, hairdressers, etc., he had managed to persuade Lieutenant Porfírio to join them for supper, something which, up until then, had been by no means certain.

Lieutenant Porfírio was what you might call an after-dinner speaker, possessing, as he did, the necessary confidence, fluency, and wit for the task. These fine gifts brought Lieutenant Porfírio certain benefits: he rarely dined at home on Sundays or on public holidays. You invited Lieutenant Porfírio on the tacit understanding that he would make a speech, just as you would expect a guest who was also a musician to play something. Lieutenant Porfírio came between dessert and coffee, and he did not come cheap, either; for if he was a good speaker, he was an even better trencherman. All things considered, his speech was amply paid for by the supper.

In the three days prior to the wedding, there had been much debate about whether the supper should precede the ceremony or vice versa. The bride's father felt that the ceremony should come after supper, and he was supported in this by young Rodrigo, who, with a wisdom worthy of a statesman, realized that, otherwise, supper would be very late. Dona Beatriz, however, thought it odd to go to church on a full stomach. This view had no theological or disciplinary basis, but Dona Beatriz had her own particular views on church matters, and she prevailed.

At around four o'clock, the guests began to arrive.

The first were the Vilela family, comprising Justiniano Vilela, a retired civil servant, Dona Margarida, his wife, and Dona Augusta, their niece.

Justiniano Vilela's head—if a breadfruit wearing a very elaborate cravat can be called a head—was an example of nature's prodigality when it came to making big heads. Some people declared, though, that his talent could not compete in size, even though a rumor to the contrary had been doing the rounds for some time. I don't know what talent those people were talking about, and the word can have various meanings, but Justiniano Vilela had certainly shown great talent in his choice of wife, who, in José Lemos's opinion, still merited ten minutes of anyone's attention, even though she was well into her forty-sixth year.

Justiniano Vilela was dressed as one usually does for such gatherings, and the only truly noteworthy thing about him were his English lace-up shoes, and since he had a horror of overly long trousers, he revealed a pair of fine, immaculate, brilliant white socks whenever he sat down.

As well as his pension, Justiniano owned a house and two houseboys, and he lived quite well on that. He disliked politics, but had firm opinions about public affairs. He played solo whist and backgammon on alternate days, spoke proudly of how things used to be in his day, and took a pinch of snuff between thumb and middle finger.

Other guests began arriving, but these were few in number, because only close friends and family would be attending the ceremony and the supper.

At half-past four, Carlota's godparents arrived, Dr. Valença and his widowed sister, Dona Virgínia. José Lemos rushed to embrace Dr. Valença, who, being a very formal, ceremonious fellow, gently pushed his friend away, whispering that, on such a day, gravity was of the essence. Then, with a serenity of which only he was capable, Dr. Valença immediately went to greet the mistress of the house and the other ladies.

He was a man of about fifty, neither fat nor thin, but endowed with a broad chest and an equally broad abdomen, which lent a still greater gravity to his face and manners. The abdomen is the most positive expression of human gravity; a thin man cannot help but make rapid movements, whereas to be seriously grave, one's movements need to be slow and measured. A truly grave man should take at least two minutes to take out a handkerchief and blow his nose. Dr. Valença took three minutes when he had a heavy cold and four when he was well. He really was the gravest of men.

I stress this because it is the best possible proof of Dr. Valença's intelligence. As soon as he had completed his law degree, he realized that the one quality guaranteed to earn other people's respect was gravity; and on inquiring into the nature of gravity, it seemed to him that it had nothing to do with profound thoughts or seriousness of mind, but with a certain "mystery of the body," as La Rochefoucauld calls it, and, the reader will add, mystery is like the flag carried by neutral forces in time of war, ensuring that no one dares to examine the cargo it conceals.

Anyone discovering so much as a wrinkle in Dr. Valença's tailcoat could feel well pleased with himself. His vest had only three buttons and formed a kind of heart-shaped opening from chest to neck. An elegant collapsible top hat completed Dr. Valença's toilette. He was not handsome in the effeminate sense that some apply to male beauty, but there was a certain correctness about the lines of his face, which was covered with a veil of serenity that suited him perfectly.

Once Dr. Valença and his sister had arrived, José Lemos asked after the bridegroom, but Dr. Valença said he hadn't seen him. It was five o'clock by then. The guests, who assumed they had arrived too late for the ceremony, were unpleasantly surprised by this delay, and Justiniano Vilela whispered to his wife that he regretted not having had something to eat beforehand. This was precisely what young Rodrigo Lemos was doing, having realized that supper would not start until seven.

Dr. Valença's sister—of whom I said but little before because she was one of the most insignificant creatures ever produced by the race of Eve— immediately wanted to go and see the bride, and Dona Beatriz went with her, leaving her husband free to strike up a conversation with Senhor Vilela's very attractive wife.

"Bridegrooms today do seem to take their time," Justiniano remarked philosophically. "When I got married, I was the first to arrive at the bride's house."

To this comment—which was entirely the child of Vilela's implacable stomach—Dr. Valença replied:

"I can perfectly understand the delay and the nervousness one must feel in the presence of one's bride."

Everyone smiled at this defense of the absent groom, and the conversation grew more animated.

At the very moment when Vilela was discussing with Dr. Valença the advantages of the old days over the present, and the young women were talking about the latest fashions, the bride entered the room, escorted by her mother and godmother, with, bringing up the rear, the very attractive Luísa, accompanied by her little brother, Antonico.

It would be both inexact of me and in poor taste if I, as narrator, were not to mention that an admiring murmur filled the room.

Carlota was a truly dazzling sight in her white dress, her garland of orange blossom, her thinnest of thin veils, and wearing no other jewels but her dark eyes, bright as diamonds of the first water.

José Lemos broke off his conversation with Justiniano's wife and gazed at his daughter. The bride was introduced to the guests and led over to the sofa, where she sat down between her godparents. Balancing his top hat on his knee and steadying it with one expensively gloved hand, Dr. Valença showered his goddaughter with praise, which made the young woman simultaneously blush and smile—an amiable alliance between vanity and modesty.

Steps were heard on the stairs, and José Lemos was preparing himself for the arrival of his future son-in-law, when the Valadares brothers appeared at the door.

Of the two brothers, the oldest, called Calisto, had a sallow complexion, an aquiline nose, brown hair, and round eyes. The younger brother, called Eduardo, only differed from his brother in having a distinctly ruddier complexion. They were both employed by the same company and were in the full bloom of middle age. There was another distinguishing feature: Eduardo wrote poetry when he was allowed time away from the accounts books, while his brother was the enemy of anything that had so much as a whiff of literature about it.

Time passed, and still no sign of either the groom or Lieutenant Porfírio. The groom was essential to the wedding, and the lieutenant to the supper. It was half-past five when Luís Duarte finally arrived. Each guest sang a private "Hallelujah."

He appeared at the door of the parlor and gave a low bow to the assembled guests, so gracefully and ceremoniously that Dr. Valença felt rather envious.

He was a young man of twenty-five, very fair-skinned, with a blond mustache and no beard at all. He wore his hair parted in the middle. His lips were so red that one of the Valadares brothers whispered to the other: "It looks like he's wearing lipstick." In short, Luís Duarte cut a figure guaranteed to please any twenty-year-old girl, and I would have no compunction in calling him an Adonis if he really were one, which he was not. At the appointed hour, bride and groom, parents and godparents set off for the church, which was nearby; the other guests remained in the house, with Luísa and Rodrigo doing the honors, although Rodrigo had to be summoned by his father, and duly appeared dressed in the very latest fashion.

"They're like a pair of turtledoves," said Dona Margarida Vilela when the wedding party had left.

"Very true," agreed the Valadares brothers and Justiniano Vilela.

Young Luísa, who was, by nature, a cheerful girl, soon livened up the proceedings, chatting animatedly to the other girls, one of whom she invited to play something on the piano. Calisto Valadares suspected that the Scriptures had made a serious omission in excluding the piano from among the plagues of Egypt. The reader can imagine the look on his face when he saw one of the girls get up and walk over to that vile instrument. He uttered a long sigh and went to study the two engravings purchased the day before.

"Magnificent!" he said, standing before *The Death of Sardanapalus*, a painting he loathed.

"Yes, it was Papa who chose it," said Rodrigo, and these were the first words he had spoken since entering the room.

"He obviously has good taste," said Calisto. "Do you know what the painting is about?"

"It's about Sardanapalus," replied Rodrigo, undeterred.

"I know that," retorted Calisto, hoping to continue the conversation, "what I meant was—"

He could not finish his sentence, because the first chords on the piano rang out.

Eduardo, who, in his role as poet, was expected to love music, too, strolled over to the piano and leaned on it in the melancholy pose of a man conversing with the muses. Meanwhile, his brother Calisto, finding it impossible to avoid the cascade of notes, went and sat down near Vilela, with whom he struck up conversation, beginning by asking what time it was by his watch. This touched Vilela's tenderest nerve.

"It's getting late," he said in a faint voice. "Nearly six o'clock."

"They can't possibly take much longer."

"Can't they! It's a long ceremony and they might not have been able to find the priest . . . Marriages should be held at home and at night."

"My feelings exactly."

The girl finished playing, and Calisto breathed easily again, while Eduardo, still leaning on the piano, applauded enthusiastically.

"Why don't you play something else?" he asked.

"Yes, Mariquinhas, play something from the *La Sonnambula*," said Luísa, making her friend sit down again.

"Yes, *La Son—*"

Eduardo did not finish the word; he saw before him his brother's two disapproving eyes, and winced. Stopping in midsentence and wincing could simply have been the sign of a painful corn. And so everyone thought, except for Vilela, who, assuming the others felt as he did, was convinced that some sharp hunger pang must have interrupted Eduardo's thoughts. And as does sometimes happen, Eduardo's pain awoke his own, so much so that Vilela's stomach issued a real ultimatum, to which he succumbed, and, taking advantage of his position as family friend, he wandered off into the house, on the excuse that he needed to stretch his legs.

A marvelous idea.

The table was already laid with a few inviting titbits, and to Vilela's eyes it seemed like a veritable cornucopia. Two pastries and a croquette were the palliatives Vilela sent to his rebellious stomach, and his viscera had to make do with that.

Meanwhile, Dona Mariquinhas was still performing miracles on the piano; Eduardo, now leaning at the window, appeared to be contemplating suicide, while his brother played with his watch chain and listened to Dona Margarida complaining about her feckless slaves. As for Rodrigo, he was pacing up and down, occasionally saying:

"Goodness, they're taking their time!"

It was a quarter past six and still no carriages; some people were already growing impatient. At twenty past six, there was a faint rattle of wheels; Rodrigo ran to the window. It was a passing cab. At twenty-five past six, everyone thought they could hear carriages approaching.

"They're here!" exclaimed a voice.

But it was nothing. What they heard seemed to be (and forgive me for marrying this noun to this adjective) a kind of aural mirage.

At six thirty-eight, the carriages arrived. There was great excitement in the parlor; the ladies ran to the windows. The men eyed each other like conspirators gathering their forces for some major undertaking. The wedding party entered. The houseboys, waiting in the hallway for the bride and groom, took their young mistress completely by surprise by showering her with rose petals. And, as there always are on such occasions, many kisses and words of congratulations were given.

José Lemos was beside himself with joy, but the news that Lieutenant Porfírio had still not arrived put something of a damper on his high spirits.

"We must send for him."

"At this hour?" murmured Calisto Valadares.

"Without Porfírio the party won't be complete," José Lemos whispered to Dr. Valença.

"Papa," said Rodrigo, "I don't think he's coming."

"That's impossible!"

"It's nearly seven o'clock."

"And supper is ready," added Dona Beatriz.

Dona Beatriz's words carried considerable weight with José Lemos, which is why he did not insist. They had no choice but to give up on the lieutenant.

However, the lieutenant was a man accustomed to awkward situations, someone you would want on your side in a tight corner. No sooner had Dona Beatriz finished speaking, with José Lemos mentally agreeing with her, than the voice of Lieutenant Porfírio was heard on the stairs. The master of the house gave a sigh of relief and satisfaction. The long-awaited guest entered the room.

The lieutenant belonged to that happy class of men who are apparently ageless; some thought he was thirty, others thirty-five, and others forty; some even went as high as forty-five, and they could all have been right, for the lieutenant's face and brown side-whiskers fitted all these hypotheses. He was thin, of medium height, and dressed rather stylishly; indeed, there was really very little to distinguish him from any other dandy. The one thing that jarred slightly was his way of walking; Lieutenant Porfírio's feet were so widely splayed that you could almost draw a straight line between right foot and left. However, everything has its compensations, and in his case, these were the flat patent-leather shoes he wore, revealing a fine pair of woolen socks whose surface was smoother than a billiard ball.

He entered with a grace that was peculiar to him. To greet the bride and groom, he bent his right arm so that the hand holding his hat was behind his back, then bowed very low, and remained in that posture, so that (from a distance) he resembled one of those old-fashioned lampposts.

Porfírio had been a lieutenant in the army before being discharged, which suited him perfectly, because he had then gone into the furniture business and made quite a sum of money. He was not particularly good-looking, but, despite this, some ladies said he was more dangerous than a can of dynamite. This was clearly not because of the way he spoke, because he had a particularly sibilant *s*, saying, for example: At your ssservisss, sssenhora . . .

When Porfírio had finished greeting everyone, José Lemos said to him: "We're expecting great things from you tonight!"

"Ah," Porfírio responded with exemplary modesty. "Who would dare to speak in the presence of such erudition?"

He said these words, meanwhile thrusting four fingers of his left hand into his vest pocket, a gesture he cultivated because he did not know what to do with that awkward arm, which is always such a trial to novice actors.

"But why are you so late?" asked Dona Beatriz.

"Reproach me if you must, dear lady, but spare me the embarrassment of having to explain a delay for which there is no excuse in the code of friendship and good manners."

José Lemos smiled and glanced around at the others as if the lieutenant's words bestowed on him some kind of reflected glory. Despite the pastries he had eaten, Justiniano Vilela still felt ineluctably drawn toward the supper table and exclaimed rather vulgarly:

"Well, at least you arrived in time for supper!"

"Yes, let's all go in, shall we?" said José Lemos, offering an arm each to Dona Margarida and to Dona Virgínia, while the other guests followed behind.

The joy of pilgrims reaching Mecca could not have been greater than that of the guests when they saw the long table, groaning with roast meats and desserts and fruit and set with china dishes and glasses. They all sat down in their allotted places. For some minutes, there was a silence such as the silence that precedes a battle, and only when this was broken did general conversation begin.

"When I introduced young Duarte to the household a year ago, who would have thought that he would one day be the delightful Dona Carlota's bridegroom?" said Dr. Valença, wiping his lips on his napkin and glancing benevolently across at the bride.

"Yes, who would have thought it?" said Dona Beatriz.

"It must have been the hand of Fate," said Dona Margarida.

"It was indeed," replied Dona Beatriz.

"If it was the hand of Fate," said the groom, "I thank the heavens for taking such an interest in me."

Dona Carlota smiled, and José Lemos thought these words in excellent taste and worthy of a son-in-law.

"Fate or chance?" asked Lieutenant Porfírio. "I favor the latter, myself."

"That's where you're wrong," said Vilela, looking up from his plate for the first time. "What you call chance is, in fact, Fate. Weddings and winding sheets are made in heaven."

"Oh, so you believe in proverbs, do you?"

"They contain the wisdom of the people," said José Lemos.

"No, they don't," said the lieutenant. "For every proverb stating one thing, there's another stating the opposite. Proverbs lie. I think it was simply a very happy happenstance, or, rather, the law of the attraction of souls that led Senhor Luís Duarte to be drawn to the charming daughter of our very own Amphitryon."

José Lemos had no idea who Amphitryon was, but confident that, if Porfírio mentioned him, he must be all right, he smiled and thanked Porfírio for what seemed to be a compliment, meanwhile helping himself to some jelly, which Justiniano Vilela assured him was excellent.

The young women were whispering and smiling, the bride and groom were absorbed in an exchange of sweet nothings, while Rodrigo was picking his teeth so loudly that his mother shot him one of those fulminating glances that were her weapon of choice.

"Some jelly, Senhor Calisto?" asked José Lemos, his spoon in the air.

"Yes, just a little," said the man with the sallow face.

"The jelly is excellent," Justiniano said for the third time, and his wife was so embarrassed by these words that she could not conceal a grimace of distaste.

"Ladies and gentlemen," said Dr. Valença, "I propose a toast to the happy couple."

"Bravo!" said a voice.

"Is that it?" asked Rodrigo. "We want a longer toast than that."

"Mama, I want some jelly!" said Antonico.

"I'm not one for making speeches. I am simply raising my glass to the bride and groom."

Everyone drank.

"I want jelly!" insisted Antonico.

Dona Beatriz felt her inner Medea stirring within her, but respect for her guests prevented any unpleasant scene. The good lady merely said to one of the servants:

"Give this to the young master, will you?"

Antonico received the dish and began eating the way children eat when they're not really hungry: he would raise a spoonful to his mouth and spend an age rolling the contents of the spoon around between tongue and palate, while the spoon, pushed to one side, formed a slight lump in his right cheek. At the same time, he kept kicking his legs, repeatedly hitting first the chair and then the table.

While this was going on—not that anyone took much notice—the conversation continued. Dr. Valença was discussing with one lady the excellence of the sherry, and Eduardo Valadares was reciting a poem to the young woman sitting next to him.

Suddenly José Lemos stood up.

"Ssshh!" hissed everyone.

José Lemos picked up a glass and said to those around the table:

"I am not prompted to speak by any feeling of pride to be addressing such an illustrious audience. I am responding to the higher duty of courtesy, friendship, and gratitude, that most preeminent, sacred, and immortal of duties."

The audience would have been cruel indeed not to applaud these words, and their applause did not ruffle the speaker in the least, for the simple reason that he knew the speech by heart.

"Yes, ladies and gentlemen, I bow before that duty, the holiest and most imperious of all duties. I drink to my friends, to those steadfast adherents of the heart, those vestal virgins, both male and female, devotees of the pure flame of friendship! To my friends! To friendship!"

To be honest, the only person who understood the utter nullity of José

Lemos's speech was Dr. Valença, who was himself no intellectual, which is why he rose to propose a toast to their host's oratorical talents.

These two toasts were followed by the customary silence, until Rodrigo turned to Lieutenant Porfírio and asked if he had perhaps left his muse at home.

"Yes," said one lady, "we want to hear you. People say you speak really well."

"Me, senhora?" replied Porfírio with all the modesty of a man who believes himself to be another golden-mouthed Saint John Chrysostom.

Once the champagne had been poured and handed around, Lieutenant Porfírio stood up. Vilela, who was some distance away, cupped one hand behind his right ear, while Calisto, fixing his eyes firmly on the tablecloth, appeared to be counting every thread. José Lemos alerted his wife, who, at that moment, was trying to tempt the implacable Antonico with a sweet chestnut; all other eyes were on the speaker.

"Ladies! Gentlemen!" said Porfírio. "I do not intend to rummage around in the very heart of history, that teacher of life, to find out what marriage was like in the earliest ages of humankind. We all know, ladies and gentlemen, what marriage is. Marriage is the rose, the queen of the garden, unfurling its red petals in order to protect us from the thistles and thorns and barbs of life . . ."

"Bravo!"

"Delightful!"

"If marriage is what I have just revealed to your auricular senses, there is no need to explain the joy, the fervor, the loving impulse, the explosions of sentiment felt by all of us seated here around this altar to celebrate our dear and much-loved friend."

José Lemos bowed his head so low that the tip of his nose touched a pear that lay in front of him on the table, and Dona Beatriz turned to Dr. Valença, who was sitting beside her, and said:

"Doesn't he speak well! He's like a walking dictionary!"

Porfírio went on:

"I fear, ladies and gentlemen, that I lack the necessary talent to speak on the subject . . ."

"Nonsense! You speak really well!" cried many of the people surrounding him.

"You are far too kind, but I still do not feel I have the necessary talent to
grapple with a subject of such magnitude."

"Nonsense!"

"Please, you're too kind," said Porfírio, bowing. "While, as I say, I may
lack that particular talent, I have more than enough goodwill, the same
goodwill that led the Apostles to plant the religion of Calvary in the world,
and thanks to that same feeling, I can sum up in just a few words my toast
to the happy couple. Ladies and gentlemen, two flowers were born in two
different flower beds, both of them beautiful, both highly scented, both full
of divine life. They were born for each other; they were the carnation and
the rose; the rose lived only for the carnation, the carnation lived only for
the rose: along came a breeze and mingled the perfumes of the two flowers,
and they, knowing they were in love, ran to meet each other. The breeze
was godfather to that union. The rose and the carnation are united in the
embrace of love, and sitting over there is the breeze honoring our gathering
here tonight."

No one was expecting this breeze; the breeze was Dr. Valença.

Loud applause greeted this speech combining Calvary with the carnation and the rose. Porfírio sat down with a sense of having done his duty.

Supper was coming to an end; it was half-past eight; a few musicians
were arriving in readiness for the ball. Still to come was a poem by Eduardo
Valadares and a few more toasts to all those present and to those few who
were absent. Now, with the liqueurs coming to the aid of the muses, battle
was engaged between Lieutenant Porfírio and Justiniano Vilela, although
the latter had to be urged to enter the arena. Once all subjects for debate
had been exhausted, Porfírio proposed a toast to the army and its generals,
and Vilela a toast to the union of all the provinces of the empire. When
everyone else got up from the table, the two of them remained behind,
warmly toasting all the practical and useful ideas of this world and the next.

The ball that followed was a very lively affair that went on until three
in the morning.

No untoward incident marred the party. At most, there was a rather
regrettable remark made by José Lemos when dancing with Dona Margarida, during which he boldly lamented her fate at having a husband who
preferred proposing endless toasts to enjoying the priceless good fortune of
being by her side. Dona Margarida smiled, and the incident went no further.

At two o'clock, Dr. Valença left with his family, and, despite the generally familiar tone of the party, he had not lost one iota of his habitual gravity all evening. Calisto Valadares escaped when Dona Beatriz's younger daughter got up to sing at the piano, and the other guests gradually drifted away.

When the party finally drew to a close, the last two tribal leaders of the dining table were still toasting all and sundry. Vilela's final toast was to the world's progress via coffee and cotton, while Porfírio raised his glass to universal peace.

However, the real toast of that memorable feast was the little baby born in January of the following year, who, if he survives his teething pains, will live to continue the Lemos dynasty.

THE ALIENIST

Chapter 1

ON HOW ITAGUAÍ GAINED A MADHOUSE

THE CHRONICLES OF ITAGUAÍ record that a long time ago there lived in the town a certain physician, Dr. Simão Bacamarte, the son of landed gentry, and the greatest physician in Brazil, Portugal, and the two Spains. He had studied at Coimbra and Padua. At thirty-four, he returned to Brazil, the king being unable to persuade him to stay in Coimbra, running the university, or in Lisbon, attending to matters of state.

"Science," he said to His Majesty, "is my sole concern; Itaguaí is my universe."

Having said this, he took himself off to Itaguaí and devoted himself body and soul to the study of science, alternating healing with reading, and demonstrating theorems with poultices. When he reached the age of forty, he married Dona Evarista da Costa e Mascarenhas, a lady of twenty-five, the widow of a magistrate, who was neither pretty nor charming. One of his uncles, an inveterate meddler in the affairs of others, was frankly surprised by his nephew's choice, and told him so. Simão Bacamarte explained to him that Dona Evarista combined physiological and anatomical attributes of the first order: good digestion, regular sleep, a steady pulse, and excellent eyesight; she was thus fit to provide him with healthy, sturdy, intelligent off-spring. If, in addition to such accomplishments—the only ones with which a sensible man should concern himself—Dona Evarista's features were some-what badly formed, then, far from regretting it, he thanked God, since he would thereby not run the risk of ignoring the interests of science in the exclusive, trivial, and vulgar contemplation of his wife.

Dona Evarista failed to live up to her husband's expectations, providing him with neither sturdy nor sickly offspring. Science is an inherently patient pursuit, and so our doctor waited three years, then four, then five. At the end of this period, he carried out a rigorous study of the matter, reread all the authoritative texts, Arab and otherwise, which he had brought with him to Itaguaí, sent inquiries to the Italian and German universities, and con-cluded by advising his wife to follow a special diet. The eminent lady, accus-tomed to eating only succulent Itaguaí pork, did not heed her husband's advice, and to her understandable but unpardonable resistance we owe the total extinction of the Bacamarte dynasty.

Science, however, has the ineffable gift of curing all ills; our physician immersed himself entirely in the study and practice of medicine. It was at this point that one of its lesser nooks and crannies caught his particu-lar attention: that pertaining to the psychic, to the examination of cere-bral pathology, also known at that time as alienism. Nowhere in the colony, or even the kingdom, was there a single expert on this barely explored, indeed almost unexplored, subject. Simão Bacamarte saw an opportunity for Lusitanian, and in particular Brazilian, science to garland itself in "ever-lasting laurels"—the expression he himself used, but only in a moment of ecstasy within the privacy of his own home; externally, he was modest, as befits a man of learning.

"The health of the mind," he declaimed, "is the worthiest occupation for a physician."

"For a *true* physician," added Crispim Soares, the town's apothecary and one of Bacamarte's close friends and supper companions.

Among the other sins of which it stands accused by the historians, the Itaguaí municipal council had made no provision for the insane. Those who were raving mad were simply locked away in their own homes, and remained uncured and uncared-for until death came to rob them of the gift of life. The tamer ones were left to wander the streets. Simão Bacamarte quickly resolved to remedy such harmful practices; he requested permission from the council to build a hospital that would provide treatment and lodgings for all the lunatics of Itaguaí and the surrounding towns and villages, in return for a stipend payable by the municipality when the patient's family were unable to do so. The proposal excited the curiosity of the whole town and met with great resistance, for it is always hard to uproot absurd or even merely bad habits.

"Look here, Dona Evarista," said Father Lopes, the parish priest, "why don't you try to interest your husband in a trip to Rio de Janeiro? All this studying can't be good for him; it gives him all sorts of strange ideas."

Greatly alarmed, Dona Evarista went to her husband and told him that she was filled by various consuming desires, in particular the desire to go to Rio de Janeiro and eat everything that he considered would help with his previously stated objective. But with the rare wisdom that distinguished him, the great man saw through this pretense and replied, smiling, that she need have no fear. He then went straight to the town hall, where the councillors were debating his proposal, and defended it with such eloquence that the majority resolved to authorize his request, and, at the same time, voted through a local tax destined to fund the treatment, board, and lodging of any of the insane who had no other means of support. It was not easy to find something new to be taxed, for everything in Itaguaí had already been earmarked. After lengthy study, the tax was imposed on the use of plumes on funeral horses. Anyone who wished to add feathers to the headdresses of horses drawing a hearse would pay two *tostões* to the council for each hour that elapsed between the time of death and the final blessing at the graveside. The town clerk got himself in a terrible muddle calculating the potential revenue arising from the new tax, and one of the councillors, who had little faith in the doctor's undertaking, asked that the clerk be relieved of such a pointless task.

"The calculations are entirely unnecessary," he said, "because Dr. Bacamarte's scheme will never come to anything. Whoever heard of putting all the lunatics together in the same building?"

The worthy councillor was mistaken, and the doctor's scheme was duly implemented. As soon as he had received permission, he began to build the house. It was in Rua Nova, which was the finest street in Itaguaí at the time; it had fifty windows on each side, a courtyard in the middle, and numerous cells to house the inmates. An eminent Arabist, the doctor had read in the Koran that Muhammad had declared that the insane were to be revered, for Allah had deprived them of their wits so that they would not sin. This struck him as a beautiful and profound idea, and he had it engraved on the front of the house. However, since he feared the parish priest's reaction, and through him that of the bishop, he attributed this sentiment to Benedict VIII, an otherwise pious fraud, which earned him, over lunch, a lengthy exposition from Father Lopes on the life of that eminent pontiff.

The asylum was given the name "Casa Verde" on account of its green shutters, this being the first time such a color had been used for that purpose in Itaguaí. It was inaugurated with great pomp; people flocked from all the towns and villages near and far, as well as from the city of Rio de Janeiro itself, to attend the ceremonies, which went on for seven days. Many patients had already been admitted, and their relatives were able to see for themselves the paternal care and Christian charity with which they would be treated. Basking in her husband's glory, Dona Evarista put on her finest clothes and decked herself in jewels, flowers, and silks. During those memorable days, she was a veritable queen; despite the rather prim social customs of the time, everyone made a point of visiting her two or even three times, and their praise went beyond mere compliments, for—and this fact is a credit to the society of the time—they saw in Dona Evarista the happy wife of an illustrious man, a man of lofty ideals, and, if they envied her, theirs was the blessed and noble envy of true admirers.

At the end of seven days, the public festivities came to an end; Itaguaí finally had a madhouse.

Chapter 2

A FLOOD OF LUNATICS

Three days later, Simão Bacamarte, now the town's official alienist, opened his heart to Crispim Soares the apothecary, and revealed to him his most intimate thoughts.

"Charity, Senhor Soares, certainly enters into my way of thinking, but only as seasoning—like salt, you might say—for that is how I interpret Saint Paul's words to the Corinthians: "And if I know all that can be known, and have not charity, I am nothing." The real purpose, though, in this Casa Verde project of mine, is to carry out an in-depth study of madness in its various degrees, classifying each type and finally discovering both the true cause of the phenomenon and its universal remedy. Therein lies the mystery of my intentions. And I believe that in this I will be doing a great service to humanity."

"A very great service indeed," said the apothecary.

"Without this asylum," continued the alienist, "I could achieve very little, but with it, my studies will have much greater scope."

"Much greater," echoed the apothecary.

And they were right. Lunatics from all the neighboring towns and villages poured into the Casa Verde. There were the violent, the meek, the monomaniacs, indeed the entire family of all those strangers to reason. By the end of four months, the Casa Verde was a hive of activity. The initial cells soon filled up, requiring a further wing with thirty-seven more cells to be added. Father Lopes admitted that he had never imagined there to be so many lunatics in the world, nor that some cases would be so totally inexplicable. There was, for example, the ignorant and uncouth young man who, every day after breakfast, would launch into an academic lecture embellished with tropes, antitheses, and apostrophes, with a few Greek and Latin flourishes and the odd snippet from Cicero, Apuleius, and Tertullian. The priest could scarcely believe his ears. What! A boy he had seen only three months before playing handball in the street!

"Oh, I agree," said the alienist, "but the truth is there before your very eyes, Your Reverence. It happens every day of the week."

"As far as I'm concerned," replied the priest, "this can only be explained by the confounding of languages in the Tower of Babel, as described in the Scriptures; since the languages were all mixed up in ancient times, it must be easy to switch between them when reason is absent."

"That could well be the divine explanation for the phenomenon," agreed the alienist after a moment's reflection, "but it is not impossible that there is also a human, indeed purely scientific, explanation, and that is what I intend to look into."

"Very well, but it troubles me, it really does."

There were three or four inmates who had been driven to madness by love, but only two stood out because of the curious nature of their symptoms. The first, a young man of twenty-five by the name of Falcão, was convinced he was the morning star; he would stand with his legs apart and his arms spread wide like the rays of a star, and stay like that for hours on end asking if the sun had come up yet so that he could retire. The other fellow paced endlessly around the rooms or courtyard, and up and down the corridors, searching for the ends of the earth. He was a miserable wretch whose wife had left him to run off with a dandy. As soon as he discovered she was gone, he armed himself with a pistol and went after them; two hours later, he found them by a lake and murdered them both with exquisite cruelty. The avenger's jealousy was satisfied, but at the price of his sanity. That was the beginning of his obsessive wanderings, relentlessly pursuing the fugitive lovers to the ends of the earth.

There were several interesting cases of delusions of grandeur, the most notable of which was the wretched son of a poor tailor, who would recount to the walls (for he never looked anyone in the face) his entire family pedigree, as follows:

"God begat an egg, the egg begat the sword, the sword begat David, David begat the purple, the purple begat the duke, the duke begat the marquis, the marquis begat the count, and that's me."

Then he would slap his forehead, snap his fingers, and repeat it again, five or six times in a row: "God begat an egg, the egg begat . . ." and so on.

Another of the same type was a humble clerk who fancied himself to be the king's chamberlain; another was the cattle drover from Minas Gerais who had a mania for distributing herds of cattle to everyone he met: he would give three hundred head to one, six hundred to another, twelve hundred to someone else, and so on. I won't mention the many cases of religious monomania, save for one fellow who, on account of his Christian name being João de Deus—John of God—went around saying he was John *the* God, and promising the kingdom of heaven to whoever would worship him and the torments of hell to everyone else. Then there was Garcia, a university graduate, who never said anything because he was convinced that if he uttered so much as a single word, all the stars would fall from the sky and set the earth on fire, for such was the power with which God had invested him.

That, at least, is what he wrote on the piece of paper provided by the alienist not so much out of charity as out of scientific interest.

For the alienist's dedication was more extraordinary than all the manias residing in the Casa Verde; it was nothing short of astonishing. Bacamarte set about putting in place two administrators, an idea of Crispim Soares's that Bacamarte accepted along with the apothecary's two nephews, whom he charged with implementing a set of rules and regulations, approved by the council, for the distribution of food and clothing, as well as keeping the accounts and other such matters. Bacamarte himself was thus free to concentrate on his medical duties.

"The Casa Verde," he said to the priest, "is now a world unto itself, in which there is both a temporal and a *spiritual* government." Father Lopes laughed at this godly quip and added, with the sole aim of making his own little joke: "Any more of that and I'll have you reported to the Pope himself."

Once relieved of his administrative burdens, the alienist embarked upon a vast enterprise, that of classifying his patients. He divided them, first, into two main categories—the violent and the meek—and from there proceeded to the subcategories of monomanias, deliria and various kinds of hallucinations. When that was done, he began a long and unremitting analysis of each patient's daily routine, when their outbursts occurred, their likes and dislikes, their words, gestures, and obsessions; he would inquire into their lives, professions, habits, how their illness had first manifested itself, any accidents suffered in childhood or adolescence, any other illnesses, any family history of mental illness; in short, an inquiry beyond that of even the most scrupulous of magistrates. And each day, he noted down a new observation, some interesting discovery or extraordinary phenomenon. At the same time, he studied the best diets, medicines, cures, and palliatives, both those handed down by his beloved Arabs and those which he himself discovered by dint of wisdom and patience. This work took up most of his time. He barely slept or ate, and even when he did eat he carried on working, either consulting an ancient text or ruminating over some particular matter; he would often spend an entire meal without saying a single word to Dona Evarista.

Chapter 3

GOD KNOWS WHAT HE IS DOING!

By the end of two months, that illustrious lady was the unhappiest of women; she fell into a deep melancholy, grew thin and sallow, ate little, and sighed at every turn. She did not dare to criticize or reproach Bacamarte in any way, for she respected him as her husband and master, but she suffered in silence and was visibly wasting away. One evening over dinner, when her husband asked her what was wrong, she replied sadly that it was nothing; then she summoned up a little courage and went as far as to say that she considered herself just as much a widow as before, adding:

"Who would have imagined that half a dozen lunatics . . ."

She did not finish the sentence, or, rather, she finished it by raising her eyes to the ceiling—those eyes which were her most appealing feature: large, dark, and bathed in a dewy light. As for the gesture itself, it was the same one she had employed on the day Simão Bacamarte had asked her to marry him. The chronicles do not say if Dona Evarista deployed that weapon with the wicked intention of decapitating science once and for all, or at least chopping off its hands, but it is a perfectly plausible conjecture. In any case, the alienist did not suspect her of having any ulterior motive. The great man was neither annoyed nor even dismayed; his eyes retained the same hard, smooth, unchanging metallic gleam, and not a single wrinkle troubled the surface of his brow, which remained as placid as the waters of the bay at Botafogo. A smile may have crossed his lips, as he uttered these words, as sweet as the oil in the *Song of Songs*:

"All right, you can go to Rio."

Dona Evarista felt the ground beneath her feet give way. She had never been to Rio, which, although but a pale shadow of what it is today, was still considerably more exciting than Itaguaí. For her, seeing Rio de Janeiro was something akin to the dream of the Hebrew slaves. Now that her husband had settled for good in that provincial town, she had given up all hope of ever breathing the airs of our fine city. And yet now there he was inviting her to fulfill her childhood and adolescent dreams. Dona Evarista could not conceal her delight at his proposal. Simão Bacamarte took her by the hand and smiled—a smile that was both philosophical and husbandly, and in which the following thought could be discerned: "There is no reliable remedy for the ailments of the soul; this woman is wasting away because she thinks I do not love her. I'll give her Rio de Janeiro, and that will console her." And since he was a studious man, he made a note of this observation.

Then a doubt pierced Dona Evarista's heart. She controlled herself, however, saying only that if he was not going, then she would not go, either, since there was no question of her undertaking a journey like that by herself.

"You can go with your aunt," said the alienist.

It should be noted that this same thought had occurred to Dona Evarista, but she had not wanted to ask or even suggest it, in the first place because it would be causing her husband even more expense, and secondly, because it would be better, more methodical, and more rational for the idea to come from him.

"Oh! But just think how much it would cost!" sighed Dona Evarista, without conviction.

"So? We've made a lot of money," said her husband. "Why, only yesterday the accountant showed me the figures. Would you like to see?"

And he showed her the ledgers. Dona Evarista was dazzled by that Milky Way of numbers. Then he showed her the coffers where the money was kept.

Goodness! There were heaps of gold; piles and piles of doubloons and mil-cruzado coins, a veritable treasure trove.

The alienist watched while she devoured the gold coins with her dark eyes, and whispered in her ear this most perfidious of remarks:

"Who would have imagined that half a dozen lunatics . . ."

Dona Evarista understood his meaning, smiled, and gave a heavy sigh:

"God must know what He is doing!"

Three months later, they set off: Dona Evarista, her aunt, the apothecary's wife, and one of their nephews, together with a priest whom the alienist had met in Lisbon and who happened to be in Itaguaí, five or six footmen, and four slave-women; this was the entourage that the townsfolk watched depart on that May morning. The farewells were a sad affair for everyone concerned, apart, that is, from the alienist. Although Dona Evarista's tears were abundant and sincere, they were not enough to move him. As a man of science, and only of science, nothing beyond science could dismay him, and the only thing bothering him on that occasion, as he cast an uneasy, policeman's gaze over the crowd, was the thought that some madman might be lurking among those of sound mind.

"Goodbye!" sobbed the ladies and the apothecary.

And so the entourage left. As the apothecary and the doctor returned home, Crispim Soares kept his gaze fixed firmly between the ears of his mule, while Simão Bacamarte's eyes were fixed on the horizon ahead, leaving his horse to deal with how to get home. What a striking image of the genius and the common man! One stares at the present, filled with tears and regrets, while the other scrutinizes the future with its promise of new dawns.

Chapter 4

A NEW THEORY

As Dona Evarista's journey brought her, tearfully, closer to Rio de Janeiro, Simão Bacamarte was studying, from every angle, a bold new idea that stood to enlarge substantially the foundations of psychology. He spent any time away from his duties at the Casa Verde roaming the streets, or going from house to house, talking to people about anything and everything, and punctuating his words with a stare that put fear into even the most heroic of souls.

One morning, about three weeks later, while Crispim Soares was busy concocting some medicine or other, someone came to tell him that the alienist wanted to see him.

"He says it's important," added the messenger.

Crispim blenched. What important matter could it be, if not some sad news of the traveling party, in particular his wife? For this point must be clearly stated, given how much the chroniclers insisted upon it: Crispim loved his wife dearly and, in thirty years of marriage, they had never been apart for even one day. This would explain the muttered private monologues he often indulged in, and which his assistants often overheard: "What on earth were you thinking of? What possessed you to agree to letting Cesária go with her? Lackey, miserable lackey! And all to get into Dr. Bacamarte's good books. Well, now you just have to grin and bear it; that's right, grin and bear it, you vile, miserable lickspittle. You just say *Amen* to everything, don't you? Well, now you've got your comeuppance, you filthy blackguard!" And many other such insults that a man should never say to anyone, still less to himself. Thus it is not hard to imagine the effect of Bacamarte's message. Soares instantly dropped what he was doing and rushed to the Casa Verde.

Simão Bacamarte received him with the joy that befits a man of learning, that is to say, a joy buttoned up to the neck with circumspection.

"I am very happy," he said.

"News of our womenfolk?" asked the apothecary, his voice trembling.

The alienist made a grand gesture and replied:

"No, it concerns something far more exalted: a scientific experiment. I say experiment, because I am not so rash as to assert my conclusions with absolute certainty, and because science, Senhor Soares, is nothing if not a constant search. So we shall call it, therefore, an experiment, but one that will change the very face of the Earth. Madness, the object of my studies, was, until now, considered a mere island in an ocean of reason; I am now beginning to suspect that it is a continent."

Upon saying this, he fell silent, the better to savor the apothecary's astonishment. Then he explained his idea at length. As he saw it, insanity afflicted a vast swath of humanity, an idea he expounded with copious arguments, texts, and examples. He cited examples both from Itaguaí itself and from history: being the rarefied intellectual he was, he recognized the dangers of drawing all his examples from Itaguaí, and sought refuge in history. He thus drew particular attention to several famous persons such as Socrates, who had his own personal demon, to Pascal, who always imagined a yawning abyss lay somewhere to his left, to Caracalla, Domitian, Caligula, and so on, a whole string of cases and people, the repulsive and the ridiculous. Since the apothecary seemed taken aback by such a promiscuous mixture, the alienist told him that it all amounted to the same thing, even adding sententiously:

"Ferocity, Senhor Soares, is merely the serious side of the grotesque."

"Witty, very witty indeed!" exclaimed Crispim Soares, throwing his hands in the air.

As for the idea of expanding the territory of insanity, the apothecary thought it somewhat extravagant, but since modesty, the principal ornament of his mind, would not suffer him to admit to anything other than a noble enthusiasm, he declared it sublime and utterly true, adding that it was definitely one for the town crier.

I should explain. At that time, Itaguaí, like all other towns, villages, and hamlets throughout the colony, had no printing press. There were, therefore, only two means of circulating news: either by nailing a handwritten notice to the doors of the town hall and the parish church, or by means of the town crier, who would roam the streets of the town with a rattle in his hand. From time to time, he would shake the rattle, townspeople would gather, and he would announce whatever he had been instructed to announce—a cure for fever, plots of arable land for sale, a sonnet, a church donation, the identity of the nosiest busybody in town, the finest speech of the year, and so on. The system had its inconveniences in terms of the inhabitants' peace and tranquility, but was preserved due to its effectiveness in disseminating information. For example, one of the municipal councillors— the very one who had been most vehemently opposed to the establishment of the Casa Verde—enjoyed a reputation as a tamer of snakes and monkeys, despite never having domesticated even one such creature. He did this simply by taking good care, every month, to employ the services of the town crier. Indeed, the chronicles say that some people attest to having seen rattlesnakes dancing on the councillor's chest, a claim that is perfectly false, but that was accepted as true entirely on account of the absolute confidence in which the system was held. As you can see, not every institution of the old regime deserves our own century's disdain.

"There is only one thing better than announcing my new theory," replied the alienist to the apothecary's suggestion, "and that is putting it into practice."

And, not wishing to diverge significantly from the alienist, the apothecary agreed that it would indeed be better to begin with action.

"There'll be time enough for the town crier," he concluded.

Simão Bacamarte reflected further for a moment, then said:

"Let's suppose, Senhor Soares, that the human spirit is an enormous seashell. My goal is to see if I can extract from it the pearl of reason. Or, in other words, to delineate definitively the boundaries of reason and insanity. Reason is the perfect equilibrium of all the faculties; beyond that lies madness, madness, and only madness.

Father Lopes, to whom the alienist also confided his new theory, declared bluntly that he could make neither head nor tail of it, that it was an absurd endeavor, and, if not absurd, then it was such a grandiose endeavor that it was not worth even embarking upon.

"Using the current definition, which is the one that has existed since time immemorial," he added, "madness and reason are perfectly delineated. We all know where one ends and the other begins. Why start moving the fence?"

Across the thin, discreet lips of the alienist danced the faintest shadow of an incipient laugh, in which disdain marched arm in arm with pity. But not a single word emerged.

Science merely extended its hand to theology, and with such self-assurance that theology no longer knew whether to believe in one or the other. Itaguaí and the universe stood on the brink of a revolution.

Chapter 5

THE TERROR

Four days later, the inhabitants of Itaguaí heard with some consternation that a certain fellow by the name of Costa had been taken to the Casa Verde.

"Impossible!"

"What do you mean, 'impossible'? He was taken there this morning."

"But surely he is the last person to deserve that . . . After all he's done!"

Costa was one of the most highly respected of Itaguaí's citizens. He had inherited four hundred thousand *cruzados* in the good coinage of King João V, a sum of money that would, as his uncle had declared in his will, provide income enough to live on "until the end of the world." No sooner had he received his inheritance than he began to share it out in the form of loans, at no interest; one thousand *cruzados* here, two thousand there, three hundred to this fellow, eight hundred to the next, so much so that, after five years, there was nothing left. Had penury befallen him suddenly, Itaguaí would have sat up and taken notice. But it came little by little; he slipped from opulence to affluence, from affluence to moderation, from moderation to poverty, and from poverty to penury, all in gradual steps. By the end of those five years, people who had once raised their hats to him as soon as they spotted him at the end of the street, would now clap him familiarly on the back, tweak his nose, and make all sorts of rude comments. And Costa would always laugh amiably. He seemed not even to notice that the least courteous men were precisely those who still owed him money; on the contrary, he would embrace them with even greater pleasure, and even more sublime resignation. One day, when one of these incorrigible debtors jeered at him and Costa simply laughed, a skeptical bystander commented, somewhat perfidiously: "You only put up with that fellow in the hope he will repay you." Costa did not hesitate for a second; he went up to the man who owed him money and canceled the debt on the spot. "Don't be surprised," interjected the bystander, "all Costa has given up is a far-distant star." Costa was perceptive enough to realize that the onlooker was mocking the worthiness of his actions, alleging that he was only relinquishing something he would never receive anyway. Costa prized his honor, and, two hours later, he found a means of proving that such a slander was untrue: he got hold of a few coins and sent them to the debtor as a new loan.

"Let's hope that now . . ." he thought, not even bothering to finish the sentence.

This last good deed of Costa's persuaded both the credulous and incredulous; no one now doubted the chivalrous sentiments of that worthy citizen. Even the most timid of paupers ventured out in their old slippers and threadbare capes to knock at his door. One worm, however, still gnawed at Costa's soul: it was the idea of that bystander disliking him. But even this came to an end: three months later, the very same bystander came and asked him for one hundred and twenty *cruzados*, promising to pay him back two days later. This was all that was left of Costa's inheritance, but it was also a noble revenge: Costa lent him the money that very instant, and without interest. Unfortunately, time ran out before he was repaid; five months later he was bundled off to the Casa Verde.

One can well imagine the consternation in Itaguaí when people learned what had happened. People spoke of nothing else; it was said that Costa had gone mad over breakfast, others said it was in the middle of the night. Accounts were given of his outbursts, which were either violent, dark, and terrifying, or gentle and even funny, depending on which version you heard. Many people rushed to the Casa Verde, where they found poor Costa looking quite calm, if a little dazed, and talking perfectly lucidly and asking why he had been taken there. Some went to see the alienist. Bacamarte applauded such sentiments of kindness and compassion, but added that science was science, and that he could not leave a madman wandering the streets. The last person to intercede on his behalf (because after what I am about to tell you everyone was too terrified to go anywhere near the doctor) was an unfortunate lady, one of Costa's cousins. The alienist told her confidentially that this worthy man was not in perfect command of his mental faculties, as could be seen from the way in which he had dissipated his fortune—

"No! Absolutely not!" the good lady said emphatically, interrupting him. "It's not his fault he spent all the money so quickly."

"Isn't it?"

"No, sir. I will tell you what happened. My late uncle was not a bad man, but when he was angry he was capable of anything, even failing to remove his hat in the presence of the Holy Sacrament. Then, one day, shortly before he died, he discovered that a slave had stolen one of his oxen. You can imagine his reaction. He was shaking all over, he turned bright red, and started foaming at the mouth—I remember it as if it were yesterday. Just then, an ugly, long-haired man, in shirtsleeves, came up to him and asked for some water. My uncle, God rest his soul, told the man that he could go drink from the river or, for all he cared, go to hell. The man looked at my uncle, raised his hand menacingly, and laid this curse upon him: 'All your wealth will last no more than seven years and a day, as sure as this thing here is the *Seal of Solomon*.' And he showed my uncle the *Seal of Solomon* tattooed on his arm. That's what caused it, sir; it was the evil man's curse that caused it."

Bacamarte fixed the woman with eyes as sharp as daggers. When she finished, he politely offered her his hand, as if to the wife of the viceroy himself, and invited her to come and speak to her cousin. The unfortunate woman believed him, and he took her to the Casa Verde and locked her up in the hallucination wing.

News of the illustrious Bacamarte's duplicity struck terror into the souls of the townspeople. No one wanted to believe that, for no reason, with no apparent animosity, the alienist had locked up in the Casa Verde a lady of perfectly sound mind, whose only crime had been to intercede on behalf of a poor unfortunate wretch. The matter was discussed on street corners and in barbershops; a whole web of romantic intrigue was concocted, tales of amorous overtures that the alienist had once made to Costa's cousin, to Costa's outrage and the lady's disdain. And this was his revenge. It was as clear as day. But the alienist's austere and studious lifestyle seemed to belie such a hypothesis. Nonsense! Surely that was just a façade. And one particularly credulous person even began to mutter that he knew a few other things, too, but he wouldn't say what they were since he wasn't absolutely certain, but he knew them nonetheless, and could almost swear they were true.

61

"Since you're such a close friend of his, can't you tell us what's happening, what happened, what reason . . . ?"

Crispim Soares was in raptures. These urgent inquiries from worried and curious neighbors and astonished friends were for him like a public coronation. There could be no doubt about it; the whole town finally knew that he, Crispim Soares, the apothecary, was the alienist's closest friend, the great man's confidant in all important matters; hence the general rush to see him. All this was evident in the apothecary's cheery face and discreet smile, a smile accompanied by silence, for he said nothing in reply, or only, at most, a few abrupt monosyllables, cloaked in that fixed, unvarying half smile, full of scientific mysteries that he could not, without danger or dishonor, reveal to any living person.

"Something's afoot," thought the most suspicious.

One such person limited himself to merely thinking this, before turning his back and going on his way. He had personal matters to attend to. He had just finished building a sumptuous new house. The house alone was enough to attract people's attention, but that was not all. There was the furniture, which he told everyone he had ordered from Hungary and Holland and which could be seen from the street, since he always left the windows wide open. And then there was the garden, a masterpiece of art and good taste. This man, who had made his fortune from the manufacture of saddles for mules and donkeys, had always dreamed of owning a magnificent house, a lavish garden, and exquisite furniture. He did not entirely give up his saddlemaking business, but sought repose from it in the quiet contemplation of his new house, the finest in Itaguaí, grander than the Casa Verde, nobler even than the town hall. Among the town's most illustrious denizens there was a wailing and gnashing of teeth whenever anyone thought of, mentioned, or praised the saddler's house—a mere donkey saddler, for goodness' sake!

"There he is again, mouth agape," said the morning passersby.

It was, in effect, Mateus's custom each morning to stretch himself out in the middle of his garden and stare lovingly at his house for a good hour, until he was summoned in for lunch. His neighbors all addressed him most respectfully, but laughed gleefully behind his back. One of them even commented that Mateus would be even better off, a millionaire in fact, if he made the donkey saddles for himself; an unintelligible witticism if ever there was one, but it made the others howl with laughter.

"There he is, making a spectacle of himself as usual," they would say as evening fell.

The reason for this was that in the early evenings, when families would take a stroll (having dined early), Mateus would position himself majestically at the window, in full view of everyone, his white suit standing out against the dark background, and he would stay like that for two or three hours until the light had completely faded. It can be assumed that Mateus's intention was to be admired and envied, although it was not something he confessed to anyone, not even to his great friends, the apothecary and Father Lopes. At least that is what the apothecary said when the alienist informed him that the saddlemaker could well be suffering from a love of stones, a mania that Bacamarte had himself discovered, and had been studying for some time. The way he stared at his house . . .

"No, sir," Soares answered vehemently.

"No?"

"Forgive me, but you are perhaps unaware that in the mornings he is *examining* the stonework, not admiring it, and, in the afternoons, it is other people who are doing the staring, at him and at the house." And he recounted the saddlemaker's habit of standing there every evening, from dusk until nightfall.

Simão Bacamarte's eyes glinted with scientific delight. Perhaps he was indeed unaware of all of the saddlemaker's habits, or perhaps, by interrogating Soares, he was seeking only to confirm some lingering doubt or suspicion. In any event, the apothecary's explanation satisfied him; but since his were the refined pleasures of a learned man, the apothecary noticed nothing to suggest a sinister intention. On the contrary, it was early evening and the alienist suggested they take a stroll together. Good heavens! It was the first time Simão Bacamarte had bestowed such an honor upon his friend. Trembling and dazed, Crispim replied that yes, indeed, why not? Just at that moment, two or three customers came in; Crispim silently cursed them; not only were they delaying the stroll, there was a risk that Bacamarte might invite one of them to accompany him, and dispense with Crispim entirely. Such impatience! Such torment! Finally, the interlopers left. The alienist steered him toward the saddlemaker's house, saw the saddlemaker standing at the window, passed slowly back and forth five or six times, pausing frequently to study the man's posture and expression. Poor Mateus noticed only that he was the object of the curiosity or perhaps admiration of Itaguaí's leading light, and struck an even grander pose. And thus, sadly, very sadly, he merely sealed his fate; the very next day he was carted off to the Casa Verde.

"The Casa Verde is nothing but a private jailhouse," commented a doctor who had no clinic of his own.

Never did an opinion take root and flourish so quickly. Private jail: this was repeated throughout Itaguaí from north to south and from east to west. It was said in fear, because during the week that followed poor Mateus's incarceration, some twenty people—two or three of whom were persons of rank—were carted off to the Casa Verde. The alienist said that only pathological cases were admitted, but few believed him. Popular theories abounded. Revenge, greed, divine retribution, the monomania of the doctor himself, a secret plot hatched by Rio de Janeiro to stamp out any germ of prosperity that might take root and flourish in Itaguaí to the disadvantage of the capital, and a thousand other explanations that explained nothing at all, but such was the daily produce of the public's imagination.

This coincided with the return from Rio de Janeiro of the alienist's wife, her aunt, Crispim Soares's wife, and all—or nearly all—of the entourage that had left Itaguaí several weeks earlier. The alienist went to greet them, along with the apothecary, Father Lopes, the municipal councillors and various other worthy officials. The moment when Dona Evarista laid eyes upon her husband is considered by the chroniclers of the time to be one of the most sublime in the annals of the human spirit, on account of the contrast in their two natures, both extreme and both admirable. Dona Evarista uttered a cry, managed to stammer out a word or two, and then threw herself upon her spouse in a movement that can best be described as a combination of jaguar and turtledove. Not so the illustrious Bacamarte, who, with clinical detachment, not for an instant unbending from his scientific rigor, held out his arms to his wife, who fell into them and fainted. This lasted only a moment, and only two minutes later, Dona Evarista was being warmly greeted by her friends, and the procession once again moved on.

Dona Evarista was the hope of Itaguaí; the town counted on her to be a moderating influence on that scourge of the Casa Verde. Hence the public acclaim, the crowds thronging the streets, the flags, the flowers, and the damask silk banners hanging from the windows. With her arm resting on that of Father Lopes—for the eminent Bacamarte had entrusted his wife to the priest and was walking pensively beside them—Dona Evarista turned her head from side to side, curious, restless, brazen even. The priest inquired about Rio de Janeiro, which he had not seen since the reign of the previous viceroy, and Dona Evarista replied enthusiastically that it was the most beautiful thing in the whole wide world. The Passeio Público gardens were now finished and were indeed a paradise; she had gone there many times, as well as to the infamous Rua das Belas Noites, and to the Marrecas fountain . . . Ah, the Marrecas fountain! Yes, there really were Marrecas ducks there, made out of metal and spouting water from their beaks. A most exquisite thing! The priest agreed that Rio de Janeiro must indeed be even lovelier now; after all, it had been very beautiful even back in the old days! And no wonder, for it was bigger than Itaguaí and, moreover, the seat of government. But nor could it be said that Itaguaí was ugly; after all, it had beautiful houses such as Mateus's, and the Casa Verde . . .

"And speaking of the Casa Verde," said Father Lopes, gliding expertly onto the topic of the moment, "your ladyship will find it remarkably full these days."

"Is that so?"

"Yes, indeed. Mateus is there . . ."

"The saddlemaker?"

"The very one. And Costa, along with his cousin, as well as many others . . ."

"They've all gone mad?"

"Or nearly mad," the priest replied judiciously.

"And?"

The priest turned down the corners of his mouth, as if to say he did not know, or did not wish to say; a vague response that could not be repeated to anyone else, since it contained no words. Dona Evarista thought it truly extraordinary that all of those people had gone mad; one or two, perhaps, but *all* of them? On the other hand, it was difficult for her to doubt it; her husband was a man of learning, and would never commit anyone to the Casa Verde without clear proof of insanity.

"Indeed . . . indeed . . ." repeated the priest at regular intervals.

Three hours later, fifty guests or so were seated around Simão Bacamarte's table for a dinner to welcome home the travelers. Dona Evarista was the obligatory subject of toasts, speeches, verses of every kind, meta-phors, hyperboles, and apologues. She was the wife of the new Hippocrates, the muse of Science, an angel, divine, the shining dawn, charity, life, and sweet consolation; her eyes were two stars, in the more modest version proposed by Crispim Soares, or two suns, according to the musings of a councillor. The alienist listened to these things, feeling mildly bored, but showing no visible signs of impatience. He merely whispered in his wife's ear that such rhetorical flourishes were not to be taken seriously. Dona Eva-rista tried hard to share her husband's opinion, but, even after discounting three-quarters of such fawning flattery, there was still more than enough to swell her pride. For example, one of the orators was a young man of twenty-five called Martim Brito, a consummate dandy well versed in amo-rous adventures and affairs; he delivered a speech in which the birth of Dona Evarista was explained in the most provocative manner. "After God gave the world both man and woman, who are the diamond and the pearl of His divine crown," he said, triumphantly drawing out this part of the sen-tence as he took in the entire table, from one end to the other, "God wished to surpass even Himself, and so He created Dona Evarista."

Dona Evarista lowered her eyes with exemplary modesty. Two ladies, considering such flattery excessive and even audacious, looked inquiringly at their host, where they indeed found the alienist's expression clouded by sus-picion, menace, and, quite possibly, bloodlust. The young man had shown great impudence, thought the two ladies. And each of them prayed to God to ward off any tragic consequences that might arise, or at the very least postpone them until the following day. Yes, that was it: postpone them. The more pious of the two ladies even admitted to herself that Dona Evarista scarcely merited such suspicion, being so far from being either attractive or witty. An insipid little simpleton. But then, if everyone liked the same color, what would happen to yellow? The thought made her tremble once again, although less than before; less, because now the alienist was smiling at Martim Brito and, when everyone got up from the table, he went over to him to exchange a few words about his speech. He congratulated the young man on his dazzling improvisation, full of magnificent flashes of wit. Was the idea about Dona Evarista's birth his own invention, or had he found it in some book? No, sir, it was his own idea; it had occurred to him on that very occasion and seemed entirely fitting as an oratorical flourish. Besides, his ideas tended to be bold and daring rather than tender or jocular. He was a man suited to the epic. Once, for example, he had composed an ode to the fall of the Marquis of Pombal's government, in which he had described the noble minister as the "harsh dragon of Nothingness," crushed by the "vindictive claws of Everything." There were others in a similar vein, always rather original, for he liked ideas that were rare and sublime, and images that were grand and noble . . .

"Poor boy!" thought the alienist. "Undoubtedly a case of cerebral lesion; not a life-threatening phenomenon, but certainly worthy of study."

Dona Evarista was astounded when, three days later, she discovered that Martim Brito had been taken to the Casa Verde. A young man with such charming ideas! The two ladies blamed it on the alienist's jealousy. What else could it be? The young man's declaration had been far too bold.

Jealousy? But how then to explain, shortly afterward, the incarceration of the highly regarded José Borges do Couto Leme, the inveterate merry-maker Chico das Cambraias, the clerk Fabrício, and others besides? The terror grew. No one knew any longer who was sane and who was mad. Whenever their husbands left the house, wives would light a candle to the Virgin Mary; and some husbands didn't even have the courage to venture out without one or two thugs to protect them. Palpable terror reigned. Those who could, left the town. One such fugitive was captured a mere two hundred paces from the town. He was a likable young man of thirty, chatty and polite, indeed so polite that whenever he greeted someone he would bow so low as to sweep the ground with his hat; in the street he would often run a distance of ten or twenty yards to shake the hand of a worthy gentleman, a lady, sometimes even a mere boy, as had happened with the chief magistrate's son. He had a vocation for bowing. Besides, he owed his good standing in the town not only to his personal attributes, which were unusual, but also to the noble tenacity with which he never gave up, even after one, two, four, or even six scowling rejections. Gil Bernardes's charms were such that, once invited into someone's house, he was disinclined to leave and his host equally disinclined to let him leave. But, despite knowing he was well liked, Bernardes took fright when he heard one day that the alienist had his eye on him; the following day he fled the town before dawn, but was quickly apprehended and taken to the Casa Verde.

"We have to put an end to this!"

"It can't go on!"

"Down with tyranny!"

"Despot! Brute! Goliath!"

These were whispers in houses rather than shouts in the street, but the time for shouts would come soon enough. Terror mounted; rebellion approached. The idea of petitioning the government to have Simão Bacamarte arrested and deported crossed several people's minds, even before Porfírio, the barber, gave full expression to it in his shop, accompanied by grand, indignant gestures. And let it be noted—for this is one of the purest pages of this whole somber story—let it be noted that ever since the Casa Verde's population had begun to grow in such an extraordinary fashion, Porfírio had seen his profits greatly increase on account of the incessant demand for leeches from the asylum; but his own personal gain, he said, must give way to the public good. And, he added: "the tyrant must be defeated!" It should also be noted that he unleashed this cry on the very day Bacamarte had committed to the Casa Verde a man by the name of Coelho who had brought a lawsuit against Porfírio.

"Can anyone tell me in what sense a man like Coelho is mad?" railed Porfírio.

No one could answer him; they all repeated one after another that Coelho was perfectly sane. Coelho's lawsuit against the barber, concerning some plots of land in the town, arose from a dispute over some old and very obscure property deeds, and not from any hatred or greed. An excellent fellow, Coelho. His only detractors were a handful of grumpy individuals who, claiming they didn't have time to chat, would duck around the corner or into a shop as soon as they caught sight of him. In truth, Coelho did love a good chat, a long chat, slowly sipped or in deep drafts, and so it was that he was never alone, always preferring those who could string two words together, but never turning his back on the less loquacious. Father Lopes, who was a devotee of Dante and an enemy of Coelho, could never watch the man tear himself away from a companion without reciting from *Inferno*, with his own witty amendment:

> La bocca sollevò dal fiero pasto
> Quel "seccatore" . . .

However, while some people knew that the priest disliked Coelho, others assumed this was just a prayer in Latin.

Chapter 6

THE REBELLION

Roughly thirty people joined forces with the barber, drafting a formal complaint and taking it to the town hall.

The council refused to accept the complaint, declaring that the Casa Verde was a public institution and that science could not be amended by administrative vote, still less by the mob.

"Go back to work," concluded the mayor. "That's our advice to you."

The agitators were furious. The barber declared that they would raise the banner of rebellion and destroy the Casa Verde; that Itaguaí could no longer serve as a cadaver to be studied and experimented on by a despot; that many estimable and even distinguished people were languishing in the cells of the Casa Verde, as well as other, humbler individuals no less worthy of esteem; that the alienist's scientific despotism was complicated by issues of greed, given that the insane, or rather those accused of insanity, were not being treated for free: their families, or, failing that, the council, were footing the bill—

"That's quite false!" interrupted the mayor.

"False?"

"About two weeks ago, we received formal notification from the eminent doctor that, since the experiments he was performing were of the highest psychological value, he would no longer accept the stipend approved by the council, just as he would no longer accept any payment from the patients' families.

The news of such a pure and noble act somewhat dampened the rebels' spirits. The alienist could very well be wrong, but clearly he was motivated by no interest other than science, and if they were to prove that mistakes had been made, then something more than noisy rabble-rousing was needed. Thus spoke the mayor, to vigorous cries of, "Hear, hear!" from the whole council. After a few moments of reflection, the barber declared that he had been given a mandate from the people and would not let matters rest until the Casa Verde, "that Bastille of human reason"—an expression he had heard from a local poet and which he now emphatically repeated—had been razed to the ground. Having said his piece, he left the building with all his followers.

The position of the councillors can easily be imagined: there was a pressing need to forestall the mob and head off revolt, battle, and bloodshed. To make matters worse, one of the councillors who had previously supported the mayor, on hearing the Casa Verde described as a "Bastille of human reason," thought it such an elegant turn of phrase that he changed his mind. It would, he said, be advisable to come up with some measures to control the Casa Verde. When the mayor expressed his indignation in energetic terms, the councillor made this observation:

"I don't know much about science, but if so many apparently sane men are being locked up as lunatics, who's to say that it isn't the alienist himself who has become alienated from reason?"

Sebastião Freitas, the dissenting councillor, was a gifted speaker and carried on talking for some time, choosing his words prudently, but emphatically. His colleagues were astonished; the mayor requested that he at least set an example of respect for the rule of law by keeping his ideas to himself in public, so as not to give form and substance to the rebellion, which at that moment was still "nothing but a swirl of scattered atoms." The appeal of this image somewhat mitigated the effect of the earlier one, and Sebastião Freitas promised to refrain from taking any overt course of action, although he reserved the right to pursue all legal avenues in order to bring the Casa Verde to heel. And, still enamored of the phrase, he repeated to himself: "A Bastille of human reason!"

Meanwhile, the protests grew. Now there were not thirty but three hundred persons accompanying the barber, whose nickname deserves mentioning at this point because it became the name of the revolt; they called him Canjica, after a kind of milky porridge, and so the movement became known as the Canjica Rebellion. The action itself may well have been limited, given that many people, by virtue of fear or upbringing, did not take to the streets, but the feeling was unanimous, or almost unanimous, and the three hundred who marched to the Casa Verde could well be compared, give or take the evident differences between Paris and Itaguaí, to those brave citizens who stormed the Bastille.

Dona Evarista got wind of the approaching mob; one of the houseboys came to tell her as she was trying on a new silk dress (one of the thirty-seven she had brought back from Rio de Janeiro), but she refused to believe it.

"Oh, it must be some revelry," she said, adjusting a pin. "Now then, Benedita, check to see if the hem is straight."

"It is, mistress," replied the slave-woman squatting on the floor. "It's just fine. Could you turn a little? Yes, it's fine."

"They're not revelers, ma'am; they're shouting, 'Death to Dr. Bacamarte the tyrant!'" exclaimed the terrified houseboy.

"Shut up, you idiot! Benedita, look there on the left side; don't you think the seam is a bit crooked? The blue stripe doesn't go the whole way down; it looks terrible like that. You'll need to unpick the whole thing and make it exactly the same as—"

"Death to Dr. Bacamarte! Death to the tyrant!" shouted three hundred voices outside. It was the mob emerging into Rua Nova.

The blood drained from Dona Evarista's face. At first she was too petrified to move. The slave-woman instinctively made for the back door. As for the houseboy whom Dona Evarista had refused to believe, he enjoyed a moment of sudden, imperceptible triumph, a deep-seated sense of moral satisfaction, on seeing that reality had taken his side.

"Death to the alienist!" shouted the voices, closer now.

Dona Evarista may not have found it easy to resist the siren calls of pleasure, but she knew how to confront moments of danger. She did not faint, but instead ran into the next room, where her husband was immersed in his studies. When she entered the room, the illustrious doctor was hunched over a text of Averroes; his eyes, shrouded in meditation, traveled from book to ceiling and from ceiling to book, blind to the outside world, but clear-sighted enough when it came to the innermost workings of his mind. Dona Evarista called to her husband twice without him paying her the slightest attention; the third time, he heard her and asked what was wrong, if she was feeling ill.

"Can't you hear them shouting?" she asked tearfully.

The alienist listened; the shouts were drawing nearer, terrifying and threatening; he immediately understood the situation. He stood up from his high-backed chair, closed his book, strode calmly and purposefully over to the bookshelf, and put the book back in its place. Inserting it slightly disturbed the alignment of the two volumes on either side, and Simão Bacamarte took care to correct this minor yet interesting imperfection. Then he told his wife to go to her room and stay there, no matter what.

"No, no," implored the worthy lady, "I want to die by your side . . ."

Simão Bacamarte insisted that it was not a case of life and death, and that even if it were, she must on all accounts stay put. The poor woman tearfully and obediently bowed her head.

"Down with the Casa Verde!" shouted the Canjicas.

The alienist walked over to the balcony at the front of the house, arriving at the same time as the mob, those three hundred faces shining with civic virtue and dark with rage. "Die! Die!" they shouted from all sides the moment the alienist appeared on the balcony. When Simão Bacamarte gestured to them to let him speak, the rebels indignantly shouted him down. Then, waving his hat to silence the crowd, the barber managed to calm his companions, and told the alienist that he could speak, adding that he must not abuse the people's patience as he had been doing up until then.

"I will say little, or even nothing at all, if that is what's required. First of all, I want to know what you are asking for."

"We're not asking for anything," replied the barber, shaking. "We're demanding that the Casa Verde be demolished, or, at the very least, that the poor unfortunates within be set free."

"I don't understand."

"You understand perfectly well, tyrant; we want to liberate the victims of your hatred, your cruel whims, your greed . . ."

The alienist smiled, but the great man's smile proved invisible to the eyes of the multitude; it was a faint contraction of two or three muscles, nothing more. He smiled and replied:

"Gentlemen, science is a serious matter, and deserves to be treated as such. I do not answer to anyone for my professional actions, save to God and the great masters of Science. If you are seeking changes in how the Casa Verde is run, I am prepared to listen; but if you are asking me to reject everything I believe in, you will go away empty-handed. I could invite some of you, as a delegation, to come and visit the poor deranged inmates with me, but I won't do so, because that would entail explaining my whole system, which is something I will never reveal to laymen, still less to rebels."

Thus spoke the alienist to the astonished crowd; they were clearly not expecting him to exhibit such determination, still less such serenity. Their amazement grew still greater when the alienist gave a solemn bow to the crowd, then turned and went slowly back inside. The barber quickly came to his senses and, brandishing his hat, invited his friends to go with him and tear down the Casa Verde. Only a few half-hearted voices responded. It was at this decisive moment that the barber felt the first stirrings of an ambition to govern; it seemed to him that by demolishing the Casa Verde and defeating the alienist, he would be able to seize control of the municipal council, confound the agents of the Crown, and make himself master of Itaguaí. For years he had been struggling to get his name included on the ballot from which the councillors were drawn, but had always been rejected because his station in life was considered incompatible with such high office. It was now or never. Besides, he had taken this mutiny so far now that defeat would mean imprisonment, or perhaps even the gallows, or exile. Unfortunately for the barber, the alienist's reply had tempered the crowd's fury. When he realized this, the barber felt a surge of indignation; he wanted to yell: "Coward! Scoundrels!" but he restrained himself and took another tack:

"Let us fight, dear friends, to the very end! The salvation of Itaguaí is in your noble and heroic hands! Let us tear down the prison of your sons and fathers, of your mothers and sisters, of your relatives and friends, and of your own good selves. If not, you will waste away on a diet of bread and water, or perhaps be flogged to death, in the dungeons of that despicable man."

The crowd grew agitated again, muttering, then shouting, then shaking its fists, before thronging around the barber. The revolt was recovering from its brief dizzy spell, and threatening once again to raze the Casa Verde.

"Onward!" cried Porfírio, with a flourish of his hat.

"Onward!" bellowed the crowd.

But something stopped them: a corps of dragoons came marching at double time into Rua Nova.

Chapter 7

SOMETHING UNEXPECTED

When the dragoons reached the Canjicas there was a moment of bewilderment; the rebels could scarcely believe that the full force of the state had been sent in against them, but the barber immediately grasped the situation and waited. The dragoons stopped, and the captain ordered the crowd to disperse. However, while some were inclined to obey, others rallied strongly around the barber, who responded with these rousing words:

"We will not disperse. If it is our corpses you want, you can have them, but only our corpses, for you will not take from us our honor, our reputation, or our rights, and with them the very salvation of Itaguaí."

Nothing could be more reckless than this response from the barber, and nothing more natural. Call it the giddy impulse of all moments of crisis. Perhaps it was also an excess of confidence, an assumption that the dragoons would not resort to violence, an assumption that the captain quickly dispelled by ordering his troops to charge the Canjicas. What followed defied description. The crowd bellowed with rage; some managed to escape by climbing into the windows of houses, others by running down the street, but most remained, howling in angry indignation, spurred on by the barber's exhortations. The defeat of the Canjicas was imminent, when, for reasons the chronicles do not reveal, a third of the dragoons suddenly switched to the rebels' side. This unexpected reinforcement gave new heart to the Canjicas, while sowing despondency among the ranks of law and order. The loyal troops had no desire to attack their own comrades, and, one by one, they crossed over to join them, so that after a few minutes, the picture had completely changed. On one side stood the captain, accompanied by only a handful of men, facing a dense throng calling for his head. There was nothing to be done; he acknowledged defeat and surrendered his sword to the barber.

The triumphant revolution lost not a single moment; the wounded were taken to nearby houses, and the mob set off toward the town hall. Troops and citizens fraternized, shouting three cheers for the king, the viceroy, Itaguaí, and their illustrious leader, Porfírio. The man himself walked in front, grasping the sword as deftly as if it were nothing but a rather long razor. Victory had surrounded him with a mysterious aura. The dignity of office had begun to stiffen his sinews.

The councillors, peering at the crowd and soldiers from the windows, assumed that the troops had subdued the rabble, and, without further ado, went back inside and approved a petition to the viceroy asking him to pay a month's wages to the dragoons, "whose bravery saved Itaguaí from the abyss into which it had been driven by a bunch of rebels." This phrase was proposed by Sebastião Freitas, the dissenting councillor whose defense of the Canjicas had so scandalized his colleagues. However, any illusion of victory was quickly shattered. The cries of, "Long live the barber," "Death to the councillors," and "Death to the doctor," revealed to them the sad truth. The chairman did not lose heart: "Whatever our own fate may be," he said, "let us remember that we serve His Majesty and the people." Sebastião Freitas suggested that they could better serve both Crown and town by slipping out the back door and going to confer with the chief magistrate, but all the other councillors rejected this proposal.

Seconds later, the barber, accompanied by some of his lieutenants, entered the council chamber and peremptorily informed the council that they had been overthrown. The councillors offered no resistance, surrendered, and were taken off to jail. The barber's followers then proposed that he assume control of the town, in the name of His Majesty. Porfirio accepted, despite (he added) being all too aware of the pitfalls of high office. He went on to say that he could not do it without the support of all those present, to which they promptly agreed. The barber went to the window and relayed these decisions to the people, who ratified them with cheers of acclamation. The barber assumed the title of "Protector of the Town in the Name of His Majesty and the People." Various important edicts were quickly issued, including official communications from the new administration and a detailed report to the viceroy filled with many protestations of loyal obedience to His Majesty. Finally, there was a short but energetic proclamation to the people:

PEOPLE OF ITAGUAÍ!

A corrupt and violent council was found to be conspiring against the interests of His Majesty and the People, and was roundly condemned by the public; as a consequence, a handful of Citizens, bravely supported by His Majesty's loyal dragoons, have this very day ignominiously dissolved said Council, and with the unanimous consent of the town, the Supreme Mandate has been entrusted to me, until such time as His Majesty sees fit to order whatever may best serve his royal Person. People of Itaguaí! All that I ask is that you give me your trust, and that you assist me in restoring peace and the public finances, so wantonly squandered by the Council that has now met its fate at your hands. You may count on my dedication and self-sacrifice, and be assured that we will have the full backing of the Crown.

Protector of the Town in the Name of His Majesty and the People
PORFÍRIO CAETANO DAS NEVES

Everyone noticed that the proclamation made no mention of the Casa Verde, and, according to some, there could be no clearer indication of the barber's evil intentions. The danger was even more pressing given that, in the midst of these momentous events, the alienist had locked up seven or eight more people, including two women, one of the men being a relative of the Protector. This was undoubtedly not intended as a deliberate challenge or act of defiance, but everyone interpreted it as such and the town was filled with the hope that, within twenty-four hours, the alienist would be in irons and that fearful prison destroyed.

The day ended merrily. While the town crier went around reading out the proclamation on every corner, people spilled out into the streets and swore to defend to the death their illustrious Porfírio. If few bothered to protest against the Casa Verde, this was merely proof of their confidence in the new government. The barber issued a decree declaring the day to be a public holiday, and because the combination of temporal and spiritual powers struck him as highly desirable, he suggested to the priest that a *"Te Deum"* might be sung. Father Lopes, however, bluntly refused.

"I trust that, in any event, Your Reverence will not join forces with the new government's enemies?" the barber said to him darkly.

To which Father Lopes replied without replying:

"How could I do that, if the new government has no enemies?"

The barber smiled; it was absolutely true. Apart from the captain, the councillors, and a handful of grandees, the whole town was on his side. Even those grandees who hadn't publicly backed him, had not come out against him, either. Not one of the municipality's officials had failed to report for duty. Throughout the town, families blessed the name of the man who would at last liberate Itaguaí from the Casa Verde and the terrible Simão Bacamarte.

Chapter 8

THE APOTHECARY'S DILEMMA

Twenty-four hours after the events narrated in the preceding chapter, the barber, accompanied by two orderlies, left the government palace—as the town hall was now called—and went to the home of Simão Bacamarte. He was not unaware that it would be more fitting for the government to send for Bacamarte; however, fearing that the alienist might not obey, he felt obliged to adopt a tolerant, moderate stance.

I will not describe the apothecary's terror upon hearing that the barber was on his way to the alienist's house. "He's going to arrest him," he thought, his anxieties redoubling. Indeed the apothecary's moral torment during those revolutionary days exceeds all description. Never had a man found himself in a tighter spot: his close acquaintance with the alienist urged him to join his side, while the barber's victory inclined him toward the other. News of the uprising itself had already shaken him to the core, for he knew how universally the alienist was hated, and the victorious rebellion was the last straw. Soares's wife, a redoubtable woman and close friend of Dona Evarista, told him in no uncertain terms that his place was at Simão Bacamarte's side; meanwhile, his heart was screaming that this was a lost cause and that no one, of his own free will, shackles himself to a corpse. "True enough, Cato did it, *sed victa Catoni*," he thought, remembering one of Father Lopes's favorite phrases. "But Cato did not attach himself to a lost cause: he himself had been the lost cause, he and his republic; moreover, his act was that of an egotist, a miserable egotist; my situation is entirely different." His wife, however, would not give in, so Crispim Soares was left with no other option than to declare himself ill and take to his bed.

"There goes Porfírio, off to Dr. Bacamarte's house," said his wife to him the following day, at his bedside. "He's got people with him."

"They're going to arrest the doctor," thought the apothecary.

One thought leads to another; the apothecary was convinced that once they'd arrested the alienist, they would come after him as an accomplice. This thought proved to be a more effective remedy than any caustic lotion. Crispim Soares sat up, pronounced himself better, and said that he was going out. Despite all his wife's efforts and protestations, he got dressed and left the house. The chroniclers are unanimous in recording that her certainty that the apothecary was about to place himself nobly at the alienist's side was a great consolation to her; they go on to note very shrewdly just how powerful our illusions can be; for the apothecary resolutely made his way not to the alienist's house, but to the government palace. On arrival, he expressed surprise on finding that the barber was not there, explaining that he had come to pledge his allegiance, having been unable to do so the previous day due to illness. With some effort he managed a cough. The functionaries who heard his declaration, knowing full well the apothecary's close links with the alienist, understood the significance of this new declaration of allegiance, and treated Crispim Soares with punctilious kindness. They assured him that the barber would return shortly; His Lordship had gone to the Casa Verde on important business, but would not be long. They offered him a chair, refreshments, and compliments; they told him that the cause of the illustrious Porfírio was the cause of every patriot, to which the apothecary responded that, yes, indeed, he had never doubted it for a minute, and would be sure to have it brought to His Majesty's attention.

Chapter 9

TWO FINE CASES

The alienist did not delay in receiving the barber, declaring that since he had no means to resist, he was ready to obey. He asked only that he should not be obliged to witness the destruction of the Casa Verde.

"You are much mistaken, Your Lordship" said the barber after a short pause, "in attributing such barbarous intentions to my government. Rightly or wrongly, public opinion believes that the majority of patients placed here are perfectly sane, but the government recognizes that this is a purely scientific matter and does not intend to attempt to regulate the matter with municipal bylaws. Furthermore, the Casa Verde is a public institution, for that is how we received it from the hands of the now-disbanded council. However, there is—as indeed there must be—an intermediate proposal that may restore the public's peace of mind."

The alienist could barely conceal his astonishment; he confessed that he had been expecting an entirely different outcome: the tearing down of the asylum, prison for him, or even exile, indeed anything but—

"You are surprised," interrupted the barber gravely, "because you have not paid close enough attention to the heavy responsibilities of government. The people, blinded by compassion, which, in such cases, provokes a perfectly legitimate sense of indignation, may demand from their government a certain series of measures, but the government, with the responsibilities incumbent upon it, should not carry them out, or at least not in their entirety. Such is the situation we find ourselves in. The valiant revolution that yesterday brought down a despised and corrupt council, clamored for the destruction of the Casa Verde, but can a government take it upon itself to abolish madness? Certainly not. And if governments cannot abolish madness, are they any better qualified to detect and identify it? Again, no—it is a matter for science. Hence, in such a delicate matter as this, the government neither can nor should dispense with the aid and counsel of Your Lordship. What we ask of you is that, together, we find some means to satisfy public opinion. Let us join forces, and the people will fall into line. One acceptable solution, unless Your Lordship has a better suggestion, would be to remove from the Casa Verde those patients who are almost cured, as well as those who are simply harmless eccentrics. In that way, and without great danger, we can show a certain degree of benign tolerance."

After a pause of about three minutes, Simão Bacamarte asked: "How many dead and injured were there in yesterday's altercations?"

The barber was taken aback by the question, but quickly replied that there had been eleven dead and twenty-five wounded.

"Eleven dead and twenty-five wounded!" the alienist repeated two or three times.

The alienist intimated that he wasn't entirely happy with the proposal, but that he would come up with an alternative within a few days. He asked a number of questions about the previous day's events, the attack, the defense, the dragoons switching sides, any resistance offered by the councillors, and so on, to which the barber gave fulsome answers, laying great emphasis on how utterly discredited the council was. The barber confessed that the new government did not yet enjoy the backing of the town's leading citizens, but then that was something where the alienist himself could make all the difference. The government, concluded the barber, would be greatly relieved if it could count on the sympathy, if not the goodwill, of the loftiest mind in Itaguaí, and, no doubt, in the entire kingdom. But none of this made a button of difference to the noble, austere features of that great man, who listened in silence, showing neither pride nor modesty, as impassive as a stone deity.

"Eleven dead and twenty-five wounded," repeated the alienist, after accompanying the barber to the door. "Here we have two fine cases of cerebral incapacity. This barber exhibits clear symptoms of shameless duplicity. As for the idiocy of those who cheered him, what further proof is needed than those eleven dead and twenty-five wounded? Yes, two fine cases!"

"Long live noble Porfírio!" shouted the thirty-odd people waiting for the barber outside.

The alienist peered out the window and managed to catch the end of the barber's short address to the excited crowd.

". . . for I will be vigilant, of this you can be certain, yes, ever vigilant in fulfilling the wishes of the people. Trust in me, and everything will be resolved in the best possible manner. I only wish to remind you of the need for order. Order, my friends, is the very foundation of government!"

"Long live noble Porfírio!" shouted the thirty voices, waving their hats.

"Two fine cases!" murmured the alienist.

Chapter 10

THE RESTORATION

Within five days, the alienist had committed to the Casa Verde around fifty supporters of the new government. The people were outraged. The government, bewildered, did not know how to react. João Pina, another barber, said openly in the streets that Porfírio had "sold his soul to Simão Bacamarte," a phrase which rallied the most ardent of the town's citizens to Pina's side. Seeing his old rival in the arts of the razor at the head of this new insurrection, Porfírio understood that all would be lost if he did not move decisively; he issued two decrees, one abolishing the Casa Verde and the other banishing the alienist. João Pina ably demonstrated, with eloquent turns of phrase, that Porfírio's actions were nothing but a ruse and should not be taken seriously. Two hours later, Porfírio was ignominiously defeated, and João Pina assumed the heavy task of government. Finding in the filing cabinets drafts of the proclamation, the loyal address to the viceroy, and other inaugural documents left by the previous government, he lost no time in having them copied and dispatched; the chroniclers specifically state, and indeed it can be safely assumed, that he took care to change the names, so that where the other barber had written "corrupt council," the new barber referred to "an impostor steeped in evil French doctrines contrary to the sacrosanct interests of His Majesty," and so on.

At this point, a detachment of troops sent by the viceroy entered the town and restored order. The alienist immediately demanded that Porfírio be handed over to him, along with fifty or so other individuals, whom he declared to be mentally deranged. Furthermore, they promised to hand over a further nineteen of the barber's followers, who were convalescing from injuries inflicted in the initial rebellion.

This moment in Itaguaí's crisis also marked the zenith of Simão Bacamarte's influence. Everything he asked for they gave him, and one of the most vivid proofs of the eminent doctor's influence can be found in the alacrity with which the councillors, restored to their positions, agreed that Sebastião Freitas should also be committed to the asylum. Aware of the extraordinary inconsistency of this particular councillor's opinions, the alienist identified the case as pathological, and locked the man up. The same thing happened to the apothecary. Ever since he had learned of Soares's instantaneous decision to back the rebellion, the alienist had weighed it against the apothecary's consistent expressions of support for him, even on the very eve of the revolt, and had him arrested too. Crispim Soares did not deny the fact, but tried to explain it away by saying that he had succumbed to an impulse of fear upon seeing the rebellion triumphant, pointing out in his own defense that he had quickly returned to his sickbed and played no further part in events. Simão Bacamarte did not argue with him, remarking to the others present that fear can also be father to insanity, and that Crispim Soares's case struck him as one of the clearest examples of such a phenomenon.

But the most obvious proof of Simão Bacamarte's influence was the docility with which the town council handed over its own chairman. This worthy official had declared in open session that he would be content with no less than a tun of blood to cleanse him of the Canjicas's effrontery, and his words reached the alienist's ears via the mouth of the town clerk, who came to him flushed with excitement. Simão Bacamarte began by putting the town clerk in the Casa Verde, and from there he went to the town hall and informed the council that the chairman of the council was suffering from "bull mania," a type of madness he intended to make a study of, to the great benefit of mankind. The council at first hesitated, but finally gave in.

From then on this harvest of men proved unstoppable. A man could not invent or repeat the simplest of lies, even when it was to the advantage of the inventor or spreader of the lie, without being thrown into the Casa Verde. Everything was madness. Composers of riddles, aficionados of puzzles and anagrams, slanderers, nosy parkers, preening dandies, and pompous officials: no one escaped the alienist's emissaries. He spared sweethearts but not strumpets, saying that the first yielded to a natural impulse, the second only to vice. A man could be a miser or a spendthrift and still be hauled off the Casa Verde; hence the claim that there was no rule for determining what constituted complete sanity. Certain chroniclers believe that Simão Bacamarte did not always act in good faith, and they cite in support of this allegation (which I cannot entirely vouch for) the fact that he persuaded the council to pass a bylaw authorizing the wearing of a silver ring on the thumb of the left hand by any person who, without any further proof, documentary or otherwise, claimed to have a drop or two of blue blood in his or her veins. These chroniclers say that Bacamarte's secret goal was to enrich a certain silversmith in the town, who was a close friend. However, while it is certainly true that the jeweler saw his business prosper following the new municipal ordinance, it is no less true that the bylaw also provided the Casa Verde with a host of new inmates; it would therefore be reckless to determine which of these was the eminent doctor's true objective. As for the reason justifying the arrest and incarceration of all those who wore the ring, that is one of the obscurest aspects of the entire history of Itaguaí. The likeliest theory is that they were locked up for going around waving their hands about for no good reason, in the streets, at home, even in church. Everyone knows that lunatics wave their hands about a lot. In any event, this is pure conjecture; there is no concrete evidence.

"Where will it all end?" exclaimed the local gentry. "Ah, if only we had supported the Canjicas . . ."

Then one morning, on the day·that the council was due to hold a grand ball, the whole town was shaken by the news that the alienist's own wife had been committed to the Casa Verde. No one could believe it; some scoundrel must surely have made it up. But no, it was absolutely true. Dona Evarista had been taken away at two o'clock in the morning. Father Lopes rushed to see the alienist and inquired discreetly about the matter.

"I've had my doubts for some time now," her husband said gravely. "Her previous matrimonial modesty, in both her marriages, cannot be reconciled with the positive frenzy for silks, velvets, laces, and precious stones she has displayed since her return from Rio de Janeiro. That was when I began to observe her closely. Her conversations revolved entirely around such fripperies; if I talked to her about the royal courts of olden times, she would immediately ask about the dresses worn by the ladies; if she received a visit from a lady when I was out, before telling me the purpose of the visit she would first describe the visitor's outfit, approving of some items and criticizing others. One day, which I am sure Your Reverence will remember, she offered to make a new dress every year for the statue of Our Lady in the parish church. These were all serious symptoms in themselves, but it was last night that her complete insanity manifested itself. She had carefully selected and made all the final alterations to the gown she was planning to wear to the municipal ball; her only hesitation was between a garnet or sapphire necklace. The day before yesterday, she asked me which one she should wear; I replied that either one would go very well. Yesterday, she repeated the question over breakfast; shortly after lunch I found her silent and thoughtful.

" 'What's the matter?" I asked her.

" 'I'd like to wear the garnet necklace, but the sapphire one is so pretty!'

" 'So wear the sapphire one.'

" 'But then what about the garnets?'

"Anyway, the afternoon and evening passed without any further developments. We had supper and went to bed. In the middle of the night, sometime around one-thirty, I woke up and she wasn't there. I got out of bed, went to our dressing room, and found her with the two necklaces, trying them on in front of the mirror, first one, then the other. She was obviously deranged, so I had her committed at once."

The alienist's response did not satisfy Father Lopes, but he said nothing. The alienist, however, understood the priest's silence and explained to him that Dona Evarista's case was one of "sumptuary mania," not incurable, and certainly worthy of study.

"In six weeks she'll be cured," he concluded. "I'm sure of it."

The eminent doctor's selfless devotion further enhanced his standing in the town. Rumors, suspicions, and doubts all crumbled into dust, for he had not hesitated to lock up his own wife, whom he loved with all his heart. No one could oppose him now, still less accuse him of having anything but strictly scientific motives.

He was a great and austere man, Hippocrates and Cato rolled into one.

Chapter 11

ITAGUAÍ'S ASTONISHMENT

And now, dear reader, prepare yourself to feel as astonished as did the townspeople of Itaguaí when it was announced that the lunatics in the Casa Verde would all be released.

"All of them?"

"All of them."

"That's impossible. Some of them, perhaps . . . but all?"

"All. That's what he said in the memorandum he sent to the council this morning."

The alienist had indeed sent an official memorandum to the council, setting out the following points, in numbered paragraphs:

1. Having consulted statistics relating to both the town and the Casa Verde, four-fifths of the population are currently residing in said establishment.

2. This displacement of population leads me to examine the fundamental basis of my theory of mental illness, pursuant to which all persons whose faculties are not in perfect equilibrium must be considered insane.

3. As a result of said examination and in the light of said statistics, I am now convinced that the true doctrine is the contrary, and that the disequilibrium of mental faculties should therefore be

considered normal and exemplary, whereas those whose mental equilibrium is undisturbed should henceforth be treated as
probably pathological.

4. In the light of this discovery, I hereby inform the council that I
   will set free the current inmates of the Casa Verde, and replace
   them with such persons as fulfill the conditions set out above.

5. I will spare no effort in the pursuit of scientific truth, and I
   expect the same dedication on the part of the council.

6. I will repay the council and individuals concerned the sum total
   of the stipend received for lodging the presumed lunatics, minus
   any amounts already spent on food, clothing, etc., which the
   council can verify upon inspection of the Casa Verde's account
   ledgers and coffers.

You can imagine the astonishment of the people of Itaguaí, and the joy
of the inmates' friends and relations. Banquets, dances, colored lanterns,
and music—no expense was spared in celebrating the happy event. I shall
not describe the festivities since they are not relevant to our purposes, but
they were magnificent, highly emotional, and prolonged.

As is always the way with human affairs, in the midst of the rejoicing
provoked by Simão Bacamarte's memorandum, no one paid any attention to
the words at the end of the fourth paragraph, which were later to prove of
such importance.

Chapter 12

THE END OF THE FOURTH PARAGRAPH

Lanterns were extinguished, families reunited, and everything seemed to
return to its rightful place. Order reigned, and the council once again governed without any external interference; its own chairman and Councillor
Freitas returned to their respective positions. Porfírio the barber, chastened
by events and having "experienced all in life," as the poet said of Napoleon
(and even more than that, because Napoleon never experienced the Casa
Verde), decided that the obscure glories of razor and scissors were prefer-

able to the brilliant calamities of power. He was, of course, prosecuted by the authorities, but the townspeople begged His Majesty to show clemency, and a pardon was duly granted. João Pina was cleared of all charges, since his actions had brought down a rebel. The chroniclers think it was this that gave birth to our adage, "When a thief robs a thief the sentence is but brief," an immoral saying, it's true, but still highly useful.

All complaints against the alienist ceased, as did any lingering traces of resentment for what he had done. Ever since he had declared the Casa Verde's inmates to be completely sane, they had all been filled with a sense of profound gratitude and fervent enthusiasm. Many of them felt that the alienist deserved special recognition for his services and even gave a ball in his honor, followed by further dinners and celebrations. The chronicles say that, at first, Dona Evarista considered asking for a separation, but the sad prospect of losing the companionship of such a great man overcame any wounded feelings, and the couple ended up even happier than before.

The friendship between the alienist and the apothecary remained equally close. The latter concluded from Simão Bacamarte's memorandum that, in times of revolution, prudence is the most important virtue, and he greatly appreciated the alienist's magnanimity in extending him the hand of friendship when he granted him his liberty.

"He is indeed a great man," said Soares to his wife, referring to the alienist's gesture.

Needless to say, Mateus the saddler, Costa, Coelho, Martim Brito, and all the others mentioned earlier were free to return to their former habits and occupations. Martim Brito, locked up on account of that overenthusiastic speech in praise of Dona Evarista, now gave another speech in honor of the eminent doctor "whose exalted genius spreads its wings far above the sun and leaves beneath it all other spirits of the earth."

"Thank you for your kind words," replied the alienist, "which only serve to remind me how right I was to release you."

Meanwhile, the council, which had replied to Simão Bacamarte's memorandum saying that it would set out its position concerning the end of paragraph four in due course, finally set about legislating on the matter. A bylaw was adopted, without debate, authorizing the alienist to detain in the Casa Verde anyone whose mental faculties were found to be in perfect equilibrium. And after the council's previous painful experience, a clause was included stating that such authorization was provisional in nature and limited to one year, so that the new theory could be put to the test, and authorizing the council to close down the Casa Verde at any time, should this be deemed advisable for reasons of public order. Councillor Freitas also proposed a provision that under no circumstances should any councillor be committed to the mental asylum, and this clause was accepted, voted through, and included in the bylaw, despite Councillor Galvão's objections. The latter's main argument was that the council, in passing legislation relating to a scientific experiment, could not exclude its own members from the consequences of the law; such an exemption was both odious and ridiculous. As soon as he uttered those two words, the other councillors erupted in howls of disapproval at their colleague's audacity and foolishness; for his part, he heard them out and simply repeated, calmly, that he would vote against the exemption.

"Our position as councillors," he concluded, "grants us no special powers, nor does it exclude us from the foibles of the human mind."

Simão Bacamarte accepted the bylaw with all its restrictions. As for the councillors being exempted, he declared that he would have been deeply saddened had he been compelled to commit a single one of them to the Casa Verde; the clause itself, however, was the best possible proof that their mental faculties did not suffer from perfect equilibrium. The same could not, however, be said for Councillor Galvão, whose wisdom in objecting to the exemption, and moderation in responding to his colleagues' abusive tirades, clearly demonstrated a well-organized brain, and on this account Bacamarte respectfully requested the council to hand him over for treatment. The council, still somewhat offended by Councillor Galvão's behavior, considered the alienist's request and voted unanimously in favor.

It goes without saying that, according to the new theory, a person could not be committed to the Casa Verde on the basis of a single incident or word; rather, a long examination was required, exhaustively covering both past and present. For example, it took thirty days after the bylaw was passed for Father Lopes to be arrested, and forty days for the apothecary's wife. This lady's detention filled her husband with indignation. Crispim Soares left his house spitting with rage, and declaring to whoever he met that he was going to box the tyrant's ears. Upon hearing this in the street, one of the alienist's sworn enemies immediately set aside his animosity and rushed to Simão Bacamarte's house to warn him of the danger. Bacamarte expressed his gratitude to his erstwhile adversary, and in a matter of minutes ascertained the worthiness and good faith of the man's sentiments, his respect and generosity toward his fellow man; he thereupon shook him warmly by the hand and committed him to the Casa Verde.

"A most unusual case," he said to his astonished wife. "Now let's wait for our good friend Crispim."

Crispim arrived. Sorrow had overcome anger, and the apothecary did not after all box the alienist's ears. The latter consoled his dear friend, assuring him that all was not lost; his wife might well have some degree of cerebral imbalance, and he, Bacamarte, would examine her very thoroughly to find out. In the meantime, though, he could scarcely let the woman roam the streets. Seeing certain advantages in reuniting them—on the basis that the husband's slippery duplicity might in some way cure the moral refinement he had detected in the wife—Bacamarte told Soares:

"You can work in your dispensary during the day, but you will have lunch and dinner here with your wife, and stay overnight, and spend all day here on Sundays and public holidays."

The proposal placed the poor apothecary in the position of Buridan's ass. He very much wanted to be with his wife, but feared returning to the Casa Verde; he remained caught in this dilemma for some time, until Dona Evarista rescued him by promising to visit her dear friend and relay messages back and forth between them. Crispim Soares gratefully kissed her hands. This gesture of cowardly egotism struck the alienist as almost sublime.

After five months, there were some eighteen persons residing at the Casa Verde, but Simão Bacamarte did not let up; he went from street to street and house to house, observing, asking questions, and taking notes, and the internment of even one new patient gave him the same pleasure he had once enjoyed when herding them in by the dozen. It was precisely this disparity that confirmed his new theory; he had finally discovered the truth about cerebral pathology. One day, he succeeded in committing the chief magistrate to the Casa Verde, but only after he had scrupulously carried out a detailed study of all his judicial decisions and spoken to all the important people in the town. On more than one occasion, he had found himself on the verge of committing someone who turned out to be perfectly unbalanced; this is what happened with a certain lawyer, in whom he had identified such a fine array of moral and mental qualities that he considered it positively dangerous to leave the man at large in society. He ordered him to be arrested, but the bailiff had doubts and asked Bacamarte if he could conduct an experiment; he went to see a friend of his who had been accused of forging a will, and advised him to engage Salustiano (the name of the lawyer in question) to defend him.

"So do you really think he'll . . . ?"

"No doubt about it. Tell him everything, the whole truth, whatever it may be, and leave the matter entirely in his hands."

The man went to see the lawyer, confessed to having forged the will, and asked him to take on the case. The lawyer agreed, studied all the papers, pleaded the case before the court, and proved beyond a shadow of doubt that the will was completely genuine. The defendant was solemnly declared innocent by the judge, and the inheritance was his. To this experiment the distinguished lawyer owed his freedom. However, nothing escapes an original and penetrating mind. Simão Bacamarte, who had already noted the bailiff's dedication, wisdom, patience, and restraint, recognized the skill and good judgment with which he had conducted such a tricky and complicated experiment, and ordered him to be committed forthwith to the Casa Verde. He did, however, give him one of the best cells.

Once again, the lunatics were lodged according to their different categories. One wing housed those madmen with a particular tendency for modesty; one was for the tolerant, one for the truthful, one for the innocent, one for the loyal, one for the magnanimous, one for the wise, one for the sincere, and so on. Naturally, the inmates' friends and family objected strongly to this new theory, and some tried to force the council to rescind its authorization. However, the council had not forgotten the language used by Councillor Galvão, and, since he would be released and restored to his former position if they rescinded the bylaw, they refused. Simão Bacamarte wrote to the councillors, not to thank them, but to congratulate them on this act of personal vindictiveness.

Disenchanted with the lawful authorities, some of the leading townspeople went secretly to Porfírio the barber and promised him their wholehearted support, as well as money and influence at court, if he would lead another uprising against the council and the alienist. The barber declined, saying that ambition had driven him to break the law on that first occasion, but that he had seen both the error of his ways and the fickleness of his followers. Since the council had seen fit to authorize the alienist's new experiment for one year, then, in the event of the council rejecting their request, they should either wait until the year was up or petition the vice-roy. He, Porfírio, could never advise resorting to means that had already failed him once and resulted in deaths and injuries that would be forever on his conscience.

"What's this you say?" asked the alienist when one of his spies told him about the conversation between the barber and the leading citizens.

Two days later, the barber was taken to the Casa Verde. "I'm damned if I do and damned if I don't!" cried the poor man.

The one-year period came to an end, and the council authorized a six-month extension to allow some new therapies to be tested. The conclusion of this episode in the chronicles of Itaguaí is of such magnitude, and so unexpected, that it deserves a full explanation of no less than ten chapters; I will, however, make do with just one, which will form both the grand finale of my account, and one of the finest-ever examples of scientific conviction and selflessness.

Chapter 13

PLUS ULTRA!

Now it was the turn of therapy. Simão Bacamarte, so assiduous and wise in finding his patients, exceeded even himself in the foresight and diligence with which he began their treatment. On this point all of the chroniclers are in complete agreement: the eminent alienist performed the most astonish-ing cures, earning him Itaguaí's most ardent admiration.

Indeed, it would be difficult to imagine a more rational system of ther-apy. Having divided the lunatics into categories according to their predomi-nant moral perfection, Simão Bacamarte set about attacking the leading attribute head-on. Take, for example, modesty. Bacamarte would apply a treatment designed to instill precisely the opposite characteristic—in this case, vanity. Rather than starting immediately with the maximum dose, he would increase it gradually, taking into account the patient's age, condi-tion, temperament, and social position. Sometimes all it took was a tailcoat, a ribbon, a wig, or a cane to restore the patient's sanity; in more stubborn cases he would resort to diamond rings, honorary titles, etc. There was one patient, a poet, who resisted everything. Simão Bacamarte was beginning to despair of finding a cure, when he had the idea of sending out the town crier to proclaim him as great a poet as Garção or Pindar.

"It's a miracle," said the poet's mother to one of her closest friends, "a blessed miracle."

Another patient, also suffering from modesty, exhibited the same resistance to medical treatment; but since he wasn't a writer (he could barely sign his name), the town-crier cure could not be applied. Simão Bacamarte had the idea of petitioning for the man to be appointed secretary of the Academy of Hidden Talents that had been established in Itaguaí. The posts of president and secretary were by royal appointment, in memory of His Late Majesty King João V, and carried with them both the title of "Your Excellency" and the right to wear a gold medallion on one's hat. The government in Lisbon initially refused the appointment, but when the alienist indicated that he was not proposing it as a legitimate distinction or honorary award, but merely as a therapeutic remedy in a difficult case, the government made an exception and granted his request, although not without extraordinary efforts on the part of the Minister for the Navy and Colonies, who just so happened to be the alienist's cousin. Yet another blessed miracle.

"Quite remarkable!" people said in the street, on seeing the healthy, puffed-up expressions of the two former lunatics.

Such was his system. The rest can be imagined. Each moral or mental refinement was attacked at the point where its perfection seemed strongest, and the effect was never in doubt. There were some instances in which the predominant characteristic resisted all attempts at treatment; in such cases the alienist would attack another element, conducting his therapies much as a military strategist would, assailing first one bastion and then another until the fortress falls.

After five and a half months, the Casa Verde was empty: everyone was cured! Councillor Galvão, so cruelly afflicted by principles of fairness and moderation, had the good fortune to lose an uncle; I say good fortune because the uncle left an ambiguously worded will and Galvão obtained a favorable interpretation by corrupting the judges and deceiving the other heirs. The alienist's sincerity was apparent on this occasion; he freely admitted that he had played no part in the cure, and that it had been all down to the healing power of nature. With Father Lopes it was an entirely different matter. Knowing that the priest knew absolutely no Hebrew or Greek, the alienist asked him to write a critical analysis of the Septuagint. The priest accepted and performed the task in short order; within two months he had written the book and was a free man. As for the apothecary's wife, she did not stay long in the cell allocated to her and where she was always treated kindly and affectionately.

"Why doesn't Crispim come to visit me?" she asked every day.

In reply they gave her one excuse after another; in the end they told her the truth. The worthy matron could not contain her shame and indignation. During her fits of rage, she would utter random words and phrases such as these:

"Scoundrel! Villain! Ungrateful cheat! Nothing but a peddler of spurious, rancid lotions and potions . . . Oh, the scoundrel!"

Simão Bacamarte recognized that, even if the accusation itself might not be true, her words were enough to show that the excellent lady was at last restored to a state of perfect mental disequilibrium, and he promptly discharged her.

Now, if you think that the alienist was delighted to see the last inmate leaving the Casa Verde, you will only be revealing how little you know our man. *Plus ultra!* was his motto: Ever Onward! It was not enough for him to have discovered the true theory of insanity; nor was he content to have restored the reign of reason in Itaguaí. *Plus ultra!* Rather than feeling elated, he grew troubled and pensive; something was telling him that his new theory held within it another, even newer theory.

"Let's see," he thought, "let's see if I can finally reach the ultimate truth."

Such were his thoughts as he paced the length of the vast room, which contained the richest library in all His Majesty's overseas possessions. The eminent alienist's majestic and austere body was wrapped in an ample damask robe, tied at the waist by a silken cord with gold tassels (a gift from a university). A powdered wig covered his broad and noble pate, polished smooth by daily scientific cogitations. His feet, neither slim and feminine nor large and uncouth, but entirely in proportion with his shape and size, were protected by a pair of shoes adorned with nothing but a plain brass buckle. Observe the contrast: his only luxuries were those of a scientific origin; everything that related to his own person bore the hallmark of simplicity and moderation, fitting virtues for a sage.

Thus it was that he, the great alienist, paced from one end of the vast library to the other, lost in his own thoughts, oblivious to anything beyond the darkest problems of cerebral pathology. Suddenly he stopped. Standing in front of a window, with his left elbow supported on the palm of his right hand, and his chin resting on the closed fist of his left hand, he asked himself:

"But were they really insane, and cured by me—or was what appeared to be a cure nothing more than the discovery of their natural mental disequilibrium?"

And, digging further into his thoughts, he reached the following conclusion: the well-organized brains he had been so successfully treating were, after all, just as unbalanced as all the rest. He could not pretend, he realized, to have instilled in his patients any sentiment or mental faculty they did not already possess; both of these things must have already existed, in a latent state, perhaps, but there nevertheless.

Upon reaching this conclusion, the eminent alienist experienced two opposing sensations, one of pleasure, the other of dejection. The pleasure was on seeing that, at the end of long and patient investigation, involving unrelenting work and a monumental struggle against the entire population, he could now confirm the following truth: there were no madmen in Itaguaí; the town possessed not one single lunatic. But no sooner had this idea refreshed his soul than another appeared, completely neutralizing the effect of the first: a doubt. What! Not one single well-adjusted brain in the whole of Itaguaí? Would such an extreme conclusion not, by its very nature, be erroneous? And would it not, moreover, destroy the entire majestic edifice of his new psychological doctrine?

The chroniclers of Itaguaí describe the illustrious Simão Bacamarte's anguish as one of the most terrifying moral maelstroms ever to afflict mankind. But such tempests only terrify the weak; the strong brace themselves and stare into the eye of the storm. Twenty minutes later, the alienist's face lit up with a gentle glow.

"Yes, that must be it," he thought.

And here is what it was. Simão Bacamarte had discovered within himself all the characteristics of perfect mental and moral equilibrium. It seemed to him that *he* possessed wisdom, patience, perseverance, tolerance, truthfulness, moral vigor, and loyalty; in other words, all the qualities that together defined a confirmed lunatic. It's true that doubts immediately followed, and he even concluded that he was mistaken; but, being a prudent man, he gathered together a group of friends and asked them for their candid opinion. Their verdict was affirmative.

"Not a single defect?"

"Not one," they replied in unison.

"No vices?"

"None."

"Absolutely perfect?"

"Absolutely."

"No," cried the alienist, "it's impossible! I don't recognize in myself the superiority you have so generously described. You're just saying these things out of kindness. I've examined myself and I can find nothing to justify the excesses of your affections."

The assembled friends insisted; the alienist resisted; finally, Father Lopes explained everything with this astute observation:

"Do you know why you can't see in yourself those lofty virtues we all so admire? It's because you have one further quality that outshines all the rest: modesty."

His words were decisive. Simão Bacamarte bowed his head, both happy and sad, and yet more happy than sad. Without further ado, he committed himself to the Casa Verde. In vain his wife and friends told him to stay, that he was perfectly sane and balanced; but no amount of begging or pleading or tears would detain him for even one moment.

"It is a matter of science," he said. "It concerns an entirely new doctrine, of which I am the very first example. I embody both the theory and the practice."

"Simão! My darling Simão!" wailed his wife, tears streaming down her face.

But the illustrious doctor, his eyes shining with scientific conviction, shut his ears to his wife's pleas, and gently pushed her away. Once the door of the Casa Verde was locked behind him, he devoted himself entirely to the study and cure of himself. The chroniclers say that he died seventeen months later, in the same state in which he entered the Casa Verde, having achieved nothing. Some even speculate that he had always been the sole lunatic in Itaguaí; but this theory, based upon a rumor that circulated after the alienist's death, has no basis beyond the rumor itself, and it is a dubious rumor at that, being attributed to Father Lopes, who had so ardently praised the great man's virtues. In any event, his funeral took place with great pomp and rare solemnity.

HOW TO BE A BIGWIG

A Dialogue

"A RE YOU SLEEPY?"

"No, Father."

"Neither am I. Let's talk awhile. Open the window. What time is it?"

"Eleven o'clock."

"And the last guest from our modest dinner has just gone home. So, my boy, you have at last reached the age of twenty-one. Yes, twenty-one years ago, on the fifth of August, 1854, you first saw the light of day, a tiny little scrap of a thing, and now you're a man with a fine mustache, a few conquests under your belt—"

"Father!"

"Now, don't act all surprised, and let's have a serious chat, man-to-man. Close the door. I have some important things to tell you. Sit down and let's talk. Twenty-one years old, a private income, and a college degree: you could go into politics, the law, journalism, farming, industry, commerce, litera-ture, or the arts. An infinite number of careers lie before you. Twenty-one, my boy, is but the first syllable of our destiny. Even Pitt and Napoleon, how-ever precocious, had not reached their peak at twenty-one. But whatever profession you choose, my only wish is that you do something great and illustrious, or at least noteworthy, that you raise yourself above the com-mon herd. Life, Janjão, is one enormous lottery; the prizes are few and the unlucky innumerable, and it is upon the sighs of one generation that the hopes of the next are built. That's life; there's no use whining or cursing; we must just accept things as they are, with their burdens and benefits, their glories and blemishes, and press on regardless."

"Yes, Father."

"However, just as it is wise, metaphorically speaking, to set some bread aside for one's old age, so it is also good social practice to keep a career in reserve, just in case the others fail entirely, or do not quite meet our ambitions. That is my advice to you, my son, on this the day when you come of age."

"And I'm grateful for it, Father. But what career do you have in mind?"

"To me, there is no career as useful or as fitting as that of bigwig. As a young man, my dream was to be a bigwig. I lacked, however, a father's advice, and so I have ended up as you can see, with no other consolation or moral support beyond the hopes I place in you. So listen to me carefully, son; listen and learn. You are young, you naturally possess the fire, the exuberance, and the impulsiveness of your years; do not reject them, but moderate them so that by the time you're forty-five, you are ready to enter the age of measure and reason. The wise man who said, "Gravity is a mystery of the body invented to conceal the defects of the mind," defined the very essence of a bigwig. Do not confuse this gravity with the other kind, which, although also present in outward appearances, is a pure reflex or emanation of the mind; the gravity of which I speak is a matter only of the body, whether natural or acquired. As for the age of forty-five . . ."

"Yes, indeed, why forty-five?"

"It is not, as you might suppose, an arbitrary number plucked out of the air; it is the normal age at which the phenomenon occurs. Generally speaking, the true bigwig begins to appear between the ages of forty-five and fifty, although some cases do occur between fifty-five and sixty, but these are rare. There are also some who emerge at forty, and others even earlier, at thirty-five or even thirty; they are not, however, at all common. I won't even mention those who become bigwigs at twenty-five; such precocity is the privilege of genius."

"I see."

"But let's get to the main point. Once you have embarked on this career, you must be extremely cautious about any ideas you may cultivate, either for your own use or for the use of others. The best thing would be not to have any ideas at all. This is something you can easily grasp by imagining, for example, an actor deprived of the use of one arm. He can, through sheer talent and skill, conceal his disability from the audience, but it would never-theless be much better for him to have both arms. The same is true of ideas; it is possible, by violent effort, to smother or conceal them permanently, but that is a very rare skill, and not one conducive to the normal enjoyment of life."

"But who says that I—"

"You, my son, if I am not mistaken, seem to be endowed with the per-fect degree of mental vacuity required by such a noble profession. I refer not so much to the fidelity with which you repeat in a drawing room opinions you have heard on the street corner, or vice versa, because this fact, while indicative of a certain absence of original thought, might well be nothing more than a slip of the memory. No, I am referring to the punctilious and statesmanlike stance you tend to adopt when expounding your views, for or against, regarding the cut of a vest, the dimensions of a hat, or the squeaki-ness (or absence thereof) of a new pair of boots. Therein lies a symptom that speaks volumes; therein lies a hope. It is not, however, inconceivable that, with age, you may come to be afflicted with some ideas of your own, and so it is important to equip your mind with strong defenses. Ideas are by their very nature spontaneous and sudden; however hard we try, they burst forth and rush upon us. This is precisely what enables the man in the street, who has a very fine nose for this kind of thing, to distinguish with absolute cer-tainty the true bigwig from the false."

"I'm sure you're right, but that is surely an insurmountable obstacle."

"No, it isn't. There is a way. You must throw yourself into a punish-ing regime of reading books on rhetoric, listening to certain speeches, and so on. Gin rummy, dominoes, and whist are all tried and tested remedies. Whist even has the rare advantage of getting one accustomed to silence, and silence is the most extreme form of circumspection. I wouldn't say the same about swimming, horse-riding, or gymnastics, even though they do force the brain to rest; but it is precisely in resting the brain that they restore its lost strength and vitality. Billiards, on the other hand, is excellent."

"How's that? Doesn't billiards also involve physical exercise?"

"I'm not saying that it doesn't, but there are some things in which obser-vation trumps theory. I recommend billiards to you only because the most scrupulously compiled statistics show that three-quarters of those who wield a billiard cue pretty much share the same opinions as the cue itself.

An afternoon stroll, particularly in places of amusement and public display, is highly beneficial, provided you don't sally forth unaccompanied. For solitude is the workshop of ideas, and if the mind is left to its own devices, even in the midst of a crowd, it is prone to lapse into some unwarranted activity or other."

"But what if I don't have a friend on hand willing and able to go with me?"

"Not to worry; there are always those habitual gathering places of idlers, where all the dust of solitude is blown away. Bookshops, perhaps because of their studious atmosphere, or for some other reason that escapes me, are not suitable for our purpose. However, it can be worthwhile visiting them from time to time, as long as you make sure everyone sees you doing it. There is a simple way of resolving this dilemma: go to a bookshop solely to talk about the rumor of the day, the funny story of the week, some salacious affair or scandal, a passing comet, or whatever it may be (unless, of course, you'd rather approach habitual readers of Monsieur Mazade's erudite columns in the *Revue des Deux Mondes*); seventy-five percent of these worthy denizens will repeat to you exactly the same opinions, and such monotony is eminently useful. By following this regime for eight, ten, eighteen months— let's call it two years—you can reduce the most prodigious of intellects to a sober, disciplined, and tedious equilibrium. I haven't mentioned vocabulary, for words are implied by the ideas they convey; it goes without saying that it should be simple, vapid, and strictly limited—definitely no purple notes or shrill colors."

"That's awful! Not being able to add a few rhetorical flourishes once in a while . . ."

"Oh, but you can; there's a whole host of figures of speech you can use: the Lernean Hydra, for example, or the head of Medusa, the cask of the Danaids, the wings of Icarus, and all those many others that romanticists, classicists, and realists employ without compunction whenever the need arises. Latin tags, historical sayings, famous verses, legal axioms, witty maxims—it's a good idea to have them readily to hand for after-dinner speeches, toasts, and so on. *Caveant, consules* is an excellent way to conclude anything with a political theme, and I would say the same of *Si vis pacem, para bellum*. Some people like to refresh an old quotation by working it into a new, original, and beautiful sentence, but I would advise against a trick like that; it will only warp the quotation's venerable charm. However, better

than all of these, which, at the end of the day, are mere trimmings, are the
clichés and traditional sayings handed down from generation to generation,
burned into both the individual and the public memory. These expressions
have the advantage of not requiring any unnecessary effort on the part of
your listeners. I won't list them all now, but will set them down in writing
later. Beyond that, your new profession will itself gradually teach you the
difficult art of thinking what has already been thought. As for the usefulness of such a system, just imagine one hypothesis. A law is passed, put into
force, but has no effect; the evil persists. Here lies a subject to whet idle
curiosities, instigate mind-numbing inquiry, the fastidious collection of documents and observations, the analysis of probable, possible, and definitive
causes, the endless study of the capacity of the individual to be reformed,
the nature of the evil, the formulation of a remedy, and the circumstances in
which it should be applied; in short, enough material for a whole edifice of
words, opinions, and nonsensical ramblings. You, however, will spare your
fellow man this long harangue by simply saying: "Reform habits, not laws!"
And this short, transparent, limpid phrase, pulled from the common purse,
instantly solves the problem, and lifts everyone's spirits like a sudden shaft
of sunlight."

"I see by this, Father, that you condemn the application of any and all
modern methodologies."

"Let me be quite clear. I do indeed condemn their application, but I
heartily approve of the phrase itself. I would say the same thing regarding
all recent scientific terminology, all of which you should learn by heart.
Although the distinguishing characteristic of a bigwig may well be a rather
unyielding attitude reminiscent of the god Terminus, whereas the sciences
are the product of everyday human endeavor, if you are to become a bigwig
later on in life, you should arm yourself with the most up-to-date weapons.
Because one of two things will happen: either these scientific terms and
expressions will be worn out from overuse in thirty years' time, or they
will keep themselves fresh and new. In the first case, they will fit you like
an old glove; in the second case, you can wear them in your buttonhole to
show that you, too, know what's what. From scraps of conversation, you will
eventually form some sort of idea about which laws, cases, and phenomena
all this terminology corresponds to; because the alternative method of scientific inquiry—from the books and theses of the experts themselves—as
well as being tedious and tiring, brings with it the danger of exposure to

new ideas, and is thus fundamentally false. Furthermore, if you were ever truly to master the spirit of those laws and formulae, you would probably be inclined to employ them with a certain moderation, like the shrewd and prosperous seamstress of whom a classical poet wrote:

> The more cloth she has the more sparingly she cuts,
> And the smaller the pile of scraps left over.

"It goes without saying that such behavior on the part of a bigwig would be most unscientific."

"My word, it's a tricky business!"

"And we're not finished yet."

"Well, then, let's carry on."

"I haven't yet spoken to you about the benefits of publicity. Publicity is a haughty and seductive mistress, and you should woo her with little gifts, sugared almonds, lavender sachets, and other tiny things expressive more of the constancy of your affections than of the boldness of your ambitions. Soliciting her favors through heroic deeds and sacrifices is something best left to Don Quixote and other such lunatics. The true bigwig takes an entirely different approach. Rather than composing a *Scientific Treatise on Sheep Breeding*, he buys a lamb and regales his friends with it in the form of a dinner, news of which cannot fail to rouse the interest of your fellow citizens. One thing leads to another, and before you know it, your name is in the newspapers five, ten, or even twenty times. Committees and delegations for congratulating war heroes, distinguished citizens, or foreigners are particularly beneficial, as are church organizations and various clubs and societies, whether devoted to mythology, hunting, or ballet. Even certain minor incidents can be mentioned, provided they serve to show you in a good light. Let me explain. If you were to fall from a carriage suffering nothing more than a nasty shock, it would be useful to trumpet the fact to all and sundry. Not on account of the incident in itself, which is insignificant, but for the purpose of reminding public affections of a name that is dear to them. Do you understand?"

"Yes, I do."

"That is your cheap, easy, workaday publicity, but there is more. Whatever the theory of art may have to say on the subject, it is beyond doubt that family sentiment, personal friendship, and public esteem all encourage the artistic reproduction of a well-loved or distinguished man's physiognomy. Nothing prevents you from being the object of such distinction, particularly if your discerning friends sense no reluctance on your part. In that case, not only are you required by the rules of common courtesy to accept the portrait or bust so offered, but you would also be ill-advised to prevent your friends from arranging a public exhibition of said portrait. In this way your name becomes firmly attached to your person; those who have read your recent speech, say, to the inaugural congress of the National Union of Hairdressers will recognize in your rugged features the author of such a weighty perora-tion, in which the "levers of progress" and the "sweat of the brow" overcame the "gaping gullets" of poverty. In the event of a delegation bringing the por-trait to your home, you should thank them for their kindness with a grateful speech and a banquet—a venerable, sensible, and honest custom. You will, of course, also invite your closest friends, your relations, and, if possible, one or two prominent figures. Furthermore, since the day is one of glory and jubilation, I do not see how you could decently refuse a place at your table to some newspaper reporters. In the unfortunate event that the duties of these gentlemen of the press have detained them elsewhere, you can help them out by yourself drafting a report of the celebrations. And should you, on account of some entirely understandable scruple, not wish to apply the requisite glowing adjectives yourself, then ask a friend or relation to do it."

"None of this is going to be easy, Father."

"You're absolutely right, son. It's difficult and will take time, lots of time, indeed years of patience and toil, but happy are they who reach the Promised Land! Those who fail will be swallowed up by obscurity. But those who triumph? And, believe me, you will triumph. You will see the walls of Jericho fall at the sound of the holy trumpets. Only then will you be able to say that you have arrived. On that day you will have become the indis-pensable ornament, the obligatory presence, the social fixture. There'll be no more need to sniff out opportunities, committees, clubs, and societies; they will come to you with the dull, crude air about them of de-adjectivized nouns, and you will be the adjective of their leaden speeches, the *fragrant* of their flowers, the *indigo* of their sky, the *upstanding* of their citizens, the *trenchant* and *meaty* of their news reports. And this is the most important thing of all, because the adjective is the very soul of language, its idealistic and metaphysical component. The noun is reality stripped naked and raw; it is the naturalism of vocabulary."

"And all this, you think, is just a standby in case all else fails?"

"That's right. It doesn't preclude any other activity whatsoever."

"Not even politics?"

"Not even politics. It is simply a matter of abiding by certain basic rules and obligations. You may belong to any party, liberal or conservative, republican or ultramontane, the one caveat being that you must not attach any specific ideas to these words, and only recognize their usefulness as biblical shibboleths."

"If I go into parliament, can I speak from the rostrum?"

"You can and you must; it is a way of attracting public attention. As for the subject of your speeches, you have a choice between pettifogging minutiae and political ideology, but with a preference for ideology. Minutiae, one must admit, are not inconsistent with the urbane dullness that is the mark of every accomplished bigwig, but, if you can, go for ideology—it's easier and much more appealing. Suppose you were to inquire into the reasons for transferring the Seventh Company of Infantry from Uruguaiana to Canguçu; you will be heard only by the minister of war, and it will take him all of ten minutes to explain the reasons for his decision. Not so with ideology. A speech on the most arcane aspects of political ideology will, by its very nature, excite the passions of politicians and the public gallery, provoking heated interjections and rebuttals. Moreover, it requires neither thought nor investigation. In this branch of human knowledge everything has already been discovered, worded, labeled, and packaged; you need only rummage around in the saddlebags of memory. But whatever you do, never go beyond the boundaries of enviable triteness."

"I'll do what I can. So no imagination, then?"

"None whatsoever. Much better to put the word around that the gift of imagination is very low-class indeed."

"And no philosophy?"

"Let's be quite clear: a smattering perhaps when writing or speaking, but in reality, none. 'Philosophy of history,' for example, is a phrase you should frequently employ, but I forbid you to arrive at any conclusions that have not already been reached by others. Avoid anything that has about it so much as a whiff of reflection, originality, or the like."

"And humor?"

"What do you mean, 'humor'?"

"Should I always be very serious?"

"It all depends. You have a jovial, fun-loving nature and there's no need to smother or suppress it entirely—you can laugh and joke once in a while. Being a bigwig doesn't necessarily require you to be a melancholic. A serious man can have his lighthearted moments too. Only—and this is a crucial point . . ."

"Go on."

"You must never use irony—that mysterious little twitch at the corners of the mouth, invented by some decadent Greek, caught by Lucian, transmitted to Swift and Voltaire, and typical of all skeptics and impudent freethinkers. No. Better to tell a rude joke, our good old friend, the chubby-cheeked, brash, and blatantly rude joke, wrapped in neither veils nor false modesty, which hits you right between the eyes, stings like a slap on the back, makes your blood pound, and snaps your suspenders with laughter. What's that?"

"It's midnight."

"Midnight? Well, then, young man, you are already entering your twenty-second year; you have definitively come of age. Let's turn in; it's late. Chew over what I've told you, son. All things considered, our conversation tonight has been worthy of Machiavelli's *The Prince*. Time for bed."

DONA BENEDITA

A Portrait

Chapter I

THE MOST DIFFICULT THING in the world, apart from governing a country, must surely be that of guessing Dona Benedita's exact age. Some said forty, some forty-five, others thirty-six. One stockbroker went as low as twenty-nine, but his judgment, clouded by hidden intentions, lacked the necessary stamp of sincerity that we all like to see in human opinions. Indeed, I only mention it to illustrate, from the very outset, that Dona Benedita was always the very model of good manners. The stockbroker's flattery served only to arouse her indignation, albeit momentarily, yes, momentarily. As for those other estimates, oscillating between thirty-six and forty-five, none of them could be contradicted by Dona Benedita's appearance, which was both maturely serious and youthfully graceful. The only surprising thing is that such speculation continued, when in order to know the truth one needed only to ask her.

Dona Benedita reached her forty-second birthday on Sunday the nineteenth of September, 1869. At six o'clock in the evening, friends and relations, some twenty or twenty-five in number, are gathered around the family table. Many of them were also present at her birthday dinners of 1868, 1867, and 1866, and they have always heard their hostess's age frankly alluded to. Moreover, there at the table, for all to see, are a young lady and a young master, her children; it is true that he, both in size and manners, is still somewhat boyish; on the other hand, the young lady, Eulália, is eighteen, although such is the severity of her manners and features that she looks twenty-one.

The joviality of the guests, the excellence of the dinner, certain matrimonial negotiations entrusted to Canon Roxo (of which more shall be said anon), and the hostess's generous nature, all these make for an intimate and happy affair. The canon stands up to carve the turkey. Dona Benedita has always abided by the custom in modest households of entrusting the turkey to one of the guests, instead of having it carved away from the table by servants, and the canon was the maestro of such solemn occasions. Nobody knew the bird's anatomy better than he, nor how to wield the knife so nimbly. Perhaps—and this is a matter for the experts—perhaps his status as a canon gave to the carving knife, in the minds of the guests, a certain prestige, which would be lacking if, for example, he were a mere student of mathematics or an office clerk. On the other hand, would a student or scribe, without the lessons of long practice, have at their disposal the canon's consummate art? That is another important question.

As for the other guests, they are sitting and chatting; the gurgle of half-sated stomachs reigns, the laughter of nature on its way to repleteness; it is a moment of relaxation.

Dona Benedita is talking, as are her visitors; however, she does not speak to all of them, but only to the one seated next to her. Her neighbor is a plump, kindly, cheerful lady, the mother of a twenty-one-year-old graduate, Leandrinho, who is sitting opposite them. Dona Benedita is not merely talking to the plump lady, she is clasping one of her hands, and not only is she clasping the plump lady's hand, she is also looking at her with vivacious, lovestruck eyes. Note that hers is not a persistent or prolonged gaze, but rather a series of small, restless, momentary glances. In any event, there is much tenderness in that gesture, and even if there weren't, nothing would be lost, because Dona Benedita repeats with her lips everything that her eyes have already said to Dona Maria dos Anjos: that she is absolutely delighted, that it is wonderful to meet her, that Dona Maria is so very kind, so very dignified, that her eyes are the very windows of her soul, and so on. One of her friends says jokingly to Dona Benedita that she is making her jealous.

"Oh, stuff and nonsense!" she replies, laughing.

And, turning back to the other woman:

"Don't you agree? No one should come between us."

And she carried on showering her with compliments, courtesies, and smiles, the offers of more of this, more of that, plans to go on a trip together or perhaps to the theater, and promises of many visits, all spoken in such warm, effusive tones that her new companion was visibly throbbing with pleasure and gratitude.

The turkey has been eaten. Dona Maria dos Anjos signals to her son, who stands up and asks them to accompany him in a toast:

"Ladies and gentlemen, there is a saying in French: *les absents ont tort*. Let us resolutely reject this, and drink to someone who is far, far away in terms of space, but close, very close indeed, to the heart of his dear wife. Let us drink to that most illustrious judge, Justice Proença."

The toast did not receive an enthusiastic response from the assembled guests, and to understand why one need only look at the sad face of their hostess. Her closest friends and relatives whispered to one another that young Leandrinho had been very thoughtless indeed; they drank the toast, but refrained from cheering, so as not, it would seem, to exacerbate Dona Benedita's suffering. In vain: Dona Benedita, unable to contain herself, burst into tears, got up from the table, and left the room. Dona Maria dos Anjos went with her. There then followed a deathly silence. Eulália begged them all to carry on as normal, saying that her mother would be back shortly.

"Mama is very sensitive," she said, "and the idea of Papa being so far away . . ."

Dismayed, Leandrinho apologized to Eulália. The fellow sitting next to him explained that Dona Benedita could not hear her husband's name mentioned without feeling a crushing blow to her heart, promptly followed by tears; Leandrinho replied that he was aware of her misfortune, but had never imagined his toast would have such a harmful effect.

"And yet it's the most natural thing in the world," explained the fellow, "for she misses her husband terribly."

"The canon," replied Leandrinho, "told me her husband went to Pará about two years ago."

"Two and a half years. He was appointed district judge by the Zacarias government. He would have preferred the appeal court in São Paulo, or perhaps Bahia, but it was not to be, and so he accepted Pará instead."

"And he hasn't been back since?"

"No."

"I presume Dona Benedita is afraid of such a long sea voyage . . ."

"I don't believe so. She's already been to Europe. No, if I recall correctly, she stayed behind in Rio to sort out some family affairs, and then stayed on, and on, and now . . ."

"But would it not have been far better to go to Pará than to suffer like this? Do you know her husband?"

"I do; a very distinguished gentleman, and still hale and hearty; he couldn't be more than forty-five. Tall, bearded, handsome. People used to say that he didn't insist on his wife joining him because he had fallen for some widow up there."

"Ah!"

"And someone even came and told Dona Benedita. Imagine how the poor lady must have felt! She cried all night, and the next day she wouldn't eat any breakfast, and made arrangements to take the very next steamship to Pará."

"But she didn't go?"

"No. She canceled three days later."

At that moment, Dona Benedita returned, on the arm of Dona Maria dos Anjos. She smiled in embarrassment, apologized for the interruption, and sat down once again with her new friend by her side, thanking her profusely for looking after her and again clasping her hand.

"I can see you only want what's good for me," she said.

"It's only what you deserve," said Dona Maria dos Anjos.

"Really?" Dona Benedita said, with a mix of vanity and modesty.

And she declared that, no, it was the other lady who was truly good, just like her name. Dona Maria dos Anjos was an angel, a real angel! And Dona Benedita underlined the word with the same loving gaze, not persistent or prolonged, but restless and intermittent. For his part, the canon, seeking to expunge all memory of the unfortunate incident, changed the topic of conversation to the weighty matter of which was the best dessert. Opinions diverged widely. Some thought the coconut dessert was best, some the one with cashew nuts, and others the orange one, etc. The author of the toast, Leandrinho, said—although not with his lips but slyly with his eyes—that the sweetest of desserts were Eulália's cheeks—a dusky, rosy-cheeked dessert. His own mother inwardly approved of those unspoken words, while the young woman's mother did not even see them, so caught up was she in her adoration of her new friend. An angel, a real angel!

Chapter II

The next day, Dona Benedita got up from her bed with the idea of writing a letter to her husband, a long letter in which she would tell him about the party, name all the guests and the different dishes, describe the reception afterward, and, more importantly, tell him about her new friendship with Dona Maria dos Anjos. The mail pouch closed at two in the afternoon, Dona Benedita had woken at nine, and, since she didn't live far away (her house was on the Campo da Aclamação), a slave would be able to deliver the letter to the post office in plenty of time. What's more, it was raining; Dona Benedita pulled back the net curtain and saw the drenched windowpanes; a persistent drizzle was falling, the sky was dark and overcast and dotted with thick black clouds. In the distance, she could see a cloth fluttering and flapping over a basket carried on the head of a black woman, from which she concluded that it was windy. A splendid day for staying at home, and, therefore, for writing a letter, two letters, or indeed all the letters a wife could possibly write to her absent husband. No one would come to tempt her away.

While she arranges the lace fringes and frills on her white linen dressing gown, which the eminent judge had given her in 1862, also on her birthday, September 19, I invite the reader to take a closer look at her. You will notice that I refrain from calling her a Venus, but nor do I call her a Medusa. Unlike Medusa, she wears her hair brushed smoothly back and fastened just above the nape of her neck. Her eyes are ordinary enough, but have a kindly expression. Her mouth is the sort that appears cheerful even when not smiling, and enjoys that other remarkable gift of showing neither remorse nor regret: one could even say it is devoid of desires, but I will say only what I want to say, and I wish to speak only of remorse and regret. This head, which neither excites nor repels, sits on a body that is tall rather than short, and neither thin nor fat, but in proportion with her build. But I won't describe her hands just yet. Why should I? You will admire them soon enough, holding pen to paper with slender, idle fingers, two of them adorned with five or six rings.

One need only see the way in which she arranges the lacy frills of her gown in order to understand that she is a persnickety woman, fond of keeping everything around her and herself tidy. I note that she has just torn the lace trimming on her left cuff, but that is because she, being impatient by nature, blurted out, "Damn and blast the thing." Those were her exact words, immediately followed by a "May God forgive me!" which took all the venom out of her. I don't say that she stamped her foot, but she might have, since that is a gesture natural to certain ladies when annoyed. In any event, her anger lasted barely a minute. She then went to her sewing box to stitch up the torn lace, but decided to make do with a pin. The pin fell to the floor; she knelt down and picked it up. There were of course others in the box, many others, but she didn't think it wise to leave pins lying on the floor. As she knelt, she caught sight of the tip of her slipper, on which there was a white mark; she sat down on the nearby chair, removed her slipper, and saw what it was: it had been chewed by a cockroach. Dona Benedita again fell into a rage, because the slipper was a very smart one, and had been given to her the year before by a dear friend. An angel, a real angel! Dona Benedita fixed her eyes on the white mark; happily their usual expression of simple charity was not so charitable as to allow itself to be entirely replaced by other, less passive expressions, and so it resumed its rightful place. Dona Benedita turned the slipper over and over, passing it from one hand to the other, lovingly at first, then mechanically, until her hands stopped moving completely, and the slipper fell into her lap, and Dona Benedita sat staring into space. At this point, the clock in the drawing room began to strike. After the first two chimes, Dona Benedita shuddered:

"Good Lord! It's ten o'clock!"

And she quickly put her slipper back on, hurriedly pinned the cuff of her gown, and went to her writing desk to begin the letter. She had put the date and "My ungrateful husband," and had barely written: "Did you think of me yesterday? I . . ." when Eulália knocked on her door, calling out:

"Mama! Mama! It's time for breakfast."

Dona Benedita opened the door, Eulália kissed her hand, then raised her own hands heavenward:

"Goodness gracious! What a sleepyhead!"

"Is breakfast ready?"

"Yes, it's been ready for ages!"

"But I gave orders that breakfast today should be later than usual . . . I've been writing to your father."

She looked at her daughter for a few moments, as if about to say something serious, or at least difficult, such was the grave, indecisive look in her eyes. But, in the end, she said nothing, and her daughter, announcing again that breakfast was served, took her by the arm and led her away.

Let us leave them to eat breakfast at leisure, and take the weight off our feet here in the drawing room, without, however, feeling the need to catalogue every item of its furniture, just as we have failed to do in any other room of the house. Not that the furniture is ugly or in bad taste; on the contrary, it is all rather good. But the overall impression is rather strange, as if the choice of furnishings were the result of some subsequently abandoned plan, or a succession of abandoned plans. Mother, daughter, and son breakfasted together. Let us leave aside the son, who is of no interest to us; a young whippersnapper of twelve years old, but so sickly that he looks more like eight. Eulália is the one who interests us, not only because of what we glimpsed in the preceding chapter, but also because, when her mother began to talk about Dona Maria dos Anjos and Leandrinho, she became very serious and, perhaps, a little sullen. Dona Benedita realized that her daughter did not like this topic of conversation and so she retreated, like someone turning a corner to avoid an undesirable encounter. She rose from the table, and her daughter followed her into the drawing room.

It was a quarter past eleven. Dona Benedita spoke with her daughter until shortly after midday, so as to have time to digest her breakfast and write the letter. As you are aware, the mail pouch closes at two o'clock. And so, a few minutes after midday, Dona Benedita told her daughter to go and practice the piano, so that she could finish the letter. Dona Benedita left the drawing room; Eulália went over to the window, glanced out at the square outside, and I can vouch for the fact that she did so with a glimmer of sadness in her eyes. It was not, however, a weak and indecisive sadness; it was the sadness of a resolute young woman who anticipates the pain her actions will cause to others, but, nevertheless, swears to go through with them, and does go through with them. I accept that not all these details could be surmised merely from Eulália's eyes, but it is for this very reason that stories are told by someone who takes it upon themselves to fill in the gaps and reveal what is hidden. True, it was certainly a vigorous sadness and equally true that a glimmer of hope would soon appear in her eyes.

"This can't go on," she murmured, coming back into the room.

At that very moment, a carriage pulled up at the front door. A lady stepped out, the doorbell sounded, a houseboy went down to open the gate, and Dona Maria dos Anjos came up the steps. When the visitor was announced, Dona Benedita dropped her pen in agitation; she hurriedly got dressed, put on her shoes, and went into the drawing room.

"Fancy coming out in this weather!" she exclaimed. "That is true friendship!"

"I didn't want to wait for you to visit me, simply to show that I'm not one to stand on ceremony, and that between you and me there must be no constraints."

This was followed by the same compliments and sweet, caressing words as on the previous day. Dona Benedita kept insisting that coming to visit her that very day was the greatest of courtesies and a proof of genuine friendship, but, she added a moment later, she wished for further proof and asked Dona Maria dos Anjos to stay for dinner. Her friend excused herself, pleading that she had to be elsewhere; furthermore, this was the very proof of friendship that she herself desired, namely, that Dona Benedita should come and dine at her house first. Dona Benedita did not hesitate and promised that she would dine with her that very week.

"I was just this minute writing your name," she continued.

"Were you?"

"Yes, I'm writing to my husband and telling him all about you. I won't repeat to you what I've written, but you can imagine that I spoke very ill of you, telling him what an unkind, insufferable, tedious woman you are, a terrible bore . . . You can just imagine!"

"I can indeed. And you can add that, despite all that and more, I send him my deepest respects."

"See how witty she is!" remarked Dona Benedita, looking at her daughter.

Eulália smiled unconvincingly. Perched on a chair facing her mother, beside the sofa on which Dona Maria dos Anjos was sitting, Eulália gave the two ladies' conversation only the degree of attention that good manners required, and not a jot more.

She came close to looking bored; every smile that appeared on her lips was wan and languid, pure duty. One of her braids—it was still morning

and she was wearing her hair in two long braids—served her as a pretext
to look away from time to time, because she would occasionally tug at it to
count the hairs, or so it seemed. At least that's what Dona Maria dos Anjos
thought, when she occasionally shot a glance in Eulália's direction, curious
and somewhat suspicious. For her part, Dona Benedita saw nothing; she had
eyes only for her dear friend, her enchantress, as she called her two or three
times: "my dear, dear enchantress."

"Enough!"

Dona Maria dos Anjos explained that she had a few other visits to make,
but her friend prevailed upon her to stay for a little longer. She was wearing
a very elegant cape of black lace, and Dona Benedita said that she had one
just the same and sent one of the slaves to fetch it. Delays, delays. But Leandrinho's mother was so pleased! Dona Benedita filled her heart with happiness; she found in her all the qualities best suited to her own personality and
her manners: tenderness, trust, enthusiasm, simplicity, a warm and willing
familiarity. The cape was brought, refreshments were offered; Dona Maria
dos Anjos would accept nothing more than a kiss and the promise that they
would dine with her that very week.

"On Thursday," said Dona Benedita.

"Promise?"

"I promise."

"What would you have me do to you if you don't come? It will need to
be a very harsh punishment."

"The harshest possible punishment would be for you never to speak to
me again!"

Dona Maria dos Anjos kissed her friend tenderly; then she hugged and
kissed Eulália, too, but with rather less enthusiasm on both sides. They were
measuring each other up, studying each other, and beginning to understand
each other. Dona Benedita accompanied her friend to the stairs, then went
over to the window to watch her get into her carriage; after settling herself in, her friend put her head out of the window, looked up, and waved
goodbye.

"Don't forget!"

"Thursday."

Eulália had already left the drawing room, and Dona Benedita rushed
to finish the letter. It was getting late; she had said nothing yet about yesterday's dinner, and it was too late to do so now. She gave a brief sum-

mary, extolling the virtues of her new friend; then, finally, she wrote the following words:

> Canon Roxo spoke to me about marrying Eulália to Dona Maria dos Anjos's son. He graduated in law this year; he's a conservative and, if Itaboraí does not resign from the government, he expects to be appointed a public prosecutor. I think it is the best possible match. Leandrinho (for that is his name) is a very polite young man; he proposed a toast to you, full of such fine words that I cried. I don't know if Eulália will want him or not; I have my suspicions about another young fellow who joined us the other day in Laranjeiras. But what do you think? Should I limit myself to advising her, or should I impose our wishes? I really think I ought to use my authority, but I don't want to do anything without your say-so. The best thing would be if you came here yourself.

She finished the letter and sealed it. At that moment, Eulália came in, and Dona Benedita gave her the letter to be sent off, without delay, to the post office. The daughter left the room with the letter, not knowing that it concerned her and her future. Dona Benedita slumped down on the sofa, exhausted. Even though there was much she had not mentioned, the letter had still turned out to be a very long one and writing long letters was such a tiresome business!

Chapter III

Yes, writing long letters was such a tiresome business! The words with which we closed the previous chapter fully explain Dona Benedita's exhaustion. Half an hour later, she sat up a little and glanced around the study, as if looking for something. That something was a book. She found the book, or, rather, books, since there were no fewer than three, two open, one marked at a certain page, all lying on different chairs. They were the three novels that Dona Benedita was reading at the same time. One of them, you will note, had required considerable effort on her part. She had heard it warmly spoken of it while she was out walking near the house; it had arrived from Europe only the day before. Dona Benedita was so excited that, despite the lateness of the hour and the distance, she turned back and went to buy the book herself, visiting no fewer than three bookshops. She returned home so eager to read it that she opened the book during dinner and read the first five chapters that same night. When sleep overcame her, she slept; the following day, she was unable to continue reading, and forgot all about the book. Now, however, a week later, and wanting to read something, there it was close to hand.

"Ah!"

And so she returns to the sofa, lovingly opens the book, and plunges eyes, heart and soul into the reading that had been so abruptly interrupted. It's only natural that Dona Benedita should love novels, and it is even more natural that she should love nice ones. Do not be surprised, therefore, when she forgets everything around her to read this one; everything, even her daughter's piano lesson, for which the piano teacher arrived and left without Dona Benedita once visiting the drawing room. Eulália said goodbye to her teacher, then went to the study, opened the door, tiptoed over to the sofa, and woke her mother with a kiss.

"Wake up, sleepyhead!"

"Is it still raining?"

"No, Mama, it's stopped now."

"Has the letter gone?"

"Yes, I told José to hurry. I bet you forgot to give my dearest love to Papa? I thought so. Well, I never forget."

Dona Benedita yawned. She was no longer thinking about the letter; she was thinking about the corset she had ordered from Charavel's, one with softer stays than the last one. She didn't like hard stays, for she had a very delicate body. Eulália talked a little more about her father, but soon stopped, and, seeing the famous novel lying open on the floor, she picked it up, closed it, and set it on the table. At that moment, a letter was brought in for Dona Benedita; it was from Canon Roxo, who wrote to ask whether they were at home that day, because he would be going to a funeral nearby.

"Of course we'll be at home!" Dona Benedita cried. "Do tell him to come."

Eulália wrote a little note in reply. Three-quarters of an hour later the canon entered Dona Benedita's drawing room. He was a good man, the canon, an old friend of the family, in which, besides carving the turkey on solemn occasions, as we have seen, he exercised the role of family advisor, and did so both loyally and lovingly. Eulália was particularly dear to him; he had known her since she was a little girl, his attentive and mischievous little friend, and he felt a paternal affection toward her, so paternal that he had taken it upon himself to see her properly married, and, thought the canon, there could be no better bridegroom than Leandrinho. That day, his idea of going to dine with them was little more than a pretext; the canon wished to raise the subject directly with the young lady herself. Eulália, either because she guessed his intentions or because the canon's presence brought Leandrinho to mind, became worried and annoyed.

But worried or annoyed does not mean sad or dispirited. She was resolute, she had a strong character, she could resist, and she did resist, declaring to the canon, when he spoke to her that night about Leandrinho, that she absolutely did not wish to marry.

"Cross your heart and hope to die?"

"Cross my heart and hope to live."

"But why?"

"Because I don't want to."

"And if Mama wants you to?"

"But I don't want to."

"Well, that's not very nice of you, Eulália."

Eulália did not reply. The canon returned yet again to the subject, praising the candidate's fine qualities, the hopes of his family, the many advantages of their marriage; she listened to all this, but said nothing. However, when the canon put the question to her directly, her response was invariably:

"I've already said all there is to say."

"You really don't want to marry?"

"No."

The canon's disappointment was deep and sincere. He wanted to see her properly married, and he could think of no better husband. He went so far as to probe her, discreetly, about whether her interest lay elsewhere. But Eulália, no less discreetly, responded that no, she had no other "interest"; she simply did not wish to marry. He believed this to be true, but also feared that it was not; he lacked sufficient experience in the ways of women to read beyond that negative. When he relayed all this to Dona Benedita, she was shocked by the abruptness of her daughter's refusal; but she quickly recovered her composure and told the priest in no uncertain terms that her daughter had no say in the matter, and that she, Dona Benedita, would do as she wished, and she wanted the marriage.

"There's no point even waiting for her father's reply," she concluded.

"I'll just tell him that she's getting married. It's as simple as that. On Thursday I will dine with Dona Maria dos Anjos, and we will arrange everything."

"I must tell you," ventured the canon, "that Dona Maria dos Anjos does not wish anything to be done by force."

"What force? No force is required."

The canon reflected for a moment.

"In any event, we must not overrule any other attachment she may have formed," he said.

Dona Benedita made no reply, but inwardly swore that, come what may, her daughter would become the daughter-in-law of Dona Maria dos Anjos. And after the canon had left, she said to herself: "Well, I never! A mere slip of a girl thinking she can rule the roost!"

Thursday dawned. Eulália, the mere slip of a girl, got out of bed feeling bright and cheerful and chatty, with all the windows of her spirit open to the blue morning air. Her mother awoke to hear a snippet from some glorious Italian melody; it was her daughter singing, happily and blithely, with all the indifference of birds who sing for themselves or for their own offspring, and not for the poet who listens and translates them into the immortal language of mankind. Dona Benedita had secretly cherished the idea of seeing her daughter downhearted and surly, and had expended a certain amount of imagination in deciding how she herself would act, pretending to be strong and forceful. Instead of a rebellious daughter, though, she found her to be talkative and amenable. It was a bad start to the day, like setting out prepared to destroy a fortress and finding instead a peaceful, welcoming city, its gates flung wide, politely inviting her to enter and break the bread of joy and harmony. It was a very bad start to the day.

The second cause of Dona Benedita's annoyance was a threatened migraine at three o'clock in the afternoon; a threat, or perhaps a suspicion of the possibility of a threat. She nearly canceled the visit, but her daughter thought it might do her good to go, and, in any event, it was too late to put it off. There was nothing else for it; Dona Benedita took her medicine, and, as she sat before the mirror brushing her hair, she was on the verge of saying that she would definitely stay at home, and she hinted as much to her daughter.

"But Mama, Dona Maria dos Anjos is expecting you," Eulália told her.

"Indeed," retorted her mother, "but I didn't promise to go there if I was indisposed."

Finally, she got dressed, put on her gloves, and issued her instructions to the servants; her head must have been hurting a lot because she was rather curt with people, like someone being compelled to do something against their will. Her daughter did her best to raise her spirits, reminding her to take her little bottle of smelling salts, urging her to go, saying how eager Dona Maria dos Anjos was to see her, repeatedly checking the little watch pinned to her waist, and so on. She would be really put out.

"Stop pestering me," her mother said.

And off she went, feeling exasperated, fervently wishing she could throttle her daughter, telling herself that daughters were the worst thing in the world. Sons were all right: they grew up and made a career for themselves; but daughters!

Happily, the meal at Dona Maria dos Anjos's calmed her down; not that it filled her with great satisfaction, because that wasn't the case at all. Dona Benedita was not her usual self; she was cold and brusque, or almost brusque; she, however, explained the difference in her own terms, mentioning the threatened migraine, which was not exactly good news, but nevertheless cheered Dona Maria dos Anjos, for this refined and profound reason: it was better that her friend's coolness was the result of an illness than a diminution in her affections. Moreover, it was nothing grave. And yet grave it was! There were no clasped hands, no loving gazes, no delicate titbits being consumed between fond caresses; in short, it was nothing like the dinner on Sunday. The meal was merely polite, not joyful; that was the most the canon could achieve. Oh, the kind, amiable canon! Eulália's mood that day filled him with hope; her playful laughter, her easy conversation, her readiness to do as asked, to play and sing, and the tender, agreeable look on her face when she listened and spoke to Leandrinho; all this greatly restored the canon's hopes. And for Dona Benedita to be indisposed today of all days! It really was bad luck.

Dona Benedita's spirits rose somewhat that evening after dinner. She talked a little more, discussed a plan to go for a stroll in the Jardim Botânico, even proposing that they go the very next day. However, Eulália warned her that it would be wise to wait a day or two for the effects of the migraine to wear off completely; and the look she got from her mother in return for her advice was as sharp as a dagger. The daughter had no fear of her mother's eyes, though. As she brushed her hair that night, thinking over the day's events, Eulália repeated to herself the words we heard her say, some days before, at the window.

"This can't go on."

And before sleeping, she smugly pulled open a certain drawer, took out a little box, opened it, and removed a card measuring only about two inches by two—a portrait. It was clearly not the portrait of a woman, not only on account of the mustache, but also the uniform; he was, at the very least, a naval officer. Whether handsome or ugly is a matter of opinion. Eulália thought him handsome, the proof being that she kissed the portrait, not once but three times. Then she gazed at it longingly, and put it back in its box.

What were you thinking, O strict and cautious mother, that you did not come and tear from the hands and lips of your daughter so subtle and mortal a venom? Standing at her window, Dona Benedita was gazing up at the night sky, amid the stars and gas lamps, with a roving, restless imagination, and filled with gnawing regrets and desires. Nothing had gone right for her since morning. Dona Benedita confessed, in the sweet intimacy of her own soul, that the dinner at Dona Maria dos Anjos's had been dreadful, and that her friend probably wasn't at her best, either. She felt certain regrets—although for what, she wasn't entirely sure—and certain desires, but for quite what, she didn't know. From time to time she gave a long, lazy yawn, like someone about to fall asleep; but if she felt anything at all it was boredom—boredom, impatience, and curiosity. Dona Benedita seriously wondered about going to join her husband; and no sooner had the thought of her husband entered her head than her heart was filled with longings and remorse, and her blood pulsed in her veins; so great was her desire to go and see the eminent judge that if her luggage had been packed and the northbound steamer had been waiting at the corner of the street, she would have embarked that very minute. No matter; there was sure to be another steamer in a week or ten days, and there was plenty of time to arrange her luggage. Since she would only be going for three months, she would not need to take very much.

It would be a relief to get away from Rio, from the sameness of the days, the lack of novelties, the same faces, even the unchanging fashions— something that always troubled her: "Why should any fashion last for more than two weeks?"

"I'll go; there's nothing more to be said. I'll go to Pará," she said softly.

Indeed, the following morning, the first thing she did was to communicate this decision to her daughter, who took the news calmly. Dona Benedita checked how many trunks she already had, wondered if she needed one more, calculated the size, and decided to buy another. In a sudden moment of inspiration, Eulália said:

"But Mama, we're only going for three months, aren't we?"

"Yes, three . . . or possibly two."

"Well, then, it isn't worth it. Two trunks will suffice."

"No, they won't."

"Well, if they aren't enough, we can always buy another one just before we leave. And you should go and choose it yourself—that would be much better than sending someone who knows nothing about trunks."

Dona Benedita thought this wise advice, and held on to her money. Her daughter smiled secretly. Perhaps she was repeating to herself the same words she had spoken at the window: "This can't go on." Her mother went to make arrangements, choosing clothes, making lists of things she needed to buy, a present for her husband, and so on. Oh, he would be so happy! In the afternoon, they went out to place orders, pay visits, buy tickets—four tickets, since they would each take a slave-woman with them. Eulália tried again to dissuade her, proposing that they delay the journey, but Dona Benedita declared that this was out of the question. At the offices of the steamship company, she was informed that the northbound steamer would leave on Friday of the following week. She asked for four tickets, opened her purse, pulled out a banknote, then two, then thought for a moment.

"We could just buy our tickets the day before, couldn't we?"

"You could, but there might not be any tickets left."

"All right, what if you set aside four tickets for us, and I'll send for them."

"Your name?"

"My name? No, better not take my name. We'll come back three days before the steamer leaves. There are sure to be tickets then."

"Possibly."

"No, there will be."

Once out in the street, Eulália remarked that it would be better to buy the tickets straightaway; and, since we know that she did not wish to travel either North or South, save on the frigate carrying the man we saw in that portrait the previous evening, one must assume that the young lady's comment was profoundly Machiavellian. It wouldn't surprise me.

Dona Benedita, meanwhile, informed her friends and acquaintances of their forthcoming journey and none of them was surprised. One did ask if, this time, she really was going. Dona Maria dos Anjos had heard about the proposed trip from the canon, but the only thing that alarmed her when her friend came to say goodbye was Dona Benedita's icy demeanor, her silence and indifference, and the way she kept her gaze fixed on the floor. A visit of barely ten minutes, during which Dona Benedita said only six words at the beginning: "We are going to the North." And one at the end: "Farewell." Followed by three sad, corpse-like kisses.

Chapter IV

The journey did not take place, for superstitious reasons. On the Sunday night, Dona Benedita realized that the steamer would be leaving on a Friday, which seemed to her a bad day to travel. They would go instead on the next steamer. However, they did not go on the next one, but this time her reasons lay entirely beyond the reach of human understanding; in such cases, the best advice is not to attempt to comprehend the incomprehensible. The fact of the matter is that Dona Benedita did not go, saying that she would go on the third steamer, unless, of course, something happened to change her plans.

Her daughter had come up with a party and a new friendship. The new friendship was with a family in Andaraí; no one knows what the party was for, but it must have been a splendid affair, because Dona Benedita was still talking about it three days later. Three days! It really was too much. As for the family, they could not have been kinder; the whole thing had made the most tremendous impression on Dona Benedita. I use this superlative because she herself used it: a document made by human hands.

"Those people made the most tremendous impression on me."

And she began going for strolls in Andaraí, enchanted by the company of Dona Petronilha, Counselor Beltrão's wife, and her sister Dona Maricota, who was going to marry a naval officer, the brother of that other naval officer whose mustache, eyes, hair, and bearing match those of the portrait the reader glimpsed earlier in that drawer. The married sister was thirty-two, and her earnestness and charming manners entirely bewitched Dona Benedita. The unmarried sister was a flower, a wax flower, another expression of Dona Benedita's, which I have left unaltered for fear of watering down the truth.

One of the most obscure aspects of this whole curious story is the speed with which friendships blossomed and events unfurled. For example, another regular visitor to Andaraí, along with Dona Benedita, was the very naval officer pictured on that little card. He was First Lieutenant Mascarenhas, whom Counselor Beltrão predicted would become an admiral. Note, however, the officer's perfidy: he came in uniform; and Dona Benedita, who adored any new spectacle, found him so distinguished, so handsome compared with the other men in civilian clothes, that she preferred him to all of them, and told him so. The officer thanked her earnestly. She told him he must come and see them; he begged permission to pay a visit.

"A visit? Why, you must come and dine with us."

Mascarenhas assented with a bow.

"Look here," said Dona Benedita, "why don't you come tomorrow?"

Mascarenhas came, and came early. Dona Benedita talked to him about life at sea; he asked for her daughter's hand in marriage. Dona Benedita was speechless, indeed shocked. She remembered, it is true, that, one day in Laranjeiras some time ago, she'd had her suspicions about him, but now her suspicions were long gone. Since then, she hadn't seen the couple speak or look at one another even once. But marriage! Was that possible? It could not be anything else; the young man's serious, respectful, and imploring behavior said clearly that he had indeed meant marriage. A dream come true! To invite to one's home a friend, and open the door to a son-in-law: it was the very height of the unexpected. And the dream was a handsome one; the naval officer was a courteous young man; strong, elegant, friendly, openhearted, and, more importantly, he seemed to adore her, Dona Benedita. What a magnificent dream! Once she had recovered from her astonishment, Dona Benedita said, yes, Eulália was his. Mascarenhas took her hand and kissed it with filial devotion.

"But what of your husband?" he asked.

"My husband will agree with me."

Everything proceeded at great speed. Certificates were obtained, banns were read, and a date for the wedding set; it would take place twenty-four hours after the judge's response was received. Dona Benedita, the good, kind mother, was beside herself with joy, busily caught up in preparing the trousseau, in planning and ordering the festivities, in choosing the guests! She rushed hither and thither, sometimes on foot, sometimes by carriage, come rain or shine. She did not linger over any one thing for very long; one day it was the trousseau, the next it was preparations for the wedding reception, the next there were visits to be made; she switched from one thing to another, then back again, and it was all somewhat frenetic. But the daughter was always there to make up for any shortcomings, to correct any mistakes, and trim back any excesses, with her own natural talent for such things. Unlike other bridegrooms, the naval officer did not get in their way; he did not take up Dona Benedita's invitation to dine with them every evening; he dined with them only on Sundays, and paid them a visit once a week. He kept in touch through long, secret letters, as he had during their courtship. Dona Benedita could not explain such diffidence when she herself had fallen head over heels in love with him; and she would avenge his strange behavior by falling even deeper in love, and telling everyone the most wonderful things about him.

"A pearl! An absolute pearl!"

"He's certainly a fine young man," they all agreed.

"Isn't he just? First-rate!"

She repeated the same thing in the letters she wrote her husband, both before and after receiving his reply to her first letter. In that reply the eminent judge gave his consent, adding that it pained him greatly that, due to a slight indisposition, he would be unable to attend the nuptials; however, he gave them his paternal blessing, and asked for a portrait of his new son-in-law.

His wishes were followed to the letter. The wedding took place twenty-four hours after his letter arrived from Pará. It was, as Dona Benedita told certain friends later on, an admirable, splendid affair. Canon Roxo officiated, and it goes without saying that Dona Maria dos Anjos was not present, still less her son. Up until the very last minute, she had expected to receive a wedding announcement, an invitation, or perhaps a visit, even if she would, naturally enough, refrain from actually attending the ceremony; but nothing came. She was frankly astonished, and scoured her memory again and again for some inadvertent slight on her part that could explain this new coolness. Finding nothing, she imagined some intrigue. But she imagined wrongly, for it was a simple oversight. On the day of the wedding, it suddenly occurred to Dona Benedita that she had forgotten to send Dona Maria dos Anjos a wedding announcement.

"Eulália, it seems we didn't send the announcement to Dona Maria dos Anjos," she said to her daughter over breakfast.

"I don't know, Mama. It was you who organized the invitations."

"Well, it seems that I didn't," said Dona Benedita. "More sugar, João."

The footman handed her the sugar, and, stirring her tea, she remembered the carriage that would be going to fetch the canon, and repeated one of the orders she had given the day before.

But fortune is a capricious thing. Two weeks after the wedding, they received news of the judge's death. I will not describe Dona Benedita's grief; it was deep and sincere. The young newlyweds, lost in their own world up in Tijuca, came down to see her; Dona Benedita wept the tears of a heartbroken and devotedly faithful wife. After the seventh-day mass, she consulted her daughter and son-in-law on the idea of her going to Pará and having a tomb built for her husband, where she could kiss the earth in which he now lay. Mascarenhas exchanged a look with his wife, and then said to his mother-in-law that it would be better for them to go together, since he was due to go to the North in three months' time on a government commission. Dona Benedita resisted somewhat, but accepted the three-month delay, meanwhile setting about giving all the necessary instructions for the building of the tomb. And so the tomb was built, but Mascarenhas's commission did not materialize, and Dona Benedita was unable to go.

Five months later, there occurred a small family incident. Dona Benedita had arranged to build a house on the road to Tijuca, and her son-in-law, using an interruption in the building work as a pretext, proposed that he should finish it. Dona Benedita agreed, and her agreement was all the more to her credit given that she was finding her son-in-law increasingly unbearable with his love of discipline, his obstinacy and impertinence. In fact, he didn't need to be obstinate; rather, he had only to rely on his mother-in-law's good nature and merely wait a few days for her to give in. But perhaps it was precisely this that vexed her. Happily, the government decided to dispatch him to the South, and the pregnant Eulália stayed with her mother.

It was around this time that a widowed merchant took it upon himself to ask Dona Benedita for her hand in marriage. The first year of widowhood had passed. Dona Benedita received his proposal kindly, albeit with little enthusiasm. She looked to her own interests; her son's age and studies would soon take him away to São Paulo, leaving her all alone in the world. The marriage would be a source of consolation and company. In her own mind, at home or out and about, she developed the idea, adorning it with her quick and lively imagination; it would be a new life for her, for it could be said that she had been a widow for a long time, even before her husband's death. The merchant had a sound reputation: it would be an excellent choice.

She did not marry. Her son-in-law returned from the South, her daughter gave birth to a strong, beautiful baby boy, who became his grandmother's passion for the next few months. Then her son-in-law, daughter, and grandson all left for the North. Dona Benedita found herself alone and sad; her son was not enough to fill her affections. Once again the idea of traveling glimmered briefly in her mind, but only like a match that quickly burned out. Traveling alone would be tiring and dull; she decided it was better to stay.

A poetry recital she happened to attend helped her shake off her torpor, and restored her to society. Society once again suggested the idea of marriage, and quickly put forward a candidate, this time a lawyer, also a widower.

"Shall I marry or shall I not?"

One night, as Dona Benedita was turning this problem over in her mind while standing at the window of the house on the shore at Botafogo, where she had moved to some months earlier, she saw a most unusual spectacle. It began as an opaque glow, like a light filtered through frosted glass, filling the inlet of the bay beyond. Against this backdrop appeared a floating, transparent figure, wreathed in mist and veiled in shimmering reflections, its shape disappearing into thin air. The figure came right up to Dona Benedita's windowsill, and, drowsily, in a childish voice, spoke these meaningless words:

"Marry . . . don't marry . . . if you do marry . . . you will marry . . . you won't marry . . . you will marry . . . get married . . ."

Dona Benedita froze in terror, but still had strength enough to ask the figure who she was. The ghostly figure began to laugh, but that laughter quickly faded, and she replied that she was the fairy who had presided over Dona Benedita's birth. "My name is Indecision," said the fairy, and, like a sigh, dissolved into the night and the silence.

THE LOAN

———

I'M GOING TO TELL YOU an anecdote, an anecdote in the true sense of the word, which common usage has since broadened out to include any brief, invented tale. This anecdote happens to be true: I can cite several people who know it as well as I do. Nor would it have remained hidden from view had some tranquil soul been capable of discerning its philosophical implications. As you know, everything has a philosophical meaning. Carlyle discovered the philosophy of vests, or, rather, of clothes, and everyone knows that numbers were used in the Pythagorean system long before the Ipiranga lottery. For my part, I think I have deciphered the meaning behind this tale of a loan; you will see if I am mistaken.

To begin with, let us amend what Seneca said. In the eyes of that stern moralist, every day is, in itself, a singular life; in other words, a life within life. I wouldn't disagree with that, but why did he not add that often a single hour can encapsulate a whole life? Observe this young man: he enters the world with great ambitions: a ministerial portfolio perhaps, his own bank, a viscount's coronet, a bishop's crozier. At fifty, we will find him working as a lowly customs inspector, or as a sacristan in some country parish. This transformation took place over a period of thirty years, and no doubt a Balzac could have fit it all into a mere three hundred pages; so why shouldn't life, which was, after all, Balzac's teacher, squeeze it into thirty or sixty minutes?

Four o'clock had struck in the office of the notary Vaz Nunes, in Rua do Rosário. The clerks had put the final flourishes to their documents, and wiped their goose quills on the piece of black silk hanging from one of the drawers; then they had closed the drawers, gathered up their papers, tidied away their books and registers, and washed their hands; those who had changed their jackets on arriving took off their work coat and put on their outdoor one, and then they all left. Vaz Nunes remained alone.

This honest notary was one of the most perceptive men of his day. He has since died, so we can praise him all we like. He had eyes like a lancet, cutting and sharp. He could read the characters of the people who came to him to notarize their contracts and agreements; he knew a testator's soul long before he had finished his will; he could scent secret plots and hidden thoughts. He wore glasses, as do all stage notaries, but, not being nearsighted, he would peer over them when he wanted to see, and through them if he preferred not to be seen. Crafty old fox, said the clerks. He was, in any event, a circumspect fellow. He was fifty years old, a childless widower, and, in the words of some of his fellow notaries, he was quietly nibbling his way through the two hundred *contos de réis* he had salted away.

"Who's there?" he asked suddenly, looking up.

Standing in the doorway was a man whom he did not immediately recognize and whom he only barely recognized afterward. Vaz Nunes invited him in; the man entered, greeted him, shook his hand, and sat down on the chair beside the desk. He did not carry himself with the customary awkwardness of a beggar; on the contrary, he gave every impression of having come with the sole purpose of giving the notary some very precious and rare commodity. Vaz Nunes nevertheless shuddered and waited.

"Don't you remember me?"

"No, I don't."

"We were with each other one night a few months ago, in Tijuca. Don't you remember? In Teodorico's house, at that magnificent Christmas Eve supper. As a matter of fact, I proposed a toast to you. Surely you remember old Custódio!"

"Ah!"

Custódio sat up straighter, having been sitting somewhat slumped. He was a man of about forty. Poorly dressed, but well groomed, neat, and very correct. He had long nails, neatly trimmed, and his hands were slender and soft, unlike the skin on his face, which was somewhat lined. Minor details, but necessary to illustrate a certain duality in the man, an air of being both a beggar and a general. Walking down the street with no breakfast and not a penny in his pocket, he behaved as if he were marching at the head of an army. The reason was none other than the contrast between nature and situation, between soul and life. Custódio had been born with a vocation to be wealthy, but with no vocation for work. He had an instinct for elegance, a love of excess, good food, beautiful ladies, luxuriant carpets, exquisite furniture, a voluptuary (and, up to a point, an artist) capable of running the Villa Torlonia or the Hamilton Gallery. But he had no money; neither money nor the aptitude or patience to earn it. And yet, on the other hand, he needed to live. *Il faut bien que je vive*, a man in search of a favor once said to Talleyrand. *Je n'en vois pas la nécessité*, the minister replied coldly. Nobody gave this answer to Custódio; they gave him money instead—someone would give him ten *mil-réis*, another would give five, another twenty, and it was principally from such small donations that he paid his bed and board.

I say "principally," because Custódio did not hold back from involving himself in various business deals, but always on condition that he could choose them, and he always chose the ones that were doomed to fail. He had an excellent nose for disasters. From among twenty businesses, he could immediately pluck the most foolhardy, and would plunge in resolutely. The bad luck that pursued him would ensure that the other nineteen would prosper, while the one he chose would blow up in his face. No matter; he would pick himself up and get ready for the next.

He had, for example, recently read an advertisement in the paper seeking a business partner willing to invest five *contos de réis* in a certain enterprise that promised, within the first six months, to return a profit of between eighty and a hundred *contos*. Custódio went to meet the person who had placed the advertisement. It was a great idea: a needle factory, a brand-new business with an exciting future. And the plans, the design of the factory, the reports from Birmingham, the lists of imports, the replies from tailors and haberdashers and other such merchants, all swam before Custódio's eyes, dazzled by figures he could not understand, and which, for that very reason, appeared to be the gospel truth. Twenty-four hours; he asked for twenty-four hours to find the five *contos*. And he left the place, flattered and fawned upon by the advertiser, who, still standing on the doorstep, continued to deluge him with a torrent of credit and debit balances. But the five *contos*—five thousand *mil-réis*, no less—proved less biddable or less fickle than a mere five *mil-réis*, shaking their heads incredulously and keeping to their coffers, paralyzed by fear and sleep. Not one penny. The

eight or ten friends he spoke to all told him they didn't have that amount
of money available, nor did they have any faith in the factory. He had just
about lost all hope when he happened to find himself in Rua do Rosário and
saw the name Vaz Nunes above the doorway of a notary's office. His heart
leapt with joy, remembering Tijuca, the notary's impeccable manners, the
kind words with which he responded to the toast, and he said to himself
that here was the man to save the situation.

"I've come to ask you to draw up a deed . . ."

Expecting a different opening gambit, Vaz Nunes did not reply, but
simply peered over his glasses and waited.

"A deed of gratitude," explained Custódio; "I've come to ask you a great
favor, an indispensable favor, and I'm counting on you, my friend . . ."

"If I can help, of course . . ."

"It's a really excellent business, a magnificent business. I would not even
deign to bother other people if the outcome were not certain. It's all set to
go; stock has already been ordered from England, and the business should
be up and running within two months; it's a new factory, you see. There are
three of us in the partnership; my share is five *contos* and I've come to ask
you to lend me that amount for six months—or even three, at a reasonable
rate of interest . . ."

"Five *contos*?"

"Yes, indeed."

"But I can't, Custódio. I simply don't have that kind of money. Business
is bad, and even if it were going really well, I wouldn't be able to lay my
hands on that amount. Who could ever expect five *contos* from a humble
notary?"

"If you really wanted to . . ."

"But I do want to. All I'm saying is that if it were a small amount, pro-
portionate to my means, I would have no hesitation in advancing it. But five
contos! Believe me, it's quite impossible."

Custódio's spirits sank. He had climbed up Jacob's ladder to heaven,
but instead of descending like the angels in the biblical dream, he had tum-
bled down and fallen flat on his face. This was his last hope, and precisely
because it had arisen so unexpectedly, he was convinced it would bear fruit,
since, like all souls who trust themselves to happenstance, Custódio was
a superstitious man. The poor wretch could feel his body being pierced
all over by every one of those millions of needles that the factory would

undoubtedly produce during its first six months. Speechless, eyes down-cast, he waited for the notary to continue, to take pity on him and give him a chance. But, sensing this, the notary remained equally silent, turning his snuff box around and around in his hand, and breathing heavily, with a certain knowing, nasal whistle. Custódio attempted every possible pose, now a beggar, now a general. The notary would not be moved. Custódio stood up.

"In that case," he said, with just a touch of resentment, "forgive me for bothering you . . ."

"There's nothing to forgive: it is I who must apologize for not being able to help you, as I would have liked. As I said, had the amount been smaller, much smaller, I would not have hesitated; however . . ."

He reached out to shake hands with Custódio, who mechanically tipped his hat with his other hand. Custódio's dull stare revealed the state of his soul, barely recovered from its fall, which had drained him of his last ounce of energy. No mysterious ladder and no heaven; everything had vanished at the snap of a notary's fingers. Farewell, needles! Reality once again gripped him with its bronze talons. He would have to return to his precarious, unplanned existence, to his old account books with their goggle-eyed zeros and wiggly-eared $-signs, that would continue to stare and listen, listen and stare, dangling before him the implacable numerology of hunger. What a fall! And into what an abyss! Realizing the truth of his situation, he looked at the notary as if to say goodbye, but an idea suddenly lit up the dark night of his brain. If it were a smaller amount, Vaz Nunes could provide it, and willingly. So why shouldn't it be a smaller amount? He had already given up the idea of the business adventure; but he could scarcely do the same with his rent arrears and his various other creditors. A reasonable sum, five hundred *mil-réis*, for example, would do nicely, if he could only persuade the notary to lend it to him. Custódio's spirits rose; he would live for the present and have nothing to do with the past, no regrets or fears, no remorse. The present was all that mattered. The present was the five hundred *mil-réis* that he would watch emerging from the notary's pocket like a certificate of emancipation.

"In that case," he said, "why don't you see what you can give me, and I'll go and ask some other friends as well. How much do you think you could afford?"

"I hardly dare say, because it can really only be a very modest amount indeed."

"Five hundred *mil-réis?*"

"No, impossible."

"Not even five hundred *mil-réis?*"

"No," said the notary firmly. "What's so surprising about that? I won't deny that I own several properties, but, my friend, I don't walk around with them in my wallet; and I have certain obligations incumbent upon me . . . Don't you have a job?"

"No, I don't."

"Look, I'll give you something better than five hundred *mil-réis*; I'll have a word with the minister of justice. I know him well, and—"

Custódio interrupted him, slapping his thigh. Whether this was a natural gesture or a crafty diversion to avoid discussing a potential job, I have absolutely no idea; nor does it seem an essential element of the story. What is essential, though, is that he persisted in his request. Could the notary really not give him five hundred *mil-réis?* He would take two hundred; two hundred would be enough, not for the factory, for he would follow his friends' advice and turn it down. Two hundred *mil-réis*, seeing that the notary was disposed to help him, would meet an urgent need, to "fill a hole," as he put it. And then he told the notary everything, meeting frankness with frankness, for that was his rule of life. He admitted that, in dealing with the business proposal, he also had in mind settling matters with a particularly persistent creditor, a devil of a fellow and a Jew, who, strictly speaking, still owed him, but had treacherously turned the tables on him. It was two hundred and something *mil-réis*; two hundred and ten, to be precise; but he would accept two hundred—

"Really, it pains me to repeat what I've already said, but there we are; even two hundred *mil-réis* is beyond my means. Even if you were to ask me for a hundred *mil-réis*, that would still exceed my capabilities at this particular time. On another occasion, possibly, I'm sure, but not right now . . ."

"You can't imagine the tricky situation I find myself in!"

"I repeat, not even one hundred *mil-réis*. I've had a lot of expenses recently. Clubs and societies, subscriptions, the Freemasons . . . You probably don't believe me, do you, given that I do own some property, but, my friend, it is indeed a fine thing to own houses, but what you don't see is all the wear and tear, the repairs, the water pipes, the tithes, the insurance, the rent arrears, and all the rest of it. They're the holes in the pot through which most of the water is lost . . ."

"If only I had a pot!" sighed Custódio.

"I'm not saying I'm not fortunate, but what I am saying is that owning houses doesn't mean you don't have worries, expenses, even creditors . . . Believe you me, I have creditors too."

"So not even a hundred *mil-réis*!"

"Not even a hundred *mil-réis*. It pains me to say so, but that's how it is. Not even a hundred *mil-réis*. Now what time is it?"

He stood up and stepped forward into the middle of the room. Custódio did likewise, impelled by necessity and desperation. He could not bring himself to believe that the notary did not have at least a hundred *mil-réis*. Who on earth doesn't have a hundred *mil-réis*? He considered making a pathetic scene, but the notary's office opened directly onto the street and he didn't want to appear ridiculous. He peered outside. In the shop across the street a man was asking the price of a frock coat; he was standing at the door because dusk was coming on and it was already dark in the shop. The clerk was holding up the item of clothing for the customer, who was examining the cloth with eyes and fingers, then the seams, the lining . . . The incident opened up a new horizon to Custódio, albeit a modest one: it was high time he replaced the jacket he was wearing. But the notary couldn't even give him fifty *mil-réis*. Custódio smiled, not scornfully or angrily, but bitterly and hesitantly. It was impossible that the man didn't have fifty *mil-réis*. Twenty, at least? Not twenty. Not even twenty! No, it was all pretense, all lies.

Custódio pulled out his handkerchief, slowly smoothed his hat, then put his handkerchief back in his pocket and straightened his tie, with a mixture of hope and resentment. He had gradually been trimming the wings of his ambitions, feather by feather, but there still remained a fine, furry down, which gave him the foolish idea that he could fly. The other man, however, remained unmoved. Vaz Nunes was checking his pocket watch with the clock on the wall, holding it to his ear, cleaning the watch face, quietly oozing impatience and annoyance from every pore. The clock's hands were creeping toward five. Finally, the hour struck, and the notary was at last able to begin his farewells. It was late; he lived far away. As he said this, he took off his alpaca jacket and put on the cashmere one, transferring from one to the other his snuffbox, handkerchief, and wallet. Oh, the wallet! Custódio saw this problematic item, caressed it with his eyes, envying the alpaca, envying the cashmere, wishing he could be the pocket, wishing he could be the leather, the material of the precious receptacle itself. There it went, plunged straight into the inside left-hand pocket of the jacket, which the notary swiftly buttoned up. Not even twenty *mil-réis*! It was impossible that he didn't have twenty *mil-réis* on him, thought Custódio; perhaps not two hundred, but certainly twenty, or ten . . .

"Right, then!" said Vaz Nunes, putting on his hat.

It was the fateful moment. Not a word from the notary, not even an invitation to dine with him; nothing. It was the end of the road. But supreme moments call for supreme efforts. Custódio felt this cliché in all its strength, and, suddenly, like a shot, he asked the notary if he couldn't at least give him ten *mil-réis*.

"Shall I show you?"

And the notary unbuttoned his jacket, took out his wallet, opened it, and removed two notes of five *mil-réis*.

"See? That's all I have," he said. "What I can do is share them with you; I'll give you one five *mil-réis* note, and I'll keep the other; will that do?"

Custódio accepted the five *mil-réis*, not glumly or with bad grace, but smiling, indeed as thrilled as if he had just conquered Asia Minor. There was his dinner taken care of. He shook the other man's hand, thanked him for his kindness, bade him farewell for now—a "for now" full of implicit meanings. Then he left; the beggar slipping out the door of the notary's office and the general marching boldly down the street, nodding fraternally to the English merchants making their way up toward the suburbs. Never had the sky seemed so blue or the evening so clear; all the men around him had a gleam of hospitality in their eyes. With his left hand he lovingly squeezed the five-*mil-réis* note in his trouser pocket, the residue of a grand ambition which, but a short time ago, had soared boldly up to the sun like an eagle, and now flapped modestly with the flightless wings of a chicken.

THE MOST SERENE REPUBLIC

(Canon Vargas's Lecture)

———

GENTLEMEN,

Before informing you of a new discovery, which I consider will bring some luster to our nation, please allow me to thank you for your prompt response to my invitation. I know that only the loftiest of interests have brought you here today, but I am also aware—and it would be ungrateful on my part not to be—that your entirely legitimate sense of scientific curiosity is mingled with a modicum of affection. I very much hope that I may prove worthy of both.

My discovery is not a recent one; it dates from the latter part of 1876. I did not reveal it then for a reason you will easily comprehend, and if it weren't for *Globo*, surely our capital's most interesting newspaper, I would not be revealing it now. The work I have come here to discuss with you still lacks a few final touches, verifications, and complementary experiments. However, when *Globo* reported that an English expert has discovered the phonetic language of insects, citing a study undertaken with flies, I immediately wrote to colleagues in Europe, and keenly await their responses. Since it is undoubtedly the case that, in the field of aerial navigation, so ably invented by our very own Father Bartolomeu, the names of foreigners have taken all the glory, while that of our compatriot is scarcely remembered even by his own people, I was determined to avoid the fate of that eminent Flying Priest, and so have come to this rostrum to proclaim loud and clear, to the entire universe, that long before that English expert, and far beyond the British Isles, I, a humble naturalist, discovered exactly the same thing, and made a much better job of it.

Gentlemen, I am about to astonish you, as I would have astonished Aristotle had I asked him: "Do you believe that a social order could ever be imposed upon spiders?" Aristotle would have replied in the negative, as will all of you, because it is simply impossible to believe that such a shy and solitary arthropod made for work alone and not for love, could ever be inducted into some form of social organization. Well, I have achieved the impossible.

I hear some laughter among the other curious murmurings. One must always strive to overcome one's prejudices, gentlemen. Spiders may strike you as inferior precisely because you do not know them. You love your dogs and hold cats and hens in high esteem, and yet you fail to notice that the humble spider neither jumps nor barks like a dog, nor meows like a cat, nor clucks like a hen. Nor does it buzz or bite like a mosquito, or rob us of our blood and sleep the way fleas do. All these creatures are the very model of vagrant parasites. Even the ant, so praised for certain qualities, preys upon our sugar and our crops, and builds its home by stealing someone else's. The spider, gentlemen, neither troubles nor defrauds us; indeed, it catches flies, our sworn enemies. The spider spins, weaves, works, and dies. What better example could there be of patience, order, foresight, respect, and, dare I say it, humanity? As for its talents, there can be no doubt. From Pliny to Darwin, naturalists the world over speak as one in praise of this tiny bug, whose marvelous web is destroyed in less than a minute by your servant's thoughtless broom. And if time permitted, I would now repeat all of these men's wise opinions; however, I have a lot to get through and so must be brief. I have them here, not quite all of them, but almost; I have, for example, this excellent monograph by Büchner, who studied the psychological lives of animals with such perspicacity. In citing Darwin and Büchner, I am, of course, merely paying due respect to two geniuses of the first order, without (as my vestments attest) in any way absolving them of the unfounded and erroneous theories of materialism.

Yes, gentlemen, I have discovered a species of spider that has the gift of speech. Initially I collected just a few of these new arthropods, then many more, and set about imposing a social order on them. The first of these marvelous specimens came to my attention on December 15, 1876. It was so large, so brightly colored, with a red dorsal patch and blue transversal stripes, so swift in its movements and at times so cheerful, that it completely captured my attention. The next day, three more appeared, and the four of them took possession of a suitable corner in my country house. I studied them at length, and was full of admiration. Nothing, however, could compare to my surprise upon discovering the arachnid language; for it is, gentlemen, a rich and varied tongue, with its own syntactical structure, verbs, conjugations, declensions, Latin cases, and onomatopoeia. I am currently engaged in meticulously compiling its grammar for use in schools and universities, based on the initial summary I prepared for my own use. It has, as you can imagine, taken extraordinary patience to overcome this most testing of challenges. I often lost heart, but my love of science gave me the strength to press ahead with a task that, I can tell you now, no man could hope to accomplish twice in his lifetime.

I will keep the technical descriptions and linguistic analysis for another time and place. The purpose of this lecture is, as I said, to safeguard the rights of Brazilian science with this timely protest, and, having done so, to tell you about the ways in which I consider my own work superior to that of that English expert. I will need to demonstrate this, and for that reason I ask for your close attention.

Within one month, I had collected twenty spiders; the following month, there were fifty-five and, by March 1877, four hundred and ninety. The two main factors involved in collecting them were: using their language as soon as I began to discern something of it, together with the sheer terror I instilled in them. My height, my flowing vestments, and my mastery of their language all made them believe that I was the god of spiders, and, from that point on, they worshipped me. And behold the benefits of their delusion. I followed their every action with great attention and detail, jotting down all my observations in a notebook, which they believed to be a record of their sins, thus reinforcing still further their virtuous behavior. My flute was also of great assistance. As you know, or should know, spiders are quite mad about music.

Mere association was not enough; I needed to give them a suitable form of government. I hesitated in my choice of system; many of the current forms seemed to me adequate, some even excellent, but they all had the disadvantage of already existing. Let me explain. Any current form of government would expose them to comparisons that might be used to belittle them. I needed either to find a brand-new system, or to reintroduce one that had long since been abandoned. Naturally, I chose the latter, and nothing seemed more fitting than a republic in the Venetian mold; I even adopted the same epithet. This obsolete system, which was, in general terms, unlike any other current system of government, had the added advantage of all complicated mechanisms, namely, it would put my young society's political skills to the test.

There was another motive behind my choice. Among the various electoral methods once used in the Venice of old was the bag and ball, which is how the sons of the nobility were initiated into matters of state. Balls bearing the candidates' names were placed in the bag, and every year a certain number were taken out, with the chosen few being deemed suitable for public service. Such a system will provoke laughter among experts in electoral suffrage, but that is not the case with me. For it precludes the follies of passion, the errors of ineptitude, and the commingling of corruption and greed. This was not my only reason for choosing it; I felt that a community so skilled in the spinning of webs would find the use of the electoral bag easy to adapt to, indeed almost second nature.

My proposal was accepted. "The Most Serene Republic" struck them as a magnificent title: high-sounding and generous, and suitably aggrandizing of their work as a collective.

I would not say, gentlemen, that my work has reached perfection, nor that it will do so in the near future. My pupils are not Campanella's solarians or More's utopians; they are a new people, who cannot in a single bound o'erleap our most venerable nations. And time is not a workman who willingly hands his tools to another; it will, though, serve far better than any paper theories, which look good on paper, but prove lame in practice. What I will say is that, notwithstanding the uncertainties of the age, the spiders continue to make progress, having at their disposal some of the virtues which I believe essential for a state to endure. One of those virtues, as I have already mentioned and as I will now demonstrate, is perseverance, the long-suffering patience of Penelope.

In effect, ever since they first grasped that the electoral act was the fundamental basis of public life, they set out to exercise it with the utmost punctiliousness. Weaving the bag was itself a national undertaking. It was five inches long, three inches wide, and woven from the finest threads into a solid, sturdy piece of work. To make it, ten ladies of the very highest rank were selected by acclamation, and given the title "mothers of the republic" along with various other privileges and perquisites. A real masterpiece, of that you can be sure. The electoral process itself is quite simple. The names of the candidates, each of whom must fulfill certain conditions, are inscribed on the balls by a public official known as the Inscriptions Officer. On election day, the balls are placed in the bag and then picked out by the Withdrawals Officer, until the required number of candidates has been chosen. What was simply an initiation ceremony in the Venice of old, here serves to fill all public positions.

At first the election passed off without incident. But soon afterward, one of the legislators declared that the election had been tainted, because the bag contained two balls each inscribed with the name of the same candidate. The assembly verified the truth of the allegation, and declared that the bag would henceforth be only two inches wide, not three, thus restricting the bag's capacity and limiting (which was as good as eliminating) the scope for fraud. However, in the following election, it transpired that the name of one of the candidates had not been inscribed on the relevant ball; whether this was due to carelessness or willful omission on the part of the public official is not known. The official insisted that he had no recollection of seeing the illustrious candidate, but nobly added that it was not impossible that he had been given the name, in which case it had not been a matter of deliberate exclusion, but of forgetfulness on his part. Faced with so ineluctable a psychological phenomenon as forgetfulness, the assembly could not bring itself to punish the official; however, in the belief that the narrowness of the bag could give rise to nefarious exclusions, it revoked the previous law and restored the bag to its full three inches.

Meanwhile, gentlemen, the first magistrate passed away and three citizens presented themselves as candidates for the position. Only two of them were important: Hazeroth and Magog, the respective leaders of the rectilinear party and the curvilinear party. I should explain these names to you. Since arachnids are masters of geometry, it is geometry that divides them politically. Some are convinced that spiders should always spin their webs with straight threads, and they adhere to the rectilinear party. Others, however, think that webs should be spun using curved threads, and they form the curvilinear party. There is a third party, which occupies the middle ground with the proposition that webs should be woven with both straight and curved threads, and is therefore called the recto-curvilinear party. Finally, there is a fourth political grouping, the anti-recto-curvilinear party, which sweeps away all such principles and proposes the use of webs woven from thin air, resulting in an entirely transparent and lightweight structure with no lines of any sort. Since geometry could only divide them, without inflaming their passions, they have adopted a purely symbolic geometry. For some, the straight line represents noble sentiments: justice, probity, integrity, and perseverance, while base or inferior sentiments such as flattery, fraud, betrayal, and perfidy are quite clearly curved. Their adversaries disagree, saying that the curved line is the line of virtue and wisdom, because it is the expression of modesty and humility, whereas ignorance, arrogance, foolishness, and boasting are straight, indeed rigidly so. The third party, less angular, less exclusive, has trimmed away the exaggerations of both sides and combined their contrasting positions, proclaiming the simultaneous nature of lines to be the exact representation of the physical and moral world. The fourth grouping simply repudiates everything.

Neither Hazeroth nor Magog was elected. The relevant balls were drawn from the bag, but were deemed invalid—Hazaroth's because the first letter of his name was missing, and Magog's because his lacked the last letter. The remaining, triumphant name was that of an ambitious millionaire of obscure political opinions, who promptly ascended the ducal throne to the general amazement of the republic. However, the defeated candidates were not content to rest on the winner's laurels; they called for an official inquiry. The inquiry showed that the Inscriptions Officer had intentionally misspelled their names. The officer confessed to both the error and the intention, explaining that it had been nothing more than a simple ellipsis; a purely literary misdemeanor, if that. Since it was not possible to prosecute someone for errors of spelling or rhetoric, it seemed sensible to review the law once again. That very same day, it was decreed that the bag would henceforth be made from a fine gauze, through which the balls could be read by the public, and *ipso facto* by the candidates themselves, who would thus have the opportunity to correct any misspellings.

Unfortunately, gentlemen, fiddling with the law brings nothing but trouble. That same door flung wide to honesty also served the cunning of a certain Nabiga, who connived with the Withdrawals Officer to get himself a seat on the assembly. There was one vacancy to be filled and three candidates; the officer selected the balls with his eyes fixed on his accomplice, who only stopped shaking his head when the ball in question was his own. That was all it took to put paid to the idea of a gauze bag. With exemplary patience, the assembly restored the thick fabric of the previous regime, but, to avoid any further ellipses, literary or otherwise, it decreed that balls with incorrect inscriptions could henceforth be validated if five persons swore an oath that the name inscribed was indeed that of the candidate in question.

This new statute gave rise to a new and unforeseen issue, as you will see. It concerned the election of a Donations Collector, a public servant charged with raising public revenue in the form of voluntary donations. Among the candidates were one called Caneca and another called Nebraska. The ball drawn from the bag was Nebraska's. There was, however, a mistake, in that the last letter was missing, but five witnesses swore an oath in accordance with the law that the duly elected candidate was the republic's one and only Nebraska. Everything seemed to be settled, until the candidate Caneca sought leave to prove that the name on the ball in question was not Nebraska's, but his own. The justice of the peace granted the hearing. As this point, they summoned a great philologist—perhaps the greatest in the republic, as well as being a good metaphysician and a rather fine mathematician—who proved the matter as follows:

"First of all," he said, "you should note that the absence of the last letter of the name 'Nebraska' is no accident. Why was it left incomplete? Not through fatigue or love of brevity, since only the final letter, a mere *a*, is missing. Lack of space? Not that, either; look closely and you will see that there is still space for another two or three syllables. Hence the omission is intentional, and the intention could only be to draw the reader's eye to the letter *k*, being the last one written, hanging there abandoned and alone, devoid of purpose. Now, then, the brain has a tendency, which no law can override, to reproduce letters in two ways: the graphic form *k*, and the sonic form, which could equally be written *ca*. Thus, by drawing the eyes to the final letter written, the spelling defect instantly embeds it in the brain as the first syllable: *Ca*. Once so embedded, the natural impulse of the brain is then to read the whole name, and thus returns to the beginning of the word, to the initial *ne* of Nebrask, giving us *Ca-ne*. There remains the middle syllable, *bras*, and it is the easiest thing in the world to demonstrate how that can be reduced to another *ca*. I will not, however, demonstrate precisely how, since you lack the necessary preparation for a proper understanding of the spiritual or philosophical meaning of such a syllable, along with its origins and effects, its phases, modifications, logical and syntactical consequences, both deductive and inductive, as well as symbolic, and so forth. But taking that as read, we are faced with the final and incontrovertible proof of my initial assertion that the syllable *ca* is indeed joined to the first two, *Ca-ne*, giving us the name Caneca."

The law was amended, gentlemen, abolishing both sworn testimonials and textual interpretations, and introducing another innovation, this time the simultaneous reduction, by half an inch, of both the length and width of the bag. The modification did not, however, avoid a minor abuse in the election of bailiffs, and the bag was restored to its original dimensions, but this time in triangular form. You will readily comprehend that such a form brings with it an inevitable consequence: many of the balls remained in the bottom of the bag. From this came the adoption of a cylindrical bag, which, later, evolved into an hourglass, which was recognized as having the same inconveniences as the triangle, and thus gave way to a crescent, and so on. Most abuses, oversights, and lacunae tend to disappear, and the rest will share the same fate, not entirely, perhaps, for perfection is not of this world, but to the degree advised by one of the most circumspect citizens of my republic, Erasmus—whose last speech I only wish I could give to you here in its entirety. Tasked with notifying the final legislative modification to the ten worthy ladies responsible for weaving the electoral bag, Erasmus recounted to them the tale of Penelope, who wove and unwove her famous web while awaiting the return of her husband Ulysses.

"You, ladies, are the Penelopes of our republic," he said in conclusion. "Aim to be as chaste, patient, and talented as she. Weave the bag again, ladies, weave it again, until Ulysses, weary of wandering, comes back to take his rightful place among us. Ulysses is Wisdom."

THE MIRROR

A Brief Outline of a New Theory of the Human Soul

———

L ATE ONE NIGHT, four or five gentlemen were debating various lofty matters, and although they all had different views, there were no frayed tempers. The house was situated on the Santa Teresa hill overlooking Rio; the room was small and lit by candles, whose glow mingled mysteriously with the moonlight streaming in from outside. Between the bustle and excitement of the city below and the sky above, where the stars were shining in the still, clear air, sat our four or five metaphysical detectives, amicably resolving the universe's knottiest problems.

Four or five, I say, and yet, strictly speaking, only four of them spoke, but there was a fifth person in the room who sat in silence, thinking or dozing, and whose only contribution to the debate was an occasional grunt of approval. The man was the same age as his companions, i.e., between forty and fifty years old; he was from the provinces, wealthy, intelligent, not uneducated, and, it would seem, shrewd and somewhat caustic. He never participated in their discussions or arguments, and always justified his silence with a paradox, saying that discussion was simply the polite form of the latent warrior instinct man had inherited from beasts. He would add that the seraphim and cherubim never disagreed, and *they* were eternal, spiritual perfection. When he gave this same answer that night, one of the others took him up on it and challenged him to prove his assertion, if he could. Jacobina (for that was his name) thought for a moment, then replied:

"All things considered, perhaps you're right."

And suddenly, in the middle of the night, this taciturn fellow began to hold forth, not for two or three minutes, but for thirty or forty. The meandering conversation had come to rest upon the nature of the soul, a point that radically divided the four friends. No two minds thought alike; not only was there no agreement, discussion became difficult, not to say impossible, on account of the multiplicity of issues branching out from the main trunk of the debate, and perhaps also on account of the inconsistency of the various positions adopted. One of the participants asked Jacobina to offer an opinion, or, at the very least, a conjecture.

"No conjecture and no opinion," he replied. "Either one can lead to disagreement and, as you all know, I never engage in arguments. But if you will listen in silence, I can tell you about an episode in my life that demonstrates the issue in question in the clearest possible terms. To begin with, there is not one soul, but two—"

"Two?"

"Yes, two. Every human creature contains two souls: one that looks from the inside out, and the other that looks from the outside in. Go on, gawk, stare, shrug your shoulders, whatever you like, but don't say anything. If you try to argue, I'll finish my cigar and go home to bed. Now, the external soul can be a spirit, a fluid, a man (or many men), an object, even an action. There are cases, for example, of a simple shirt button being a person's external soul, or it could be the polka, a card game, a book, a machine, a pair of boots, a song, a drum, etc. Clearly, the function of this second soul, like the first, is to transmit life; together they complete the man, who is, metaphysically speaking, an orange. Whoever loses one half, automatically loses half of his existence, and there have been instances, quite common ones, in which the loss of the external soul implies the loss of one's entire existence. Shylock, for example. The external soul of that particular Jew was his ducats; to lose them was the same as dying. 'I shall never see my gold again,' he says to Tubal; 'thou stick'st a dagger in me.' Consider carefully his choice of words: for him, the loss of the ducats, his external soul, meant death. One must, of course, remember that the external soul does not always stay the same—"

"No?"

"Indeed not, sir; it changes both in nature and in state. I am not alluding to certain all-consuming souls, such as one's country, of which Camões famously said that he would not only die in his country, but with it; or

power, which was Caesar's and Cromwell's external soul. These are forceful, all-excluding souls, but others, though still forceful, are changeable in
nature. There are gentlemen, for example, whose external soul in their earliest years is a rattle or a hobbyhorse, but later on in life it will be their
seat on the board of a charity. For my part, I know a lady—and a charming
creature she is too—who changes her external soul five or six times a year.
During the season it's the opera, and when the season is over, she swaps her
external soul for another: a concert, a ball at the Cassino, a trip to Rua do
Ouvidor or Petrópolis—"

"Excuse me, but who is this lady?"

"The lady is the devil's kin and bears the same name: her name is
Legion. And there are many other such cases. I myself have experienced
these changes. I won't recount them now because it would take too long;
I will confine myself to the episode I mentioned earlier. At the time, I was
twenty-five years old . . ."

Eager to hear the promised tale, his four companions forgot all about
their raging controversy. Blessèd curiosity! Thou art not only the soul of
civilization; thou art the apple of concord, a divine fruit that tastes quite
different from the apple of mythology. The room, until then buzzing with
physics and metaphysics, is now a becalmed sea; all eyes are on Jacobina,
who trims his cigar while collecting his thoughts. Here's how he began:

"I was twenty-five years old and poor, and had just been made a second
lieutenant in the National Guard, the very lowest rank of commissioned
officer. You cannot imagine what a huge event this was in our house. My
mother was so happy and so proud! She insisted on addressing me as *her*
lieutenant. Cousins, aunts, uncles, everyone was bursting with the purest, sincerest joy. In the town, to be sure, there were several disgruntled
fellows—a wailing and gnashing of teeth, as it says in the Scriptures—the
reason being that there had been many candidates for the post, and these
other fellows were the losers. I suppose some of their annoyance was less
understandable, though, and arose simply from a feeling of resentment that
someone else should be singled out for distinction. I remember how some
young men, even friends of mine, looked at me askance for quite some time
afterward. On the other hand, many people were pleased by my appointment, the proof of which is that the whole of my rather splendid uniform
was paid for by friends. It was then that one of my aunts, Dona Marcolina,
Captain Peçanha's widow, who lived on a remote and isolated farm many

leagues from town, begged me to come and see her, and to bring my uniform. I went, accompanied by a footman, who returned to town a few days
later, because no sooner had Auntie Marcolina lured me to her house than
she wrote to my mother telling her that she wouldn't let me go for at least
a month. And how she hugged me! She, too, called me *her* lieutenant. She
pronounced me a handsome devil and, being a rather jolly sort herself, even
confessed to envying the girl who would one day be my wife. She declared
that there was not a man in the entire province who was my equal. And it
was always lieutenant this, lieutenant that, every hour of the day or night.
I asked her to call me Joãozinho as she used to, but she shook her head,
exclaiming that, no, I was 'Senhor Lieutenant' and that was that. One of
her brothers-in-law, her late husband's brother, who lived in the house, also
refused to address me in any other way. I was 'Senhor Lieutenant' not in
jest but perfectly seriously, and in front of the slaves as well, who naturally
followed suit. I sat at the head of the table and was always served first. It was
absurd, really. Such was Auntie Marcolina's enthusiasm that she went so far
as to have a large mirror placed in my room—a magnificent, ornate piece of
work, quite out of keeping with the rest of the house, which was furnished
simply and modestly. It had been given to her by her godmother, who had
inherited it from her mother, who had bought it from one of the Portuguese
noblewomen who came to Brazil in 1808 with the rest of King João VI's
court. I don't know how much truth there was in this story, but that was
the family tradition. Naturally, the mirror was very old, but you could still
see the gilding, eaten away by time, a couple of carved dolphins in the top
corners of the frame, a few bits of mother-of-pearl, and other such artistic
flourishes. All rather old, but very good quality."

"Was it large?"

"Indeed it was. And as I say, it was really very kind of her, because the
mirror had previously been in the parlor, and was the best piece in the
house. But there was no dissuading my aunt; she replied that it would not
be missed, that it was only for a couple of weeks, and, after all, it was the
least the 'Senhor Lieutenant' deserved. The fact is that all these little atten-
tions, shows of affection, and kindnesses brought about a transformation in
me, aided and abetted by the natural vanity of youth, as I'm sure you can
imagine."

"Well, no, actually."

"The officer eliminated the man. For several days, the two hung in the balance, but it wasn't long before my original nature gave way to the other; only a tiny part of my humanity remained. What had happened was that my external soul, which, up until then, had been the sun, the air, the rolling countryside, and the eyes of young women, changed entirely and became the bowing and scraping that went on around the house, everything that spoke to me of my rank, and nothing about me, the man. Only the officer remained; the private citizen had vanished into thin air, and into the past. Hard to believe, isn't it?"

"I find it hard even to understand," replied one of his listeners.

"You will in due course. Actions are better at explaining feelings: actions are everything. After all, even the very best definition of love is no match for a kiss from the girl you're courting, and, if memory serves me right, an ancient philosopher once demonstrated movement by walking. So let's cut to the chase. Let us see how, as the consciousness of the man was slowly being obliterated, that of the officer was becoming intensely alive. Human suffering and human joys, if that's all they were, barely won from me so much as an apathetic nod or a condescending smile. After three weeks, I was a different person, changed utterly. I was all lieutenant and nothing else. Then one day, Auntie Marcolina received some grave news. One of her daughters, married to a farmer who lived five leagues away, was ill, perhaps dying. Farewell, nephew! Farewell, Lieutenant! The distraught mother immediately made arrangements to travel, asked her brother-in-law to go with her, and me to take charge of the farm. I believe that had she not been so upset she would have done the opposite, leaving the brother-in-law behind and taking me with her. As it turned out, however, I was left on my own, with a couple of household slaves. I immediately felt a great sense of oppression, as if the four walls of a prison had suddenly closed around me. It was my external soul contracting, you see, for now it was limited to a handful of half savages. The officer continued to hold sway within me, albeit less intensely alive and less fiercely conscious. The slaves put a note of humility into their bows and curtsys, which somewhat made up for the lack of family affection and the interruption of domestic intimacy. That same night, they noticeably redoubled their cheerful expressions of respect and admiration. It was 'Massa' Lieutenant every other minute. Massa Lieutenant very handsome, Massa Lieutenant soon be colonel, Massa Lieutenant marry pretty girl, general's daughter; a concerto of praise and prophesies that left me feeling ecstatic. Ah, the traitors! Little did I suspect the scoundrels' secret intentions."

"What? To kill you?"

"If only."

"Worse?"

"Just listen. The following morning I awoke to find myself alone. The scoundrels, whether egged on by others or of their own accord, had plotted to run away in the night, and had done precisely that. I found myself completely alone, with no one else within the four walls of the house, staring out at the deserted yard and empty countryside beyond. Not a single human breath. I searched the house, the slave quarters, everywhere, but found nothing and no one, not a single pickaninny. Only some cocks and hens, a pair of mules philosophizing about life as they flicked away the flies, and three oxen. The slaves had even taken the dogs. Not a single human being. Do you think this was better than dying? Well, I can tell you it was worse. Not that I was afraid; I swear to you that I wasn't; in fact, I was almost devil-may-care, to the point of not feeling anything at all during those first few hours. After that, I felt sad for Auntie Marcolina's financial loss, and was in somewhat of a quandary as to whether I should go and see her and give her the bad news, or stay and take care of the house. I opted for the latter course of action, so as not to leave the house completely defenseless, and because, if my cousin was seriously ill, I would only be increasing her mother's distress without providing any remedy. Besides, I expected Uncle Peçanha's brother to return that day or the next, since he'd already been gone thirty-six hours. But the morning passed with no sign of him, and during the afternoon I began to feel decidedly odd, like someone who has lost all sensation in his nerves and can no longer feel his muscles move. Uncle Peçanha's brother did not return that day, or the next, or for the rest of the week. My solitude took on overwhelming proportions. Never had the days been so long; never had the sun scorched the earth with such wearying ferocity. The hours passed as slowly as centuries on the old clock in the parlor, whose pendulum, *tick-tock*, *tick-tock*, tapped away at my inner soul like the endlessly snapping fingers of eternity. When, many years later, I read an American poem, one of Longfellow's, I think, and came across the famous refrain: '*Never, for ever! – For ever, never!*' I confess that I felt a shiver run down my spine at the memory of those terrifying days. Auntie Marcolina's clock was just like that: '*Never, for ever! – For ever, never!*' It wasn't merely the tick-tock of the pendulum, but a dialogue from the abyss, a whispering voice from the void. And then there were the nights! Not that they were any quieter. They were as silent as the days, but the nights were filled with darkness and an even narrower, or perhaps vaster, solitude. *Tick-tock, tick-tock.* No one in any of the rooms, no one on the veranda, in the hallways, the yard; no one anywhere at all. Are you laughing?"

"Yes, for it seems you *were* a little scared after all."

"Oh! If only I could have felt scared! At least I would have been alive. But the main thing I remember is that I couldn't even feel fear, or at least not fear as it is commonly understood. It was an inexplicable sensation. I was like a dead man walking, a sleepwalker, a mechanical toy. Sleep itself was another matter. Sleep brought me relief, but not for the usual reason: that sleep is death's brother. I think I can explain the phenomenon as follows: in eliminating the need for an external soul, sleep gives free rein to the internal one. In my dreams, I would put on my uniform surrounded by family and friends, who would praise my elegant attire, address me as lieutenant; then a family friend would come and promise me a promotion to captain or major, and I would be filled with life again. But when I woke to the cold light of day, that sense of my newly reunified self faded with my dreams—because my internal soul had lost its exclusive power of action, and was once again dependent upon the other, the external soul, which stubbornly refused to return. And it did not return. I would wander about outside to see if there was any sign of life. *Sœur Anne, sœur Anne, ne vois-tu rien venir?* Nothing, absolutely nothing, just like that old French fairy tale. Only the dust of the road and the grassy hilltops. I would return to the house, at my wits' end, and lie down on the sofa in the parlor. *Tick-tock, tick-tock.* I would stand up, pace the room, drum my fingers on the windowpanes, whistle. At one point, I considered writing something, a political article, a novel, an ode, perhaps; I didn't choose which, but sat down and scribbled a few words and random phrases that I could use to spice up the style. But the style, like Auntie Marcolina, would not come. *Sœur Anne, sœur Anne* . . . Nothing at all. All I could see was the ink turning blacker and the page whiter."

"But didn't you have anything to eat?"

"Not much; just fruit, ground-up cassava, preserves, a few roots roasted on the fire, but I would have endured it all quite cheerfully had it not been for the terrible mental state I was in. I recited verses, speeches, passages in Latin, Gonzaga's love poems, whole stanzas by Camões, sonnets, a thirty-volume anthology in all. Sometimes I did gymnastic exercises, other times I pinched my legs, but the effect was only a physical sensation of weariness or pain, nothing more. There was only silence, a vast, enormous, infinite silence, only underscored by the eternal *tick-tock* of the clock. *Tick-tock, tick-tock . . ."*

"Yes, that would be enough to drive anyone mad."

"There's worse to come. I should tell you that ever since I'd been alone, I had not once looked in the mirror. I wasn't avoiding it deliberately, for I had no reason to do so; it was an unconscious impulse, a dread of finding two of me, at the same time, in that solitary house. If that is the true explanation, then there is no better proof of man's contradictory nature, for, a week later, I got it into my head to look at the mirror with precisely the aim of seeing myself twice over. I looked and recoiled. The glass itself seemed to be conspiring with the rest of the universe; it didn't show me as a sharp, complete image, but as something vague and hazy, diffuse, a shadow of a shadow. The laws of physics will not allow me to deny that the mirror did indeed reproduce my shape and features accurately, for it must have done, but that was not what my senses told me. Then I did feel afraid; I attributed the phenomenon to my strained nerves; I feared I would go mad if I stayed any longer. 'I must leave,' I said to myself. And I raised my arm in a gesture that was both ill-tempered and decisive. I saw the gesture repeated in the mirror, but it was somehow dispersed, frayed, mutilated . . . I began to get dressed, muttering to myself, clearing my throat, shaking my clothes brusquely, and cursing my recalcitrant buttons, just in order to say something. From time to time, I glanced furtively at the mirror, only to see the same blurred outlines, the same confused shapes. I carried on getting dressed. Suddenly some inexplicable flash of inspiration, some spontaneous impulse, planted an idea in my head. Can you guess what it was?"

"No, tell us."

"I was staring desperately at the mirror, contemplating my own dissolving, incomplete features, a mass of loose and shapeless lines, when the idea came to me . . . No, you'll never guess."

"Go on, tell us."

"I had the idea of putting on my lieutenant's uniform. I did so, every last bit of it, and, as I stood in front of the mirror, I raised my eyes and . . . I hardly need say it: the mirror now showed my whole figure, with not a feature or a line out of place; it was me, my own self, the lieutenant, who had finally rediscovered his external soul. This soul, missing since my aunt's departure, scattered and dispersed since the slaves ran away, was now pieced back together in the mirror. Imagine a man who, little by little, emerges from a coma, opens his eyes without seeing, then begins to see, begins to distinguish people from objects, but cannot recognize any of them individually, then, finally, realizes that this fellow is so-and-so, and that one is what's-his-name, here's a chair, there's a sofa. Everything returns to what it was before his deep sleep. So it was with me. I looked in the mirror, moved from side to side, stepped back, waved, smiled, and the glass reflected everything. I was no longer an automaton, I was a living being. From that point on, I was another person. Every day, at a certain time, I would put on my lieutenant's uniform and sit in front of the mirror, reading, looking, and meditating; after two or three hours, I would take my uniform off again. By sticking to this regime, I was able to get through more than six days of solitude without the slightest problem."

By the time his companions had come to their senses again, the narrator had already left.

A VISIT FROM ALCIBIADES

Letter from District Judge "X" to the Rio Chief of Police
Rio de Janeiro, September 20, 1875

SIR,

I trust you will forgive my shaky handwriting and slovenly style; you will soon understand the reason why.

Today, this very evening, just after dinner, while I was waiting for the Cassino to open, I lay down on the sofa and opened a volume of Plutarch. You, sir, who were my schoolroom companion, will remember that ever since I was a boy I have had a passion for Greek, a passion or indeed a mania, which was the name you gave it, and one so intense that it often led me to fail in other subjects. I opened the book and, as always happens when I read some ancient text, I found myself transported back to the period in question, right into the thick of the action or whatever else was going on. Perfect after-dinner reading. In no time at all, one finds oneself on a Roman road, under a Greek portico, or in a grammarian's workshop. Modern times, the Herzegovina uprising, the Carlist Wars, Rua do Ouvidor, the Chiarini Circus—all vanish into thin air. Fifteen or twenty minutes of ancient life, and all for free. A veritable literary *digestif*.

That is precisely what happened this evening. The book fell open at the life of Alcibiades. I allowed myself to be seduced by the flow of those Attic cadences; within moments, I was entering the Olympic Games, marveling at that flower of Athenian manhood as he drove his chariot magnificently, with the grace and determination he had always shown on the battlefield, or when curbing his fellow citizens or his own sensual urges. Oh, to be alive then, sir! But then the slave-boy came in to light the gas, and that was enough to put all the archaeology of my imagination to flight. Athens was relegated to history, while my gaze fell from the clouds, or, rather, came to rest upon my white duck trousers, my alpaca jacket, and my cordovan leather shoes. And then I thought to myself:

"What would that illustrious Athenian make of modern-day dress?"

I have been a spiritualist for some months now, because, convinced that all systems are pure nothingness, I decided to adopt the most enjoyable one. The time will come when it is not only enjoyable, but also useful for solving historical problems: it is far quicker to summon the spirits of the dead than to expend one's own critical energies to no good end, because no rationale or theory can better explain the intention of an act than the author of the act himself. Such was my goal this evening. Wondering what Alcibiades might have thought was a sheer waste of time, with no benefit beyond the pleasure of admiring my own cleverness. I therefore decided to summon up the Athenian, and asked him to appear in my house forthwith, without delay.

And here begins the extraordinary part of the adventure. Alcibiades lost no time in answering my call; two minutes later, he was there, in my parlor, standing by the wall, but he was not the intangible shadow I had expected to summon using our schoolboy methods; it was the real Alcibiades, flesh and blood, the man himself, authentically Greek, dressed like the ancients, and full of that blend of courtesy and audacity with which he used to harangue the great assemblies of Athens, and occasionally its fools. You, sir, who know so much about history, cannot ignore the fact that there were, indeed, some fools in Athens. Yes, even Athens had fools, a precedent that perhaps gives us something of an excuse. I swear I could not believe it; no matter what my senses told me, I could not believe that it was not a ghost standing there before me, but Alcibiades himself, restored to life. I still nurtured the hope that it was nothing more than the effects of indigestion, a simple excess of gastric fluids, magnified through the lens of Plutarch. And so I rubbed my eyes, stared, and . . .

"What do you want from me?" he asked.

On hearing this, the hairs on the back of my neck stood up. The figure

spoke, and spoke Greek, the purest Attic. There was no doubting that it was
the man himself, dead for twenty centuries, brought back from the grave,
and as alive as if he had come straight from cutting off his poor dog's tail, as
he so famously did. It was clear that, without a moment's thought, I had just
taken a great stride forward along the path of spiritualism. But, silly me, I
didn't, at first, realize this, and I allowed myself to be caught off guard. He
repeated the question, looked around him, and sat down in an armchair. He
saw that I was cold and trembling (as I still am even now), and spoke to me
rather tenderly, even trying to laugh and joke so as to put me at my ease. As
deft as ever! What more can I say? A few minutes later, we were chatting
away in ancient Greek, he reclining nonchalantly in his chair, I earnestly
begging all the saints in heaven to send some sort of distraction—a servant,
a visitor, a local constable, or even, should it prove necessary, for a fire to
break out.

Needless to say, I gave up on the idea of consulting him on modern-
day dress; I had summoned a ghost, not a "real-life" man, as children say.
I limited myself to replying to his questions; he asked me for news about
Athens, and I obliged; I said that Athens was finally the capital of a unified
Greece; I told him about the long years of Muslim domination, then about
independence, Botsaris, and Lord Byron. The great man hung on my every
word and, when I expressed surprise that the dead had told him nothing of
all this, he explained to me that when one stood at the gates of the other
world, one's interest in this world waned considerably. He had met neither
Botsaris nor Lord Byron—firstly, because there is such a vast multitude of
spirits that it's very easy to miss someone, and secondly, because there the
dead are grouped not according to nationality or some similar category, but
according to their temperament, customs, and profession. Thus he, Alcibiades, forms part of a group of elegant, passionate politicians, alongside the
Duke of Buckingham, Almeida Garrett, our very own Maciel Monteiro,
etc. Then he asked me about current affairs; I briefly told him what I knew;
I spoke of the Hellenic parliament and the rather different way in which
his compatriot statesmen, Voulgaris and Koumoundouros, are going about
imitating Disraeli and Gladstone in taking turns at government, and, just
like them, trading oratorical blows. Alcibiades, a magnificent orator himself,
interrupted me:

"Bravo, Athenians!"

I enter into such minutiae only so as to omit nothing that might give you a more precise understanding of the extraordinary events I am describing. I have already mentioned that Alcibiades was listening to me avidly; I should also add that he was clever and shrewd, very quick on the uptake. He was also somewhat sarcastic, or at least that's how he came across at one or two points in our conversation. But, in general, he showed himself to be simple, attentive, polite, sensitive, and dignified. And quite the dandy, too, as dandyish as in ancient times; he was always glancing sideways at the mirror, just as women and others do in our own century, admiring his buskins, adjusting his cloak, and striking sculptural poses.

"Go on," he would say to me, whenever I paused.

But I couldn't. Having entered into the realm of the inextricable and the marvelous, I believed that anything was possible, and just as he had come to meet me in this world, I couldn't see why I couldn't go and join him in eternity. I froze at this idea. For a man who has just had his dinner and is waiting for the Cassino to open, death would be a joke in the very worst possible taste.

"If only I could get away . . ." I thought to myself. Then I had an idea: I told him I was going to a ball.

"A ball? What's a ball?"

I explained.

"Ah! You're going to dance the Pyrrhic dance!"

"No," I replied. "The Pyrrhic dance has been and gone. My dear Alcibiades, every century changes its dances just as it changes its ideas. We no longer dance as we did a century ago; probably the twentieth century won't dance as we do now. The Pyrrhic dance is long gone, like Plutarch's men and Hesiod's gods."

"Even the gods?"

I explained that paganism had come to an end, that the august academies of the last century had still given it shelter, but with little real soul or conviction, and that even Arcadian drunkenness—*Evoe! Father Bassareus! Evoe!*, etc.—the honest pastime of certain peace-loving district judges, had been eradicated. From time to time, I added, some writer of poetry or prose alluded to the remnants of the pagan theogony, but only for show or amusement, while science had reduced the whole of Olympus to the merely symbolic. Dead, all dead.

"Even Zeus?"

"Even Zeus."

"Dionysus? Aphrodite?"

"All dead."

Plutarch's man stood up and took a few paces, containing his indignation, as if saying to himself, as someone else once did: "Ah! I must be there, too, along with my Athenians!" And from time to time, he would murmur: "Zeus, Dionysus, Aphrodite . . ." I then recalled that he had once been accused of disobeying the gods, and wondered to myself where this posthumous and, therefore, artificial indignation came from. I was forgetting—me, a devotee of Greek!—I was forgetting that he was also a consummate hypocrite, an illustrious fraudster. However, I scarcely had time to think this, because Alcibiades suddenly stopped his pacing and declared that he would go to the ball with me.

"To the ball?" I repeated in astonishment.

"Yes, to the ball. Let's go to the ball."

I was terrified and told him that it was impossible, that they wouldn't let him in wearing that outfit; he would look ridiculous; unless, of course, he wanted to go there to perform one of Aristophanes's comedies, I added, laughing so as to hide my fear. What I really wanted was to leave him there in the house, and, once I was outside, rather than going to the Cassino, I would come straight to see you. But the wretched man would not budge; while listening to me, he stared down at the floor, as if deep in thought. I stopped talking; I began to think that the nightmare would soon end, that the apparition would disappear, and that I would be left there alone with my trousers, my shoes, and my century.

"I want to go to the ball," he repeated. "I can't go back without comparing dances."

"My dear Alcibiades, I really don't think it wise. It would certainly be a great honor, and give me enormous pride, to introduce you, the most genteel and charming of Athenians, to the Cassino. But the other men, the young lads and lasses, the older folk . . . Well, it's just impossible."

"Why?"

"I've already told you; they will think you're a lunatic or a comedian, because of your clothes . . ."

"What about them? Clothes change. I'll go in modern clothes. Don't you have anything you can lend me?"

I was about to say no, but then it occurred to me that the most urgent thing was to get out of the house and that, once outside, I'd have more chance of escaping, and so I told him that I did.

"Well, then," he replied as he stood up, "I'll go in modern clothes. All I ask is that you get dressed first, so that I can learn and then copy you."

I, too, stood up, and asked him to follow me. He paused in astonishment. I saw that only then had he noticed my white trousers, and was staring at them, eyes bulging, mouth agape; after a long pause, he asked why I was wearing those cloth pipes. I replied that it was for reasons of comfort and convenience, adding that our century, more reserved and practical than artistic, had decided to dress in a manner compatible with our sense of decorum and gravity. Furthermore, not everyone could be Alcibiades. I think this flattered him, for he smiled and shrugged.

"In that case . . ."

We made our way to my dressing room, and I quickly began to change my clothes. Alcibiades reclined lazily on a divan, complimenting me on it, the mirror, the wicker chair, and the paintings. As I say, I got dressed quickly, keen to get out of the house and jump in the first cab that passed.

"Black pipes!" he exclaimed.

These were the black trousers I had just put on. He shrieked and laughed, a sort of giggle mingling surprise with scorn, which greatly offended my modern sensibilities. Because, as I'm sure you will agree, sir, while we may consider our own times worthy of criticism, even execration, we do not like it when one of the ancients comes and makes fun of it to our faces. I did not answer the Athenian; I merely frowned a little and carried on buttoning my suspenders. Then he asked me why on earth I wore such an ugly color.

"Ugly, but serious," I told him. "And observe the elegance of the cut, see how it falls over the shoe, which is patent leather, albeit black, and very shapely too."

And, seeing him shaking his head, I added:

"My dear friend," I said, "you can certainly insist that your Olympian Jupiter is the eternal emblem of majesty: his is the domain of ideal, disinterested art, superior to the passing of the ages and the men who inhabit them. But the art of dressing is another matter. What may appear absurd or ungainly is perfectly rational and beautiful—beautiful in our way, for we no longer wander the streets listening to poets reciting verses, or orators giving speeches, or philosophers explaining their philosophies. You yourself, were you to grow used to seeing us, would end up liking us, because—"

"Stop, you wretch!" he yelled, hurling himself at me.

I felt the blood drain from my face, until I realized the reason for this violent response. It was all down to a misunderstanding. As I looped the tie around my neck and began to tie the knot, Alcibiades assumed, as he told me afterward, that I was about to hang myself. And he did, indeed, turn very pale, trembling and sweating. Now it was my turn to laugh. I chuckled, and explained the use of a necktie to him, noting that it was a white tie, not black, although we did wear black ties on certain occasions. Only after I'd explained all this would he agree to give it back to me. I put it on and then put on my vest.

"For the love of Aphrodite!" he exclaimed. "You are the oddest thing I've ever seen, alive or dead. You're entirely the color of night—a night with only three stars," he continued, pointing to the buttons on my shirtfront. "The world must be a very melancholy place for you to choose to wear such a sad, dead color. We were a far jollier lot, we lived . . ."

He couldn't finish the sentence; I had just put on my tailcoat, and the Athenian's consternation surpassed description. His arms drooped by his sides, he struggled for air, unable to utter a word, and stared at me with wide, bulging eyes. Believe me, sir, I was truly afraid now, and made even more haste to leave the house.

"Are you finished?" he asked.

"No, there's still the hat."

"Oh! Please let it be something that'll make up for all the rest!" replied Alcibiades in a pleading voice. "Please, please! Has all the elegance we bequeathed to you been whittled away to a pair of closed pipes and another pair of open pipes (as he said this he lifted up my coattails), and all in this boring, depressing color? No, I can't believe it! Please let there be something that makes up for it. What is it you say that's missing?"

"My hat."

"Well, whatever it is, put it on, dear fellow, put it on."

I obeyed; I went over to the coat stand, took down my hat, and put it on my head. Alcibiades looked at me, swayed, and fell. I rushed to the illustrious Athenian's side to help him up, but (and it pains me to say this) it was too late; he was dead, dead for the second time. I therefore request, sir, that you see fit to issue the requisite orders for the corpse to be taken to the morgue, and proceed with the *corpus delicti*. Please excuse my not coming to your house in person at this hour (it being ten o'clock at night), on account of the deep shock I have just experienced, and rest assured that I will do so tomorrow morning, before eight o'clock.

THE DEVIL'S CHURCH

Chapter 1

A MARVELOUS IDEA

A N OLD BENEDICTINE MANUSCRIPT tells how, one day, the Devil had the idea of founding a church. Although he was making steady and substantial profits, he felt humiliated by the rather isolated role he had played down the centuries, with no organization, no rules, no canon law, and no rituals, indeed nothing much at all. He lived, so to speak, on divine leftovers, on human oversights and favors. Nothing fixed, nothing regular. Why shouldn't he have his own church? A Devil's Church would be the best way to take on the other religions and destroy them once and for all.

"Yes, a church of my own," he concluded. "Scripture against Scripture, breviary against breviary. I'll have my own mass, with wine and bread aplenty, my own sermons, bulls, novenas, and all the other ecclesiastical bells and whistles. My creed will be the universal nucleus of souls, my church a tent of Abraham. And then, while other religions quarrel and split, my church will stand united and alone, with no Muhammad or Luther to oppose me. There are many ways to affirm a belief, but only one way to deny it."

As he said this, the Devil shook his head and stretched out his arms in a magnificently manly gesture. Then he remembered that he really ought to go and see God, to tell him his plan and throw down this challenge; he raised his eyes, burning with hatred and bitter with revenge, and said to himself: "Yes, it is time." And with a beat of his wings—which set off a rumble that shook all the provinces of the abyss—he flew swiftly up from the shadows into the infinite blue.

Chapter 2

BETWEEN GOD AND THE DEVIL

When the Devil arrived in Heaven, God was just welcoming an old man. The seraphim who were busily garlanding the recent arrival immediately stopped what they were doing, and the Devil stood waiting at the entrance with his eyes fixed on the Lord.

"What do you want with me?" asked the Lord.

"I haven't come for your servant Faust," replied the Devil, laughing and pointing at the old man, "but for all the Fausts of this and every century."

"Explain yourself."

"The explanation is easy, Lord. But let me first say this: take in this worthy old man, give him the best place in Heaven, command your most tuneful zithers and lutes to receive him with their divinest choruses . . ."

"Do you have any idea what he did?" asked the Lord, his eyes filled with tenderness.

"No, but he's probably one of the last who will come to you. It won't be long before Heaven is like an empty house, on account of its high rent. I'm going to build a cheap boardinghouse; in short, I'm going to set up my own church. I've had enough of my lack of organization, my haphazard, spur-of-the-moment kingdom. It's time I won a complete and final victory. And so I have come to tell you this, in all loyalty, so that you can't accuse me of any deception. Good idea, don't you think?"

"You came to tell me, not seek my approval," commented the Lord.

"Yes, you're right," replied the Devil. "But vanity likes to hear its master's applause. True, in this case it will be the applause of a defeated master, and as such . . . Lord, I'm going down to Earth. I'm going to lay my foundation stone."

"Go ahead."

"Do you want me to come and let you know how it all works out?"

"That won't be necessary. Just tell me, since you've been so fed up with your lack of organization for so very long, why is it that you have only thought of founding a church now?"

The Devil gave a triumphant, mocking smile. He was savoring some cruel idea, some stinging remark stored away in the saddlebag of his memory which, in that brief instant of eternity, made him believe he was superior even to God. But he suppressed his laughter and said:

"I have only just concluded a study I began several centuries ago, and I see now that the virtues, those daughters of Heaven, are in many respects comparable to queens whose velvet mantles are edged with cotton fringes. Now, I propose to tug them by those fringes, and bring them all to my church; after them will come the queens dressed in purest silk . . ."

"Pompous old windbag!" murmured the Lord.

"Look here. Many of those bodies who kneel at your feet in churches throughout the world wear the bustles of drawing room and street; their cheeks are rouged with the same powder, their handkerchiefs carry the same scents, and their eyes sparkle with curiosity and devotion, torn between the holy book and the tempting mustache of sin. See the passion—or disdain, at least—with which that gentleman over there makes sure everyone knows about the favors he liberally bestows: clothes, boots, coins, or any of the other necessities of life. But I don't want to seem to be dwelling on the little things; I am not talking, for example, about the smug serenity of this man here, president of a lay brotherhood, who, when taking part in any religious procession, piously carries pinned to his chest both your love and a medal. I have more important business to deal with . . ."

At this, the seraphim ruffled their wings, heavy with boredom and sleep. The archangels Michael and Gabriel gazed at the Lord imploringly. God interrupted the Devil.

"You talk in clichés, which is the worst thing that could happen to a spirit of your sort," replied the Lord. "All that you say or may say has been said and resaid by the world's moralists. It's been done to death, and if you have neither the ability nor the originality to breathe new life into it, it would be better for you to be quiet and keep your thoughts to yourself. See? The faces of all my legions show clear signs of the tedium you're inflicting on them. The old man here looks thoroughly fed up, and do you know what he did?"

"I've already said that I don't."

"After an honest life, he died a truly sublime death. Caught in a shipwreck, he was going to seize hold of a plank and save himself, when he spied
a couple of newlyweds, in the flower of youth, already grappling with death.
He gave them that plank and plunged into eternity. No one was watching,
only the water and the sky above. Where in that do you find your cotton
fringe?"

"As you know, Lord, I am the spirit who denies."

"Do you deny this death?"

"I deny everything. Misanthropy can look like charity, because, to a
misanthrope, leaving life to others is actually a way of despising them . . ."

"A windbag, and a crafty one at that!" exclaimed the Lord. "Go on, go
and set up your church. Call upon all the virtues, gather together all the
fringes, summon all of mankind . . . But go! Go!"

In vain, the Devil tried to say something more, but God had silenced
him, and, upon a divine signal, the seraphim filled Heaven with the harmonious sound of their singing. The Devil suddenly found himself in midair;
he furled his wings and, like a bolt of lightning, plunged to Earth.

Chapter 3

GOOD NEWS FOR MANKIND

Once on Earth, the Devil did not waste a single minute. He hurriedly
donned a Benedictine cowl—as being a habit of good repute—and began
to spread a new and extraordinary doctrine with a voice that echoed down
through the bowels of the century. He promised his faithful disciples all of
Earth's delights, all its glories, and all its most intimate pleasures. He admitted that he was indeed the Devil, but did so in order to rectify mankind's
view of him and to deny the stories pious old women told about him.

"Yes, I am the Devil," he said again and again. "Not the Devil of sulfu-
rous nights, of bedtime stories, or childish terrors, but the one and only true
Devil, the very genius of nature, who was given that name to drive him from
the hearts of men. See how gentle and graceful I am. I am your true father.
Come with me: embrace the name that was invented to shame me, make
it your trophy and your banner, and I will give you everything, absolutely
everything . . ."

Thus he spoke in order to arouse enthusiasm and awaken the indifferent, in short, to gather the multitudes around him. And they came; and once they were with him, the Devil began to set out his doctrine. The doctrine was what one would expect from the mouth of a spirit of denial, at least in terms of substance. As for its form, it was at times clever and at others cynical and shameless.

He proclaimed that the accepted virtues should be replaced with others, the natural and legitimate ones. Pride, Lust, and Sloth were restored, as was Greed, which he declared was nothing but the mother of Thrift, the sole difference being that the mother was robust and the daughter a scrawny wretch. The best argument in favor of Wrath was the existence of Homer, for without the fury of Achilles, there would have been no *Iliad*. "Sing, O goddess, the anger of Achilles son of Peleus." He said the same of Gluttony, which produced the best bits of Rabelais and many fine verses in Diniz's *Hyssope*. It was such a superior virtue that no one now remembers Lucullus's battles, only his banquets; it was Gluttony that made him immortal. But still, setting aside these literary or historical justifications and focusing only on the intrinsic value of such a virtue, who would deny that it feels much better to fill one's mouth and belly with good food than to get by on meager morsels, or the saliva of fasting? For his part, the Devil promised to replace the Lord's vineyard, a merely metaphorical expression, with the Devil's vineyard in the literal sense, for his followers would never want for the fruit of the finest vines. As for Envy, he preached coolly that it was the greatest virtue of all and the source of infinite prosperity; a precious virtue that would come to supplant all the others, even talent itself.

The crowd chased excitedly after him. With great blasts of eloquence, the Devil instilled in them the new order of things, changing all their notions, making them love the things that were wicked and hate those that were wholesome.

There was nothing more curious, for example, than his definition of fraud. He called it man's left arm, the right arm being force. His conclusion was simply that many men were left-handed, and that was that. Not that he required everyone to be left-handed, for no one was to be excluded. Some could be left-handed, others right-handed; he'd accept everyone, except those who were neither one thing nor the other. His most profound and rigorous explanation, however, was that of Venality. One casuist of the time

even confessed that his explanation was a monument of logic. Venality, said
the Devil, was the exercise of a right superior to all others. If you can sell
your house, your ox, your shoe, or your hat—things that legally and juridically belong *to* you but are not part *of* you—why shouldn't you be allowed
to sell your opinion, your vote, your word, or your faith, things which are
more than mere possessions, because they form part of your own consciousness, that is, your very self? To deny this is to lapse into absurdity and contradiction. For are there not women who sell their hair? Can a man not sell
some of his blood for transfusion to another who is anemic? And why should
blood and hair, mere physical parts, enjoy a privilege that is denied to character, man's moral portion? Having thus set out the principle behind Venality, the Devil lost no time in expounding its practical and financial benefits.
He then indicated that, in light of social prejudice, it would be appropriate
to disguise the exercise of such a well-founded right; this would, of course,
amount to practicing Venality and Hypocrisy at the same time, and would
therefore be doubly deserving.

Up and down he went, examining and rectifying everything. Naturally
he fought against the forgiveness of sins and other such principles of charitable kindness. He didn't absolutely prohibit the spreading of calumnies
without reward, but urged that it should always be done in return for some
sort of payment, whether financial or otherwise. However, in cases where
the calumny resulted from nothing more than an uncontrollable explosion
of impetuous imagination, he forbade any recompense, since that was equiv-
alent to being paid for merely sweating. He condemned all forms of respect
as potential elements of social and personal politeness—except, of course,
where there was some sort of advantage to be drawn from it. But this exception was itself soon eliminated by the realization that the desire for personal
gain converted a display of respect into straightforward flattery, and the relevant intention was therefore the latter and not the former.

To complete his work, the Devil realized that he needed to sever all
bonds of human solidarity—the idea of loving one's neighbor was a major
obstacle to his new institution. He therefore demonstrated that this rule
was a mere invention of parasites and insolvent tradesmen; one should show
nothing but indifference toward one's fellow man, and, in some cases, hatred
and contempt. He even demonstrated that the notion of "neighbor" was
erroneous, and cited the refined and learned Neapolitan priest Ferdinando

Galiani, who wrote to a certain *marquise de l'ancien régime*: "Neighbor be damned! There's no such thing as neighbor!" The only situation in which the Devil permitted loving one's neighbor was when it concerned loving other men's wives, because that kind of love has the peculiarity of being nothing more than the individual's love for himself. And since some disciples may have found that such a metaphysical explanation would escape the understanding of the masses, the Devil resorted to an illustration: one hundred people take shares in a retail bank, but, in reality, none of the shareholders looks after the business, only their own dividends: this is what happens to adulterers. This illustration was included in the book of wisdom.

Chapter 4

FRINGES AND FRINGES

The Devil's prediction came true. As soon as someone tugged the fringe of those virtues whose velvet cloak was fringed with cotton, they duly threw their cloaks into the nettles and joined the new church. The others duly followed and the institution grew over time. The church had been founded and its doctrine was being propagated; there was not one region of the globe that did not know of it, not one language into which it had not been translated, and not one race that did not love it. The Devil gave a triumphant cheer.

However, one day, many years later, the Devil noticed that many of his faithful followers were secretly practicing the old virtues again. They didn't practice all of them, or practice them in their entirety, but they did practice some of them, partially, and, as I say, in secret. Certain gluttons were retreating to eat frugally three or four times a year, on days of Catholic obligation; many misers were giving alms under cover of darkness or on sparsely populated streets; various embezzlers of the public purse were reimbursing small amounts; now and then fraudsters spoke the honest truth, although with their usual sly expression just so that people would think they were still being tricked.

This discovery shocked the Devil. He investigated the evil more closely, and saw that it was spreading rapidly. Some cases were simply incomprehensible, like that of a Levantine apothecary who had slowly poisoned a whole generation and then, with the profits of his nefarious trade, had come to the aid of his victims' children. In Cairo, the Devil found an otherwise impeccable camel thief covering his face so that he could attend the mosque. The Devil confronted him at the entrance to the mosque and berated him for such outrageous behavior, but the man denied everything, saying he was only going there so as to steal a dragoman's camel; indeed, he did steal it, in full view of the Devil, but then gave it as a present to a muezzin, who prayed to Allah on the thief's behalf. The Benedictine manuscript cites many other extraordinary discoveries, including the following one that completely confounded the Devil. One of his best apostles was a Calabrian gentleman, fifty years old and an eminent forger of documents, who owned a fine house in the Roman Campagna filled with paintings, statues, a library, etc. He was fraud personified; he would even take to his bed so as not to admit that he was in good health. However, this man not only failed to cheat at cards, he even gave bonuses to his servants. Having attracted the friendship of a canon, he went to make his confession to him every week in a deserted side chapel, and although he did not reveal to him any of his secret activities, he crossed himself twice, once upon kneeling and again when he stood up. The Devil could scarcely believe such treachery, but there was no doubting what had happened.

He did not stop for an instant. The shock gave him no time to reflect, to draw comparisons, or to infer from the present situation something analogous in the past. Once again he flew straight up to Heaven, trembling with rage, anxious to discover the hidden cause of such a peculiar occurrence. God listened to him with infinite benevolence, not interrupting or criticizing him, or even gloating over his satanic agony. He looked the Devil straight in the eye and said:

"Well, what do you expect, my poor Devil? The cotton cloaks now have silk fringes, just as the velvet cloaks had cotton ones. What do you expect? It's the eternal human contradiction."

FINAL CHAPTER

MANY SUICIDES HAVE the excellent custom of not departing this life without setting out the reason and circumstances that have turned them against it. Those who go silently rarely do so out of pride; in most cases they either lack time or don't know how to write. It is an excellent custom for two reasons: first, it is an act of courtesy, for this world is not a ball from which a man can sneak away before dancing the cotillion; second, the newspapers collect and publish these posthumous scribbles, and thus the deceased lives on for a day or two, sometimes even a week.

Notwithstanding the excellence of the custom, it was originally my intention to go silently, because, having been unlucky my whole life, I feared that any final words might cause complications in the hereafter. But a recent incident made me change my plans, and I am leaving behind not one document, but two. The first is my will, which I have just finished drafting and sealing; it's here on the table, beside the loaded pistol. The second is this outline of an autobiography. Note that I am leaving the second document only because it is needed to clarify the first, which would seem absurd or unintelligible without some commentary. In my will I state that my few books, old clothes, and the little house I own in Catumbi, which I rent out to a carpenter, should be sold and the proceeds used to buy new boots and shoes to be distributed in the manner indicated, which, I confess, is rather extraordinary. Without an explanation for such a legacy, I risk doubt being cast on the will's validity. The reason behind the legacy stems from a recent incident, and the incident, in turn, is connected to my entire life.

My name is Matias Deodato de Castro e Melo, son of Sergeant-Major Salvador Deodato de Castro e Melo and Dona Maria da Soledade Pereira, both deceased. I come from Corumbá, in the state of Mato Grosso; I was born on March 3, 1820, and am, therefore, fifty-one years of age today, March 3, 1871.

As I said, I am an unlucky fellow, if not the unluckiest of all men. There is even an old proverb that I have quite literally fulfilled. It happened in Corumbá, when I was nearly eight years old. I was swinging back and forth in my hammock during siesta time, in a little room directly under the roof tiles. Now, either because the hook was loose, or because I was swinging too vigorously, the hammock came away from one of the walls and I found myself flat on the floor. I had fallen on my back, but even so I managed to break my nose, because a loose piece of roof tile, which was just waiting for an opportunity to fall, took advantage of the commotion to come crashing down as well. The wound inflicted was neither serious nor of long duration; indeed, my father teased me mercilessly about it. When Canon Brito came to sip a cool glass of *guaraná* with us that evening and was told all about the episode, he cited the proverb, saying that I was the first person actually to achieve the absurd feat of falling flat on my back *and* breaking my nose. Neither the canon nor my father could have imagined that the incident was simply a sign of things to come.

I won't dwell on the other misfortunes that blighted my childhood and youth. I want to die at noon, and it is already eleven o'clock. Besides, I've sent my manservant out, and he might come back early and interrupt the execution of my deadly project. If I had time, I would recount in detail several painful episodes, including a beating I received by mistake. It concerned the rival of a friend of mine—a rival in love and, naturally, one who had been defeated. My friend and the lady in question were most indignant when they found out about the beating I had received, but secretly they were rather pleased that I had been beaten and not him. Nor will I speak of certain illnesses I have suffered. I will hasten to the point when my father, having been poor all his life, died in extreme poverty, and my mother survived him by less than two months. Canon Brito, who had just been elected to the Chamber of Deputies, proposed taking me with him to Rio de Janeiro with the idea of making a priest of me; however, five days after we arrived, he died. You see what I mean when I say I have always been unlucky.

There I was, at sixteen years of age, all on my own, friendless and penniless. A canon at the Imperial Chapel tried to get me employment as a sacristan, but although I had often served at mass in Mato Grosso and knew some Latin, I was not admitted due to a lack of vacancies. Others encouraged me to study law, and I accepted with grim determination. I even had some help to begin with, and when that stopped, I soldiered on and finally managed to get my bachelor's degree. Now, don't tell me that this was an exception in my life of misfortune, because my academic qualification brought me to an even sorrier state of affairs; however, since destiny was determined to punish me whatever my chosen profession, I do not blame my law degree for that. It's true that I was very pleased to obtain it; my tender age and a certain superstitious belief in the need to improve oneself made of that roll of parchment the diamond key that would open every door to good fortune.

And, to begin with, my bachelor's degree was not the only piece of paper in my pocket. No, sir; beside it there were ten or fifteen others, the fruits of a love affair begun in Rio de Janeiro during Holy Week of 1842, with a widow seven or eight years my senior, but fiery, good-humored, and rich. She lived with her blind brother on Rua do Conde; I can't say any more than that. All my friends were aware of this relationship; two of them even read the letters, which I showed them on the pretext of admiring the widow's elegant style, but really so that they could read the marvelous things she said to me. In everyone's opinion, our marriage was a certainty, an absolute certainty; the widow was merely waiting for me to finish my studies. When I graduated, one of these friends congratulated me, underlining his certainty with this definitive sentence:

"Your marriage is pure dogma."

And, laughing, he asked if, on account of that dogma, I could lend him fifty *mil-réis*, which he needed urgently. I didn't have fifty *mil-réis* on me, but that word "dogma" was still reverberating so sweetly within me that I didn't rest all day until I had obtained the money. I happily took it to him myself, and he received it gratefully. Six months later, it was he who married the widow.

I won't tell you how I suffered then, only that my first impulse was to shoot them both. I did shoot them in my imagination, and watched them dying, gasping, begging for my forgiveness. This was a purely hypothetical revenge; in reality, I did nothing. They married, and went to the hills of

Tijuca to watch the rising of their honeymoon moon. I was left rereading the widow's letters. "As God is my witness," said one of them, "my love is eternal, and I am yours, eternally yours . . ." And, in my bewilderment, I muttered blasphemies to myself: "Ours is a jealous God; he will suffer no eternity but his, and that is why he repudiated the widow's words; nor will he suffer any dogma but Catholic dogma, and that is why he repudiated my friend's words." This was how I explained the loss of my fiancée and the fifty *mil-réis*.

I left the capital and went to practice as a country lawyer, but not for long. Misfortune rode behind me on my mule, and wherever I got off, it got off with me. I saw its finger in everything, in the cases that never came my way, in the ones that did come but were worth little or nothing, and in the ones that were worth something but were invariably lost. Besides the fact that clients who win are generally more grateful than the other sort, my succession of defeats discouraged other litigants from contacting me. After a year and a half, I returned to Rio and set myself up with an old companion from my student days, Gonçalves.

Gonçalves was the least juridically minded fellow imaginable, and the least suited to grappling with matters of law. In fact, he was an utter good-for-nothing. If one were to compare mental activity to an elegant house, Gonçalves was incapable of even ten minutes of polite drawing-room conversation—he would always be sneaking off down to the pantry to gossip with the servants. However, this baseness was compensated by a certain lucidity and agility in grasping less arduous or less complex subjects, together with a facility of expression and an almost uninterrupted good humor—something which for me, a poor devil beaten down by fortune, was not to be sneezed at. In the early days, when we had no cases to work on, we passed the time in excellent conversation, lively and animated, in which he always took the better part, whether discussing politics or—a subject that was of particular interest to him—women.

But slowly the cases began to arrive; among them a dispute about a mortgage. It concerned the house of a customs official, Temístocles de Sá Botelho, who had no other assets and didn't want to lose his property. I took charge of the matter. Temístocles was delighted with me, and, two weeks later, when I told him I wasn't married, he laughed and said he wanted nothing to do with bachelors. He said one or two other things, too, and invited me to dinner that Sunday. I went, and fell in love with his daughter, Dona

Rufina, a very pretty girl of nineteen, but rather shy and insipid. Perhaps it's her upbringing, I thought. We married a few months later. I didn't, of course, invite misfortune to the wedding, but inside the church, among the neatly trimmed beards and luxuriant side-whiskers, I thought I saw the sardonic face and glancing eyes of my cruel adversary. It was for this reason that, when the time came to utter the sacred and irreversible vows of marriage, I trembled and hesitated before, finally, stammeringly repeating the priest's words . . .

I was married. It is true that Rufina lacked brilliance and elegance; it was immediately apparent, for example, that she would never be a society hostess. She did, however, possess the qualities of a good housewife, and that was all I asked for. A quiet life was enough for me, and as long as she filled that life, all would be well. But this was precisely the fly in the ointment. If you will permit me a chromatic illustration, Rufina's soul was not black like Lady Macbeth's, or red like Cleopatra's, or blue like Juliet's, or white like Beatrice's, but gray and dull like the lumpen mass of humanity. She was kind only out of apathy, faithful but not out of virtue, friendly but never intentionally tender. An angel might carry her up to heaven, or the devil down to hell, in either case without any struggle on her part, and without her meriting either glory in the first case or shame in the second. Hers was the passivity of a sleepwalker. She was not in the least bit vain. Her father had hatched the marriage because he wanted his son-in-law to be a man with a profession; she accepted me just as she would have accepted any sacristan, magistrate, general, civil servant, or lieutenant, and not out of impatience to be married, but out of obedience to her family and, to a certain extent, so as to be like everyone else. All the other women had husbands, so she wanted one too. Nothing could have been more antipathetic to my nature, but married I was.

Happily—ah! a "happily" in this the final chapter of an unlucky man is, it's true, something of an anomaly. But carry on reading and you will see that the adverb is simply a matter of style, not of life; it is a way of moving the story along, nothing more. What I am going to say will not alter what has already been said. I *will* say that Rufina's domestic qualities were greatly to her credit. She was modest; she did not care for balls, or walks, or gazing out of windows. She kept to herself. She didn't toil away at domestic chores, nor was this necessary, for my work provided her with everything, and all her dresses and hats came from "the French ladies," as we used to call the seamstresses in those days. In between giving orders to the servants, Rufina would sit for hours and hours, letting her spirits yawn, killing time, that hundred-headed hydra that would never die. But, I repeat, despite all her shortcomings, she was a good housewife. As for me, I played the role of the frogs in *Aesop's Fables* who wanted a king, the difference being that when Jupiter threw me down a lump of wood, I didn't ask him for another king, knowing he'd send a snake that would come and swallow me up. "Long live the lump of wood!" I said to myself. I only mention these things to show the steadfast logic of my fate.

Time for another "happily," I think, and this time it isn't just a way of moving between two sentences. Happily, after a year and a half, a sign of hope appeared on the horizon, and, judging by the excitement the news aroused in me, it was a supreme and unique sign of hope. The thing I most desired was on its way. What thing? A child. My life changed in an instant. Everything smiled upon me as on the day of a wedding. I prepared a royal reception for the baby; I bought an expensive cradle finely carved from ebony and ivory; then, little by little, I bought all the other items for the layette; I set the seamstresses to work on the finest cambrics, the warmest flannels, a lovely little lace bonnet; I bought him a pram, and I waited and waited, ready to dance before him like David dancing before the Ark . . . Ah, woe is me! The Ark entered Jerusalem empty; the child was stillborn.

The person who consoled me in my despair was Gonçalves, who was to have been the child's godfather, and was our friend, companion, and confidant. "Be patient," he said, "I'll be godfather to the next one." And he comforted me, and talked to me about other things with the tenderness of a true friend. Time did the rest. Gonçalves himself told me later on that if the child was destined to be unlucky, as I was convinced he would be, then he was better off stillborn.

"What makes you think he wouldn't have been born unlucky?" I retorted.

Gonçalves smiled; he didn't believe in my rotten luck. In fact he had no time to believe in anything; he devoted himself entirely to being happy. He had finally begun to apply himself to the law; he was now pleading cases, presenting petitions, attending court, all because, as he used to say, he needed to live. And he was always happy. My wife found him very amusing; she would laugh at his little stories and jokes, which at times were somewhat risqué. At first I reprimanded him privately, but eventually I grew used to them. After all, who wouldn't pardon the talents of a friend, and such a jovial friend at that? I must say that, eventually, he began to rein himself in, and, from then on, I began to find him a far more serious companion. "You're in love," I said to him one day, and he, turning pale, replied that he was, and added with a smile, albeit weakly, that he, too, must marry. Over supper that evening, I returned to the subject.

"Rufina, did you know that Gonçalves is getting married?"

"It's just his little joke," Gonçalves said, interrupting me.

I cursed my indiscretion, and neither he nor I mentioned it again. Five months later . . .—you must excuse the rapid transition, but there is no means of lengthening it out—five months later, Rufina fell seriously ill and, within a week, she had died of a rampant fever.

And here's a strange thing: while she lived, our differing temperaments weakened the ties between us, which were based principally on necessity and habit. Death, with its great spiritual power, changed everything. Rufina now seemed to me like the bride in the *Song of Songs* who descends from Lebanon, and the divergence between us was replaced by a complete fusion of our beings. I seized upon the image; it filled my soul, and with it she filled my life, where once she had occupied so little space and for so little time. It was a defiant challenge to my evil star; I was building the fortress of destiny on solid, indestructible rock. Please understand me: everything that had, up until then, depended on the exterior world was naturally precarious: roof tiles fell when hammocks swayed, surplices turned their backs on sacristans, widows' vows fled arm in arm with friends' dogmas, lawyers' cases came but fleetingly or sank without trace; finally, children were born dead. But the image of a dead woman was immortal, and with it I could defy the malicious gaze of misfortune. I held happiness captive in my hands, its great condor wings beating the air, while owl-like misfortune flapped its wings and vanished into night and silence . . .

One day, however, while convalescing from a fever, I had the notion of drawing up an inventory of my dead wife's possessions. I began with a little box that hadn't been opened since she had died five months previously. I found inside a large number of odds and ends: needles, threads, scraps of lace, a thimble, a pair of scissors, a prayer of Saint Cyprian, a list of clothes, other bits and pieces, and a bundle of letters tied with a blue ribbon. I undid the ribbon and opened the letters: they were from Gonçalves . . . Ah, it's noon already! I must finish; my manservant will be back at any moment, and then that would be that. No one can imagine how time rushes by in these circumstances; minutes fly like fleeting empires, and, more importantly on this occasion, the leaves of paper fly with them.

I won't dwell on the discarded lottery tickets, the aborted business deals, the interrupted love affairs; still less on fate's other petty grudges. Weary and dismayed, I realized that I would not find happiness anywhere; I went even further: I believed that it did not exist anywhere on Earth, and, since yesterday, I have been preparing myself for my great plunge into eternity. This morning, I had breakfast, smoked a cigar, and leaned out the window. After ten minutes, I saw a well-dressed man walk by, and he kept looking down at his feet. I knew him by sight; he had been the victim of many great misfortunes, but he smiled as he walked, and stared his feet, or, rather, his boots. They were new, patent leather, beautifully made, and no doubt impeccably stitched. From time to time, he looked up at the windows, or at people's faces, but his eyes quickly darted back to his boots, as if drawn to them by a law of attraction stronger than his own will. He was a happy fellow; one could see the blissful expression on his face. He was clearly happy; and yet he may have had no breakfast; he might not even have so much as a penny in his pocket, but he was happy gazing at his boots.

Could happiness be a pair of boots? That man, so buffeted by life, had finally found fortune smiling on him. Nothing is worth nothing. No worldly preoccupation, no social or moral dilemma, neither the joys of the new generation nor the sorrows of the old, neither poverty nor class warfare, no artistic or political crisis, nothing is worth as much to him as a pair of boots. He gazes at them, he breathes them in, he glows, in them he treads the surface of an orb that belongs only to him. Thence comes the dignity of his posture, the firmness of his step, and a certain air of Olympian tranquility. Yes, happiness is a pair of boots.

So here you have the explanation for my will. Those of a superficial nature will say that I'm crazy, that the testator's closing words are pure suicidal delirium; but I am speaking here to the wise and to the unfortunate. And there's no point suggesting that I would be better off wearing the boots myself rather than bequeathing them to others; no, because then there would be only me. By distributing them, I make a certain number of people fortunate. Roll up, roll up, O unfortunate ones! May my final wish be granted. Farewell, and put your boots on!

POSTHUMOUS PICTURE GALLERY

I

THE DEATH OF Joaquim Fidélis caused indescribable consternation throughout the suburb of Engenho Velho, and particularly in the hearts of his dearest friends. It was so unexpected. He was in fine fettle, had an iron constitution, and, the very night before he passed away, had been attending a ball where he had been seen happily chatting away. He had even danced, at the request of a lady in her sixties, the widow of a friend of his, who took him by the arm and said:

"Come on, then, let's show these youngsters that their elders still know a thing or two!"

Joaquim Fidélis protested with a smile, but did as he was told and danced. It was two o'clock in the morning when he left, wrapping his sixty years in a warm winter cape (for it was June 1879), covering his bald head with the hood, lighting a cigar, and hopping nimbly into his carriage.

He may well have nodded off in the carriage, but, once home, despite the late hour and his heavy eyelids, he went to his desk, opened a drawer, took out one of many notebooks, and, in three or four minutes, wrote some ten or eleven lines. His last words were these: "Altogether a vile ball; some aging reveler forced me to dance a quadrille with her; at the door, a dark-skinned country bumpkin asked me for a present. Simply vile!" He put the notebook back in the drawer, undressed, got into bed, fell asleep, and died.

Yes, indeed, the news dismayed the whole neighborhood. So beloved was he, with his fine manners and his ability to be able to talk to anyone; he could be educated with the educated, ignorant with the ignorant, boyish with the boys, even girlish with the girls. And then, most obligingly, he was always ready to write letters, speak to friends, patch up quarrels, or lend money. In the evenings, a handful of close acquaintances from Engenho Velho, and sometimes other parts of the city, would gather in his house to play ombre or whist and discuss politics. Joaquim Fidélis had been a member of the Chamber of Deputies until its dissolution by the Marquis of Olinda in 1863. Unable to get reelected, he abandoned public life. He was a conservative, a label he had difficulty in accepting because it sounded to him like a political Gallicism. He preferred to be called one of the "Saquarema Set." But he gave it all up, and it seems that, in recent times, he detached himself first from the party, and, eventually, from the party's politics. There are reasons to believe that, from a certain point onward, he was merely a profound skeptic.

He was a wealthy and educated man. He had qualified as a lawyer in 1842. Now he did nothing, but read a great deal. There were no women in his house. Widowed after the first outbreak of yellow fever, he refused to countenance a second marriage, to the great sorrow of three or four ladies, who for some time had hopes in that regard. One of them perfidiously managed to make her beautiful 1845 ringlets last until well after her second grandchild was born; another younger woman, also a widow, thought she could hold on to him with concessions that were as generous as they were irretrievable. "My dear Leocádia," he would say whenever she hinted at a marital solution, "why don't we carry on just as we are? Mystery is what gives life its charm." He lived with a nephew called Benjamin, the orphaned son of one of his sisters who had died when the child was still very young. Joaquim Fidélis brought him up and made him study hard, so much so that the boy graduated with a law degree in the year of 1877.

Benjamin was utterly dumbfounded. He could not bring himself to believe that his uncle was dead. He rushed to his bedroom, found the corpse lying in bed, cold, eyes wide open, and a faintly ironic curl to the left-hand corner of his mouth. He wept profusely. He was losing not just a relative but a father, a tenderhearted, dedicated father, one of a kind. Finally, Benjamin wiped away his tears and, since it upset him to see the dead man's eyes open and his lip curled, he rectified both defects. Thus death took on a more tragic but less original expression.

"No! I don't believe it!" cried Diogo Vilares, one of the neighbors, shortly after hearing the news.

Diogo Vilares was one of Joaquim Fidélis's five closest friends. He owed to him the job he had held since 1857. Diogo was followed by the four others in quick succession, all speechless and unable to believe what had happened. The first was Elias Xavier, who had obtained a knighthood, thanks, it was said, to the deceased's timely intervention; then came João Brás, another deputy who, under the rather peculiar rules of the time, had been elected to the Chamber thanks to Joaquim Fidélis's influence. Last of all came Fragoso and Galdino, who, in lieu of diplomas, knighthoods, or jobs, owed him other favors instead. Fidélis had advanced Galdino a small amount of capital, and had arranged a good marriage for Fragoso. And now he was dead! Gone forever! Standing around the bed, they gazed at his serene face and recalled their last get-together the previous Sunday, so intimate and yet so jolly! And, even more recently, the night before last, when their customary game of ombre had lasted until eleven o'clock.

"Don't come tomorrow," Joaquim Fidélis had said to them. "I'm going to Carvalhinho's ball."

"And after that?"

"I'll be back the day after tomorrow."

And, as they left, he gave each of them a box of excellent cigars, as he sometimes did, with a little bag of sweets for the children and two or three fine jokes . . . All lost! Vanished! Gone!

Many persons of note came to the funeral: two senators, a former minister, a few noblemen, wealthy businessmen, lawyers, merchants, and doctors; but the coffin was carried by Benjamin and those five close friends. None of them would yield this honor to anyone, considering it their final and inalienable duty. The graveside eulogy was given by João Brás; it was a touching address, slightly too polished for such an unexpected event, but nonetheless excusable. When everyone had deposited their shovelful of earth on the coffin, the mourners slowly slipped away from the graveside, apart from those six, who stayed to oversee the gravediggers as they went indifferently about their work. They stayed there until the grave had been filled to the very top and the funeral wreaths laid out upon it.

II

The seventh-day mass brought them together again at the church. When the mass was over, the five friends accompanied the deceased man's nephew home. Benjamin invited them to stay for breakfast.

"I hope that Uncle Joaquim's friends will also be my friends," he said.

They went in and, while they ate, they talked about the dead man, each one recounting some story, some witty remark; they were unanimous in their praise and fond regrets. Since each of them had asked for a little memento of the deceased, when they finished breakfast they all went through into his study and chose something: an old pen, a glasses case, a little pamphlet, or some other personal token. Benjamin felt greatly consoled. He informed them that he intended to keep the study exactly as it was. He hadn't even opened the desk yet. He did so then, and, with the others, drew up a list of the contents of some of the drawers. There were letters, loose papers, concert programs, menus from grand dinners; all of it in an enormous muddle. Among other things they found some notebooks, numbered and dated.

"A diary!" exclaimed Benjamin.

It was indeed a diary of the deceased's thoughts and impressions, a sort of collection of secret memories and confidences that the man had shared only with himself. The friends were greatly moved and excited; reading them would be just like conversing with Joaquim again. Such an upright character! And the soul of discretion! Benjamin began reading, but his voice broke, and João Brás had to carry on.

Their interest in what they heard soothed the pain of death. It was a book worthy of being published. It was filled with political and social observations, philosophical reflections, anecdotes about public men such as Feijó and Vasconcelos, others of a rather racier nature, the names of ladies, among them Leocádia's; an entire repertoire of events and comments. They all admired the dead man's talent, his graceful style, and the fascinating subject matter. Some were in favor of having it printed; Benjamin agreed, on condition that they excluded any elements that might be unsavory or excessively personal. And they continued reading, skipping whole sections and pages, until the clock struck noon. They all stood up. Diogo Vilares had been due at his office hours ago; João Brás and Elias also had to be else-

where. Galdino went off to his shop. Fragoso had to change out of his black
clothes and take his wife shopping on Rua do Ouvidor. They agreed to meet
again and continue their reading. Some of the details had given them an itch
for scandal, and itches need to be scratched, which is precisely what they
intended to do, by reading.

"Until tomorrow, then," they said.

"Yes, until tomorrow."

Once he was alone, Benjamin carried on reading the manuscript.
Among other things, he marveled at the portrayal of the Widow Leocádia,
a masterpiece of painstaking observation, even though the date coincided
with the time when they were still lovers. It was proof of a rare impartial-
ity. The deceased, it turned out, was a master of portraits. The notebooks
were full of them, stretching back to 1873 or 1874; some were sketches of
the living, others of the dead, some were of public men like Paula Sousa,
Aureliano, Olinda, etc. They were brief and to the point, sometimes only
three or four lines, drawn with such confident fidelity and perfection that
the image seemed almost like a photograph. Benjamin carried on reading.
Suddenly he came across Diogo Vilares, about whom he read the following:

DIOGO VILARES—I have referred to this friend many times and
will do so yet again, provided he doesn't kill me with boredom, a
field in which I consider him a true professional. Many years ago,
he asked me to get him a job and I did. He did not warn me of the
currency in which he would repay me. Such singular gratitude! He
went so far as to compose a sonnet and publish it. He wouldn't
stop talking about the favor I'd done him, paying me endless compliments; finally, though, he relented. Later on, we became more
closely acquainted. I got to know him even better. C'est le genre
ennuyeux. Not a bad partner at ombre, though. They tell me he
owes nothing to anyone. A good family man. Stupid and credulous.
Within the space of four days, I've heard him describe a government
as both excellent and detestable, depending on who he is speaking
to. He laughs a lot and usually inappropriately. When they meet
him for the first time, everyone begins by assuming he is a serious
fellow; by the second day, they snap their fingers at him. The reason
is his face, or, more particularly, his cheeks, which lend him a certain air of superiority.

Benjamin's first reaction was that he'd had a lucky escape. What if Diogo Vilares had been there? He reread the description and could scarcely believe it. But there was no denying it: the name was definitely Diogo Vilares and it was written in his uncle's own hand. And he wasn't the only friend mentioned, either; he flicked through the manuscript and came across Elias:

ELIAS XAVIER—This Elias is a subordinate fellow, destined to serve someone, and serve him smugly, like a coachman to a fashionable household. He vulgarly treats my personal visits with a certain arrogance and disdain: the policy of an ambitious lackey. From the first weeks I knew him, I realized that he wanted to make himself my intimate friend, and I also understood that on the day he really became one, he would throw all the others out in the street. There are times when he calls me to one side to talk to me secretly about the weather. His aim is clearly to instill in the others a suspicion that there are private matters between us, and he achieves precisely this, because all the others bow and scrape before him. He is intelligent, good-humored, and refined. He's an excellent conversationalist. I don't know anyone with a sharper intellect. He is neither cowardly nor slanderous. He only speaks ill of someone when his own interests are at stake; when such interests are absent, he holds his tongue, whereas true slander is gratuitous. He is dedicated and persuasive. He has no ideas, it's true, but that's the difference between him and Diogo Vilares: Diogo simply parrots the ideas he hears, whereas Elias knows how to make them his own and choose the opportune moment to introduce them into the conversation. An event in 1865 provides a good illustration of the man's shrewdness. He was due to be granted a knighthood by the government for providing some freed slaves for the war in Paraguay. He had no need of me, but he came to see me on two or three occasions, with a dismayed and pleading air, to ask me to intercede on his behalf. I spoke to the minister, who told me: "Elias knows the document has already been drafted and only awaits the Emperor's signature." I understood then that this was simply a way of showing how deeply indebted he was to me. A good partner at whist; a touch quarrelsome, but he knows what he's doing.

"Well, really, Uncle Joaquim!" exclaimed Benjamin, getting to his feet. A few moments later, he thought to himself: "Here I am reading the unpublished book of his heart. I only knew the public edition, revised and expurgated. This is the original, internal text, exact and authentic. But who would have thought it of Uncle Joaquim!"

He sat down again, slowly reread the portrait of Elias, pondering its features. While he lacked the necessary knowledge to evaluate the truth of the sketch, he thought that, in many aspects, at least, the portrait was a true likeness. He compared these iconographic notes, so crude and cold, with his uncle's warm, elegant manners, and felt gripped by a certain fear and disquiet. What, for example, might his uncle have said about him? With this thought, he again leafed through the manuscript, skimming over various ladies and public men, and came upon Fragoso—an extremely brief sketch that came immediately after Galdino and four pages before João Brás. He remembered that the former had, only a short time before, taken a pen as a memento; perhaps the very pen with which the dead man had drawn his portrait. The sketch was only a few lines long, as follows:

FRAGOSO—Honest, saccharine manners, and handsome. Wasn't difficult to marry him off; he gets on very well with his wife. I know he adores me—almost as much as he adores himself. Polished, insipid, and commonplace conversation.

GALDINO MADEIRA—The warmest heart in the world and a spotless character, but the qualities of his mind destroy all the others. I lent him some money for family reasons and because money is not something I lack. There is in his brain a hole of some sort, through which his mind slips and falls into a vacuum. He is incapable of three minutes' consecutive thought. He subsists mainly on images and borrowed phrases. The "teeth of calumny" and other such expressions are his perennial delight—as worn out as the mattress in a cheap boardinghouse. He is easily vexed at cards, and, once vexed, makes a point of losing, making it clear that this was deliberate. He doesn't dismiss any employees, however bad. If he didn't have bookkeepers, it's doubtful he could keep track of his earnings at all. A friend of mine, who is a civil servant, owed him some money for more than two years and used to say to me with a grin that, whenever Galdino saw him in the street, instead of asking for his money, he would ask him how things were going at the ministry.

JOÃO BRÁS—Neither foolish nor stupid. Very attentive, despite having no manners. Cannot bear to see a minister's carriage go by; he turns pale and averts his eyes. I believe he's ambitious, but at his age, with no settled career, ambition is slowly turning to envy. In the two years he served as a deputy, he performed his duties honorably: he worked hard and made several good speeches; not brilliant, but solid, full of facts, and well thought out. Proof that he retains a residue of ambition lies in his ardent pursuit of certain prominent, honorific posts; a few months ago, he allowed himself to be appointed honorary president of a São José lay brotherhood, and according to what I hear, he performs his duties with exemplary zeal. I believe he is atheist, but I can't be sure. He smiles little and discreetly. He lives a pure and rigorous life, but his character has one or two fraudulent notes to it, which he lacks the skill to conceal; he lies easily about trivial matters.

At last, with a feeling of dread, Benjamin found himself described in this diary.

This nephew of mine [said the manuscript] is twenty-four years of age, engaged on a project for judicial reform, has abundant hair, and he adores me. I adore him no less. Discreet, loyal, and kind—even to the point of gullibility. As firm in his affections as he is fickle in his opinions. Superficial and a lover of novelty; very fond of legal vocabulary and formulas.

He tried to reread this, but couldn't bear to; those few lines were like gazing into a mirror. He stood up, went over to the window, looked out at the garden, and came back inside to contemplate once again his own features. He reread what his uncle had written: it was rather scant and thin, but not slanderous. If someone had been there with him, it's likely that the young man's feelings of mortification would have been less intense, because the need to dispel the impressions formed by the others would have given him the necessary strength to react against what was written. Alone, however, he had to bear it with no contrasting light and shade. Then he wondered whether his uncle might have composed these pages when he was simply in a bad mood; he compared them to others in which the phrasing was less harsh, but he had no idea whether or not the milder tone was deliberate.

To confirm his hypothesis, he recalled his uncle's customary good manners, the happy hours he had spent alone with him or in conversation with his friends. He tried to summon up his uncle's face, the kindly, amused look in his eyes, and his rather solemn sense of humor; but instead of those innocent, friendly features, all he could see was his uncle lying dead, stretched out on the bed, his eyes open and his lip curled. He tried to banish this image from his mind, but it refused to budge. Unable to drive it away, Benjamin tried mentally to close the man's eyes and straighten his mouth; but no sooner had he done so than the eyelids would lift once again, and the lips resume that ironic sneer. It was no longer the man he had known, but the author of those portraits.

Benjamin ate and slept badly. The five friends returned the following afternoon to continue their reading. They arrived eager and impatient, asking many questions and insisting on seeing the notebooks. Benjamin, however, put them off, making one excuse after another; unfortunately for him, there in the room, behind the others, he could still see the dead man's eternally curling lip, and this made him seem even more awkward and withdrawn. Benjamin's demeanor toward the others turned chilly, for he wanted them to leave, and to see if that vision would disappear with them. Thirty or forty minutes went by. Eventually, the five friends looked at each other and decided to go; they bade him a ceremonious farewell, and returned to their houses deep in conversation:

"What a difference from his uncle! What a gulf separates them! Puffed up by his inheritance, no doubt! Well, we'll leave him to it. Alas, poor Joaquim Fidélis!"

THE CHAPTER ON HATS

———

GÉRONTE: *In which chapter, may I ask?*
SGANARELLE: *In the chapter on hats.*

—MOLIÈRE

SING, O MUSE, of the dismay of Mariana, wife of the distinguished Conrado Seabra, on that April morning in 1879. What could be the cause of such upset? A simple hat, light and not inelegant; in short, a bowler hat. Conrado, a lawyer with offices on Rua da Quitanda, wore it to the city every day, and it went with him to all his court hearings; he only refrained from wearing it at receptions, the opera, funerals, and formal social visits. Otherwise, it was a constant feature, and had been so for the entire five or six years of his marriage. Until, on that particular April morning, after finishing their breakfast, Conrado began to roll a cigarette, and Mariana announced with a smile that she had something to ask him.

"What is it, my angel?"

"Would you be capable of making a sacrifice for me?"

"I could make ten or twenty of them!"

"Then stop wearing that hat to the city."

"Why? Is it ugly?"

"I wouldn't say ugly, but it's only meant to be worn locally, when going for a stroll around the neighborhood, in the evenings or at night. But in the city, for a lawyer, well, it hardly seems—"

"Don't be so silly, sweetie!"

"It may be silly, but will you do it as a favor? Just for me?"

Conrado struck a match, lit his cigarette, and tried to change the subject with an affable wave of his hand, but his wife persisted, and her insistence, at first gently imploring, quickly became harsh and imperious. Conrado was shocked. He knew his wife; she was usually such a passive creature, sweet and gently amenable as the situation demanded, capable of wearing a bonnet, a wimple, or a royal tiara with the same divine indifference. The proof of this is that, having been part of a rather fast set during the two years before marrying, once she did marry, she quickly settled into homelier habits. She did go out from time to time, mainly at the behest of her husband, but she was only truly at ease in her own home. Furniture, curtains, and ornaments made up for the lack of children; she loved them like a mother, and such was the harmony between person and surroundings that she took particular pleasure in everything being in its proper place, the curtains hanging in the same neat folds, and so on. For example, one of the three windows that gave onto the street was always left half open, and it was always the same one. Even her husband's study did not escape her fastidious demands, for she carefully maintained, and at times restored, his books, so that they were always in the same state of disorder. Her mental habits were equally uniform. Mariana possessed very few ideas and read only the same books again and again: Macedo's *Moreninha*, seven times; Walter Scott's *Ivanhoe* and *The Pirate*, ten times each; *Le Mot de l'Énigme* by Madame Craven, eleven times.

In the light of all this, how can one explain this business with the hat? The previous evening, while her husband was attending a meeting of the bar association, Mariana's father came to their house. He was a kindly old man, wiry and somewhat ponderous, a retired civil servant who was consumed by nostalgia for the days when employees wore frock coats to the office. Even now, a frock coat was what he wore to funerals, not for the reasons a reader might suspect, such as the solemnity of death or the gravity of a final farewell, but for the less philosophical reason that this was how things used to be. He always gave the same reason, whether it was frock coats at funerals, or having dinner at two o'clock in the afternoon, or twenty other such foibles. He was so chained to his habits that, on his daughter's wedding anniversary, he would go to their house at six o'clock, having already dined and digested, and watch them eat and, at the end, take a little dessert, a glass of port, and some coffee. Given that he was Conrado's father-in-law, how could he possibly approve of his son-in-law's bowler hat? He put up with it in silence, in consideration of the man's other qualities, but nothing more. That day, however, he had caught sight of it in the street, conversing with other hats—top hats belonging to distinguished gentlemen—and never had it seemed so vile. That night, finding his daughter alone, he opened his heart to her, dubbing the bowler hat the "abomination of abominations," and urging her to banish it.

Conrado was unaware that this was the origin of the request. Knowing his wife's docile nature, he did not understand her resistance, and, because he was willful and authoritarian, her stubbornness irritated him deeply. Even so, he kept these feelings to himself, preferring simply to scoff; he spoke to her with such scathing irony and disdain that the poor lady felt utterly humiliated. Twice Mariana tried to leave the table and twice he forced her to stay, the first time by grabbing her lightly by the wrist, the second time by subduing her with a withering look. And he said with a smile:

"Now, then, sweetie, I have a philosophical reason for not doing as you ask. I have never told you this before, but I will now tell you everything."

Mariana bit her lip and said no more; she picked up a knife and began to tap it slowly on the table, just to have something to do, but her husband wouldn't even allow her this; he delicately took the knife from her and went on:

"Choosing a hat is no random act, as you might suppose; it is governed by a metaphysical principle. Do not think that a man who buys a hat does so freely and voluntarily; the truth is that he is obeying an obscure form of determinism. The illusion of liberty is deeply embedded in the purchaser's psyche, and shared by hatters, who, after watching a customer try on thirty or forty hats, then leave without buying a single one, imagine that he is merely searching for the most elegant combination. The metaphysical principle is this: the hat completes the man; it is an extension of his head, a combination decreed *ab eterno* and that no man may put asunder without committing an act of mutilation. This is a profound question that no one has yet considered. Wise men have studied everything from asteroids to worms, or, in bibliographical terms, from Laplace—you mean you've never read Laplace?—well, from Laplace and his *Mécanique Céleste* to Darwin and his curious book about worms, and yet they've never thought to pause in front of a hat and study it from every angle. No one has noticed that there is a whole metaphysics of hats. Perhaps I should write an essay on the subject myself. However, it's now a quarter to ten and I really must go, but do think about it and you'll see what I mean. Who knows? Perhaps it's not even the hat that complements the man, but the man who complements the hat."

Mariana finally wrested back her independence and got up from the table. She had not understood a word of his barbed terminology, nor his peculiar theory, but she sensed his sarcasm and, inside, she wept with humiliation. Her husband went upstairs to get dressed to go out, came back down a few minutes later, and stood in front of her with the infamous hat on his head. Mariana really did think it made him look seedy, vulgar, and not at all serious. Conrado ceremoniously bade her good day and left.

The lady's irritation had subsided considerably, but her feelings of humiliation remained. Mariana did not wail and weep, as she thought she would, but, thinking it all over, she recalled the simplicity of her request and Conrado's sarcastic response, and, while she recognized that she had been somewhat demanding, she found no justification whatsoever for such excesses. She paced back and forth, unable to stand still; she went into the drawing room, approached the half-open window, and watched her husband standing in the street waiting for the streetcar, with his back to the house and that eternal, despicable hat on his head. Mariana felt herself overcome with hatred for that ridiculous item; she couldn't understand how she had put up with it for so many years. And she thought of all those years of docility and acquiescence to her husband's whims and desires, and wondered if that might not be the very thing that had led to his reaction that morning. She called herself a fool and a ninny; if she had behaved like so many other wives, Clara or Sofia, for example, who treated their husbands as they deserved to be treated, none of this would have happened. One thought led to another, and to the idea of going out. She got dressed and went to visit Sofia, an old school friend, just to clear her head, and certainly not to divulge anything.

Sofia was thirty, two years older than Mariana. She was tall, sturdy, and very sure of herself. She greeted her friend with the usual show of affection and, when Mariana said nothing, she guessed at once that something was very much amiss. Adieu to Mariana's best intentions! Within twenty minutes she had told her friend everything. Sofia laughed, shrugged her shoulders, and told her it wasn't her husband's fault at all.

"Oh, I know, it's my fault entirely," agreed Mariana.

"Don't be silly, my dear! You've just been far too soft with him. You must be strong, for once; take no notice; don't speak to him for a while, and when he comes to patch things up, tell him he must first change his hat."

"Goodness, but it seems such a trivial thing . . ."

"At the end of the day, he's just as right as all the others. Take that chump Beatriz: Hasn't she gone and disappeared off to the country, just because her husband took a dislike to an Englishman who was in the habit of riding past their house every afternoon? Poor Englishman! Naturally, he didn't even notice she'd gone. We women can live very happily with our husbands, in mutual respect, not frustrating each other's desires and without resorting to stubborn outbursts or despotism. Look, I get on very well with my Ricardo, perfectly harmoniously. Whatever I ask him to do, he does immediately, even when he doesn't want to; I only need to frown and he obeys. He wouldn't give me any trouble over a hat! Certainly not! Where would that lead? No, he'd jolly well get a new hat, whether he wanted to or not."

Mariana listened enviously to this delightful description of conjugal bliss. The clarion call of Eve's rebellion reverberated within her, and meeting her friend gave her an irresistible itch for independence and free will. To complete the picture, Sofia was not only very much her own mistress, but also the mistress of everyone else too; she had eyes for all the Englishmen, whether on horseback or afoot. She was an honest woman, but also a flirt; the word is rather crude, but there's no time now to find a more delicate one. She flirted left, right, and center, out of a necessity of nature, a habit of her maiden days. It was the small change of love, and she distributed it to all the paupers who knocked on her door: a nickel to one, a dime to another, never as much as five *mil-réis*, still less anything more substantial. These charitable urges now induced her to propose to Mariana that they take a stroll together, see the shops, and admire some fine, dignified hats while they were at it. Mariana accepted; a little demon was firing up within her the furies of revenge. Moreover, her friend had Bonaparte's powers of persuasion and gave her no time to reflect. Of course she would go; she was tired of living like a prisoner in her own home. She, too, wanted to live a little.

While Sofia went to dress, Mariana remained in the drawing room, restless and rather pleased with herself. She planned out what remained of her week, marking the day and time for each appointment like fixtures on an official journey. She stood up, sat down, went over to the window, while she waited for her friend.

"Has she died or something?" she said to herself from time to time.

Once, when she went to the window, she saw a young man pass by on horseback. He wasn't English, but he made her think of Beatriz, whose husband had taken her off to the country due to his distrust of an Englishman, and she felt swelling within her a hatred of the entire masculine race—except, perhaps, for young men on horseback. To be honest, this one was far too affected for her taste; he stuck out his legs in the stirrups just to show off his boots, and rested one hand on his waist as if he were a mannequin. Mariana noted these two defects, but thought that his hat made up for them. Not that it was a top hat; it was a bowler, but entirely appropriate for equestrian purposes. It was not covering the head of a distinguished lawyer on his way to the office, but that of a man simply enjoying himself or passing the time.

The slow, leisurely click of Sofia's heels came down the stairs. "Ready!" she said a moment later upon entering the drawing room. She really did look lovely. We already know she was tall. Her hat gave her an even more commanding air, and a devilish black silk dress, molding the curves of her bust, made her even more striking. Next to her, Mariana disappeared somewhat—one needed to look carefully to see that she did in fact have very pretty features, beautiful eyes, and a natural elegance. The worst of it was that Sofia instantly monopolized all attention, and if there were only a limited amount of time to observe them both, Sofia grabbed it all for herself. This remark would be incomplete if I did not add that Sofia was perfectly aware of her superiority, and for this very reason appreciated the charms of women like Mariana, because they were less obvious or effusive. If this is a flaw, it is not for me to correct it.

"Where are we going?" asked Mariana.

"Don't be silly! We're going for a little trip into town. Now, let's see: I'm going to have my picture taken, then I'm going to the dentist. No, let's go to the dentist first. Don't you need to go to the dentist?"

"No."

"Or have your picture taken?"

"I've got lots already. And why do you need a picture? To give to 'you-know-who'?"

Sofia realized that her friend's resentment had not abated and, as they walked, she took care to add some more fuel to the fire. She told Mariana that, while it wouldn't be easy, there was still time to free herself. And that she would teach her a way of slipping the shackles of tyranny. It was best not to do it in a single bound, but slowly and surely, so that the first he'd know about it was when she was standing over him with her foot placed firmly on his neck. It would be a matter of a few weeks, three or four at the most. Sofia was ready and willing to help her. And she told Mariana again not to be so soft, that she was no one's slave, and so on. As she walked, Mariana's heart sang to itself the *"Marseillaise"* of matrimony.

They reached Rua do Ouvidor. It was just after noon. There were crowds of people walking, or just standing around, the usual hustle and bustle. Mariana felt a little overwhelmed, as she always did. Uniformity and tranquility, the foundations of her life and character, took their usual knocks from all that hurly-burly. She could scarcely thread her way through the groups of people, still less know where to fix her gaze, such was the jumble of people and the profusion of shops. She stuck close to her friend, and, not noticing that they had passed the dentist's, was anxious to reach the place and get inside. It would be a refuge, certainly better than the hullabaloo of Rua do Ouvidor.

"Really, this street!" she kept saying.

"What?" responded Sofia airily, turning her head toward her friend, and her eyes toward a young man on the sidewalk opposite.

As an experienced navigator of these choppy waters, Sofia slipped through and around the groups of people with great skill and composure. Her figure commanded attention: those who knew her were pleased to see her again, while those who did not, stopped or turned to admire her *élan*. And the bounteous lady, full of charity, swept her eyes from left to right, to no great scandal, since Mariana's presence gave everything a veneer of decency. She babbled away, barely seeming to hear Mariana's replies, commenting on everything and everyone they passed: people, shops, hats . . . For under the midday sun on Rua do Ouvidor, there were many hats, for both ladies and gentlemen.

"Look at that one," Sofia would say.

And Mariana would promptly look, although not quite knowing where to look, because everywhere was a swirling kaleidoscope of hats. "Where's the dentist's?" she asked her friend. She had to repeat her question before Sofia told her that they had already passed the surgery; now they were going to the end of the street; they would come back later, and finally they did.

"Ouf!" sighed Mariana as they entered the hallway.

"My goodness! What's the matter? Anyone would think you were just up from the country!"

There were already some patients in the dentist's waiting room. Mariana couldn't see a single face she recognized, and went to the window to avoid the gaze of strangers. From the window she could enjoy the street without all the pushing and shoving. She leaned back; Sofia came to join her. Some men's hats down below turned to stare up at them; others, passing by, did the same. Mariana felt annoyed by their insistence, but, when she noticed that they were staring principally at her friend, her irritation dissolved into a kind of envy. Meanwhile, Sofia was telling her all about some of the hats—or, more precisely, their romantic adventures. One of them was highly thought-of by Miss so-and-so; another was madly in love with Madam you-know-who, who was also in love with him, so much so that they were sure to be seen on Rua do Ouvidor on Wednesdays and Saturdays between two and three in the afternoon. Mariana listened in bewilderment. The hat was indeed rather handsome, and wore a beautiful necktie, and had an air about it that was somewhere between elegant and raffish, but . . .

"I can't swear to it, mind," Sofia continued, "but that's what people are saying."

Mariana gazed pensively at the hat in question. It was now joined by three more, of equal poise and elegance; the four were probably talking about them, and in favorable terms too. Mariana blushed deeply, looked away, then back again, then retreated into the room. As she did so, she noticed two ladies who had just arrived, and with them a young man who promptly stood up and came to greet her effusively. He had been her very first suitor.

He would be about thirty-three now. He had been away from Rio, first to somewhere in the interior, then to Europe, then as governor of one of the southern provinces. He was of medium height, pale, with a rather skimpy beard and clothes that were straining at the seams. He was holding a new top hat: black, serious, gubernatorial, ministerial even; a hat befitting his person and his ambitions. Mariana, however, could hardly look at him. She became so flustered and disorientated by the presence of a man whom she had known in such special circumstances, and had not seen since 1877, that she was unable to take in anything at all. She proffered him the tips of her fingers, apparently murmured some kind of response, and was about to rejoin Sofia at the window, when her friend turned from the window and came toward her.

Sofia also knew the new arrival. They exchanged a few words. Mariana whispered impatiently in her friend's ear that perhaps it would be better to leave their teeth for another day, but Sofia said no; it would only take half an hour, or three-quarters at most. Mariana felt very uncomfortable: the presence of that man tied her in knots, throwing her into a state of conflict and confusion. It was all her husband's fault. If he hadn't been so stubborn, and, even worse, made fun of her, none of this would have happened. Mariana swore she would have her revenge. She thought about her house, so pretty and peaceful, where she could be right now, as usual, without all this pushing and shoving in the street, without having to be so dependent on her friend . . .

"Mariana," said Sofia, "Senhor Viçoso insists that he's very thin. Don't you think he's put on weight since last year? Don't you remember him from last year?"

Senhor Viçoso was the name of the erstwhile suitor, now chatting with Sofia and casting frequent glances in Mariana's direction. She shook her head. He seized the opportunity to draw her into the conversation, remarking that, as a matter of fact, he hadn't seen her for several years. He underlined these words with a rather sad, meaningful gaze. Then he opened up his tool kit of topics and pulled out the opera. What did they think of the cast? In his opinion they were excellent, except for the baritone; the baritone seemed to him rather dull. Sofia protested, but Senhor Viçoso insisted, adding that, in London, where he'd heard him for the first time, he'd thought the same thing. The ladies, of course, were quite another matter; both the soprano and the contralto were first-rate. And he discussed the various operas he had seen, referring to the most famous passages, praising the orchestra, particularly in *Les Huguenots* . . . He had spotted Mariana on the last night, sitting in the fourth or fifth box on the left, wasn't that so?

"Yes, we were there," she murmured, emphasizing the plural.

"Although I haven't seen you at the Cassino even once," he continued.

"Oh, she's become quite the little peekaboo!" interrupted Sofia, laughing.

Viçoso had greatly enjoyed the last ball at the Cassino, and shared his recollections of it minutely; Sofia did likewise. The most elaborate *toilettes* were described by both of them in particular detail, followed by the various people they had seen, the different characters, and a few barbed comments, albeit anodyne enough not to harm anyone. Mariana listened without the slightest interest; two or three times she even got up and went over to the window, but the hats were so numerous and so inquisitive that she sat back down again. Silently, she called her friend some rather ugly names; I won't give them here because it's unnecessary and, moreover, in rather bad taste to reveal what one young lady might think of another in a moment of irritation.

"And the races at the Jockey Club?" asked the former governor.

Mariana again shook her head. She hadn't been to the races that year. Well, she had missed a treat, especially the one before last; it had been a very lively affair and the horses really top-notch. Better even than the races at Epsom, which he'd attended when he was in England. Sofia said that, yes, indeed, the race before last really had been a credit to the Jockey Club, and confessed that she had enjoyed herself immensely; it had been positively thrilling. The conversation drifted on to two concerts taking place that very week, then it took the ferry and climbed the hills to Petrópolis, where two diplomats provided ample hospitality. When they spoke of a minister's wife, Sofia remembered to flatter the former governor and declare that he, too, must marry, since he would soon be in government. Viçoso squirmed with pleasure and smiled, shaking his head; then, looking at Mariana, he said that he would probably never marry. Mariana turned bright red and stood up.

"You seem in a great hurry," Sofia said to her. "What time is it?" she continued, turning toward Viçoso.

"Nearly three!" he exclaimed.

It was getting late; he had to go to the Chamber of Deputies. He went over to speak to the two ladies he had been accompanying, cousins of his, and made his excuses; he came back to say goodbye to Sofia and Mariana, but Sofia said that she was leaving too. She simply couldn't wait a moment longer. In fact, the idea of going to the Chamber of Deputies had begun to scintillate inside her head.

"Shall we all go to the Chamber?" she proposed to Mariana.

"Oh, no," replied Mariana. "I couldn't. I'm so tired."

"Come on, let's go. Just for a little bit; I'm very tired, too, but . . ."

Mariana resisted a little longer, but resisting Sofia—like a dove arguing with a hawk—was completely pointless. There was nothing for it; she went. The street was busier now, people passing this way and that on both sides of the street, and getting in each other's way at the street corners. The ever-solicitous former governor escorted both ladies, having offered to find them somewhere to sit in the gallery.

Mariana's soul felt ever more torn apart by all this confusion of people and things. She had completely lost her original motivation, and the resentment that had propelled her into that audacious, short-lived flight began to slow its wings, or give up entirely. Once again she thought of her house, so quiet, so tidy, everything in its place, with no pushing or shoving, and, most of all, no unexpected changes. Her impatience grew, and with it her anger. She wasn't listening to a word Viçoso was saying, even though he was talking rather loudly, and principally to her. She couldn't hear and she didn't want to hear. She merely prayed to God to make the time pass quickly. They arrived at the Chamber and went up to the gallery. The rustle of skirts attracted the attention of the twenty or so deputies who were still in the Chamber listening to a speech about the budget. As soon as Viçoso excused himself and left, Mariana quickly told her friend not to play a trick on her like that again.

"Like what?" asked Sofia.

"Like having me run around all over the place like some madwoman. What have I got to do with the Chamber of Deputies? Why should I care about speeches I don't even understand?"

Sofia smiled, fluttered her fan, and received the full attention of one of the ministers. Many eyes gazed at her whenever she visited the Chamber, but this particular minister's eyes had a particularly warm, pleading expression. It may be assumed, therefore, that she did not receive his gaze unexpectedly; it could even be said that she sought it out of curiosity. While she was acknowledging this legislative attention, she replied gently to her friend that she was very sorry and had meant well, and had simply wanted to restore Mariana's independence.

"But if you find me irritating, then don't come out with me again," Sofia concluded.

And, leaning forward a little, she said:

"Look at the minister of justice."

Mariana had no choice but to look at the minister of justice. He was bravely enduring a speech by a government supporter, in which the speaker was extolling the merits of the criminal justice system and, along the way, painstakingly summarizing all the old colonial legislation on the subject. There were no interruptions; just a polite, resigned, cautious silence. Mariana's eyes drifted from one side to the other, utterly bored; Sofia was constantly saying things to her, as an excuse for making all kinds of elegant gestures. After fifteen minutes, the Chamber stirred into life, thanks to a remark made by the speaker and an objection from the opposition. Heckles were exchanged, the temperature rose, and there ensued an uproar that lasted nearly a quarter of an hour.

Mariana did not find this diversion in the least diverting; indeed, her placid, equable nature was thrown into a spin by such unexpected commotion. She even got up to leave, then sat down again. She was ready now to stay until the end, repentant and resolved to keep her marital woes to herself. Doubts began to creep in. She had been right to ask her husband to change his hat, but was it worth all this heartache? Was it reasonable to make such a fuss? He had been cruel and sarcastic, but it was, after all, the first time she had put her foot down and, naturally, the novelty had irritated him. At any rate, it had been a mistake to spill the beans to her friend. Sofia might go and tell others . . . The thought sent a chill down Mariana's spine; her friend's indiscretion was assured; she herself had heard Sofia tell many tales about hats, male and female, engaged in much more than a simple marital tiff. Mariana felt the need to flatter her, and covered up her impatience and annoyance with a mask of hypocritical docility. She, too, began to smile and make random observations about this or that deputy, and in this uneasy truce they reached the end of the speech and the session.

It was gone four o'clock. "Time for home," said Sofia. Mariana agreed, although she seemed in no hurry, and they made their way back along Rua do Ouvidor. Walking up the street and catching the streetcar completed Mariana's mental exhaustion, and she only began to breathe more easily when she saw that she really was on her way home. Shortly before Sofia got off, Mariana asked her keep to herself what she had told her, and Sofia promised that she would.

Mariana gave a sigh of relief. The dove was free of the hawk. Her soul was aching from all the pushing and shoving, dizzy from all those disparate people and things. What she needed was equilibrium and peace. She was nearly home; as she watched the neighboring houses and gardens pass by, Mariana felt her spirits lift. At last she arrived; she entered the garden, and took a deep breath. This was her world, except for a flowerpot that the gardener had moved.

"João, put that flowerpot back where it was," she said.

Everything else was in order, the entrance hall, the drawing room, the dining room, the bedrooms, everything. First of all, Mariana sat down, in various different places, looking carefully at all the objects, so still and orderly. After a whole day of swirling variety, the monotony restored her peace of mind, and had never before seemed so delightful. The truth was she'd made a mistake. She tried to relive the day's events, but couldn't; her soul was gently slipping back into its home comforts. At most, she thought about Viçoso, whom she now, rather unfairly, thought ridiculous. She undressed slowly and lovingly, precisely removing and putting away each item of clothing. Once she was undressed, she thought again about the quarrel with her husband. All things considered, she realized that it had been mainly her fault. Why such stubbornness over a hat that her husband had been wearing for years? And, besides, her father was a terrible fusspot.

"I'll wait and see the look on his face when he comes home," she thought.

It was half-past five; he wouldn't be long. Mariana went to the front room, peered out the window, listened for the streetcar, but heard nothing. She sat down by the window with *Ivanhoe* in her hands, trying, and failing, to read. Her eyes skimmed to the end of the page, then back to the beginning; firstly, because she couldn't grasp the meaning, and secondly, because time and again her eyes would wander from the page to admire the perfect folds of the curtains or some other feature of the room. Ah, blessèd monotony, cradling her in thy eternal bosom.

Eventually the streetcar stopped outside the house and her husband got off; the garden gate creaked open. Mariana went to the window and peered out. Conrado was walking slowly up the garden path, looking to left and right, his hat on his head—not the famous hat he always wore, but another one, the one his wife had asked him to wear that very morning. It came as a rude shock to Mariana, just like the flowerpot in the garden being moved, or as if she'd come across a page of Voltaire in her copy of *Moreninha* or *Ivan-hoe*. It was a jarring note in the harmonious sonata of life. No, that hat would never do. Really, whatever had possessed her to make him get rid of the old one that suited him so well? Even if it wasn't perhaps the most appropriate of hats, it had served him for many years, and framed his face so well . . . Conrado came in through a side door. Mariana flung her arms around him.

"So, is it over?" he asked, circling her waist.

"Listen, darling," she replied, giving him the divinest of kisses, "throw that hat away; the other one's much nicer."

EX CATHEDRA

———

"Y OU'LL GO BLIND like that, Godfather."

"What?"

"You'll go blind; you read as if there were no tomorrow. Go on, give me the book."

Caetaninha took the book from his hands. Her godfather turned on his heel and went into his study, where there was no shortage of books. He shut the door behind him and carried on reading. It was his vice; he read to excess—morning, noon, and night, at lunch and dinner, in bed, after his bath, while walking or standing up, in the house and in the garden; he read before reading and he read after reading. He read every sort of book, but especially law (for he was a law graduate), mathematics, and philosophy; recently, he had also taken up the natural sciences.

Worse than going blind, he went mad. It was toward the end of 1873, up in Tijuca, that he began to show signs of mental derangement. But since the episodes were few and insignificant, it was only in March or April 1874 that his goddaughter noticed the change. One day, over lunch, he interrupted his reading to ask her:

"What's my name again?"

"What's your name?" she repeated, shocked. "Your name is Fulgêncio."

"From this day forth, you shall call me Fulgencius."

And, once more burying his nose in the book, he carried on with his reading. Caetaninha discussed the matter with the house-slaves, who told her they had suspected for some time that he wasn't well. You can imagine the young lady's fears, but her fear soon passed, leaving only pity, which merely made her feel still fonder of him. Also, his mania was harmless enough, for it extended only to books. Fulgêncio lived for the written word, the printed word, the doctrinal and the abstract, for principles and formulas. Over time, he reached the point of theoretical hallucination, although not yet superstition. One of his maxims was that freedom would not die as long as there remained one piece of paper on which to declare it. One day, waking up with the idea of improving the condition of the Turks, he drafted a constitution and sent it to the British envoy in Petrópolis, as a gift. On another occasion, he applied himself to studying the anatomy of the eyes, to see if they really could see, and concluded that they could.

Tell me how, under such conditions, Caetaninha's life could possibly be happy? It's true that she wanted for nothing, because her godfather was a rich man. It was he himself who had brought her up from the age of seven, when he lost his wife; he taught her reading and writing, then French, a little history and geography (which is tantamount to saying almost nothing), and charged one of the house-slaves with teaching her embroidery, lace-making, and sewing. So much is true. But Caetaninha was now fourteen, and, if toys and slaves had once been enough to amuse her, she was reaching the age when toys lose their appeal and slaves their interest, and when no amount of reading and writing can make a paradise of a secluded house up in Tijuca. She sometimes went down to the city, but these were rare occasions, and always very rushed; she didn't visit the theater or go to dances, and she neither made nor received visits. Whenever she saw a riding party of ladies and gentlemen pass by on the road, her soul would jump up behind one of the riders, while her body stayed put by the side of her godfather, who carried on reading.

One day, when she was in the garden, she saw a young man stop at the front gate. He was riding a small mule, and he asked if this was Senhor Fulgêncio's house.

"Indeed it is, sir."

"May I speak with him?"

Caetaninha replied that she would go and see; she entered the house and went to the study, where she found her godfather ruminating over a chapter of Hegel with the most devoutly voluptuous expression on his face.

"A young man? What young man?" Caetaninha told him that it was a young man dressed in mourning.

"In mourning?" repeated the old man, snapping the book shut; it must be him.

I forgot to say (but there is time for everything) that a brother of Fulgêncio's had passed away three months earlier, up north, leaving an illegitimate son. Since the brother, a few days before dying, had written to Fulgêncio asking him to take care of the soon-to-be orphan, Fulgêncio sent for the boy to come to Rio de Janeiro. Upon hearing that a young man in mourning had arrived, he concluded that he must be his nephew, and concluded correctly. It was indeed him.

So far, nothing has happened that would seem out of place in any innocently romantic tale: we have an old lunatic, a lonely, sighing damsel, and now the unexpected arrival of a nephew. So as not to descend from the poetic sphere in which we find ourselves, I shall omit to mention that the mule on which Raimundo was mounted was led back by a slave to the place it had been hired from; I shall skim over the arrangements for the young man's accommodation, limiting myself to saying that since the uncle, by virtue of his devotion to reading, had entirely forgotten that he had sent for the boy, no preparations whatsoever had been made to receive him. However, the house was large and well appointed, and, an hour later, the young man was comfortably lodged in a beautiful room overlooking the kitchen garden, the old well, the laundry, copious lush greenery, and an immense blue sky.

I don't believe I have yet revealed the new guest's age. He is fifteen years old, with just a hint of fuzz on his upper lip; in fact, he's almost a child. So if Caetaninha quickly became flustered, and the slave-women began rushing hither and thither, peering around doors and talking about "the ole master's nephew come from far away," it's because nothing much happened in that house, not because he was a grown man. This was also Fulgêncio's impression, but here's the difference. Caetaninha was unaware that the vocation of such fuzz is to become a mustache, or if she thought of it at all, she did this so vaguely that it's not worth mentioning here. This was not the case with old Fulgêncio. He understood that here was material for a husband, and he resolved to marry the pair of them. But he also saw that, unless he took them by the hand and instructed them to fall in love, chance might move things in a different direction.

One thought begets another. The idea of marrying them combined with one of his recent opinions, viz., that calamities and setbacks in matters of the heart come from love being conducted in a purely empirical manner, with no scientific basis. A man and a woman who were aware of the physical and metaphysical reasons for such a sentiment would be more inclined to receive and nourish it effectively than a man and a woman who knew nothing of the phenomenon.

"My young charges are still wet behind the ears," he said to himself. "I have three or four years ahead of me, and I can start preparing them now. We shall proceed in a logical manner; first, the foundations, then the walls, then the roof . . . rather than starting with the roof . . . Someday we will learn to love just as we learn to read. When that day comes . . ."

He was dazed, dazzled, and delirious. He went to his bookshelves, took down various volumes on astronomy, geology, physiology, anatomy, jurisprudence, politics, and linguistics, opening them, leafing through them, comparing them, and taking a few notes here and there, until he had formulated a program of instruction. It was composed of twenty chapters, and included general concepts of the universe, a definition of life, a demonstration of the existence of man and woman, the organization of societies, the definition and analysis of passion, and the definition and analysis of love, along with its causes, needs, and effects. In truth, they were rather tricky subjects, but he knew how to tame them by using plain, everyday language, giving them a purely familiar tone, just as Fontenelle did when he wrote about astronomy. And he would say emphatically that the essential part of the fruit was the pulp, not the peel.

All of this was highly ingenious, but here is the most ingenious bit. He did not ask them if they wanted to learn. One night, looking up at the sky, he commented on how brightly the stars were shining; and what were the stars? Did they perhaps know what the stars were?

"No, sir."

From here it was but a short step to beginning a description of the universe. Fulgêncio took that step so nimbly and so naturally that the two youngsters were delighted and charmed, and begged him to continue the journey.

"No," said the old man. "We won't exhaust it all today; these things can only be understood slowly. Maybe tomorrow, or the day after . . ."

Thus, stealthily, he began to execute his plan. The two students, astounded by the world of astronomy, begged him every day to continue, and, although Caetaninha was a little confused at the end of this first lesson, she still wanted to hear the other things her godfather had promised to tell them.

I will say nothing about the growing familiarity between the two students, since that would be too obvious. The difference between fourteen and fifteen is so small that the two bearers of those respective ages had little more to do than take each other by the hand. This is what happened.

After three weeks, it was as if they had been raised together. This alone was enough to change Caetaninha's life, but Raimundo brought her still more. Less than ten minutes ago, we saw her looking longingly at the riding parties of ladies and gentlemen passing along the road. Raimundo put an end to such longings by teaching her to ride, despite the reluctance of her godfather, who feared some accident might befall her. Nevertheless, he gave in and hired two horses. Caetaninha ordered a beautiful riding habit; Raimundo went into the city to buy her gloves and a riding crop, with his uncle's money (obviously), which also provided him with the boots and other men's apparel he needed. It was soon a pleasure to behold them both, gallant and intrepid, riding up and down the mountain.

At home, they were free to do as they wished, playing checkers and cards, tending to the birds and the plants. They often quarreled, but, according to the house-slaves, these were silly squabbles that they got into just so that they could make up afterward. Such was the extent of their quarrels. Raimundo sometimes went into the city on his uncle's instructions. Caetaninha would wait for him at the front gate, watching anxiously. When he arrived, they would always argue, because she wanted to take the largest parcels on the pretext that he looked tired, and he wanted to give her the lightest one, claiming that she was too delicate.

After four months, life had changed completely. One could even say that only then did Caetaninha begin to wear roses in her hair. Before this, she would often come to the breakfast table with her hair uncombed. Now, not only did she comb and brush her hair first thing, she would even, as I say, wear roses—one or even two, which were either picked by her the previous night and kept in water, or picked that very morning by Raimundo, who would then bring them to her window. The window was high up, but, by standing on tiptoe and reaching out his arm, Raimundo managed to hand her the roses. It was at around this time that he acquired the habit of tormenting his incipient mustache, tugging at it, first on one side and then on the other. Caetaninha would rap him on the knuckles to make him desist from such an unseemly practice.

Meanwhile, their lessons followed a regular pattern. They already had a general notion of the universe, and a definition of life that neither of them understood. Thus they reached the fifth month. In the sixth, Fulgêncio began his demonstration of the existence of man. Caetaninha could not help giggling when her godfather asked if they knew that they existed and why; but she quickly became serious, and replied that she did not.

"What about you?"

"No, me neither," confirmed the nephew.

Fulgêncio began a general, and profoundly Cartesian, demonstration. The following lesson took place in the garden. It had rained heavily in the preceding days, but the sun now flooded everything with light, and the garden resembled a beautiful widow who has swapped her mourning veil for that of a bride. As if wanting to imitate the sun (great things naturally copy each other), Raimundo shot her a long, all-embracing gaze, which Caetaninha received, quivering, just like the garden. Fusion, transfusion, diffusion, confusion, and profusion of beings and things.

While the old man spoke—straightforward, logical, and plodding, relishing his words, and with his eyes fixed on nowhere in particular, his two students made strenuous efforts to listen, but found themselves hopelessly distracted by other things. First, it was a pair of butterflies fluttering in the breeze. Would you please tell me what is so extraordinary about a pair of butterflies? Admittedly, they were yellow, but this alone is insufficient to explain the distraction. Nor was their distraction justified by the fact that the butterflies were chasing each other—to the left, to the right, then up, then down—given that butterflies, unlike soldiers, never travel in a straight line.

"Man's understanding," Fulgêncio was saying, "as I have just explained . . ."

Raimundo gazed at Caetaninha, and found her gazing at him. Each of them seemed awkward and confused. She was the first to lower her eyes. Then she raised them again, so as to look at something else farther off, such as the garden wall; on their way there, given that Raimundo's eyes lay in their path, she glanced at them as briefly as she could. Luckily, the wall presented a spectacle that filled her with surprise: a pair of swallows (it was the day for couples) were hopping along it with the elegance peculiar to winged beings. They chirruped as they hopped, saying things to each other, whatever it might be, perhaps this: that it was a very good thing that there was no philosophy in garden walls. Suddenly one of them took off, probably the female, and the other, naturally the male, was not going to let himself be left behind: he spread his wings and flew off in the same direction. Caetaninha looked down at the grass.

When the lesson finished a few minutes later, she begged her godfather to continue and, when he refused, took him by the arm and invited him to take a turn in the garden.

"No, it's too sunny," protested the old man.

"We'll walk in the shade."

"It's terribly hot."

Caetaninha suggested they remain on the veranda, but her godfather said to her mysteriously that Rome was not built in a day, and ended up saying that he would only continue the lesson two days hence. Caetaninha retired to her room and stayed there for three-quarters of an hour, with the door closed, either seated or standing at the window or pacing back and forth, or else looking for something she was already holding in her hand, and even going so far as to imagine herself riding up the road alongside Raimundo. At one point, she saw the young man standing by the garden wall, but, on closer inspection she realized it was a pair of beetles buzzing through the air. One of the beetles was saying to the other:

"Thou art the flower of our race, the flower of the air, the flower of flowers, the sun and moon of my life."

To which the other replied:

"No one exceeds thee in beauty and grace; thy buzzing is an echo of divine voices; but leave me . . . leave me . . ."

"Why should I leave thee, O soul of these sylvan glades?"

"I have told thee, king of pure breezes, leave me."

"Do not speak to me like that, thou charm and ornament of the forest. Everything above and around us is saying that thou shouldst speak to me another way. Dost thou not know the song of blue mysteries?"

"Let us listen to it upon the green leaves of the orange tree."

"The leaves of the mango tree are lovelier."

"Thou art more beautiful than both."

"And thee, O sun of my life?"

"Moon of my being, I am whatever thou wilt have me be . . ."

This is how the two beetles were talking. She listened to them, engrossed. When they disappeared, she turned away from the window, saw what time it was, and left her bedroom. Raimundo had gone out; she went to wait for him at the front gate for ten, twenty, thirty, forty, fifty minutes. When he returned, they said very little; they met and parted two or three times. The last time it was she who took him to the veranda, to show him a trinket she thought she'd lost and had just found. Readers, please do her the justice of believing that this was a blatant lie. Meanwhile, Fulgêncio brought the next lesson forward and gave it on the following day between lunch and dinner. Never had he spoken so clearly and simply, which was just as it should be, for it was the lesson concerning the existence of man, a profoundly metaphysical chapter, in which it was necessary to consider everything and from every possible angle.

"Do you understand?" he asked.

"Perfectly."

And the lesson carried on to its conclusion. When it was over, the same thing happened as the day before. As if she were afraid of being alone, Caetaninha begged him to continue the lesson, or to take a turn about the garden with her. He refused both requests, patted her paternally on the cheek, and went and shut himself up in his study.

"Next week," the old man thought as he turned the key, "next week I will make a start on the organization of societies; all of next month and the one after will be devoted to the definition and classification of passion; in May we will move on to love . . . by then it will be time . . ."

While he was saying this and closing the study door, a sound echoed forth from the veranda—a thunderclap of kisses, according to the caterpillars in the garden. Mind you, to caterpillars the slightest noise sounds like thunder. As for the authors of the noise, nothing definitive is known. It seems that a wasp, seeing Caetaninha and Raimundo together at that moment, confused coincidence with consequence and deduced that it was them, but an old grasshopper demonstrated the absurdity of such a proposition, citing the fact that he had heard many kisses, long ago, in places where neither Raimundo nor Caetaninha had ever set foot. We may all agree that this latter argument was utter nonsense, but such is the prestige of good character that the grasshopper was applauded for having once again defended both truth and reason. And, on that basis, maybe it was indeed so. But a thunderclap of kisses? Let's imagine there were two; let's even imagine three or four.

THE ACADEMIES OF SIAM

H AVE YOU HEARD of the academies of Siam? All right, I know Siam never had any academies, but let's just suppose it did, and that there were four of them, and then listen.

I

Whenever they saw swarms of milky-hued fireflies rising up through the night sky, the stars would often say that these were the sighs of the king of Siam, who was amusing himself with his three hundred concubines. And, winking at each other, they would ask:

"Pray tell us, O regal sighs, what is the beautiful Kalaphangko up to tonight?"

To which the fireflies would reply gravely:

"We are the sublime thoughts of the four academies of Siam; we bring with us all the wisdom of the universe."

One night, there were so many fireflies that the stars took fright and hid in their bedrooms, and the fireflies took over part of outer space, where they stayed forever and called themselves the "Milky Way."

This enormous rising cloud of thoughts was the result of the four academies of Siam trying to solve a very peculiar puzzle: Why are there feminine men and masculine women? And it was the nature of their young king that led them to ask this question. Kalaphangko was virtually a lady. Everything about him breathed the most exquisite femininity: he had velvety eyes, a silvery voice, gentle, amenable manners, and an abiding horror of war. The Siamese warlords grumbled, but the nation lived very happily; everywhere there were dances, plays, and songs, following the example of the king, who cared for little else, which rather explains the stars' misinterpretation of those sighs.

Then, suddenly, one of the academies came up with a solution to the problem:

"Some souls are masculine, others are feminine. The anomaly we have before us is a case of mistaken bodies."

"I disagree," shouted the other three. "The soul is neuter; it has nothing to do with external differences."

Nothing more was needed for the alleys and waterways of Bangkok to turn red with academic blood. First came controversy, then insults, and finally fistfights. It wasn't so bad when the insults began; no one hurled abuse that was not scrupulously derived from Sanskrit, which was the academic language, the Latin of Siam. From then on, though, they lost all shame. The rivalry turned very nasty indeed, rolled up its sleeves, and descended into mudslinging, stone-throwing, punches, and vile gestures, until, in exasperation, the sexual academy (i.e., that which espoused the sexuality of souls) decided to put an end to the other three academies, and prepared a sinister plan . . . O winds that blow, scatter forth these leaves of paper, that I may not recount the tragedy of Siam! For—woe is me!—I can scarcely bear to write of such a dastardly revenge. They secretly armed themselves and went to find the members of the other academies, just as the latter, sitting hunched in thought over the famous puzzle, were dispatching a cloud of fireflies up to heaven. They gave no warning and showed no pity, but fell upon them, foaming with rage. Those who fled did not flee for long; pursued and attacked, they died on the riverbank, aboard barges, or in dark alleyways. Altogether there were thirty-eight corpses. An ear was cut off from each of the leaders, and these were made into necklaces and bracelets for their own victorious president, the sublime U-Tong. Drunk on victory, they celebrated the deed with a great feast, at which they sang this magnificent hymn: "Glory be to us, for we are the rice of science and the lamp of the universe."

The city awoke to this horrifying news. Terror gripped the masses. No one could forgive such a cruel and despicable act; some even doubted their own eyes. Only one person approved of it all: the beautiful Kinnara, the flower of the royal concubines.

II

Lying languidly at the feet of the beautiful Kinnara, the young king asked her to sing.

"I'll sing no other song than this: I believe that souls have a sex."

"What you believe is absurd, Kinnara."

"So, Your Majesty believes that souls are neuter?"

"That is equally absurd. No, I don't believe in the neuter soul, or the sexual soul, either."

"But then what does Your Majesty believe in?"

"I believe in your eyes, Kinnara. They are the sun and light of the universe."

"But you must choose: either you believe that souls have no sex, and must, therefore, punish the only surviving academy, or you believe that souls do have a sex, and must, therefore, pardon it."

"What a delightful mouth you have, my sweet Kinnara! I believe in your mouth; it is the very fount of wisdom."

Kinnara leapt angrily to her feet. Just as the king was the feminine man, she was the masculine woman—a buffalo in swan's feathers. Just now it was the buffalo that strode across the bedchamber, but, a moment later, it was the swan that stopped and, tilting her neck, asked and obtained from the king, between two gentle caresses, a decree in which the doctrine of the sexual soul was declared legitimate and orthodox, and the other doctrine absurd and perverse. On that same day, the decree was sent to the victorious academy, to all the pagodas and mandarins, and distributed throughout the kingdom. The academy hung out lanterns, and peace was restored.

III

Meanwhile, the beautiful Kinnara had an ingenious and secret plan. One night, while the king was studying some papers of state, she asked him if taxes were being paid on time.

"*Ohimè!*" he exclaimed, repeating a word he had heard from an Italian missionary. "Alas, very few taxes have been paid, but I didn't want to have the defaulters beheaded . . . No, not that . . . Blood? Blood? No, I want no blood . . ."

"And what if I were to find you a solution to all of this?"

"What solution?"

"Your Majesty has decreed that souls are masculine and feminine," said Kinnara, after first giving him a kiss. "Suppose that our bodies have been switched. All we need is to return each soul to the body that belongs to it. Let us exchange souls and bodies . . ."

Kalaphangko scoffed at the idea, and asked her just how they would achieve such an exchange. She replied that she would use the method of Mukunda, the king of the Hindus, who placed himself in the corpse of a Brahmin while a jester entered Mukunda's. It's an old legend passed down to the Turks, Persians, and Christians. Yes, but how was the invocation worded? Kinnara declared that she knew the wording, because an old Buddhist monk had found a copy of it in the ruins of a temple.

"What do you think?"

"I don't actually believe in my own decree," he retorted, laughing, "but go ahead; if it's true, let's switch. But only for six months, no more. At the end of six months, we'll change back."

They agreed to make the exchange that very night. While the city slept, they sent for the royal barge, stepped aboard, and let themselves drift away. None of the rowers saw them. When Dawn appeared, urging on the golden-red cows drawing her glittering chariot, Kinnara offered up the mysterious invocation. Her soul detached itself from her body and hovered in the air, waiting for the king's body to become vacant too. Her own body lay slumped on the rug.

"Ready?" asked Kalaphangko.

"Ready. I'm here in the air, waiting for you. Please excuse my undignified state, Your Majesty . . ."

But the king's soul did not hear the rest. Sprightly and shimmering, it left its physical vessel and entered Kinnara's body, while her soul took possession of the royal remains. Both bodies sat up and gazed at each other, and one can only imagine their amazement. It was the same situation as Buoso and the serpent in Dante's *Inferno*, but see here my audacity. The poet silences Ovid and Lucan, because he considers his metamorphosis worthier than either of theirs. I am silencing all three of them. Buoso and the snake never meet again, whereas my two heroes continue talking and living together after the switch—which, though I say so myself, is obviously even more Dantesque.

Kalaphangko said: "This business of looking at myself and calling myself 'Your Majesty' is very strange. Does Your Majesty not feel the same?"

Both of them were content, like people who have finally found their proper home. Kalaphangko luxuriated in Kinnara's feminine curves. Kinnara flexed her muscles in Kalaphangko's solid torso. Siam finally had a king.

IV

Kalaphangko's first action (from now on, it should be understood that "Kalaphangko" means the king's body and Kinnara's soul, whereas "Kinnara" means the body of the beautiful Siamese lady and Kalaphangko's soul) was to bestow the very highest honors upon the sexual academy. He did not elevate its members to the status of mandarins, for they were men given to philosophy and literature rather than action and administration, but he decreed that everyone must prostrate themselves before them, as was the custom with mandarins. He also presented them with rare and valuable gifts, such as stuffed crocodiles, ivory chairs, emerald tableware, diamonds, and sacred relics. Grateful for all these favors, the academy also requested the official right to use the title "Light of the World," which was duly granted.

Once this was done, Kalaphangko turned his attention to the public finances, justice, religion, and ceremonial matters. The nation began to feel the "heavy weight," to use the words of our distinguished poet, Camões— for no less than eleven tax dodgers were forthwith beheaded. The others, who naturally preferred their heads to their money, rushed to pay their taxes, and order was quickly restored. The courts and legislation were greatly improved. New pagodas were built, and religion seemed to gain a new impetus, since Kalaphangko, imitating the ancient Spanish arts, ordered the burning of a dozen poor Christian missionaries who were wandering those parts; the bonzes called this action the "pearl" of his reign.

What he lacked was a war. On a more or less diplomatic pretext, Kalaphangko attacked a neighboring kingdom, in what was the shortest and most glorious campaign of the century. On his return to Bangkok, he was greeted with splendid celebrations. Three hundred boats decorated with blue and scarlet silk went out to receive him. On the prow of each boat stood a golden dragon or swan, and all the boats were crewed by the city's finest inhabitants. Music and cheering filled the air. At night, when the festivities had ended, his beautiful concubine whispered in his ear:

"My young warrior, repay me for the pangs of longing that I felt in your absence; tell me that the greatest of celebrations is your sweet Kinnara."

Kalaphangko responded with a kiss.

"Your lips have the chill of death or disdain on them," she sighed.

It was true; the king was distracted and preoccupied, for he was plotting a tragedy. It was getting close to the time when they should return to their own bodies, and he was thinking of escaping that clause in their agreement by killing his beautiful concubine. He hesitated because he did not know if he, too, would suffer upon her death, given that it was his body, or even if he would have to succumb with her. Such were Kalaphangko's thoughts. But the idea of death cast a shadow over his brow, while, imitating the Borgias, he clutched to his breast a little vial of poison.

Suddenly he remembered the learned academy; he could consult it, not directly, but hypothetically. He summoned the academicians; they all came except their president, the illustrious U-Tong, who was ill. There were thirteen of them; they prostrated themselves and, in the Siamese manner, said:

"Mere despicable straws that we are, we hasten to answer the call of Kalaphangko."

"Arise," said the king benevolently.

"No, the place for dust is underfoot," they insisted, their knees and elbows on the ground.

"Then I will be the wind that lifts up the dust," replied Kalaphangko, and, with a gracious, tolerant gesture, he stretched out his hands to them.

He then started to talk about a variety of matters, so that the main topic of interest should appear to arise naturally of its own accord. He spoke of the latest news from the west and the Laws of Manu. Referring to U-Tong, he asked them whether he really was as great a sage as he seemed; when he received only a reluctant, mumbled response, he ordered them to tell him the whole truth. They confessed, with exemplary unanimity, that U-Tong was one of the most sublime idiots in the kingdom—a shallow, worthless mind who knew nothing and was incapable of learning. Kalaphangko was shocked. An idiot?

"It pains us to say so, but that is what he is; a shallow, withered intellect. He has, however, a pure heart, and a noble, elevated character."

When he had recovered from his shock, Kalaphangko told the academicians to leave, without asking them the question he had intended to ask. An idiot? He would somehow have to unseat him from the academy without offending him. Three days later, U-Tong was summoned by the king. The king inquired kindly after his health. He then said that he wanted to send someone to Japan to study some documents; it was a matter which could only be entrusted to a person of enlightenment. Which of his colleagues at the academy seemed to him most suitable for such a task? One can see the king's cunning plan: he would hear two or three names, and then conclude that he preferred U-Tong himself to all of them. But here's what U-Tong replied:

"My royal lord and master, if you will pardon my coarse language: the men you speak of are thirteen camels, except that camels are modest and they are not. They compare themselves to the sun and the moon. But, in truth, neither the sun nor the moon has ever shone on such worthless fools. I understand Your Majesty's surprise, but I would be unworthy of my position if I did not say this with all due loyalty, albeit confidentially . . ."

Kalaphangko's jaw dropped. Thirteen camels? Thirteen, thirteen! U-Tong's only kind word was for their hearts, all of which he declared to be excellent; no one was superior to them in terms of character. With an elegant, indulgent gesture, Kalaphangko dismissed the sublime U-Tong from his presence, and remained pensive. What his thoughts were, no one knew. What we do know is that he sent for the other academicians, but this time separately, to conceal his intentions and obtain a franker exchange of views. The first to arrive, although unaware of U-Tong's opinion, was entirely in agreement, with but one emendation, that there were twelve camels, or thirteen if one counted U-Tang himself. The second academician expressed the same opinion, as did the third and all the others. They differed only in style: some said camels, others used circumlocutions and metaphors that meant the same thing. However, none of them cast any aspersions on anyone's moral character. Kalaphangko was speechless.

But this was not the final shock to greet the king. Since he could not consult the academy, he attempted to make his own deliberations. He devoted two whole days to this, but then the beautiful Kinnara revealed that she was going to be a mother. This news made him recoil from the crime he had been planning. How could he destroy the chosen vessel of the flower that would bloom the following spring? He swore to heaven and earth that the child would be born and would flourish. The end of the week arrived, and with it the moment for each of them to return to their original bodies.

As on the previous occasion, they boarded the royal barge at night, and let themselves drift downstream, both of them against their will, not wanting to give up the body they had and return to the other. When the shimmering cows of Dawn's chariot began to tread slowly across the sky, they offered up the mysterious invocation, and each soul was returned to its former body. On returning to hers, Kinnara felt a maternal instinct, just as she had felt a paternal instinct when she occupied Kalaphongko's body. It even seemed to her that she was simultaneously mother and father of the child.

"Father and mother?" repeated the king, restored to his former self.

They were interrupted by delightful music in the distance. It was a junk or a canoe coming upriver, for the music was fast approaching. By then the sun was flooding the waters and green riverbanks with light, giving the scene an air of life and rebirth, which to some extent made the two lovers forget this return to their former selves. And the music kept coming closer, clearer now, until a magnificent boat appeared around a bend in the river, decorated with feathers and fluttering pennants. Aboard were the fourteen members of the academy (including U-Tong), all chanting in unison that old hymn: "Glory be to us, for we are the rice of science and the light of the world!"

The beautiful Kinnara (formerly Kalaphangko) was wide-eyed with astonishment. She could not understand how fourteen males, gathered together in an academy, could be both the light of the world, and yet, individually, a bunch of camels. She consulted Kalaphangko, but he could think of no explanation. If someone happens to find one, they would be doing a great service to one of the most gracious ladies in the Orient by sending it to her in a sealed letter, addressed, for greater security, to our consul in Shanghai, China.

FAME

———

"OH! SO YOU'RE PESTANA? said Sinhazinha Mota, raising her hands in surprise and admiration. And then, correcting her over-familiar tone, she quickly followed this up with: "You must forgive me for being so forward, but . . . is it really you?"

Embarrassed and annoyed, Pestana replied that yes, it was indeed him. He had just left the piano, mopping his brow with his handkerchief, and had nearly reached the window, when the young lady stopped him. It was not a ball, just an intimate gathering for a handful of guests, no more than twenty, all told, who had come to dine with the Widow Camargo at Rua do Areal on the occasion of her birthday, November 5, 1875. Such a kind and cheerful widow! She loved to laugh and have fun, even though she had just reached the fine old age of sixty; indeed this turned out to be the last time she did laugh and have fun, for she died during the first few days of 1876. Yes, such a kind and cheerful widow! Such spirit and enthusiasm: no sooner had they finished dinner than she launched into organizing the dances, asking Pestana to play a quadrille! She scarcely needed to finish her request, for Pestana bowed graciously and hastened to the piano. After the quadrille, she gave him barely time to draw breath before she bustled over once again to ask a very particular favor.

"Just say the word, madam."

"Would you play that polka of yours, *Keep Your Hands to Yourself, Mister?*"

Pestana grimaced, then, quickly disguising his displeasure, gave a stiff, silent bow, and returned, unenthusiastically, to the piano. On hearing the first few bars, a new wave of gaiety swept the room, the gentlemen rushed over to the ladies, and the pairs launched furiously into the latest polka. It was absolutely the latest thing, for it had been published only a couple of weeks earlier and there was hardly a corner of the city where it had not been heard. It had even attained that highest of accolades, being whistled and hummed in the streets at night.

Sinhazinha Mota had not for one moment thought that the Pestana she had seen at the dining table and then at the piano, with his snuff-brown frock coat and long black curly hair, his somewhat wary eyes and smoothly shaven chin, could possibly be the *composer* Pestana; a friend had only told her this when Pestana got up from the piano after finishing the polka. Hence her admiring question. As we have seen, he responded with some embarrassment and annoyance. Unperturbed, Sinhazinha Mota and her friend heaped so many extravagant compliments upon him that even the most humble of vanities would have been pleased. Pestana, however, received their words with growing annoyance until, pleading a terrible headache, he asked to be excused. Neither the young ladies nor his hostess could persuade him to stay. He was offered homemade remedies and a little rest, but would have none of it; he insisted on leaving, and he left.

Out in the street, he walked quickly away, afraid they might still call him back; he only slowed down once he had turned the corner of Rua Formosa. But there, too, his polka awaited him in all its jollity. From a smallish house on the right-hand side, only a few yards away, came the notes of his latest composition, played on a clarinet. There was the sound of dancing, too. Pestana paused for a few moments, considered turning back, but carried on walking, quickening his pace and crossing to the other side of the street. The notes faded into the distance, and Pestana turned into Rua do Aterrado, where he lived. As he reached his house, he saw two men coming toward him. One of them, almost brushing past Pestana, started whistling the same polka, *con brio*; the other man joined in and the two of them headed noisily and cheerily off down the street, while the tune's composer ran despairingly into his house.

Once inside, he breathed again. His old house, his old staircase, his old black manservant, who came to inquire whether he wanted any supper.

"No, no supper," Pestana bawled at him. "Just make me some coffee and go to bed."

He got undressed, put on a nightshirt, and went to the room at the back of the house. When the servant lit the gas lamp in the room, Pestana smiled and nodded his heartfelt greetings to the ten or so portraits hanging on the wall. Only one was an oil painting; it was a portrait of the priest who had raised him, taught him Latin and music, and who, if you believed idle gossip, was Pestana's father. He had certainly left him as an inheritance this old house, along with its bits and pieces of antique furniture, some dating from the reign of Pedro I. The priest had himself composed a couple of motets; he was mad about music, both sacred and profane, and this passion he instilled in the boy, or perhaps transmitted to him by blood, if those wagging tongues were right. However, as you will see, my story does not concern itself with such matters.

The other portraits were of classical composers: Cimarosa, Mozart, Beethoven, Gluck, Bach, Schumann, and three more; some of them were engravings, others lithographs, all badly framed and of differing sizes, but arranged on the wall like saints in a church. The piano was the altar and upon it lay open the evening gospel: a Beethoven sonata.

The coffee arrived; Pestana gulped down the first cup and went over to the piano. He looked up at the portrait of Beethoven and began to play the sonata, as if caught up in a kind of wild ecstasy, but with absolute perfection. He repeated the piece, then paused, stood up, and went to one of the windows. Then he returned to the piano; now it was Mozart's turn. He picked up a sheet of music and performed it in the same manner, his soul transported to another place. Haydn took him up to midnight and his second cup of coffee.

Between midnight and one o'clock, Pestana did little except stand at the window and gaze at the stars, or back at the portraits in the room. From time to time he went to the piano and, without sitting down, played a few random chords, as if searching for a thought. But the thought did not appear and he returned to the window. To him the stars resembled a host of musical notes fixed in the night sky waiting for someone to reach out and unstick them; a time would come when the sky would be empty, and the Earth would be a constellation of musical scores. Nothing, no image, no reverie or reflection reminded him of Sinhazinha Mota, who, at that very moment, was drifting off to sleep thinking about him, that famous composer of so many well-loved polkas. Perhaps the idea of marriage deprived that young lady of several moments of sleep? And why shouldn't it? She was about to turn twenty, and he was thirty, a good age. The young lady fell asleep to the sound of the polka, which she knew by heart, whereas its composer was thinking of neither the polka nor of her, but of the great classics of old, while he endlessly quizzed the heavens and the night, asking the angels and, as a last resort, the devil himself. Why could he not write just one of those immortal pages?

At times, the dawn of an idea seemed to rise up from the depths of his unconscious, and he would run to the piano in order to set it down whole, translate it into sounds, but in vain; the idea vanished. At other times, sitting at the piano, he would let his fingers run wild, to see what fantasias blossomed from them, as they had from Mozart's hands. But nothing, absolutely nothing; inspiration failed him, his imagination slumbered. If by any chance an idea did appear, fully formed and beautiful, it was merely the echo of another piece repeated from his memory, and which he thought he had invented. Then he would leap angrily to his feet and swear that he would give up his art, go and plant coffee or push a cart around the streets. But ten minutes later there he would be once again at the piano, with his eyes fixed on Mozart, trying to mimic his genius.

Two, three, four o'clock. Sometime after four he went to bed; he was weary, disheartened, dead with fatigue; he had to give lessons the following day. He only slept a little, awoke at seven, got dressed, and ate breakfast.

"Would Sir like the cane or the umbrella?" the servant asked, following orders, for his master was often distracted.

"The cane."

"But it looks like rain today, sir."

"Rain," Pestana repeated mechanically.

"Yes, sir. Seems so. The sky's quite dark."

Pestana looked at the servant vaguely, his mind elsewhere. Suddenly:

"Wait right there."

He ran to the room with the portraits, opened the piano, sat down, and spread his hands over the keyboard. He began to play something of his own making, a real and spontaneous inspiration, a polka, a rambunctious polka, as the papers would say. The composer did not hold back: his fingers plucked the notes from the air, entwining them, shaping them; you could say his muse was simultaneously composing and dancing. Pestana forgot all about his lessons, his servant waiting for him with the cane and the umbrella, forgot even the portraits hanging gravely on the wall. He simply composed, at the keyboard or on paper, with none of the previous evening's vain efforts, no frustration, asking nothing of heaven or of Mozart's impassive eyes. No weariness at all. Life, wit, and novelty gushed from his soul like an unquenchable stream.

Soon the polka was finished. He made a few minor changes when he returned for dinner, but already he was humming the tune as he walked down the street. He liked it; the blood of his father and his musical vocation flowed through this new and original composition. Two days later, he took it to the publisher of his other polkas, of which there were already over thirty. The editor thought it delightful.

"It will be a huge success."

The matter of a title arose. When Pestana composed his first polka, in 1871, he had wanted to give it a poetical title; his choice was *"Drops of Sunshine."* The publisher shook his head and told him that titles must themselves be destined for popular tastes, either by allusion to some current event or some catchy expression. He suggested two: *"The Law of September 28,"* or *"Fine Words Butter No Parsnips."*

"But what does *'Fine Words Butter No Parsnips'* mean?" asked the composer.

"Oh, it means nothing at all, but soon enough it'll be all the rage."

Still new to the ways of the world, Pestana refused both titles and kept his polka, but it was not long before he composed another, and the itch of publicity led him to have both of them published, with whatever titles the publisher considered most attractive or appropriate. And thus the pattern was set.

Now, when the composer delivered his brand-new polka and they came to discussing the title, the publisher remembered that, for quite some time, he had been keeping one aside for the next tune Pestana brought him. It was intriguing and expansive, yet jaunty: *"Hey Missus, Hang On to Your Hamper."*

"And I've already thought up another good one for next time," he added.

The first edition sold out as soon as it appeared. The composer's fame was enough to guarantee sales, and in itself the tune was well suited to the genrè, being original, danceable, and easily learned by heart. Within one week it was famous. For the first few days Pestana was truly in love with his new creation; he enjoyed humming it to himself, would stop in the street to listen to it being played in some house, and get annoyed when it was played badly. Soon the theater orchestras were playing it, and he even went to one of the performances. Nor was he displeased to hear it whistled, one night, by a shadowy figure coming down Rua do Aterrado.

The honeymoon lasted only a quarter moon. As on previous occasions, and even more quickly than before, the old masters in the portraits made him bleed with remorse. Angry and ashamed, Pestana raged against the muse who had so often consoled him, she with her impish eyes and warm embraces, so easygoing and so gracious. Back came his self-disgust and his loathing of anyone who asked him to play his latest polka, and he resumed his efforts to compose something along classical lines, even if it was only a page, just one, but one that would deserve to be bound between those of Bach and Schumann. A futile enterprise, a vain effort. He plunged himself into that Jordan, but emerged from it unbaptized. He wasted night after night, confidently and stubbornly convinced that it was only a matter of willpower, and that if he could only let go of the easy stuff . . .

"To hell with polkas; let the devil dance to them," he said to himself one morning, at dawn, as he was getting into bed.

But the polkas did not want to go quite that far. They came to Pestana's house, to the very room where the portraits hung, bursting in so profusely that he scarcely had time to set them down, have them published, enjoy them for a few days, get bored with them, and return to the same old well-springs whence nothing flowed. And thus his life swung between those two extremes until he married, and after he married too.

"Who's he marrying?" Sinhazinha Mota asked her uncle the notary, who gave her this news.

"A widow."

"Is she old?"

"Twenty-seven."

"Pretty?"

"No, but not ugly, either. Just so-so. I'm told he fell in love with her because he heard her sing at the last feast day of Saint Francis of Paola. But I also heard that she possesses another great gift, less rare and not as worthy: she has consumption."

Notaries should not attempt wit, or at least not the caustic sort. At this last piece of news, his niece felt a drop of soothing balm, which cured her twinge of envy. It was all true. A few days later, Pestana married a widow age twenty-seven, a fine singer and a consumptive. She would be the spiritual wife of his creative genius. Celibacy was doubtless the cause of his sterile, errant ways, he told himself; artistically he considered himself a wandering outcast of the dead of night; his polkas were merely his foppish fancies. Now, finally, he was going to beget a whole family of works that were serious, profound, inspired, and finely polished.

Such hopes had budded in the very first hours of love, and blossomed at the first dawn of married life. "Maria," his soul stammered, "give me what I could find neither in the solitude of night, nor in the turmoil of day."

Straightaway, to celebrate their union, he had the idea of composing a nocturne. He would call it *Ave Maria*. It was as though happiness brought with it the beginnings of inspiration; not wanting to say anything to his wife before it was ready, he worked in secret, which was difficult, since Maria, also a fervent music lover, would come and play with him, or simply listen, for hours and hours, in the room with the portraits. They even put on a few weekly concerts, with three of Pestana's musician friends. One Sunday, however, he could contain himself no longer and called his wife into the room to play her a passage from the nocturne; he did not tell her what it was, nor who it was by. Suddenly, stopping, he looked at her inquiringly.

"Don't stop," said Maria. "It's Chopin, isn't it?"

Pestana went pale, stared into space, repeated one or two passages, and stood up. Maria sat down at the piano, and, struggling slightly to remember, played the piece by Chopin. The idea and the motif were the same; Pestana had discovered them in some dark alleyway of his memory, that perfidious old city. Sad and despairing, he left the house and headed toward the bridge, in the direction of São Cristóvão.

"Why struggle?" he asked himself. "I'll stick to polkas . . . Long live the polka!"

Passersby hearing this stared at him as if he were mad. He carried on walking, delirious, tormented, an eternal shuttlecock between his ambition and his vocation. He passed the old slaughterhouse; when he came to the railroad crossing, he had the notion of walking up the tracks and waiting for the first train to come and crush him. The guard made him turn back. He came to his senses and went home.

A few days later—a clear, fresh morning in May 1876—at six o'clock in the morning, Pestana felt a familiar tingling in his fingers. He slipped slowly out of bed so as not to wake Maria, who had been coughing all night and was now sound asleep. He went to the room with the portraits, opened the lid of the piano, and, as quietly as he could, knocked out a polka. He had it published under a pseudonym; in the following two months he composed and published two more. Maria knew nothing about it; she carried on coughing and dying, until one night she passed away in the arms of her distraught and despairing husband.

It was Christmas Eve. Pestana's suffering was only made worse by the sounds of a dance nearby, where several of his best polkas were being played. The dancing was bad enough; hearing his own compositions gave it all a perverse air of irony. He heard the rhythm of the footsteps and imagined the accidentally salacious movements of the dancers, movements that some of his compositions quite frankly called out for; all this as he sat by her pale corpse, mere skin and bones, laid out on the bed. Every hour of the long night passed like that, fast or slow, moistened by tears and sweat, by eau de cologne and Labarraque's disinfectant, springing ceaselessly back and forth as if to the sound of a polka written by the great invisible Pestana.

After the burial, the widower had only one goal: to abandon his music forever once he had composed a *Requiem*, which he would perform on the first anniversary of Maria's death. Then he would take up some other job: clerk, postman, street peddler, anything that would make him forget his murderous art, so deaf to his aspirations.

He began the great work. He put everything into it: boldness, patience, thought, and even the occasional flight of fancy, as he had done in times gone by, imitating Mozart, whose *Requiem* he reread and studied. Weeks and months went by. The work, which at first went quickly, slowed its pace. Pestana had his good days and bad. At times he found the music lacking in some way, a sacred soul, ideas, inspiration, or method; at other times his spirits rose and he worked frantically. Eight, nine, ten, eleven months, and the *Requiem* was still not finished. He redoubled his efforts, neglected his teaching and his friends. He had reworked the piece many times, but now he wanted to finish it, no matter what. Two weeks, one week, five days to go . . . The anniversary dawned and he was still working on it.

He had to make do with a simple spoken mass, for him alone. It is hard to say whether all the tears that came stealthily to his eyes were those of the husband, or if some were the composer's. In any event, he never looked at the *Requiem* again.

"What for?" he asked himself.

Another year passed. At the beginning of 1878, the publisher came to see him.

"It's been two years," he said, "since you've given us one of your lively tunes. Everyone is wondering if you have lost your talent. What have you been doing with yourself?"

"Nothing."

"I know what a blow your wife's death must have been, but it's been two years now. I'm here to offer you a contract: twenty polkas over the next twelve months; the usual fee, and a higher percentage of the sales. And at the end of the year, we can renew it."

Pestana nodded his agreement. He was giving very few lessons, had sold the house to pay off debts, and daily necessities were eating up what little remained. He accepted the contract.

"But I need the first polka straightaway," explained the publisher. "It's urgent. Did you hear that the Emperor has dismissed the Duke of Caxias? The liberals have been summoned to form a government; they're going ahead with electoral reform. The polka will be called '*Hurrah for Direct Elections!*' It's not political, just a good title for the occasion."

Pestana composed the first piece for the contract. Despite his lengthy silence, he had lost neither his originality nor his inspiration. It had the same touch of genius. The other polkas followed one by one at regular intervals. He had kept the portraits and their subjects' repertoire, but he avoided spending all his nights at the piano, so as not to fall into new temptations. Now he would always ask for a free ticket whenever there was a good opera or recital on; he would sit in a corner and simply savor the sounds that would never again blossom in his own mind. From time to time, on returning home, his head filled with music, the unsung maestro in him would awaken once again; he would sit at the piano and aimlessly play a few notes, then, twenty or thirty minutes later, go to bed.

And so the years passed, until 1885. Pestana's fame made him the undisputed master of the polka, but first place in such a village did not suffice for this Caesar, who would still have preferred not the second, but the hundredth place in Rome. He had the same mood swings regarding his compositions as before, the difference being that now they were less violent. No more wild enthusiasm during the first few hours, nor revulsion after the first week; just a degree of pleasure followed by a certain ennui.

That year, he caught a slight fever. After a few days, the fever rose, and became life-threatening. He was already in grave danger when the publisher appeared, unaware that Pestana was ill; he had come to give him the news that the conservatives were back in power, and to ask him to write a polka for the occasion. The nurse, an impoverished theater clarinetist, informed him of Pestana's condition, and the publisher realized it was best to say nothing. It was the patient himself who insisted that he tell him what he had come for; the publisher obeyed.

"But only once you're fully recovered," he concluded.

"Just as soon as the fever subsides a little," said Pestana.

There was a few seconds' pause. The clarinetist quietly tiptoed over to prepare the medication; the publisher stood up and took his leave.

"Goodbye."

"Look," said Pestana, "since it's quite likely that I'll be dead in the next few days, I'll do you two polkas straightaway; the other will come in handy for when the liberals are back."

It was the only joke he had made in his entire life, and it came none too soon, for he died at five minutes past four the following morning, at peace with his fellow men and at war with himself.

THE GENTLEMAN'S COMPANION

So you really think that what happened to me in 1860 could be made into a story? Very well, but on the sole condition that nothing is published before my death. You'll only have to wait a week at most, for I'm really not long for this world.

I could even tell you my whole life story, which contains various other interesting episodes, but that would require time, energy, and paper, and I only have paper; my energy is low and time for me is like the guttering flame of a night lamp. Soon the sun will rise on a new day, a terrible sun, impenetrable as life itself. Farewell, my dear friend; read on and wish me well, forgive anything that offends, and don't be surprised if not everything smells of roses. You asked me for a human document and here you have it. Do not ask me for the empire of the Great Mogul or a photograph of the Maccabees. Ask me, on the other hand, for my dead man's shoes, and they will be yours and yours alone.

As you know, these events took place in 1860. Sometime around August of the preceding year, when I was forty-two, I became a theologian—or rather, I began copying out theological tracts for a priest in Niterói, an old friend from school, who thereby tactfully provided me with room and board. During that month of August 1859, he received a letter from a fellow priest in a certain provincial town, who asked him if he knew of a discreet, intelligent, patient fellow who would be willing to go and serve as gentleman's companion to a Colonel Felisberto, in return for a decent wage. My friend duly consulted me, and I gladly accepted, for I was already becoming fed up with copying out Latin quotations and ecclesiastical formulas. I returned to Rio to say goodbye to a brother of mine, then set off for the provinces.

When I arrived in the town, I heard dire reports about the colonel. He was, it seemed, a quite unbearable man, eccentric and demanding; no one, it was said, could stand him, not even his friends. He had been through more gentleman's companions than medicines. Indeed, he had punched two of them in the face. I replied that I was not afraid of healthy folk, still less of the sick; and after discussing matters with the priest, who confirmed what I had heard and recommended an attitude of meekness and loving charity, I proceeded to the colonel's residence.

I found him stretched out in a chair on the veranda, breathing heavily. He did not receive me badly; at first he said nothing and merely fixed me with his eyes like a watchful cat. Then a malevolent smile spread across his harsh features. Finally, he told me that none of his previous gentleman's companions had been any use at all—always sleeping, answering back, chasing after the female slaves. Two of them had been downright thieves!

"Are you a thief?"

"No, sir."

Then he asked me my name. I told him and he looked startled. Colombo? No, sir: Procópio José Gomes Valongo. Valongo? He thought this a preposterous name and proposed calling me just plain Procópio, to which I replied that he could call me whatever he pleased. I'm telling you this detail not just because I think it gives you an idea of what he was like, but also because my reply made a very favorable impression on the colonel. He himself said so to the priest, adding that I was the most agreeable of all the gentleman's companions he'd had. The honeymoon lasted for seven days.

On the eighth day, my life became exactly the same as that of my predecessors. It was a dog's life, with no sleep, no thoughts of my own, and being constantly showered with insults, which, at times, I laughed at with an air of resignation and deference, for I had noticed that this was one way of mollifying him. His rudeness stemmed as much from his illness as from his temperament, for he suffered from a litany of complaints: an aneurism, rheumatism, and three or four lesser afflictions. He was nearly sixty, and from the age of five everyone had indulged his every whim. Had he been merely grumpy, that would have been fine; but he had a mean streak in

him, and took pleasure in the pain and humiliation of others. At the end
of three months I'd had enough and decided to leave; I waited only for the
right opportunity.

It wasn't long in coming. One day, when I failed to give him his embro-
cation at the correct time, he grabbed his stick and struck me two or three
times. That was the last straw; I quit there and then and went to pack my
bags. Later, he came to my room and begged me to stay, saying that there
was no need to take offense at an old man's bad temper. He was so insistent
that I stayed.

"I'm in a terrible pickle, Procópio," he told me that night. "I won't live
much longer. One foot in the grave, you might say. But you must go to my
funeral, Procópio; I absolutely insist. You must go, and you must pray at my
graveside. If you don't," he added with a chuckle, "I'll come back at night
and torment you. Do you believe in spirits from the other world, Procópio?"

"Certainly not!"

"Why wouldn't you believe, you donkey?" he retorted excitedly, opening his eyes very wide.

If these were the truces, just imagine the wars! He stopped hitting me
with the stick, but the insults were just as bad, if not worse. With time I
became inured to them and stopped noticing; I was an ass, a dolt, an idiot,
a good-for-nothing lazybones, everything under the sun. There wasn't even
anyone to share these insults with me. He had no relatives; there had been
a nephew up in Minas Gerais, but he had died of consumption sometime
between the end of May and the beginning of July. His friends came by
occasionally to flatter and indulge him; a five- or ten-minute visit, nothing more. So there was no one but me, just me, for an entire dictionary of
expletives. More than once I resolved to leave, but each time, at the priest's
insistence, I ended up staying.

Not only were relations between us becoming increasingly strained, I
was also keen to return to Rio. At forty-two I wasn't yet ready to become
a complete recluse tending to a petulant old invalid in the back of beyond.
To get an idea of my isolation, suffice it to say that I didn't even read the
newspapers; apart from the odd piece of news that reached the colonel, I
was totally cut off from the rest of the world. I therefore decided to return
to the capital at the first opportunity, even if it meant crossing swords with
the local priest. Seeing as I'm making a general confession, I should perhaps

add that, since I was spending nothing and saving up all of my wages, I was eager to come and squander them here in the city.

Such an opportunity seemed imminent. The colonel's health was steadily deteriorating and he had drawn up his will, managing to offend the notary almost as much as he had me. His manners became ever coarser, and the brief lapses of peace and affability were now rare. I had already lost the meager dose of pity that had made me overlook the sick man's excesses; inside, I was seething with hatred and revulsion. At the beginning of August, I resolved definitively to go; the priest and the doctor, while accepting my reasons, asked me to stay just a little longer. I granted them one month; at the end of the month I would leave, no matter what the patient's condition. The priest took it upon himself to find my replacement.

Now here comes the event itself. On the evening of the twenty-fourth of August, the colonel fell into a fit of rage and knocked me down, calling me all sorts of vile names, threatening to shoot me, even ending up by throwing a bowl of porridge at me because he said it had gone cold. The bowl hit the wall and shattered into pieces.

"You'll pay for that, you thief!" he bellowed.

He rumbled on in this manner for quite some time. At eleven o'clock he fell asleep. While he slept, I pulled from my pocket an old translation of a d'Arlincourt novel which I had happened to find lying about. I sat down in his room to read it, a short distance from the bed, since I would have to wake the colonel at midnight to give him his medicine. Whether it was the effects of tiredness or the book itself, before I had reached the end of the second page, I, too, fell asleep. The colonel's shouts woke me with a start and I sprang to my feet, still half asleep. He seemed delirious and kept on shouting, finally flinging the water jug at me. There was no time to duck; the jug caught me hard on the left cheek. Blinded by pain, I lunged at the invalid and grabbed him by the throat; we struggled, and I strangled him.

When I realized he had stopped breathing, I stepped back in alarm and cried out, but no one heard me. I shook him then, trying to bring him back to life, but it was too late; the aneurism must have burst, and the colonel was dead. I went into the adjoining room and for two hours did not dare return to the bedroom. I cannot even begin to describe what went through my mind during that time. I was in a complete daze, a kind of vague, vacant delirium. It seemed to me that the walls had faces, and I could hear muffled voices. The victim's cries, both before and during the struggle, continued to reverberate inside me, and whichever way I turned, the air seemed to shake with convulsions. Do not imagine that I'm simply making up colorful imagery for mere stylistic effect; I am telling you that I distinctly heard several voices crying: "Murderer! Murderer!"

Otherwise, the house was silent. The slow, staccato tick tick of the clock only emphasized the silence and solitude. I put my ear to the bedroom door hoping to hear a groan, a word, an insult, anything that would indicate that he was alive and restore some peace to my conscience. I would have willingly taken ten, twenty, a hundred blows from the colonel's fists. But nothing, absolutely nothing; all was silent. I began to pace the room once again; I sat down, my head in my hands, wishing I had never come to this place. "Damn and blast their wretched job!" I exclaimed. And I cursed the priest from Niterói, the doctor, the local priest, everyone who had gotten me the job and begged me to stay just a little longer. I clung to their complicity.

When I began to find the silence too terrifying, I opened a window in the hope of hearing the sound of the wind, but there was no wind. The night was utterly still and the stars shone with the indifference of those who remove their hats when a funeral passes by but carry on with their conversation. I leaned out of the window for some time, staring into the darkness, mentally reviewing my life in the hope that this might ease my present anguish. Only then can I say that I thought clearly about my possible punishment. A heinous crime weighed upon me and certain retribution awaited. At this point, fear was added to my feelings of remorse. I felt my hair stand on end. A few minutes later, I saw three or four human shapes peering in at me from yard, as if ready to pounce; I stepped back into the room, the shapes vanished into thin air; it was a hallucination.

Before day broke, I carefully cleaned the wound on my cheek. Only then did I dare return to the bedroom. Twice I drew back, but, finally, there was no avoiding it and I went in; even then I couldn't go near the bed. My legs shook, my heart pounded; I considered fleeing the scene, but that would be tantamount to confessing my guilt, when what I urgently needed to do was to remove all traces of it. I went over to the bed and looked at the corpse, at its staring eyes and open mouth, as if it were uttering those eternal, centuries-old words: "Cain, what hast thou done with thy brother?" I saw the marks of my fingernails on his neck; I buttoned his nightshirt as high as I could and drew the sheet up to his chin. Then I called one of the slaves, told him the colonel had died in the night, and sent word to the local priest and the doctor.

My first thought was to leave immediately, on the pretext that my brother was ill, for I had indeed received a letter from him a few days earlier saying he was not feeling well. But I realized that such a sudden departure might arouse suspicions, and so I stayed. I laid out the body myself, with the help of a shortsighted old Negro. I sat with the body, afraid others might notice something. I wanted to scrutinize their faces for some flicker of suspicion, and yet I dared not look at anyone. Everything made me jittery: the quiet footsteps stealing into the room, the whispers, the priest's rituals and mumbled prayers. When the time came to close the coffin, my hands trembled so much that someone commented pityingly to their neighbor:

"Poor Procópio! See how moved he is, despite all he had to put up with."

Fearing this might be an ironic remark, I was desperate to get it all over with. We moved outside. Passing from the half darkness of the house into the bright light of the street terrified me, convinced now that my crime would be impossible to hide. I fixed my eyes on the ground and kept walking. When it was all over, I breathed a sigh of relief. I was at peace with my fellow men, if not with my conscience; the next few nights were naturally ones of anxiety and affliction. I need hardly say that I came straight back to Rio de Janeiro and that I lived here in terror, even though I was far removed from the scene of the crime. I never laughed and barely spoke; I ate badly and suffered from hallucinations and nightmares . . .

"Let the dead rest in peace," people would say to me. "There's no reason to be so upset."

And I took full advantage of this illusion, singing the praises of the dead man, calling him a fine old fellow, a little rough around the edges, perhaps, but with a heart of gold. And as I praised him, I almost persuaded myself that this was true, at least for a few moments. Another interesting aspect, which may be of some interest to you, is that, although I wasn't a religious man, I had a mass said for the eternal rest of the colonel's soul, at the Church of the Blessed Sacrament. I didn't send out any invitations, or mention it to anyone; I went to hear it alone, kneeling throughout and crossing myself many times. I paid the priest double the usual amount and distributed alms at the door of the church, all in the name of the deceased. I wasn't trying to deceive anyone, the proof being that I went to the mass alone. I should also add that I never mentioned the colonel without saying, "God rest his soul!" And then I would tell a couple of lighthearted anecdotes about him and some of his more amusing outbursts.

Seven days after arriving in Rio de Janeiro, I received the letter from the priest that I showed you, telling me they'd found the colonel's will and that I was his sole heir. You can imagine my astonishment. I thought I had misread the letter; I showed it to my brother and some friends; they all interpreted it in exactly the same way. It was there in writing: I was the colonel's sole heir. I even wondered if it was a trap, but quickly realized that there were other means of ensnaring me if the crime had been discovered. Furthermore, I knew the priest to be an honest man and a most unlikely instrument for such a scheme. I reread the letter countless times; there it was in black and white.

"How much was he worth?" my brother asked me.

"I don't know, but he was rich."

"Well, he's certainly proved himself to be your friend."

"He has . . . yes, he has . . ."

Thus, by some strange irony of fate, all the colonel's worldly goods came into my possession. I considered refusing the inheritance. Taking even a penny from his estate seemed odious to me, worse even than being a hired killer. I thought about it for three days, and every time I bumped up against the argument that my refusal might arouse suspicion. At the end of the three days, I settled on a compromise: I would accept the inheritance and secretly give it all away, little by little. It wasn't just a matter of scruples; it was also a way of redeeming my crime through an act of virtue—by doing so, my accounts would be settled.

I made preparations and set off for the town. The closer I got, the more vividly I recalled the whole sad adventure; an air of tragedy surrounded the town, and the colonel's shadow seemed to loom out at me from every side. My imagination re-created every word, every gesture, the whole horrendous night of the murder . . .

Murder or self-defense? Surely the latter, for I had been defending myself from an attack, and in my defense . . . It was an unfortunate accident, just one of those things. I gladly seized upon this idea. And I weighed up all the aggravating circumstances, the blows, the insults . . . I knew very well that the fault lay not with the colonel, but with his illness, which had made him surly, even wicked. But I forgave him everything; nothing, though, could erase what had happened that fateful night. However, I took into account that the colonel could not in any event have lived much longer; he was clearly at death's door—he himself knew it and said so. How long would he have lived? Two weeks? One? Perhaps even less? It wasn't a life, it was a tattered old toe-rag of a life, if even that could describe the poor man's continual suffering. And who knows, perhaps our struggle and his death were simply coincidental? It was possible, even probable; indeed it could not have been otherwise. I seized upon this idea too.

When I reached the town, I felt my heart sink, and I wanted to turn back, but I pulled myself together and carried on. Everyone congratulated me. The priest explained the various provisions of the will, the usual charitable gifts and legacies, all the while praising my Christian patience and devotion in serving the colonel, a man who, for all his harsh behavior, had nonetheless shown his gratitude.

"Indeed," I said, looking away.

I was dumbstruck. Everyone praised my dedication and patience. The initial formalities of drawing up the estate detained me in the town for some time. I appointed a lawyer and everything proceeded smoothly. During this time, there was much talk of the colonel. People came to tell me things about him, in rather less moderate terms than the priest; I defended the colonel, pointing out his few virtues, yes, he could be stern perhaps . . .

"Stern, you say? Well, he's dead now and good riddance, but he was the very devil, that's for sure."

And they described incidents of extraordinary, even perverse, cruelty. What could I say? At first I listened with curiosity; then I began to feel a singular pleasure, which I made a genuine effort to drive out. I continued to defend the colonel, explain his actions, and attribute certain things to local rivalries. He was, I confessed, somewhat violent . . .

"Somewhat? He was a vicious snake-in-the-grass!" said the barber. The tax collector, the pharmacist, the notary, and everyone else agreed. Other stories followed, encompassing the entire life of the dead man. Older people recalled his cruelties as a little boy. And that secret, silent, insidious pleasure grew inside me like a kind of moral tapeworm, which for all that I tried to extract it, ring by ring, would always recover and keep on growing.

The legal formalities kept me busy, and, besides, since no one in the town had a good word to say about the colonel, I began to find the place less forbidding than I had at first. Once I took possession of my inheritance,

I converted it into bonds and cash. Many months passed, and the idea of distributing it all in charitable gifts and worthy donations no longer held me in such a firm grip; I even began to consider this rather presumptuous. I trimmed back the initial plan; I gave something to the poor, new vestments to the parish church, and a donation to the Santa Casa Hospital: thirty-two *contos* in all. I also had a tomb built for the colonel, all marble, the work of a Neapolitan sculptor who was here in Rio until 1866, before going off to die, I believe, in Paraguay.

The years have rolled by and my memories have grown faded and gray. I still sometimes think about the colonel, but without the terror of those early days. I told several doctors about the colonel's illnesses and they all agreed that death would have been imminent; they were only surprised he hadn't succumbed earlier. I may have unwittingly exaggerated his ailments, but the truth is he was going to die, no matter what happened . . .

Anyway, farewell, dear friend. If you judge these scribblings of any value, then repay me with my own marble tomb, on which you may carve as an epitaph this little amendment I have made to the Sermon on the Mount: "Blessed are they that possess: for they shall be comforted."

MR. DIPLOMAT

———

THE BLACK SERVING WOMAN entered the dining room, approached the table where all the guests were seated, and whispered to her mistress. It must have been something urgent, because the lady of the house immediately got up.

"Shall we wait for you, Dona Adelaide?"

"Do carry on, Senhor Rangel; there's no need to wait. I'll take my turn when I get back."

Rangel was reading from the book of fortunes. He turned the page and read out another question: "Is someone secretly in love with you?" There was general fidgeting; the young ladies and gentlemen smiled at each other. The year was 1854, it was the eve of São João, and we were in a fine house on Rua das Mangueiras. João was also the name of the host, João Viegas, and he had a daughter named after him, Joaninha. Every year, the same group of friends and family gathered, a bonfire was lit in the garden, potatoes were roasted as custom required, and fortunes were told. There would be supper and sometimes dancing or parlor games to follow; it was all very convivial. João Viegas was a clerk at one of the civil courts in Rio.

"Come on, who's going to start the ball rolling?" he said. "Dona Felismina, surely. Let's see if you have a secret admirer."

Dona Felismina gave a somewhat forced smile. She was well into her forties and had neither money nor looks, and beneath her veil of piety she was constantly on the lookout for a husband. It was a rather cruel joke, but understandable. Dona Felismina was the perfect example of those gentle, forgiving creatures who seem to have been born to be the butt of other people's jokes. She picked up the dice and threw them with a patient but skeptical air. "Number ten!" cried two voices. Rangel ran his eyes down the page, found the corresponding box, and read: Yes, it was someone she should seek out at church on Sunday, when she went to mass. The whole table congratulated Dona Felismina, who smiled dismissively, but was secretly rather hopeful.

Others took the dice, and Rangel proceeded to read each person's fortune. He read in a pretentious, affected manner. From time to time, he removed his spectacles and wiped them very slowly with the corner of his cambric handkerchief—either simply because it was rather fine cambric or because it gave off a delicate scent of jasmine. His fondness for such airs and graces had merited him the nickname "Mr. Diplomat."

"Go on, Mr. Diplomat, *do* please continue!"

Rangel started; he was so absorbed in perusing the row of young ladies across the table from him that he had forgotten to read out one of the predictions. Was he in love with one of them? Let us take things from the beginning, step by step.

He was a bachelor, by virtue of circumstance rather than vocation. As a young man he had enjoyed several passing flirtations, but, as time passed, the itching for rank and status had set in, and it was this that prolonged his bachelorhood until he was forty-one, the age at which we now see him. He hoped for a bride superior to both him and the circles in which he moved, and he wasted his time in waiting for her. He even attended dances given by a rich and celebrated lawyer for whom he transcribed documents, and who made him his protégé. At these dances, however, he occupied the same subaltern position he held at the office; he would spend the evening wandering the hallways, peering into the ballroom, watching the ladies pass by, devouring with his eyes a multitude of magnificent shoulders and elegant figures. He envied the other men and imitated them. He would leave full of enthusiasm and determination. When there were no dances, he would attend religious processions, where he could feast his eyes on some of the most eligible young ladies in the city. He was also to be found in the courtyard of the imperial palace on gala days, watching the great ladies and gentlemen of the court, together with ministers, generals, diplomats, and high court judges; he recognized everyone and everything, both the individuals themselves and their carriages. He would return from church or palace just as he returned from a ball, feeling impetuous and passionate, ready to grasp the laurels of fortune.

The worst of it is that between hand and branch stood that wall of which the poet spoke, and Rangel was not a man to leap over walls. Everything that he did, from razing cities to carrying off their womenfolk, he did only in his imagination. More than once he imagined himself a minister of state, wallowing in a surfeit of salutations and decrees. One year, on the second of December, as he was returning from the birthday parade on Largo do Paço, he even went so far as to proclaim himself emperor; to this end he envisaged a revolution, in which some blood was spilled, but only a little, followed by a benevolent dictatorship, in which he merely took revenge for a few minor grudges from his days as a court clerk. However, all his daring deeds were but fairy tales. In reality, he was a quiet, discreet fellow.

By the time he reached forty, he had given up on his grandiose ambitions, but his essential nature remained the same, and, notwithstanding his desire to marry, he failed to find a bride. More than one lady would have accepted him willingly, but he lost them all because he was too cautious, too circumspect. One day, he noticed Joaninha, who was nearly nineteen and had a pair of eyes that were both beautiful and meek—undefiled by any masculine conversation. Rangel had known her since she was a child; he had carried her in his arms in the Passeio Público and to see the fireworks at Lapa. How could he speak to her of love? But, on the other hand, his relations with the family were such that a marriage should be easy to arrange; it was either her or nothing at all.

This time, the wall was not high and the branch within his grasp; he needed only to stretch out his arm with a modicum of effort and pluck it from its stem. Rangel had been engaged in this undertaking for several months. He would not, however, reach out his arm without first checking all around him to see that no one was coming, and if he spied someone, he would hide his intentions and continue on his way. Whenever he did reach out, a gust of wind would set the branch swaying or a little bird would make a rustling noise in the dry leaves, and that was all it needed for him to withdraw his hand. And so time passed and his passions deepened, giving him many hours of anguish, always followed by higher hopes. And so, on this very night, the Feast of Saint John, he is carrying with him his first love letter, ready to deliver. Two or three good opportunities have already presented themselves, but he keeps putting off the moment; the night is still young! Meanwhile, he carries on reading out fortunes with all the solemnity of a high priest.

Around him, everyone is cheerful and jolly. Some are whispering, others are laughing or talking over each other. Uncle Rufino, the joker in the family, is going around the table with a feather, tickling the ears of the young ladies. João Viegas is waiting impatiently for his friend Calisto, who is late. Where on earth has he got to?

"Everyone out! I need the table. Let's all go through to the drawing room."

Dona Adelaide had returned and it was time to lay the table for supper. All the guests migrated to the other room, and it was when she walked that the charms of the clerk's daughter could most truly be appreciated. Rangel followed her, besotted and puppy-eyed. She went to the window for a few moments, while a little parlor game was being set up, and he followed: it was his opportunity to slip her the letter.

In a large house across the street a ball was taking place, and the dancing had started. Joaninha was watching; Rangel watched too. Through the windows they could see the couples passing to and fro, swaying to the music, the ladies in their silks and laces, the gentlemen refined and elegant, some wearing medals. From time to time there was a flash of diamonds, swift and fleeting, amid the swirl of the dance. Couples talking, epaulets gleaming, men bowing, fans beckoning; all this could be glimpsed through the windows, which did not reveal the entire ballroom, but the rest could be imagined. He, at least, knew all of it, and described everything to the clerk's daughter. The demons of grandeur, which had seemed to be lying dormant, started once again to perform their prancing pantomimes in our friend's heart, and, lo and behold, began to seduce the young lady's heart too.

"I know someone who would be entirely at home over there," murmured Rangel.

"Why, you, of course," replied Joaninha, without a hint of guile.

Rangel smiled, flattered, and didn't know what to say. He looked at the footmen and liveried coachmen in the street, huddled in groups or leaning against the sides of the carriages. He began pointing out the various carriages to Joaninha: this one's the Marquis of Olinda's, that one belongs to the Viscount of Maranguape, and look, here comes another one, turning into the street from Rua da Lapa. It pulls up opposite: the footman jumps down, opens the carriage door, removes his hat, and stands at attention.

From inside the carriage emerges a bald pate, a head, a man, two medals, then a richly dressed lady; they step into the entrance hall and ascend the grand staircase, carpeted and adorned with two large vases at its foot.

"Joaninha, Senhor Rangel . . .".

That blasted game! And just as he was formulating in his head some knowing comment regarding the couple ascending the stairs, from which he would have slipped naturally into giving her the letter . . . Rangel obeyed the summons and sat down opposite the young lady. Dona Adelaide, who had taken charge of the game, was collecting names; each person was to be a flower. Of course, Uncle Rufino, ever the jester, chose for himself the pumpkin flower. Rangel, wishing to avoid such trivialities, weighed up the potential of each flower and, when the lady of the house asked him for his, answered slowly and softly:

"Jasmine, senhora."

"What a shame Calisto isn't here!" sighed the court clerk.

"Did he actually say he was coming?"

"He did; indeed, he came to the office yesterday for the sole purpose of telling me he would be arriving late, but that he would definitely make it; he had to stop by first at some jolly down in Rua da Carioca."

"Room for two?" boomed a voice from the hallway.

"Thank goodness for that! Here he is, the man himself!"

João Viegas went to open the door; it was indeed Calisto, accompanied by an unknown young man, whom he presented to the general gathering: "This is Queirós; he works at the Santa Casa Hospital; no relation of mine whatsoever, although he does look awfully like me—people are always mixing us up . . ." Everyone laughed; it was one of Calisto's little jokes, for he was as ugly as sin, whereas Queirós was a handsome young man of twenty-six or twenty-seven, with dark hair, dark eyes, and a strikingly slender figure. The young ladies drew back a little. Dona Felismina unfurled her sails.

"We're playing a parlor game and you two gentlemen are very welcome to join us," said the lady of the house. "Will you play, Senhor Queirós?"

Queirós said he would be delighted and looked around at the other guests. He knew some of them, and exchanged a few words of greetings. He told João Viegas that he had been wanting to meet him for quite some time, on account of a favor his father owed him from many years before, concerning a legal matter. João Viegas had forgotten all about it, even when Queirós told him what the favor had been, but he enjoyed hearing such things said in public, and basked for a few minutes in quiet, smug contentment.

Queirós threw himself into the game. Within half an hour he had made himself one of the family. He was a lively fellow, who talked easily, and his manners were natural and spontaneous. He charmed the whole gathering with his vast repertoire of penalties, and indeed there was no one better than him at leading the game, rushing from one side to the other with such vivacity and animation, putting groups together, moving chairs, chatting with the young ladies as if they had all been playmates since childhood.

"Dona Joaninha sits here, on this chair; Dona Cesária stands over on that side, and Senhor Camilo comes in through this door . . . No, not that way. Look: like this, and then . . ."

Sitting stiffly on his chair, Rangel was speechless. Where had this hurricane blown in from? And the hurricane continued to blow, lifting the men's hats and tousling the ladies' hair, and all of them laughing merrily: Queirós here, Queirós there, Queirós everywhere. Rangel went from stupefaction to mortification. Slowly, the scepter was falling from his grasp. He didn't look at the other man, didn't laugh at anything he said, and answered him only curtly. Inside, he was seething with rage and cursing the man, one of those happy fools who knows how to amuse people and make them laugh, because that's what happens at parties. But not even telling himself these and even worse things restored his peace of mind. In the innermost depths of his self-esteem, he was really suffering. Worse still, the other man saw this, and, worst of all, knew he was the cause of it.

Just as he dreamt of future glories, Rangel also dreamt of revenge. In his head, he pounded Queirós to a pulp. Then he imagined some sort of disaster befalling his rival; a sudden pain would do, something serious enough to get rid of the interloper entirely. But no pain appeared, nothing at all; the wretch seemed to grow merrier by the minute, and the whole room fell under his spell. Even Joaninha, normally so timid, quivered with excitement in Queirós's hands, as did the other young ladies; all the guests, men and women, seemed to be at his beck and call. When he mentioned dancing, all the young ladies rushed over to Uncle Rufino and asked him to play a quadrille on his flute, just one, promising not to ask for any more.

"I can't, I've got a callus on my finger."

"The flute?" exclaimed Calisto. "Ask Queirós to play something and then you'll see what a flute can really do. Go and get your flute, Rufino. Come on, everyone, listen to Queirós. You can't imagine how hauntingly he plays!"

Queirós played *"Casta Diva."* "Utterly ridiculous," Rangel muttered to himself, "even the kids in the street are whistling that tune." He shot Queirós a sideways glance, trying to determine whether any serious man would ever stand with his arms like that, and concluded that the flute was indeed a grotesque instrument. He also looked at Joaninha and saw that, like everyone else, her eyes were on Queirós, enraptured, carried away by the sounds of the aria. He shuddered, although without quite knowing why. Joaninha's expression was no different from everyone else's, and yet he felt something which added a further complication to his dislike of the inter-loper. When Queirós finished playing, Joaninha clapped less loudly than the others, and Rangel was unsure whether to attribute this to her usual shyness or to some other emotion. He urgently needed to give her that letter.

Supper was served. The guests entered the dining room in no particular order and, happily for Rangel, he found himself opposite Joaninha, whose eyes were more beautiful than ever and so bright they scarcely seemed the same eyes at all. Rangel savored them in silence, and carefully pieced back together the dream that wretch Queirós had so abruptly shattered with a snap of his fingers. Once again he saw himself by her side, in the house he would rent for them, their little love nest, adorned with all the golden ornaments of his imagination. He would even win a prize in the lottery and spend it all on silks and jewels for his dear wife, the lovely Joaninha, Joaninha Rangel, Dona Joaninha Rangel, Dona Joana Viegas Rangel, or even Dona Joana Cândida Viegas Rangel—he couldn't leave out the Cândida.

"Come on, a toast, Mr. Diplomat. Give us one of your famous toasts!"

Rangel awoke from his reverie; the whole table joined in Uncle Rufino's request; Joaninha herself was begging him to propose a toast, just like last year's. Rangel promised to oblige, just as soon as he had polished off his chicken wing. There were general stirrings and murmurings of praise; when one of the young ladies confided that she had never heard Rangel speak, Dona Adelaide replied in astonishment:

"Really? Goodness gracious, you can't imagine how well he speaks: so very clearly, and with such well-chosen words, and such refinement!"

As he ate, he rehearsed a few thoughts and fragments of ideas that would form the basis of his fine phrases and metaphors. When he was ready, he stood up with an air of self-satisfaction. At last, they were coming knocking at his door. The merry-go-round of anecdotes and mindless jokes was over and they had come to him for something dignified and serious. He looked around and saw all eyes fixed expectantly on him. Not quite all; Joaninha's were turned toward Queirós, whose eyes met hers halfway, along with a cavalcade of promises. Rangel blanched. The words died in his throat, but speak he must; everyone was eagerly, silently waiting for him.

His efforts failed to impress. He merely toasted their host and his daughter. The latter he called "a divine inspiration, transported from immortality to reality," a phrase he had used three years earlier, but that should by now have faded from memory. He spoke also of the sanctuary of family, the altar of friendship, and of gratitude being the flowering of pure hearts. What it lacked in meaning, it made up for in empty grandiloquence. All in all, it was a speech that should have stretched to a good ten minutes, but which he dispatched in five, then sat down.

That wasn't the end of it. Queirós stood up two or three minutes later for another toast, and this time the silence was even more immediate and complete. Joaninha stared into her lap, embarrassed at what he might say. Rangel shuddered.

"Senhor Rangel, the illustrious friend of this house," said Queirós, "drank to the two people who share the name of the saint we commemorate today; I drink to the person who is a saint every day of the year, Dona Adelaide."

Loud applause greeted this worthy sentiment, and Dona Adelaide, greatly flattered, was congratulated by each and every guest. Her daughter did not stop at congratulations. "Mama! Dearest Mama!" she exclaimed, getting up from her seat and going over to hug and kiss her mother three or four times—a sort of letter, as it were, to be read by two people.

Rangel's anger turned to despondency and, as soon as supper was finished, he decided it was time to leave. But hope, that green-eyed demon, begged him to stay, and he stayed. Who knows? It might blow over, a St. John's Eve flirtation; he was, after all, a good friend of the family, held in high esteem, and the young lady's hand was his for the asking. Furthermore, that Queirós fellow might well not have the means to marry. What was that job of his at the hospital? Something menial, perhaps? He glanced at Queirós's clothes, running his eyes over the seams, scrutinizing the embroidery on his shirt, examining the knees of his trousers to see if they were worn from use, also his shoes, and he concluded that Queirós was a capricious young man who probably spent all his money on himself, whereas marriage was a serious business. Also, he might well have a widowed mother, unmarried sisters. Rangel had only himself to provide for.

"Play a quadrille, Uncle Rufino."

"I can't. After a meal, playing the flute always gives me indigestion. Let's play lotto."

Rangel declared he could not play lotto on account of a headache, but Joaninha came over to him and asked him to be her partner. "Half the winnings for you, half for me," she said, smiling; he smiled, too, and accepted. They sat down side by side. Joaninha talked, laughed, looked up at him with her beautiful eyes, and glanced restlessly around at her at the other guests. Rangel felt a little better, and in no time at all felt entirely better. He marked off the numbers randomly, missing some of them, which she pointed out with her finger—a nymph's finger, he said to himself, and his mistakes became deliberate, just so he could see her finger and hear her scold him: "You're not paying attention, Senhor Rangel; do watch out or we'll lose all our money!"

Rangel thought of slipping her the letter under the table, but since nothing had been said between them, she would be taken too much by surprise, and that would spoil everything. Best to say something first. He looked around the table: all the faces were bent over their cards, attentively following the numbers. Then he leaned to his right and looked down at Joaninha's cards, as if checking something.

"You have two squares left," he whispered.

"No, I haven't. I have three."

"Oh, yes, quite right. Three. Now, listen—"

"And you?"

"I have two."

"What do you mean, 'two'? You have four."

There were indeed four; she leaned closer as she pointed to them, almost brushing her ear against his lips; then she looked up at him laughing and shaking her head: "Oh, Senhor Rangel! Senhor Rangel!" Rangel listened with exquisite delight; her voice was so soft, her tone so amicable that he forgot everything, seized her by the waist, and launched them both into the eternal waltz of the chimeras. House, table, guests, all vanished as if they were mere fancies, leaving the two of them as the one true reality, turning and turning in space beneath a million stars that shone for them and them alone.

No letter, nothing. As dawn approached, they all went to the window to watch the guests leaving the ball across the street. Rangel recoiled in horror.

He saw Queirós and the lovely Joaninha brush fingers. He tried to explain this away as a mere illusion, but no sooner had he demolished one such illusion than up sprang another and another, breaking over him like never-ending waves. He could scarcely believe that a single night, a few hours, could be enough to bind two creatures together like that, but the proof was there in their gestures, their eyes, their words, their laughter, and even in the regret with which they parted in the early hours of the morning.

He left, feeling bewildered. A single night! A few hours! When he arrived home late, he lay down on his bed, not in order to sleep, but to sob. Only now, alone, did all his affectations desert him; no longer was he the haughty Mr. Diplomat, he was the crazed madman, tossing and turning on his bed, screaming and bawling like a child, made truly miserable by his sad autumnal love. The poor devil, made of daydreams, indolence, and pretension, was, in substance, as wretched as Othello, and had met a still crueler fate.

Othello killed Desdemona; our lover, whose hidden passions went unnoticed by anyone, served as a witness when, six months later, Queirós married Joaninha.

Neither events nor the passing years changed his essential nature. When the Paraguayan War broke out, he often thought about enlisting as an officer with the volunteers, but he never did; although there can be no doubt that he won several battles and ended up a brigadier.

LIFE!

T HE END OF TIME. Ahasuerus, sitting on a rock, stares out at the distant
horizon, across which two eagles are flying. He meditates, then dreams.
The day draws slowly to a close.

AHASUERUS: And so I reach the end of time, for here lies the very
threshold of eternity. The earth is deserted and forsaken; no other
man breathes the air of life. I am the last; now I can die. Death!
What a wonderful thought! For centuries upon centuries have I
lived, weary and tormented, ever the wanderer, but behold, the
centuries have come to an end, and with them, I, too, will die.
Farewell, old nature! Blue sky, reborn clouds, roses of a single day
and every day, everlasting waters, enemy earth who would not
eat my bones, farewell! The wanderer will wander no more. God
will forgive me, if he so wishes, but death consoles me. Jagged as
my pain rises yonder mountain; the hunger of those passing eagles
must be as desperate as my despair. Will ye, divine eagles, die too?
PROMETHEUS: All mankind must have died; the earth is bare of them.
AHASUERUS: And yet I hear a voice . . . A man's voice? Merciless heavens, am I not the last? Here, he approaches. Who are you? In your
wide eyes there is something of the mysterious light of the archangels of Israel; you are not a man . . .

PROMETHEUS: No.

AHASUERUS: Are you, then, one of the divine race?

PROMETHEUS: You said it, not I.

AHASUERUS: I do not know you, but what does that matter? You are not a man and so I can still die; for I am the last, and behind me I close the door of life.

PROMETHEUS: Life, like ancient Thebes, has a hundred doors. You close one, others will open. You say you are the last of your species? Another species will come, a better one, made not from the same clay, but from the same light. Yes, O last of mankind, the plebeian element will perish forever, and the elite will be what returns to reign over the earth. The times will be set right. Evil will end; the winds will no longer scatter the germs of death, nor the weeping and wailing of the oppressed, but only the song of everlasting love and the blessing of universal justice . . .

AHASUERUS: What do all these posthumous delights matter to the species that will die with me? Believe me, you who are immortal, to bones that rot in the earth, all the purple of Sidon is worthless. What you are telling me is even better than the world dreamed of by Campanella, in whose ideal city there was crime and sickness; yours excludes all moral and physical injuries. May the Lord hear you! But let me go now and die.

PROMETHEUS: Go, then, go. But why such haste to end your days?

AHASUERUS: It is the haste of a man who has lived for thousands of years. Yes, thousands of years. Even men who lived for only a few decades invented a term for that sense of weariness, *tedium vitae*, which they could never truly have known, not at least in all its vast and unyielding reality, because to acquire such a profound aversion to existence it is necessary to have walked, as I have, through every generation and through every ruin.

PROMETHEUS: Thousands of years?

AHASUERUS: My name is Ahasuerus. I was living in Jerusalem when they took Jesus Christ to be crucified. As he passed by my door, he stumbled under the weight of the cross he was carrying, and I drove him on, shouting at him not to stop, not to rest, but to go on up to the hill where he would be crucified . . . Then a voice

from heaven told me that I would be condemned to wander ceaselessly until the end of time. So great was my sin, for I showed no
pity for the man who was going to die. I didn't even know why he
must die. The Pharisees said the son of Mary had come to destroy
the law, and that he must be killed; poor fool that I was, I wanted
to show off my zeal, and that is what provoked my actions on that
day. Later, as I made my way through all the ages and all the cities
of the earth, how often did I see the same thing happen again and
again! Whenever zeal entered a humble soul, it became something
cruel or ridiculous. That was my unpardonable sin.

PROMETHEUS: A grievous sin indeed, but the punishment was generous. Other men read only one of life's chapters; you have read
the entire book. What does one chapter know of another chapter? Nothing. But he who has read every chapter connects them
all together and draws conclusions. If some pages are melancholy,
others are jovial and happy. After bitter tears comes laughter, out
of death springs life, storks and swallows change climate without ever abandoning it entirely; thus is everything reconciled and
restored. You saw this, not ten times, not a thousand times, but
every time; you saw the magnificence of the earth healing the
affliction of the soul, and the joy of the soul overcoming the desolation of things. Such is the alternating dance of nature, which
gives its left hand to Job and its right hand to Sardanapalus.

AHASUERUS: What do you know about my life? Nothing; you know
nothing of human life.

PROMETHEUS: I know nothing of human life? Don't make me laugh!
Come on, then, everlasting man, explain yourself! Tell me everything; you left Jerusalem . . .

AHASUERUS: I left Jerusalem. I began my pilgrimage through the ages.
I traveled everywhere, encountered all races, beliefs, and tongues; I
traveled in sunshine and in snow, among civilized peoples and bar-
barians, to islands and to continents; wherever mankind breathed,
there breathed I. I never worked again. Work is a refuge, and I
never again knew such a refuge. Every morning brought with it my
daily coin . . . See? Here is the last one. Be gone with you, worthless thing! (*He hurls the coin into the distance.*) I did not work, only

wandered, always, always, always wandering, day after day, year after year, down through all the years and all the centuries. Eternal justice knew what it was doing, for to eternity it added idleness. Each generation bequeathed me to the next. Languages that had died lay with my name embedded in their bones. With each passing age everything was forgotten; heroes vanished into myths, into a distant shade, and history slowly dissolved, retaining only two or three faint and far-off outlines. And in one way or another I saw it all. You spoke of chapters? Happy are those who read their lives in only one chapter. Those who departed at the birth of empires took with them an impression of their perpetuity; those who died when those empires were declining were buried with the hope of their restoration; but do you know what it is like to see the same thing over and over again, the same alternation of prosperity and desolation, desolation and prosperity, endless funerals and endless hallelujahs, sunrise after sunrise, sunset after sunset?

PROMETHEUS: But you did not suffer, I believe, and it is at least something not to have suffered.

AHASUERUS: Yes, but I saw other men suffer, and, toward the end, cries of joy had much the same effect on me as the ramblings of a madman. Calamities of flesh and blood, endless conflicts; I saw everything pass before my eyes, to the point where night has made me lose my taste for day, and I can no longer distinguish flowers from weeds. To my weary retina everything looks the same.

PROMETHEUS: But nothing harmed you personally; it was I who, for time immemorial, suffered the effects of divine wrath.

AHASUERUS: You?

PROMETHEUS: I am Prometheus.

AHASUERUS: You are Prometheus?

PROMETHEUS: And what was my crime? From mud and water I made the first men, and then, out of compassion, I stole for them the fire of heaven. That was my crime. Jupiter, who reigned over Olympus at the time, condemned me to the cruelest of tortures. Come, climb up upon this rock with me.

AHASUERUS: This is a fable you are telling me. I know this Hellenistic dream.

PROMETHEUS: Old man of little faith! Come and see these chains that bind me; an excessive punishment, given that no crime was committed, but proud divinity is a terrible thing. Anyway, look, here they are . . .

AHASUERUS: You mean that Time, which corrodes everything, did not want these chains?

PROMETHEUS: They were the work of divine hands: Vulcan forged them. Two messengers from heaven came and chained me to the rock, and an eagle, like that one over there flying across the horizon, pecked at my liver, without ever consuming it entirely. This I endured for countless ages. You cannot imagine the agony.

AHASUERUS: Is this a trick? You really are Prometheus? So it was not some dream concocted by the ancient imagination?

PROMETHEUS: Look at me; touch these hands. See if I exist.

AHASUERUS: So Moses lied to me. You, Prometheus, you created the first men?

PROMETHEUS: That was my crime.

AHASUERUS: Yes, it was your crime, you artificer of hell; it was a crime for which there is no possible atonement. Here you should have remained for all time, chained and being endlessly devoured; you who are the source of all the evils that afflict me. I lacked pity, it is true, but you, who brought me into existence, you, perverse divinity, were the original cause of everything.

PROMETHEUS: Your impending death clouds your reason.

AHASUERUS: Yes, it really is you; you have the Olympian forehead of a strong and handsome Titan: it really is you . . . Are these your chains? I see no sign of your tears.

PROMETHEUS: I shed them for your race.

AHASUERUS: It shed many more on account of you.

PROMETHEUS: Listen to me, O last of your ungrateful line!

AHASUERUS: What do I want with your words? I want to hear your groans, you perverse divinity. Here are your chains. See how I lift them up? Hear the clanking of the irons? Who unchained you?

PROMETHEUS: Hercules.

AHASUERUS: Hercules . . . Let us see if he performs the same service now that you will once again be chained.

PROMETHEUS: You must be mad.

AHASUERUS: Heaven gave you your first punishment; now earth will
     give you your second and last. Not even Hercules will be able to
     break these irons again. See how I shake them about in the air like
     feathers; for I represent the strength of millennia of despair. All of
     humanity is within me. Before I fall into the abyss, I will write the
     world's epitaph on this rock. I will summon the eagle and it will
     come; I will tell it that, on departing this life, the very last man is
     leaving it a gift from the gods.

PROMETHEUS: Poor ignorant man; you are refusing a throne! No, you
     cannot refuse it.

AHASUERUS: Now you are the madman. Come on, kneel. Let me bind
     your arms. Yes, like that, don't resist. Breathe, breathe deeply.
     Now your legs . . .

PROMETHEUS: Go on, go on! These are earthly passions that turn
     against me, but I am not a man and know nothing of ingratitude.
     You will not change one letter of your fate; it will be fulfilled in
     its entirety. You will be the new Hercules. I, who proclaimed the
     glory of the first one, also proclaim yours; and you will be no less
     generous than he.

AHASUERUS: Are you mad?

PROMETHEUS: The truth men do not know is the madness of whoever
     proclaims it. Go on, finish it!

AHASUERUS: Glory never pays for anything, and then it dies.

PROMETHEUS: This glory will never die. Go on, finish what you're
     doing; teach the sharp beak of the eagle how to devour my
     entrails, but listen . . . No, don't listen; you cannot understand me.

AHASUERUS: No, speak, speak.

PROMETHEUS: The passing world cannot understand the eternal, but
     you will be the link between the two.

AHASUERUS: Tell me everything, I'm listening.

PROMETHEUS: I will tell you nothing. Go on, tighten the chains on
     my wrists so that I cannot escape, so that you will find me here
     when you return. You want me to tell you everything? I have
     already told you that a new race will inhabit the earth, made
     from the finest spirits of the extinct race; the multitude of oth-

ers will perish. A noble family, lucid and powerful, it will be the perfect blend of the divine and the human. A new era will be born, but between that old era and this a link is needed, and that link is you.

AHASUERUS: Me?

PROMETHEUS: Yes, you, the chosen one, the king. Yes, indeed, Ahasuerus, you shall be king. The wanderer shall find rest. He who was scorned by men shall govern them.

AHASUERUS: Cunning Titan, you wish to deceive me. Me, a king?

PROMETHEUS: Yes, you. Who else could it be? The new world needs something from the old world, and no one can explain those two worlds better than you. Thus there will be no break between the two humanities. From the imperfect will come the perfect, and your mouth will tell it of its origins. You will tell the new mankind of all the good and evil of the old. You will spring to life once again like the tree whose dead leaves have been removed to reveal only the lush green ones, but in this case the lushness will be eternal.

AHASUERUS: A shining vision! Can it really be me?

PROMETHEUS: Yes, really.

AHASUERUS: These eyes . . . these hands . . . a new and better life . . . Sublime vision! Well, it is only fair, Titan. The punishment was fair, but so is the glorious remission of my sin. I shall live? Me? A new and better life? No, surely you mock me.

PROMETHEUS: Well, then, leave me; one day you will return, when these immense heavens open for the spirits of new life to descend. You will find me here, at peace. Go.

AHASUERUS: Will I greet the sun again?

PROMETHEUS: This very sun which now is setting. Our friend the sun, eye of the ages, will never again close its eyelids. Gaze upon it, if you can.

AHASUERUS: I cannot.

PROMETHEUS: Later you will, when the circumstances of life have changed. Then your eyes will be able to gaze safely at the sun, because future mankind will be a concentration of all that is best in nature: robust and delicate, shimmering and pure.

AHASUERUS: Swear to me you're not lying.

PROMETHEUS: You will see if I am lying.

AHASUERUS: Speak, tell me more; tell me everything.

PROMETHEUS: Describing life is not the same as feeling it; you will have it in abundance. The bosom of Abraham described in your old Scriptures is none other than this perfect world beyond. There you will see David and the prophets. There you will tell the astonished multitudes not only the great events of the extinct world, but also the evils that they will never know: illness and old age, deceit, selfishness, hypocrisy, tedious vanity, unimaginable foolishness, and all the rest. The soul, like the earth, will have an incorruptible sheath.

AHASUERUS: I will once again see this immense blue sky!

PROMETHEUS: Look, how beautiful it is!

AHASUERUS: As beautiful and serene as eternal justice. O magnificent sky, more beautiful even than the tents of Kedar, I will see you again and forevermore; you will gather up my thoughts as in ages past; you will grant me clear days and friendly nights . . .

PROMETHEUS: Sunrise upon sunrise.

AHASUERUS: Speak, speak! Tell me more. Tell me everything. Let me loosen these chains . . .

PROMETHEUS: Unchain me, new Hercules, last man of one world and first of the next. That is your destiny; neither you nor I, nor anyone else, can change it. You are greater even than your Moses. From the heights of Nebo, ready to die, he gazed upon all the lands of Jericho that would belong to his posterity; and the Lord said unto him: "You have seen it with your eyes, but you will not cross into it." You will cross into it, Ahasuerus; you will reach Jericho.

AHASUERUS: Place your hand upon my head, look into my eyes; fill me with the reality and force of your prediction; let me feel something of this full, new life . . . King, you said?

PROMETHEUS: Chosen king of a chosen people.

AHASUERUS: It is no more than just amends for the utter scorn in which I have lived. Where one life spat mud at me, another will

crown my head with a halo. Go on, tell me more . . . tell me
more . . . (*He continues dreaming. The two eagles approach.*)

FIRST EAGLE: Woe is he, this the last man on earth, for he is dying and
yet still dreams of life.

SECOND EAGLE: He only hated life so much because he loved it dearly.

THE CANON,
OR THE METAPHYSICS OF STYLE

"COME FROM LEBANON, my spouse, come from Lebanon, come . . .
The mandrakes give their smell. At our doors we have every breed
of dove . . .

"I charge you, O daughters of Jerusalem, if ye find my beloved, that ye
tell him I am sick of love . . ."

And so it was, to the melody of that ancient drama of Judah, that a noun
and an adjective searched for each other inside the head of Canon Matias.
Do not interrupt me, hasty reader; I know you won't believe anything I'm
about to say. I will, however, say it, despite your little faith, because the day
of public conversion will come.

On that day—sometime around 2222, I imagine—the paradox will take
off its wings and put on the thick coat of common truth. At that point, this
page will merit not just favor, but apotheosis. It will be translated into every
tongue. Academies and institutes will make a little book out of it, to be
used throughout the centuries, with bronze pages, gilt edges, letters of inlaid
opal, and a cover of unpolished silver. Governments will decree that it be
taught in schools and colleges. Philosophers will burn all previous doctrines,
even the most definitive, and will embrace this, the one true psychology, and
everything will be complete. Until then, I will pass for a fool, as you will see.

Matias, honorary canon and a preacher by trade, was composing a sermon when this psychic idyll began. He is forty years of age and lives in
the Gamboa District surrounded by books. Someone came to ask him to

give a sermon at a forthcoming festival; at the time, he was enjoying reading a weighty spiritual tome that had arrived on the last steamer and so he
refused their request; but they were so insistent that he gave in.

"Your Reverence will rattle it off in no time at all," said the principal
organizer of the festival.

Matias smiled meekly and discreetly, as should all clerics and diplomats.
Bowing low, the organizers took their leave and went to announce the festival in the newspapers, with the declaration that Canon Matias, "one of the
ornaments of the Brazilian clergy," would preach the Gospel. The phrase
"ornaments of the clergy" quite put the canon off his breakfast when he read
the morning papers, and it was only because he had given his word that he
sat down to write the sermon.

He began unwillingly, but after only a few minutes he was already
working with passion. Inspiration, its eyes turned toward heaven, and
meditation, its eyes turned to the floor, stand on either side of his chair,
whispering a thousand grave and mystical things in his ear. Matias carries
on writing, sometimes slowly, sometimes quickly. The sheets of paper fly
from his hands, vibrant and polished. Some have a few corrections, others have none at all. Suddenly, on the point of writing an adjective, he
stops; he writes another and scores it out, then another, which meets the
same fate. Here lies the nub of the idyll. Let us climb inside the canon's
head.

Ouf! Here we are. Not that easy, was it, dear reader? So don't go believing those people who troop up to the top of Corcovado and claim that from
that great height man seems utterly insignificant. A false and hasty conclusion; as false as Judas and other such diamonds. Do not believe it, beloved
reader. No Corcovados or Himalayas are worth much when set beside the
head that measures them. Here we are. Notice that it is indeed the canon's
head. We have the choice of one or other cerebral hemisphere, but let's go
into this one, which is where nouns are born. Adjectives are born in the
other one, on the left-hand side. This is one of my own discoveries, possibly
the principal one, but it is a starting point, as we will see. Yes, sir, adjectives
are born on one side and nouns on the other, and the entire destiny of words
is based on sexual difference—

"Sexual difference?"

Yes, ma'am. Words have a gender. Indeed, I am currently in the process of finishing my great psycho-lexico-logical dissertation, in which I expound and demonstrate this discovery. Words are of different sexes . . .

"But do they then love each other?"

They do indeed. And they get married. Their marriage is what we call style. You must confess, ma'am, that you have understood nothing.

"I confess I haven't."

Well, then, join me inside the canon's head. Just now there is some whispering going on over there. Do you know who is whispering? It is the noun from just a few minutes ago, the one the canon wrote down on the piece of paper just before his pen hesitated. The noun is summoning a certain adjective, which fails to appear: "Come from Lebanon, come . . ." That is how it speaks, for it is inside the head of a priest; if it were in a layman's head, the language would be Romeo's: "Juliet is the sun . . . Arise, fair sun." But in an ecclesiastical brain, the language is that of Scripture. At the end of the day, though, what do such formulations matter? Lovers in Verona or in Judah all speak the same language, just as the thaler or the dollar, the florin or the pound, are all the same money.

So let us carry on through these circumvolutions of the ecclesiastical brain, on the trail of the noun seeking an adjective. Sílvio calls to Sílvia. Listen: in the distance it sounds like someone else is whispering; lo, it is Sílvia calling to Sílvio.

Now they can hear each other and they begin to seek each other out. What a difficult and intricate path this is, in a brain so chock-full of things old and new! There is such a hubbub of ideas in here that it almost drowns out their voices; let us not lose sight of ardent Sílvio over there, going up and down, slipping and jumping; when he stumbles, he grabs hold of some Latin roots over there, he leans against a psalm, yonder he climbs aboard a pentameter, and on he goes, carried along by an irresistible inner force.

From time to time, a lady—another adjective—appears to him and offers him her graces ancient or modern; but, alas, she is not the right one, not the one and only, the one destined *ab eterno* for this union. And so Sílvio carries on, looking for that special one. Pass by, ye eyes of every hue, ye shapes of every caste, ye hairstyles fit for Day or Night; die without an echo, sweet ballads yearningly played upon the eternal violin; Sílvio is not asking for any old love, casual or anonymous; he is asking for one specific love, named and predestined.

Don't be frightened, reader; it's nothing to worry about, it's just the canon standing up, going over to the window, and taking a break from all his labors. While he's there he forgets about the sermon and about everything else. The parrot on its perch beside the window repeats its usual words to him and, out in the courtyard, the peacock puffs himself up in the morning sun. The sun, for its part, recognizing the canon, sends him one of its faithful rays as a greeting. The ray arrives and stops in front of the window: "Illustrious canon, I bring you the compliments of the sun, my lord and father." Thus all of nature seems to applaud the return of that galley-slave of the mind. He himself rejoices, gazes up at the pure air and feasts his eyes on greenery and freshness, all to the sound of a little bird and a piano. Then he speaks to the parrot, calls to the gardener, blows his nose, rubs his hands, and leans forward. He has forgotten all about Sílvio and Sílvia.

But Sílvio and Sílvia have not forgotten each other. While the canon concerns himself with other things, they continue to search for each other, without him suspecting a thing. Now, however, the path is dark. We pass from the conscious to the unconscious, where the confused elaboration of ideas takes place, where reminiscences sleep or doze. Here swarms formless life, the germs and the detritus, the rudiments and the sediments; it is the immense attic of the mind. Here they slip and slide, searching for each other, calling and whispering. Give me your hand, madam reader; you, too, sir, hold tight, and let us slip and slide with them.

Vast and alien, *terra incognita*. Sílvio and Sílvia rush onward past embryos and ruins. Groups of ideas, deducing themselves in the manner of syllogisms, lose themselves in the tumult of memories of childhood and the seminary. Other ideas, pregnant with more ideas, drag themselves still more heavily along, assisted by other, virgin ideas. Things and men merge; Plato brings the spectacles of a scribe from the ecclesiastical court; mandarins of all classes distribute Etruscan and Chilean coins, English books, and pale roses; so pale that they do not seem the same as the ones the canon's mother planted when he was a child. Pious memories and family memories cross paths and commingle. Here are the distant voices of his first mass; here are the country rhymes he heard the black women sing at home; the tattered remnants of faded sensations, a fear here, a pleasure there, over there a distaste for things that arrived singly, but now lie in an obscure, impalpable heap.

"Come from Lebanon, my bride . . ."

"I charge you, O daughters of Jerusalem . . ."

They could hear each other growing ever closer. Here they reach the deep strata of theology, philosophy, liturgy, geography, and history, of ancient lessons and modern notions, all mixed together, dogma and syntax. Here the secret, pantheistic hand of Spinoza; there the scratch mark left by the Angelic Doctor's fingernail; but none of this is Sílvio or Sílvia. They plow on, carried along by an inner force, a secret affinity, through all the obstacles and over all the abysses. But sorrows will also come. Here are dark sorrows that did not linger in the canon's heart, like moral stains, surrounded by the yellow or purple tints of universal pain, the pain of others, if such pain has a color. They slice through all of this with the speed of love and desire.

Do you sway and stumble, gentle reader? Fear not, the world is not collapsing; it is the canon sitting down again. Having cleared his head, he returns to his desk and rereads what he wrote; now he takes up his pen, dips it in the ink, and lowers it to the paper, to see which adjective he will attach to the noun.

Now is precisely the moment when the two lovesick lovers will draw closest. Their voices rise, as does their enthusiasm, the entire *Song of Songs* passes their lips, tinged with fever. Joyous phrases, sacristy anecdotes, caricatures, witticisms, nonsense, mere foolishness, nothing holds their attention, or even makes them smile. On and on they go, while the space between them narrows. Stay where you are, blurred outlines of dunderheads who made the canon laugh and whom he has long since forgotten; stay, vanished wrinkles, old riddles, the rules of card games, and you, too, the germs of new ideas, outlines of conceits, the dust of what must once have been a pyramid; stay, jostle, hope, and then despair, for to them you are nothing. They have eyes only for each other.

They seek and they find. Sílvio has finally found his Sílvia. They see each other and fall into each other's arms, panting with exhaustion, but satisfied with their reward. They join together, arms about each other, and return, pulsating, from unconscious to conscious. "Who is this that cometh up from the wilderness, leaning upon her beloved?" asks Sílvio, as in the *Song*; and she, with the same erudite turn of phrase, replies that it is "the seal upon thine heart" and that "love is as strong as death itself."

At this the canon trembles. His face lights up. His pen, filled with emotion and respect, joins the adjective to its noun. Sílvia will now walk side by side with Sílvio in the sermon that the canon will one day preach, and hand in hand they will go to the printer's, if, that is, he ever gets around to putting together a collection of his sermons, which remains to be seen.

THE CANE

D AMIÃO RAN AWAY from the seminary at eleven o'clock on a Friday morning in August. I don't know which year it was exactly, but certainly before 1850. After only a few minutes, he stopped running, suddenly filled with embarrassment. He had not considered how people might react to the sight of a fleeing, frightened seminarian. Being unfamiliar with the streets, he walked aimlessly up and down, and finally stopped. Where could he go? He could not go home, because his father, after giving him a sound beating, would send him straight back to the seminary. He had not planned where exactly he might take refuge, because he had intended making his escape at some later date; however, a chance incident had precipitated his departure. Where could he go? There was his godfather, João Carneiro, but he was a spineless creature, incapable of doing anything on his own initiative. He had been the one to take him to the seminary in the first place, presenting him to the rector with these words:

"I bring you a great man of the future."

"We welcome great men," the rector said, "as long as they are humble and good. True greatness lies in simplicity. Come in, boy."

That had been his introduction to the seminary. Shortly afterward, he had run away. We see him now standing in the street, frightened, uncertain, not knowing where to turn for shelter or advice; in his mind he reviewed his various relatives and friends, but none seemed quite right. Then a thought occurred to him:

"I'll appeal to Sinhá Rita! She'll send for my godfather and tell him she wants me to leave the seminary. Perhaps that way . . ."

Sinhá Rita was a widow and João Carneiro's mistress. Damião had a vague understanding of what this meant, and it occurred to him that he might be able to take advantage of the situation. But where did she live? He was so disoriented that it took him a few minutes to find the house, which was in Largo do Capim.

"Good heavens! Whatever's the matter?" cried Sinhá Rita, sitting bolt upright on the sofa on which she was reclining

Damião had burst in unannounced, looking utterly terrified, for when he reached Sinhá Rita's house, he saw a priest coming down the street, and, in sheer panic, he violently pushed open Sinhá Rita's front door, which, fortunately for him, was neither locked nor bolted. Once inside, he peered through the shutters to watch the priest, who had clearly failed to notice him and walked on by.

"Whatever's the matter, Senhor Damião?" she said again, for she had recognized him now. "What are *you* doing here?"

Damião, who was trembling so much he could barely speak, told her not to be afraid, it was nothing very important, and he would explain everything.

"All right, sit down and explain yourself, then."

"First, I swear that I haven't committed a crime of any kind . . ."

Sinhá Rita stared at him in alarm, and all the young girls in the room—boarders and day pupils—froze over their lace-making pillows, their bobbins and hands suddenly motionless. Sinhá Rita earned her living largely from teaching lace-making, cutwork, and embroidery. While the boy was catching his breath, she ordered the girls to go back to their tasks, while she waited for Damião to speak. Finally, he told her everything, about how much he hated the seminary and how he was certain he would not make a good priest. He spoke with great passion and begged her to save him.

"But how? I can't do anything."

"You could if you wanted to."

"No," she said, shaking her head, "I'm not getting involved in family matters; besides, I hardly know your family, and they say your father has a very nasty temper on him!"

Damião saw that he was lost. In desperation, he knelt at her feet and kissed her hands.

"Please help me, Sinhá Rita. Please, for the love of God, by everything you hold most sacred, by the soul of your late husband, save me from death, because I will kill myself if I have to go back."

Flattered by the boy's pleas, Sinhá Rita tried to reason with him. The life of a priest was a very holy and pleasant one, she said; in time, he would see that it was best to overcome his dislike of the seminary and then, one day—

"No, never!" insisted Damião, shaking his head and again kissing her hands and saying it would be the death of him.

Sinhá Rita hesitated for a while longer. Then she asked why he could not speak to his godfather.

"My godfather? He's even worse than Papa. He never listens to me. I shouldn't think he listens to anyone . . ."

"Doesn't listen, eh?" Sinhá Rita responded, her pride wounded. "I'll show you if he listens or not."

She summoned a slave-boy and ordered him to go straight to Senhor João Carneiro's house, and if the gentleman wasn't at home, then he should ask where he could be found and run and tell him that she needed to speak to him urgently.

"Off you go."

Damião sighed loudly and sadly. To justify the authority with which she had issued these orders, she explained to him that Senhor João Carneiro had been a friend of her late husband and had brought her several new pupils. Then, when he remained leaning in the doorway, looking glum, she tweaked his nose and said, smiling:

"Don't you worry, my little priest, it'll all be fine."

According to her birth certificate, Sinhá Rita was forty years old, but her eyes were only twenty-seven. She was a handsome, lively woman, who enjoyed both her food and a joke; however, when she had a mind to, she could be extremely fierce. She tried to cheer the boy up and, despite the situation, this did not prove difficult. Soon they were both laughing; she was telling him stories and asking him to reciprocate, which he did with considerable humor. One particularly extravagant tale, which required him to pull funny faces, made one of Sinhá Rita's pupils laugh so much that she neglected her work. Sinhá Rita picked up a cane lying next to the sofa and threatened her:

"Remember the cane, Lucrécia!"

The girl bowed her head, waiting for the blow, but the blow did not come. It had only been a warning. If, by the evening, she had not finished her work, then Lucrécia would receive the usual punishment. Damião looked at her; she was a scrawny little black girl, all skin and bone, with a scar on her forehead and a burn mark on her left hand. She was about eleven years old. Damião noticed, too, that she kept coughing, quietly, as if not wanting to disturb their conversation. He felt sorry for her and decided to take her side if she did not finish her work. Sinhá Rita would be sure to forgive her . . . Besides, she had been laughing at *him*, so it was his fault, if being funny can be a fault.

At this point, João Carneiro arrived. He blanched when he saw his godson there, and looked at Sinhá Rita, who came straight to the point. She told him he had to remove the boy from the seminary, that the child had no vocation for the ecclesiastical life, and it was far better to have no priest at all than a bad priest. One could just as easily love and serve Our Lord in the outside world. For the first few minutes, João Carneiro was too taken aback to reply; in the end, however, he did open his mouth to scold his godson for coming and bothering "complete strangers" and threatened him with punishment.

"What do you mean, 'punishment'!" Sinhá Rita broke in. "Punish him for what? Go on, talk to his father."

"I can't promise anything; in fact, I think it's highly unlikely, if not impossible . . ."

"Well, I'm telling you that it has to be possible. If you really try," she went on in a rather insinuating tone, "I'm sure you can sort something out. You just have to ask nicely and he'll give in. Because, Senhor João Carneiro, your godson is not going back to the seminary."

"But, senhora—"

"Go on, off you go."

João Carneiro did not want to go, but neither could he stay. He was caught between two opposing forces. He really didn't care if the boy ended up being a cleric, a lawyer, or a doctor, or something else entirely, however useless, but he was being asked to do battle with the father's deepest feelings and could not guarantee the result. If he failed, that would mean another battle with Sinhá Rita, whose final words had a threatening note to them: "your godson is not going back to the seminary." Either way, there was sure to be a ruckus. João Carneiro stood there, wide-eyed, his eyelids twitching, his chest heaving. He kept shooting pleading glances at Sinhá Rita, glances in which there was just a hint of censure. Why couldn't she ask him for something else, anything? Why couldn't she ask him to walk in the rain all the way to Tijuca or Jacarepaguá? But to persuade a father to change his mind about his son's career . . . He knew the boy's father well, and knew that he was perfectly capable of smashing a glass in his face. Ah, if only the boy would just drop down dead of an apoplectic fit! That would be a solution—cruel, yes, but final.

"What do you say?" demanded Sinhá Rita.

He made a gesture as if asking for more time. He stroked his beard, looking for some way out. A papal decree dissolving the Church or, at the very least, abolishing all seminaries, that would do the trick. João Carneiro could then go home and enjoy a quiet game of cards. It was like asking Napoleon's barber to lead the Battle of Austerlitz . . . Alas, the Church was still there, so were the seminaries, and his godson was still standing waiting by the wall, eyes downcast, with no convenient apoplectic fit in sight.

"Go on, off you go," said Sinhá Rita, handing him his hat and cane.

There was nothing for it. The barber put away his razor, buckled on his sword, and went off to battle. Damião breathed more easily, although, outwardly, he remained grave-faced, eyes fixed on the floor. This time, Sinhá Rita pinched his chin.

"Come on, don't be so glum, let's have something to eat."

"Do you really think he'll succeed?"

"He has to," retorted Sinhá Rita proudly. "Come along, the soup's getting cold."

Despite Sinhá Rita's natural joviality and his own naturally playful self, Damião felt less happy over supper than he had earlier on. He had no confidence in his spineless godfather. Nevertheless, he ate well and, toward the end, was once again telling jokes as he had in the morning. Over dessert, he heard the sound of people in the next room, and asked if they had come for him.

"No, it'll be the ladies."

They got up and went into the drawing room. The "ladies" were five neighbors who came every evening after supper to have coffee with Sinhá Rita and stayed until nightfall.

Once the pupils had finished their supper, they returned to their lace-making pillows. Sinhá Rita presided over this gaggle of women, some of whom were resident and others not. The whisper of bobbins and the chatter of the ladies were such worldly sounds, so far removed from theology and Latin, that the boy let himself be carried along by them and forgot about everything else. At first the ladies were a little shy, but soon recovered. One of them sang a popular ballad accompanied on the guitar by Sinhá Rita, and the evening passed quickly. Before the soirée ended, Sinhá Rita asked Damião to tell them the story she had particularly liked. The same one that had made Lucrécia laugh.

"Come on, Senhor Damião, don't play hard to get. Our guests are just about to leave. You'll really love this one, ladies."

Damião had no option but to obey. Despite the expectation created by Sinhá Rita's words—which rather diminished the joke and its effect—the story did nevertheless make the ladies laugh. Pleased with himself, Damião glanced over at Lucrécia to see if she had laughed as well, but she had her head bent over her work, intent now on finishing her task. She certainly wasn't laughing, or perhaps only to herself, in the same way she kept her cough to herself.

The ladies left, and darkness fell. Damião's heart also grew blacker with the onset of night. What would be happening at his father's house? Every few minutes he went over to peer out of the window, but returned each time feeling more discouraged. No sign of his godfather. His father had doubtless sent him packing, then summoned a couple of slaves and gone to the police station to demand that a constable come with him to arrest his son and take him back to the seminary. Damião asked Sinhá Rita if there was a back entrance to the house and ran out into the garden to see if he could climb over the wall. He also asked if there was an escape route down Rua da Vala or if she could perhaps speak to one of her neighbors, who might be kind enough to take him in. The problem was his cassock: could Sinhá Rita lend him a jacket or an old overcoat? Sinhá Rita did indeed have a jacket, left behind by João Carneiro, either as a souvenir or out of sheer absentmindedness.

"I have an old jacket of my husband's," she said, laughing, "but why are you so frightened? It will all work out, don't you worry."

At last, when night had fallen, a slave arrived bearing a letter for Sinhá Rita from his godfather. No agreement had yet been reached; the father had reacted furiously and tried to smash everything in the room; he had roared out his disapproval, saying that if his lazy rapscallion of a son refused to go back to the seminary, he would have him thrown in jail or sent to the prison ship. João Carneiro had battled very hard to persuade Damião's father not to rush into a decision, but to sleep on it and ponder deeply whether it was right to give the Church such a rebellious, immoral child. He explained in the letter that he had only used such language as a way of winning the argument. Not that he considered the argument won, by any means, but tomorrow he would go and see the man again and try to win him around. He concluded by saying that, meanwhile, the boy could stay at his house.

Damião finished reading the letter and looked at Sinhá Rita. She's my last hope, he thought. Sinhá Rita ordered a bottle of ink to be brought, and she wrote this response on the bottom half of João Carneiro's letter: "My dear Joãozinho, either you save the boy or you'll never see me again." She sealed the letter with glue and gave it to the slave for him to deliver with all speed. She again tried to cheer up the reluctant seminarian, who had again donned the monkish hood of humility and consternation. She told him not to worry, that she would sort things out.

"They'll see what I'm made of! No one's going to get the better of me!"

It was time to collect in the lace work. Sinhá Rita examined each piece, and all the girls had completed their daily task. Only Lucrécia was still at her lace-making pillow, furiously working the bobbins, even though it was too dark to see. Sinhá Rita went over to her, saw that the work was unfinished, and flew into a rage, seizing her by one ear.

"You lazy girl!"

"Please, senhora, please, for the love of God and Our Lady in Heaven."

"You idler! Our Lady doesn't protect good-for-nothings like you!"

Lucrécia broke away and fled the room. Sinhá Rita went after her and caught her by the arm.

"Come here!"

"Please, senhora, please forgive me!"

"No, I won't forgive you!"

And they came back into the room: Lucrécia dragged along by her ear, struggling and crying and pleading; and Sinhá Rita declaring that she must be punished.

"Where's that cane?"

The cane was next to the sofa. From the other side of the room, Sinhá Rita, not wanting to let the girl go, shouted to Damião.

"Senhor Damião, give me that cane, will you?"

Damião froze. Oh, cruel moment! A kind of cloud passed before his eyes. Had he not sworn to help the young girl, who had only fallen behind with her work because of him?

"Give me the cane, Senhor Damião!"

Damião began to walk over to the sofa. The young black girl begged him by all that he held most sacred, his mother, his father, Our Lord . . .

"Help me, sir!

Sinhá Rita, face aflame, eyes bulging, was demanding the cane, still not letting go of the girl, who was now convulsed by a coughing fit. Damião was terribly touched by her plight, but . . . he had to get out of that seminary. He went over to the sofa, picked up the cane, and handed it to Sinhá Rita.

MIDNIGHT MASS

I'VE NEVER QUITE understood a conversation I had with a lady many years ago, when I was seventeen and she was thirty. It was Christmas Eve. Having arranged to attend midnight mass with a neighbor, I had agreed that I would stay awake and call for him just before midnight.

The house where I was staying belonged to the notary Meneses, whose first wife had been one of my cousins. His second wife, Conceição, and her mother had both welcomed me warmly when, months before, I arrived in Rio de Janeiro from Mangaratiba to study for my university entrance exams. I led a very quiet life in that two-story house on Rua do Senado, with my books, a few friends, and the occasional outing. It was a small household, consisting of the notary, his wife, his mother-in-law, and two slave-women. They kept to the old routines, retiring to bed at ten and with everyone sound asleep by half-past. Now, I had never been to the theater, and more than once, on hearing Meneses announce that he was going, I would ask him to take me with him. On such occasions, his mother-in-law would pull a disapproving face, and the slave-women would titter; he, however, would not even reply, but would get dressed, leave the house, and not return until the following morning. Only later on did I realize that the theater was a euphemism in action. Meneses was having an affair with a lady who was separated from her husband and, once a week, he slept elsewhere. At first Conceição had found the existence of this mistress deeply wounding, but, in the end, she had resigned herself and grown accustomed to the situation, deciding that there was nothing untoward about it at all.

Good, kind Conceição! People called her "a saint," and she did full justice to that title, given how easily she put up with her husband's neglect. Hers was a very moderate nature, with no extremes, no tearful tantrums, and no great outbursts of hilarity. In this respect, she would have been fine as a Muslim woman and would have been quite happy in a harem, as long as appearances were maintained. May God forgive me if I'm misjudging her, but everything about her was contained and passive. Even her face was average, neither pretty nor ugly. She was what people call "a nice person." She never spoke ill of anyone and was very forgiving. She wouldn't have known how to hate anyone, nor, perhaps, how to love them.

On that particular Christmas Eve, the notary went off to the theater. It was around 1861 or 1862. I should have been in Mangaratiba on holiday, but I had stayed until Christmas because I wanted to see what midnight mass was like in the big city. The family retired to bed at the usual time, and I waited in the front room, dressed and ready. From there I could go out into the hallway and leave the house without disturbing anyone. There were three keys to the front door: the notary had one, I would take the second, and the third would remain in the house.

"But Senhor Nogueira, what will you do to fill the time?" Conceição's mother asked.

"I'll read, Dona Inácia."

I had with me a novel, *The Three Musketeers*, in an old translation published, I think, by the *Jornal do Commercio*. I sat down at the table in the middle of the room, and by the light of an oil lamp, while the rest of the house was sleeping, I once again climbed onto D'Artagnan's scrawny horse and set off on an adventure. I was soon completely intoxicated by Dumas. The minutes flew past, as they so rarely do when one is waiting; I heard the clock strike eleven, but barely took any notice, as if it were of no importance. However, the sound of someone stirring in the house roused me from my reading: footsteps in the passageway between the parlor and the dining room. I looked up and, soon afterward, saw Conceição appear in the doorway.

"Still here?" she asked.

"Yes, it's not yet midnight."

"Such patience!"

Conceição came into the room, her bedroom slippers flip-flapping. She was wearing a white dressing gown, loosely tied at the waist. She was quite thin and this somehow lent her a romantic air, rather in keeping with my adventure story. I closed the book, and she went and sat on the chair next to mine, near the couch. When I asked if I had unwittingly woken her by making a noise, she immediately said:

"No, not at all. I simply woke up."

I looked at her and rather doubted the truth of this. Her eyes were not those of someone who had been asleep, but of someone who had not yet slept at all. However, I quickly dismissed this observation—which might have borne fruit in someone else's mind—never dreaming that I might be the reason she hadn't gone to sleep and that she was lying so as not to worry or annoy me. She was, as I said, a kind person, very kind.

"It must be nearly time, though," I said.

"How do you have the patience to stay awake while your neighbor sleeps? And to wait here all alone too. Aren't you afraid of ghosts? I bet I startled you just now."

"I was a little surprised when I heard footsteps, but then you appeared immediately afterward."

"What were you reading? Don't tell me, I know: it's The *Three Musketeers*."

"Exactly. It's such a good book."

"Do you like novels?"

"I do."

"Have you read *The Dark-Haired Girl*?"

"By Macedo? Yes, I have it at home in Mangaratiba."

"I love novels, but I don't have much time to read anymore. What novels have you read?"

I began listing a few titles. Conceiçao listened, leaning her head against the chair back, looking at me fixedly through half-closed eyelids. Now and then, she would run her tongue over her lips to moisten them. When I finished speaking, she said nothing, and we sat in silence for a few seconds. Then, still gazing at me with her large, intelligent eyes, she sat up straight, interlaced her fingers, and rested her chin on them, her elbows on the arms of the chair.

"Perhaps she's bored," I thought. Then, out loud, I said:

"Dona Conceição, I think it must be nearly time, and I—"

"No, no, it's still early. I just looked at the clock and it's only half-past eleven. You still have time. If you ever do miss a night's sleep, can you get through the next day without sleeping at all?"

"I have in the past."

"I can't. If I miss a night's sleep, I'm no use for anything the next day and have to have a nap, even if it's only for half an hour. But then I'm getting old."

"What do you mean, 'old,' Dona Conceição?"

I spoke these words with such passion that it made her smile. She usually moved very slowly and serenely, but now she sprang to her feet, walked over to the other side of the room, and paced up and down between the window looking out onto the street and the door of her husband's study. Her modestly rumpled appearance made a singular impression on me. Although she was quite slender, there was something about that swaying gait, as if she were weighed down by her own body; I had never really noticed this until then. She paused occasionally to examine the hem of a curtain or to adjust the position of some object on the sideboard; finally, she stopped in front of me, with the table between us. Her ideas appeared to be caught in a very narrow circle; she again remarked on her astonishment at my ability to stay awake; I repeated what she already knew, that I had never attended midnight mass in Rio and did not want to miss it.

"It's just the same as mass in the countryside, well, all masses are alike, really."

"I'm sure you're right, but here it's bound to be more lavish and there'll be more people too. After all, Holy Week is much prettier in Rio than it is in the countryside. Not to mention the feasts of Saint John or Saint Anthony . . ."

She gradually leaned forward, resting her elbows on the marble tabletop, her face cupped in her outspread hands. Her unbuttoned sleeves fell back to reveal her forearms, which were very pale and plumper than one might have expected. This was not exactly a novelty, although it wasn't a common sight, either; at that moment, however, it made a great impression on me. Her veins were so blue that, despite the dim light, I could count every one. Her presence was even better at keeping me awake than my book. I continued to compare religious festivals in the countryside and in the city, and to give my views on whatever happened to pop into my head. I kept changing the subject for no reason, talking about one thing, then going back to something I'd mentioned earlier, and laughing in the hope that this would make her smile, too, thus affording me a glimpse of her perfect, gleaming white teeth. Her eyes were very dark, almost black; her long, slender, slightly curved nose gave her face an interrogative air. When I raised my voice a little, she told me off:

"Ssh! You might wake Mama!"

Much to my delight, though, she didn't move from where she was, our faces very close. It really wasn't necessary to speak loudly in order to be heard; we were both whispering, I even more softly than her, because I was doing most of the talking. At times, she would look serious—very serious—even frowning slightly. She eventually grew tired and changed position and place. She walked around to my side of the table and sat down on the couch. I turned and could just see the toes of her slippers, but only for the time it took her to sit down, because her dressing gown was long enough to cover them. I remember that the slippers were black. She said very softly:

"Mama's room is quite some way away, but she sleeps so very lightly, and if she were to wake up now, it would take her ages to get back to sleep."

"I'm the same."

"What?" she asked, leaning forward to hear better.

I went and sat on the chair beside the couch and repeated what I'd said. She laughed at the coincidence of there being three light sleepers in the same house.

"Because I'm just like Mama sometimes: if I do wake in the night, I find it hard to go back to sleep, I toss and turn, get up, light a candle, pace up and down, get into bed again, but it's no use."

"Is that what happened tonight?"

"No, not at all," she said.

I couldn't understand why she denied this, and perhaps she couldn't, either. She picked up the two ends of her dressing-gown belt and kept flicking them against her knees, or, rather, against her right knee, because she had crossed her legs. Then she told some story about dreams, and assured me that she had only ever had one nightmare, when she was a child. She asked if I ever had nightmares. The conversation continued in this same slow, leisurely way, and I gave not a thought to the time or to mass. Whenever I finished some anecdote or explanation, she would come up with another question or another subject, and I would again start talking. Now and then she would hush me:

"Ssh! Speak more softly!"

There were pauses too. Twice I thought she had dropped asleep, but her eyes, which had closed for an instant, immediately opened again with no sign of tiredness or fatigue, as if she had merely closed them in order to see more clearly. On one such occasion, I think she became aware of my rapt gaze, and she closed her eyes again, whether quickly or slowly I can't recall. Other memories of that night appear to me as truncated or confused. I contradict myself, stumble. One memory does still remain fresh, though; at one point, she, who I had only thought of as "nice-looking" before, looked really pretty, positively lovely. She was standing up, arms folded; out of politeness, I made as if to stand up, too, but she stopped me, placing one hand on my shoulder and obliging me to sit down again. I thought she was about to say something, but, instead, she shivered, as if she suddenly felt cold, then turned and sat in the chair where I had been sitting when she entered the room. From there, she glanced up at the mirror above the couch and commented on the two engravings on the wall.

"They're getting old, those pictures. I've already asked Chiquinho to buy some new ones."

Chiquinho was her husband. The pictures exemplified the man's main interest. One was a representation of Cleopatra, and I can't remember the other one, but both were of women. They were perhaps rather vulgar, but, at the time, I didn't think them particularly ugly.

"They're pretty," I said.

"Yes, but they're rather faded now. And frankly I would prefer two images of saints. These are more suited to a boy's bedroom or a barber's shop."

"A barber's shop? But you've never been in one, have you?"

"No, but I imagine that, while they're waiting, the customers talk about girls and love affairs and, naturally, the owner brightens up the place with a few pretty pictures. The ones over there just don't seem appropriate in a family home. At least, that's what I think, but then I often have strange thoughts. Anyway, I don't like them. In my prayer niche I have a really beautiful statuette of Our Lady of the Conception, my patron saint, but you can't hang a sculpture on the wall, much as I would like to."

This talk of prayer niches reminded me of mass, and it occurred to me that it might be getting late, and I was just about to mention this. I did, I think, get as far as opening my mouth, but immediately closed it again to listen to what she was saying, so gently, touchingly, softly, that my soul grew indolent and I forgot all about mass and church. She was talking about her devotions as a child and as a young girl. She then moved on to stories about dances, about outings she'd made, memories of Paquetá, all woven almost seamlessly together. When she grew tired of the past, she spoke about the present, about her household duties and the burdens of family life, which, before she married, she had been told were many, but which were not, in fact, burdensome at all. She didn't mention that she was twenty-seven when she married, but I knew that already.

She was no longer pacing up and down as she had been to begin with, but stayed almost frozen in the same pose. She no longer kept her large eyes fixed on me, but glanced around at the walls.

"This room needs repapering," she said after a while, as if talking to herself.

I agreed, simply in order to say something and to try to shake off that strange, magnetic sleep or whatever it was trammeling my tongue and my senses. I both wanted and didn't want to end that conversation; I made an effort to take my eyes off her, and I did so out of a sense of respect, but then, fearing that she might think I was bored, when I wasn't at all, I quickly brought my gaze back to her. The conversation was gradually dying. Out in the street, utter silence reigned.

We sat without speaking for some time, I don't know for how long. The only sound came from the study, the faint noise of a mouse gnawing away at something, and this did at last rouse me from my somnolent state; I tried to speak, but couldn't. Conceição appeared to be daydreaming. Then, suddenly, I heard someone banging on the window outside, and a voice shouting:

"Midnight mass! Midnight mass!"

"Ah, there's your friend," she said, getting up. "How funny! You were the one who was supposed to wake him up, but there he is waking you. Off you go. It must be time."

"Is it midnight already?" I asked.

"It must be."

"Midnight mass!" came the voice again, accompanied by more banging on the window.

"Quick, off you go. Don't keep him waiting. It was my fault. Good night. See you tomorrow."

And, with the same swaying gait, Conceição slipped silently back down the corridor. I went out into the street, where my neighbor was waiting. We set off to the church. More than once during mass, the figure of Conceição interposed itself between me and the priest, but let's put that down to my seventeen years. The following morning, over breakfast, I described the mass and the congregation, but Conceição showed not a flicker of interest. During the day, she was her usual natural, benign self and made no mention of our conversation the previous night. At New Year, I went home to Mangaratiba. By the time I returned to Rio in March, the notary had died of apoplexy. Conceição was living in Engenho Novo, but I neither visited her nor met her again. I later heard that she had married her late husband's articled clerk.

CANARY THOUGHTS

A KEEN ORNITHOLOGIST, Macedo by name, once told some friends a
story so extraordinary that none of them believed him. Some even
thought Macedo had lost his mind. Here is a summary of that tale.

I was walking down a street at the beginning of last month—he said—
when a cab came careering past and almost knocked me over. I escaped by
jumping into the doorway of a junk shop. Neither the clatter of horse and
cab nor my sudden irruption into his shop roused the owner, who was in the
back, dozing in a folding chair. He was a ruin of a man, with a grubby, straw-
colored beard and, on his head, a tattered cap that had doubtless failed to
find a buyer. He appeared to be a man without a past, unlike some of the
objects he was selling, and yet he did not exude the air of austere, embit-
tered sadness you might expect of a man who did once have a life.

The shop was dark and crammed with the bent, broken, grimy, rusty
objects one usually finds in such places, and all in the state of semi-disorder
one would expect. However banal, though, this motley collection of detritus was not without interest. Filling the area around the shop door were pots
without lids, lids without pots, buttons, shoes, locks, a black skirt, straw
hats and fur hats, picture frames, a pair of binoculars, tailcoats, a fencing
foil, a stuffed dog, slippers, gloves, various nondescript vases, some epaulets, a velvet bag, two coat racks, a catapult, a thermometer, some chairs, a
lithograph of a portrait by Sisson, a backgammon set, two wire masks for
some future carnival, as well as other things I either didn't even see or have

forgotten, all leaning or hanging or on display in equally ancient glass cases. Farther in there was still more shabby merchandise, mostly larger pieces of furniture, dressers and chairs and beds piled one on top of the other, lost in the gloom.

I was just about to leave when I spotted a cage hanging in the doorway. Like everything else, it was very old, and, in keeping with the general desolation, it should really have been empty, but it wasn't. A canary was hopping about inside. The little creature's color, animation, and grace lent a touch of life and youth to the surrounding junk. He was the last surviving passenger from a shipwreck, washed up on that shore, happy and unscathed. As soon as I saw him, he began to jump from perch to perch, as if to say that in the midst of that cemetery there was at least one ray of sunlight. I do not attribute that image to the canary, and I use it only because I am speaking now to rhetorically minded people; as he told me later on, he knew nothing of either cemeteries or sunlight. Carried away by the sheer pleasure he gave me, I felt indignant at his fate and murmured bitterly:

"What base owner could have had the heart to sell him for a few coins? Or what indifferent servant, not wishing to keep this, his late master's companion, gave him away for free to a small boy, who, in turn, sold him on so that he could buy a lottery ticket?"

The canary paused on the perch and trilled:

"Whoever you are, you're clearly not in your right mind. I had no owner, nor was I given to a child who then sold me on. Those are the imaginings of a sick mind; go cure yourself, my friend—"

"What?" I asked, interrupting him, without even having time to feel amazed. "So your owner didn't sell you to this shop? And it wasn't poverty or idleness that brought you to light up this cemetery like a ray of sunlight?"

"I don't know what 'sunlight' or 'cemetery' mean. If the other canaries you've known used the first of those words, so much the better, because it's a lovely word, but I think you're wrong."

"Excuse me, are you saying you came here of your own accord, without anyone's help, unless, of course, that man sitting over there is your owner?"

"My owner? That man is my servant, he gives me food and water every day and with such regularity that if I had to pay him for his services, it would cost me a pretty penny, but canaries don't pay their servants. Indeed, since the world belongs to canaries, it would be ridiculous for us to pay for something that already exists in that world."

Astonished by these responses, I didn't know which to find most amazing, his language or his ideas. His words emerged from him as charming trills, but entered my ears as if couched in our human language. I looked around to make sure I was indeed awake; yes, it was the same street, the same sad, damp, gloomy shop. Still hopping back and forth, the canary was waiting for me to speak. I asked him then if he didn't miss the infinite blue sky . . .

"My dear fellow," trilled the canary, "what does 'infinite blue sky' mean?"

"Tell me, then, what you think of this world. What *is* the world?"

"The world," responded the canary with a somewhat professorial air, "the world is a junk shop, with a small, square wicker cage hanging from a nail; the canary is the master of the cage he inhabits and of the surrounding shop. Everything else is illusion and lies."

At this point, the old man woke up and came shuffling over to me. He asked if I wanted to buy the canary, and I asked him if he had acquired it in the same way he had acquired the other things he was selling, and he told me that, yes, he had bought it from a barber, along with a set of razors.

"The razors are in very good condition," he said.

"No, I only want the canary."

I paid the asking price, took the canary home with me, bought a vast, circular cage made of wood and wire, which I ordered to be painted white and placed on the veranda, from where the bird could see the garden, the fountain, and a scrap of blue sky.

I intended to make a long study of this phenomenon, but would say nothing to anyone else until I had reached the point where I could dazzle the whole century with my extraordinary discovery. I began to alphabet-ize the canary's language, to study its structure, its links with music, the creature's aesthetic feelings, his ideas and memories. Having completed this initial philological and psychological analysis, I immersed myself in the his-tory of canaries, their origins, their early history, the geology and flora of the Canary Islands, whether he had any knowledge of navigation, and so on. We talked for long hours, with me taking notes, and him waiting, hopping about, and trilling.

Since I had no other family than my two servants, I had ordered them not to interrupt me, not even with a letter or an urgent telegram or an impor-tant visitor. They both knew about my scientific interests and so found these instructions perfectly normal and did not suspect for a moment that the canary and I could understand each other.

Needless to say, I slept very little, waking two or three times in the night to pace aimlessly, feverishly about. Finally, I would return to my work, rereading, expanding, and amending my thoughts. I had to correct more than one of the canary's observations, either because I had misunderstood or because he had not expressed himself clearly enough. His definition of the world was one such example. Three weeks after he came to live in my house, I asked him to repeat his definition of the world.

"The world," he said, "is a fair-sized garden with a fountain in the middle, a few flowers and shrubs, a little grass, clear air and a scrap of blue up above; the canary, who is the master of this world, lives in a vast white circular cage, from which he views all these things. Everything else is illusion and lies."

The language he used underwent a few changes, too, and I realized that certain of my conclusions, which I had thought quite straightforward, were, in fact, positively rash. I could not yet write the article I intended to send to the National Museum, to the Historical Institute, and to various German universities, not because I lacked material, but because I still needed to compile and confirm all these observations. Latterly, I did not even leave the house or answer letters and I had no time for friends or relatives. I was pure canary. Each morning, one of the servants was tasked with cleaning the cage and giving the canary his food and water. The canary said nothing to him, as if he knew that the servant lacked any scientific training. Besides, the servant carried out this task in a very summary fashion, for he was not a lover of birds. One Saturday, I woke up feeling ill, my head and back aching. The doctor ordered complete rest; I had been overtaxing my brain and must neither read nor think; I must not even attempt to find out what was going on in the city and the world. I remained like this for five days, and on the sixth, I left my bed, only to discover that the canary had escaped while the servant was cleaning out its cage. My first impulse was to strangle my servant; overcome with rage, I slumped into a chair, my head spinning, unable to speak. The servant defended himself, swearing that he had taken every possible care, but that the bird had cunningly escaped . . .

"Didn't you look for him?"

"We did, sir. At first he flew up onto the roof, and I went after him, then he flew over to a tree and hid. I've been asking everywhere, the neighbors, the local farmers, but no one has seen him."

You can imagine my anguish. Fortunately, though, I had by then recovered from my exhausted state and, after only a few hours, I was able to go out onto the veranda and into the garden. Not a sign of the canary. I made inquiries, I went here, there, and everywhere, I advertised, but all in vain. I had already compiled my notes for the article, however truncated and incomplete, when I happened to visit a friend, who lived in one of the largest and most beautiful mansions in the area. We went for a stroll in the garden before supper, when I heard a voice trill out this question:

"Hello, Senhor Macedo, where did you disappear to?"

It was the canary. He was perched on the branch of a tree. You can imagine my feelings and what I said to him. My friend thought I had gone mad, but what did I care what my friends thought? I addressed the canary tenderly, begging him to come back and resume our conversation, in our world composed of garden, fountain, veranda, and white circular cage . . .

"What garden? What fountain?"

"The world, my dear friend."

"What world? I see you have lost none of your bad professorial habits. The world," he concluded solemnly, "is an infinite blue space, with the sun up above."

I indignantly retorted that, if he was to be believed, the world was everything and anything; it had even been a junk shop . . .

"A junk shop?" he trilled mockingly. "Do such things exist?

FATHER AGAINST MOTHER

LIKE MANY OTHER social institutions, slavery brought with it certain trades and implements. I will mention only a few of those implements because of their connection with a particular trade. There was the neck iron, the leg iron, and the iron muzzle. The muzzle covered the mouth as a way of putting a stop to the vice of drunkenness among slaves. It had only three holes, two to see through and one to breathe through, and was fastened at the back of the head with a padlock. Along with the vice of drunkenness, the muzzle also did away with the temptation to steal, because slaves tended to steal their master's money in order to slake their thirst, and thus two grave sins were abolished, and sobriety and honesty saved. The muzzle was a grotesque thing, but then human and social order cannot always be achieved without the grotesque or, indeed, without occasional acts of cruelty. The tinsmiths would hang them up at the doors of their shops. But that's enough of muzzles for the moment.

The neck iron was fitted to slaves who made repeated attempts to escape. Imagine a very thick collar, with a thick rod either to the right or the left that extended as far as the head and was locked from behind with a key. It was, of course, heavy, but was intended not so much as a punishment as a sign. Any slave who ran away wearing one of these would instantly be identified as a repeat offender and quickly recaptured.

Half a century ago, slaves often ran away. There were large numbers of them, and not all enjoyed enslavement. They would sometimes be beaten,

and not all of them liked being beaten. Many would merely receive a repri-
mand, either because someone in the household would speak up for them
or because the owner wasn't necessarily a bad man; besides, a sense of own-
ership moderates any punishment, and losing money is not itself without
pain. There were always runaways, though. In a few rare cases, a contraband
slave who had just been bought in the Valongo slave market would immediately escape and race off down the streets, even though he didn't know
the town at all. Those who stayed put—usually the ones who already spoke
Portuguese—would arrange to pay a nominal "rent" to their master and then
earn their living outside the house as street vendors.

A reward was offered to anyone who returned a runaway slave. Advertisements were placed in the local newspapers, with a description of the
fugitive, his name, what he was wearing, any physical defects, the area where
he had last been seen, and the amount of the reward. When no amount was
given, there would be a promise: "will be handsomely rewarded" or "will
receive a generous reward." The advertisement would often be accompanied
at the top or the side by a drawing of a black figure, barefoot and running,
with, on his shoulder, a stick with a small bundle attached. It also carried a warning that anyone sheltering the runaway would feel the full force
of the law.

Now, pursuing fugitive slaves was one of the trades of the time. It might
not have been a very noble profession, but, since it involved helping the
forces who defend the law and private property, it had a different sort of
nobility, the kind implicit in retrieving what is lost. No one took up that
trade in the pursuit of entertainment or education; other reasons lay behind
such a choice for any man who felt tough enough to impose order on disorder: poverty, a need for money, a lack of any other skills, pure chance, and,
occasionally, the desire to be useful, at least to one of the parties.

Cândido Neves—known to his family as Candinho—is the person
caught up in this tale of an escaped slave; he had already sunk into poverty
when he began recapturing fugitive slaves. He had one grave fault: an inabil-
ity to hold down any job or trade; he had no staying power, although he himself put this down to bad luck. He started out wanting to be a typographer,
but soon saw that it would take a long time to become really good, and that
even then he might not earn enough, or so, at least, he told himself. Then
a career in commerce seemed a good idea, and he eventually found a job as
a clerk in a notions store. However, being obliged to attend to and serve all

and sundry wounded his self-esteem, and, after five or six weeks, he left of his own volition. Bookkeeper to a notary, office boy in a department attached to the Ministry of Internal Affairs, postman, and other positions were all abandoned shortly after he took them up.

When he fell in love with Clara, all he had were debts, although not as yet that many, for he lived with a cousin, a wood-carver by trade. After several attempts to get work, he decided to take up his cousin's trade, and had already had a few lessons. It was easy enough to get his cousin to give him a few more, but, because he wanted to learn quickly, he learned badly too. He never made anything very fine or complicated, just claw-and-ball feet for sofas or mundane carvings for chair backs. He wanted to be working when he eventually married, and marriage was not far off.

He was thirty years old, and Clara was twenty-two. She was an orphan and lived with her Aunt Mônica, with whom she made a living as a seamstress. Her work was not so arduous that she had no time for flirtations, but none of her potential suitors proved serious. Whole evenings passed with her looking at them and with them looking at her, until it grew dark and she had to return to her sewing. What she noticed was that she did not really miss any of them and none filled her with desire; she didn't even know the names of some. She did, of course, want to marry, but, as her aunt said, it was like fishing with a rod and waiting for a fish to bite, but all the fish swam straight past, apart from the occasional one who stopped, swam around the bait, looked at it, sniffed, then swam away to inspect other bait.

Love, however, always recognizes its intended recipient. When she saw Cândido Neves, she felt at once that he was the husband for her, the one, true husband. They met at a dance; this—to take an image from Candinho's first job as a typographer—was the opening page of that book, one that would leave the presses badly composed and even more badly bound. The marriage took place eleven months later, and it was the most splendid party their relatives had ever attended. More out of envy than out of friendship, Clara's friends tried to dissuade her from the path she was about to take. They did not deny that her husband was a decent enough fellow, nor that he loved her, nor even that he had certain other virtues, but, they said, he was rather too fond of having a good time.

"Thank heavens for that," retorted Clara, "at least I'm not marrying a corpse."

"No, not a corpse, but . . ."

The friends did not explain further. After the wedding, the newlyweds moved into some shabby lodgings with Aunt Mônica, who spoke to them about the possibility of their having children. They wanted only one, even though it would, of course, be an added burden.

"If you have a child, you'll all die of hunger," her aunt said to her niece.

"Our Lady will provide," said Clara.

Aunt Mônica should have issued this warning or, rather, threat when Candinho came to ask for Clara's hand in marriage, but she, too, liked a good time, and the wedding would, after all, be an opportunity for a party, which it was.

All three of them enjoyed a laugh. The couple, in particular, would laugh at almost anything. Even their bright, snow-white names—Clara, Neves, Cândido—were the subject of jokes, and while jokes might not put food on the table, they did make them laugh, and laughter is easily digested. Clara took in more sewing, and Cândido did odd jobs here and there, but never found any fixed employment. They still did not give up their dream of having a child. The child, however, unaware of their hopes, was still waiting, hidden in eternity. One day, though, it did finally announce its presence, and regardless of whether it was male or female, it would be the blessèd fruit that would bring the couple the happiness they sought. Aunt Mônica was horrified, but Cândido and Clara laughed at her anxieties.

"God will help us, Auntie," insisted the mother-to-be.

The news spread from neighbor to neighbor. All that remained now was to wait for the great day to dawn. Clara worked even harder than before, well, she had no choice, since, on top of her paid work, she was also busily making the baby's layette out of odds and ends. Indeed, she thought of little else, measuring out diapers, sewing dresses. What little money they earned was slow to come in. Aunt Mônica did help, but only reluctantly.

"You're in for a wretched life, you'll see," she would sigh.

"But other people have children, don't they?" Clara would ask.

"They do, and those children are always guaranteed to find food on the table, too, however scant . . ."

"What do you mean, 'guaranteed'?"

"I mean because their father has a guaranteed job, trade, or occupation, but what does the father of this poor unfortunate creature do with his time?"

As soon as Cândido Neves heard about this conversation, he went to see the aunt, not in anger, but nonetheless rather less meekly than usual, and he asked if, since living with them, she had ever once gone hungry.

"The only time you've fasted was during Holy Week, and that's only because you chose not to have supper with us. We've never gone without our salt cod . . ."

"I know, but there's only the three of us."

"And soon we'll be four."

"It's not the same thing."

"What would you have me do, beyond what I'm already doing?"

"Something that would bring in a steady wage. Look at the cabinetmaker on the corner, or the haberdasher, or the typographer who got married on Saturday, they all have guaranteed employment. Now, don't be angry. I'm not saying you're lazy, but your chosen trade is so uncertain. There are some weeks when you don't earn a penny."

"Yes, but other nights make up for that entirely, or even more so. God is by my side, and any fugitive slave knows I mean business. They rarely resist and some give themselves up straightaway."

He was proud of this, and spoke of hope as if it were money in the bank. Then he laughed and made the aunt laugh, too, for she was, by nature, a cheerful soul and was already looking forward to another party when the child was baptized.

Cândido Neves had abandoned his job as a wood-carver, as he had so many others before, both better and worse. Catching runaway slaves had a certain charm. He was not obliged to spend long hours sitting down, and all the job required was strength, a quick eye, patience, courage, and a length of rope. He would read the advertisements, copy them down, stick the piece of paper in his pocket, and set off in search of fugitives. He had a keen memory too. Once he had fixed in his mind the features and habits of a slave, it did not take long to find him, secure him, tie him up, and bring him back. Strength and agility were what counted. On more than one occasion, he would be standing on a corner, chatting, and along would come a slave, looking no different from any other slave, and yet Cândido would recognize him at once as a runaway, his name, his master, his master's house, and the size of the reward; he would immediately interrupt the conversation and set off after the villain. He wouldn't stop him there and then, but would wait for the right place to nab both slave and reward. Occasionally the slave would fight tooth and nail, but, generally speaking, Candinho emerged from such encounters without a scratch.

One day, though, his earnings began to dwindle. Runaway slaves no longer surrendered themselves only to Cândido Neves's hands. There were newer, more skillful hands around. As the business grew, other unemployed men took themselves and a length of rope and went off to the newspapers to copy out the advertisements and go hunting. Even in his own neighborhood, he had more than one competitor. In short, Cândido's debts began to grow, and, without the instant or almost instant reward he had garnered before, life became much harder. They ate poorly and on credit; they ate late. The landlord would send around for the rent.

Clara was so busy sewing for other people that she barely had time to mend her husband's clothes. Aunt Mônica helped her niece, of course, and when Cândido arrived home in the evening, she could tell from his face that he had earned nothing. He would have supper, then go straight out again, on the trail of some fugitive or other. On a few rare occasions, a blindness brought on by necessity caused him to pick the wrong man and pounce on a loyal slave going about his master's business. Once, he captured a free black man, and although he apologized profusely, he was soundly beaten by the man's relatives.

"That's all you need!" cried Aunt Mônica when she saw him and after he had told them about his mistake and its consequences. "Give it up, Candinho, find another way of earning a living, another job."

Candinho would have much preferred to do something else, although not for the same reasons, but simply for the sake of variety; it would be a way of changing skins or personality. Alas, he could find no job that could be learned quickly.

Nature continued to take its course, the fetus was growing and was soon a weight in its mother's belly. The eighth month came, a month of anxieties and privations, then the ninth, but I won't go into that. It would be best simply to describe its effects, which could not have been crueler.

"No, Aunt Mônica!" roared Candinho, rejecting a piece of advice I find painful even to write down, although not as painful as it was for Candinho to hear. "Never!"

It was in the last week of the final month when Aunt Mônica advised the couple that, as soon as the baby was born, they should take it to the

foundling wheel at the convent on Rua dos Barbonos, where they took in
abandoned babies. Abandoned. There could have been no crueler word for
those two young parents expecting their first child, looking forward to kissing and caring for it, watching it laugh and grow and prosper and play . . .
In what sense would that child be abandoned? Candinho stared wild-eyed
at the aunt and ended up thumping the table hard with his fist, so hard that
the rickety old table almost collapsed. Clara intervened.

"Auntie doesn't mean any harm, Candinho."

"Of course I don't," retorted Aunt Mônica. "I'm just saying what I think
would be best for you. You owe money for everything; you've no meat in the
house, not even any beans. If you're not bringing in a wage, how is the family to grow? After all, there's still time. Later on, when you've found some
steadier job, any future children will receive as much care and attention as
this one, possibly more. He'll be well cared for, he'll lack for nothing. Giving
him to the foundling hospital isn't like abandoning him on the shore or on a
dung heap. They don't kill children there, no child dies of neglect, whereas
here, living in poverty, he's sure to die . . ."

With a shrug, Aunt Mônica turned and went to her room. She had
hinted at such a solution before, but this was the first time she had spoken
with such candor and such passion, or so callously, if you like. Clara reached
out her hand to her husband, as if to comfort him; Cândido Neves pulled a
face and muttered something about her aunt being mad. This tender scene
was interrupted by someone banging on the street door.

"Who is it?" asked Cândido.

It was the landlord, to whom they owed three months' rent, and who
had come in person to threaten his tenant. His tenant invited him in.

"That won't be necessary . . ."

"No, please, come in."

The landlord came in, but would not accept the proffered chair; he
glanced around at the furniture to see if there was anything worth pawning,
but found very little. He had come for the unpaid rent and could wait no
longer; if they didn't pay up in the next five days, he would put them out in
the street. He hadn't worked hard all his life just to give others an easy time
of it. To look at him, you would never think he was a landlord, but his words
gave the lie to his face, and, rather than argue, poor Cândido Neves chose
to say nothing. He gave a slight bow, which was both promise and plea. The
landlord would not be swayed.

"Pay me in five days, or you're out!" he repeated, reaching for the door handle and leaving.

Candinho also left. At such moments, he never gave in to despair. He always relied on being able to get some loan or other, even though he didn't know how or from whom. He also went back to check the newspaper advertisements. There were several, some already old, but he had looked for all those runaways before with no success. He spent a few profitless hours, then returned home. At the end of the fourth day, he had still not managed to scrape together any money, and so he decided to try his luck with friends of the landlord, but all he received was that same order to quit the house.

The situation was critical. They couldn't find alternative lodgings or anyone who might take them in; they would definitely be out on the street. They had not, however, counted on Aunt Mônica. She had somehow or other found accommodation for the three of them in the house of a rich old lady, who promised to let them have the use of four rooms, behind the coach house and looking out onto a courtyard. Even more astutely, Aunt Mônica had said nothing to the couple, so that, in his despair, Cândido Neves would be forced to take the baby to the foundling wheel and find some steadier way of earning money; so that he would, in short, mend his ways. She listened patiently to Clara's complaints, but without offering her any consolation, either. On the day they were evicted, she would surprise them with the news of this gift and they would sleep far better than expected.

And so it was. Once evicted from their house, they went straight to the new lodgings, and, two days later, the baby was born. Cândido felt both enormously happy and enormously sad. Aunt Mônica insisted that they take the child straight to the foundling hospital on Rua dos Barbonos. "If you don't want to do it, I'll take him." Cândido begged her to wait, promising that he would take him later. Yes, the baby was a boy, just as his parents had wanted. Clara quickly gave the child some milk, but then it began to rain, and Candinho said that he would take the baby to the foundling wheel the next day.

That night, he went over all the notes he had taken about runaway slaves. Most of the rewards were mere promises; some did specify an amount, but it was always some very paltry sum. One, though, offered a hundred *milréis*. The slave in question was a mulatta; there was a description of her face and clothes. Cândido Neves had looked for her before, but given up, imagining that perhaps some lover had taken her in. Now, though, he felt encouraged both by the thought of that generous reward and by the desperate straits he was in. The next morning, he went out to patrol Rua da Carioca and the adjoining square, as well as Rua do Parto and Rua da Ajuda, which was the area where, according to the advertisement, she had last been seen. He found no trace of her, but a pharmacist on Rua da Ajuda recalled having sold an ounce of some drug three days before to a woman answering that description. Playing the part of the slave's master, Cândido Neves politely thanked the pharmacist. He had no better luck with any of the other fugitives for whom the reward was either unspecified or low.

He returned to their rather gloomy, temporary lodgings. Aunt Mônica had made some food for Clara, and had the baby all ready to be taken to the foundling hospital. Although Candinho had agreed to this, he could barely conceal his grief. He could not eat the food Aunt Mônica had kept for him; he simply wasn't hungry, he said, and it was true. He thought of a thousand ways that would allow him to keep his son, but none of them worked. He thought about the slum in which they lived. He consulted his wife, but she seemed resigned. Aunt Mônica had painted a picture for her of what awaited their child—still greater poverty and with the child possibly dying as a result. Cândido Neves had no option but to keep his promise; he asked Clara to give the child the last milk he would take from his mother. Once fed, the little one fell asleep, and his father picked him up and headed off toward Rua dos Barbonos.

More than once, he considered simply taking him back to the house; he also kept him carefully wrapped up, kissing him and covering his face to protect him from the damp night air. As he entered Rua da Guarda Velha, Cândido Neves slowed his pace.

"I'll delay handing him over for as long as possible," he murmured.

However, since the street was not infinite in length, he would soon reach the end; it was then that it occurred to him to go down one of the alleyways connecting that street to Rua da Ajuda. He reached the bottom of the alleyway and was about to turn right, in the direction of Largo da Ajuda, when, on the opposite side, he saw a woman: the runaway slave. I will not even attempt to describe Cândido Neves's emotions, because I could not do so with the necessary intensity. One adjective will have to suffice; let's say "overwhelming." The woman walked down the street, and he followed; the pharmacy we mentioned earlier was only a few steps away. He went in, spoke to the pharmacist, and asked if he would be so kind as to look after the baby for a moment; he would return soon.

"Yes, but—"

Cândido Neves did not give him time to say anything more; he left at once, crossed the street, and continued on to a point where he could arrest the woman without making too much of a scene. At the end of the street, when she was about to head off down Rua de São José, Cândido Neves drew nearer. Yes, it was definitely her, the fugitive mulatta.

"Arminda," he called, for that was the name given in the advertisement.

Arminda innocently turned around, and it was only when he removed the length of rope from his pocket and grabbed her arms that she realized what was happening and tried to flee. By then it was too late. With his strong hands, Cândido Neves had bound her wrists together and was ordering her to walk. She tried to scream, and she did perhaps call out more loudly than usual, but saw at once that no one would come to free her; on the contrary. She then begged him, for the love of God, to let her go.

"I'm pregnant, sir!" she cried. "If you yourself have a child, I beg you for the love of that child to let me go. I'll be your slave and serve you for as long as you like. Please, sir, let me go!"

"Walk on!" repeated Cândido Neves.

"Let me go!"

"Look, I don't have time for this. Walk on!"

There was a struggle at this point, because she, heavy with her unborn child, kept moaning and resisting. Anyone passing by or standing in a shop doorway would have realized what was going on and would, naturally, have done nothing to help. Arminda was telling him that her master was a very bad man and would probably beat her, and in her present state that would be even harder to endure. Yes, there was no doubt about it, he would have her beaten.

"It's your own fault. Who told you to get pregnant and then run away?" Cândido Neves asked.

He was not in the best of moods because he had his own child waiting for him at the pharmacy, and, besides, he had never been a great talker. He continued to drag her down Rua dos Ourives toward Rua da Alfândega, where her master lived. On the corner, she struggled still more fiercely, planting her feet against the wall and trying vainly to pull away from him. All that she achieved, though, with the house now so near, was to delay her arrival a little. They did at last arrive, she reluctant, desperate, panting. Even then, she knelt down, but again to no avail. Her master was at home and ran out to see what all the noise and shouting were about.

"Here's your runaway," said Cândido Neves.

"So it is."

"Master!"

"Come on, in you come!"

In the hallway, Arminda stumbled and fell. And there and then her master opened his wallet and took out two fifty-*mil-réis* notes, which Cândido Neves immediately pocketed, while the master again ordered Arminda to come into the house. Instead, on the floor where she lay, overcome by fear and pain, she went into labor and gave birth to her now-dead child.

That unripe fruit entered the world amid the cries and moans of the mother and the despairing gestures of the master. Cândido Neves watched the whole spectacle. He had no idea of the time, but whatever the hour, he urgently needed to go back to Rua da Ajuda, which is precisely what he did, quite indifferent to the consequences of the disaster he had just witnessed.

When he arrived at the shop, he found the pharmacist alone, with no son to return to him. Cândido's first instinct was to throttle the man. Fortunately, the pharmacist quickly explained that the child was inside with the family, and when both men went in, Cândido Neves furiously snatched up the baby, much as he had grabbed the runaway slave a little earlier—a very different fury, of course, the fury of love. He brusquely thanked the pharmacist; then, with his son in his arms and the reward in his pocket, he raced off, not to the foundling hospital, but back to their temporary lodgings. When Aunt Mônica heard his explanation, she forgave him for bringing the child back, given that he also brought with him the hundred *mil-réis*. She did have a few harsh words to say about the slave-woman, though, both for running away and for having miscarried. Kissing his son and shedding genuine tears, Cândido Neves, on the other hand, blessed the fugitive and gave barely a thought to her dead child.

"Not all children make it," his heart told him.

MARIA CORA

Chapter I

I ARRIVED HOME one night feeling so tired that I even forgot to wind my watch. My forgetfulness may have had something to do with a certain lady I had met at the comendador's house, but those two reasons, of course, cancel each other out. Thinking keeps you from sleeping, and sleeping stops you from thinking, so only one of those reasons can be the real one. Let's just say that neither of them was, and concentrate on the main point: my stopped watch and me waking in the morning to the sound of the house clock chiming ten.

At the time (1893), I was living in a boardinghouse in Catete. There were many such residences in Rio at the time. Mine was small and tranquil. With my four hundred *mil-réis* I could have afforded a house all to myself, but, firstly, I was already living in the boardinghouse when I won that money at cards, and, secondly, I was a forty-year-old bachelor so accustomed to boardinghouse life that I would have found it impossible to live alone. Marriage was equally impossible. Not that there was any shortage of candidates. Since the end of 1891, more than one lady—and not of the plainer variety, either—had looked at me with tender, friendly eyes. One of the comendador's daughters was particularly attentive. I didn't encourage any of them, though; the bachelor life is my very soul, my vocation, my habit, my destiny. I would only love if ordered to or for my own amusement.

A couple of adventures a year are quite enough for a heart half inclined toward sunset and night.

Perhaps that is why I did pay some attention to the lady I had seen at the comendador's house on the previous evening. She was a strong, dark-haired creature, between twenty-eight and thirty, and somberly dressed; she arrived at ten o'clock, accompanied by an old aunt. Since it was the first time she had been there—it was my third—she was greeted with rather more ceremony than the other guests. I asked someone if she was a widow.

"No, she's married."

"Who to?"

"The owner of a large estate in Rio Grande do Sul."

"Name?"

"Him? He's Fonseca, and she's Maria Cora."

"Didn't her husband come with her?"

"No, he's in Rio Grande."

That was all I could glean; but what intrigued me most were her physical attractions, the very opposite of what romantic poets and seraphic artists would dream of. I spoke to her for a few minutes about matters of no importance, but long enough to hear her very singsong voice, and to learn that she had republican leanings. I didn't like to admit that I had no leanings at all, and so mumbled something suitably vague about the future of the country. When she spoke, she had a way of moistening her lips with her tongue; whether this was intentional, I don't know, but it was both charming and piquant. Seen from close up, her features were less perfect than they had seemed at a distance, but they were also more hers, more original.

Chapter II

In the morning, I found that my watch had stopped. When I reached town, I walked down Rua do Ouvidor as far as Rua da Quitanda, and, as I was about to turn right to go to my lawyer's office, I glanced at my watch, forgetting that it had stopped.

"Oh, what a bore!" I cried.

Fortunately, to the left, on Rua da Quitanda, between Rua do Ouvidor and Rua do Rosário, was the shop where I had bought that watch, and by whose clock I always set my own. Instead of going in one direction, I went in the other. It was only half an hour out of my way; I wound my watch, set it to the right time, exchanged a few words with the clerk at the counter, and, as I was leaving, I saw, standing outside a novelty shop opposite, the somberly dressed lady I had met at the comendador's house. I greeted her, and she returned my greeting somewhat hesitantly, as if she did not immediately recognize me, and then she continued on up Rua da Quitanda, still on the other side of the road.

Since I had a little time to spare (slightly less than thirty minutes), I started following Maria Cora. I'm not saying I was already in the grip of some violent force, but I cannot deny giving in to an impulse of curiosity and desire, a remnant from my lost youth. Watching her walking along, wearing the same somber colors she had worn the night before, I found her even more impressive. She kept up a pace that was neither fast nor slow, but certainly one that allowed me to admire her lovely figure, which was more perfect than her face. She walked up Rua do Hospício to an optician's, where she went inside, remaining there for ten minutes or so. I kept a safe distance, furtively watching the doorway. Then she left and set off briskly, turning down Rua dos Ourives toward Rua do Rosário, then up to Largo da Sé; from there, she walked on to Largo de São Francisco de Paula. You will think all these details unnecessary, not to say tedious, but they fill me with a particularly intense feeling, as the first steps on a long and painful road. You'll have noticed that she avoided walking up Rua do Ouvidor, which is the route everyone and anyone would take at that or any other hour in order to go to Largo de São Francisco de Paula. She crossed the square in the direction of the Escola Politécnica, but, halfway there, was met by a carriage, which was waiting for her outside the college; she got in, and the carriage left.

Like other earthly paths, life has its crossroads. At that moment, I found myself at a particularly complicated one, except that I didn't have time to choose a direction—neither time nor opportunity. I still don't know how it was that I found myself in a cab, telling the driver to follow her carriage.

Maria Cora lived in a part of Rio called Engenho Velho, in a good, solid, fairly old house surrounded by a garden. I could tell that she lived there, because her aunt was looking out of one of the windows. When she stepped from the carriage, Maria Cora told the driver (my cab happened to be passing hers at that point) that she would not be going out again that week, but asked him to come for her on Monday at noon. Then she walked straight into the garden, as if she were the mistress of the house, and paused to talk to the gardener, who began earnestly explaining something to her.

I turned back once she had gone into the house, and only farther down the hill did I think to look at my watch; it was almost half-past one. I reached Rua da Quitanda at a trot, and got out at the door to my lawyer's office.

"I thought you weren't coming," he said.

"I'm sorry. I met a friend who insisted on recounting some tiresome business or other."

This was not the first time in my life that I had lied, nor would it be the last.

Chapter III

I often met Maria Cora after that; first, at the comendador's house and, later, at other houses. Maria Cora was not a complete recluse, but occasionally went on outings and visited friends and acquaintances. She also received visitors, not on any fixed day, but every now and then, although these gatherings only ever consisted of five or six close friends. The general view of her was that she was a person of strong feelings and austere habits. Add to this her sharp, brilliant, virile nature and her capacity for dealing with difficulties and hard work, not to mention quarrels and struggles; in the words of a poet and regular visitor, she was: "one part pampa and one part *pampeiro*," a reference to the icy wind that blows across the pampas in southern Brazil. The original line rhymed, but I took from it only the underlying idea. Maria Cora liked to hear herself described like this, although she didn't always display those qualities, nor did she dwell on stories of herself as an adolescent. Her aunt, on the other hand, did sometimes lovingly tell the occasional anecdote, saying that her niece was exactly like her when she was a girl. Justice demands that I declare, here and now, that her aunt, although ill, was still full of life and vigor.

It did not take long for me to fall in love with the niece. It doesn't pain me to admit this, because it is the one page in my life that merits any interest. I will make my story brief; and I will invent nothing and tell no lies.

I loved Maria Cora. I didn't tell her how I felt straightaway, but, like all women, she probably realized or guessed how I felt. Even if she had made this realization before my visit to the house in Engenho Velho, there are still no grounds for disapproving of her for inviting me there one evening. She may have been completely indifferent to my state of mind; she may also have enjoyed feeling loved, even though she had not the slightest intention of reciprocating that love. The fact is that I went there on that first evening and on other evenings too; her aunt took a liking to me and my ways. The silly, gabby poet who also visited said once that he was tuning his lyre in readiness for the aunt's marriage to me. The aunt laughed, and, wanting to stay in her good graces, I had to laugh, too, and, for about a week, the topic provided material for much banter. By then, though, my love for her niece had reached new heights.

Shortly afterward, I learned that Maria Cora was separated from her husband. They had married eight years before, and it had been a real love match. For five years, they lived very happily together. Then, one day, her husband had an affair that destroyed their domestic peace. João da Fonseca fell in love with a circus performer, a Chilean woman, Dolores, who did stunts on horseback. He left house and estate and went after her. Six months later, he returned, entirely cured of love, but only because Dolores had fallen in love with a newspaper editor without a penny to his name, and for whom she left Fonseca and all his wealth. His wife had sworn never to take him back, and this is what she said to him when he returned:

"It's all over between us. We must separate."

At first João da Fonseca agreed, but he was a proud forty-year-old, for whom such a suggestion was in itself an affront. That same evening, he began making the necessary arrangements; however, the following morning, his wife's beauty again stirred his heart and—not imploringly, but rather as if he were forgiving her—he suggested that they wait for six months. If, at the end of that period, the feelings that had provoked the separation remained unchanged, then they would part. Maria Cora did not want to accept this emendation, but her aunt, who lived in Porto Alegre and had gone to spend a few weeks with them, acted as go-between. Three months later, they were reconciled.

"João," his wife said to him on the day after their reconciliation, "as you can see, my love is greater than any feelings of jealousy, but you have to understand that if you deceive me again, I will never forgive you."

João da Fonseca's conjugal passion was reborn; he promised his wife everything and more. "I'm forty years old," he said, "I'm hardly going to have such an affair again, especially one that had such painful consequences. You'll see, this is forever."

They resumed their life together and were as happy as they had been at the start, he would have said even happier. So strong was his wife's passion for him that he came to love her as he had before. They lived like this for two years. By then his ardor had waned, and a few fleeting love affairs came between them. Contrary to what she had said, Maria Cora forgave him these minor flings, which, besides, were not as long-lasting or as important as the Dolores affair. They did have quarrels, though, major ones. There were violent scenes. It seems that, more than once, she even threatened to kill herself; but, although she didn't lack the necessary courage to do so, she made no actual attempt on her life, because it would have grieved her to leave the very cause of her distress, namely, her husband. João da Fonseca realized this and possibly exploited the power he had over his wife.

Politics further complicated this situation. João da Fonseca was on the side of the revolution, knew several of its leaders, and personally detested some of their opponents. Because of certain family ties, Maria Cora was against the Federalists. These opposing views were not enough to cause them to part, nor can it be said that it soured their life together. She, who was passionate about everything, was no less passionate in condemning the revolution, calling its leaders and officials by the very coarsest of names; and he, equally given to excess, responded with equal loathing, and yet these political tiffs would merely have added to their numerous domestic disagreements had not a new Dolores appeared on the scene—this time a woman called Prazeres, who was neither Chilean nor an acrobat—thus reviving the bitter times they had lived through before. Prazeres had connections with the rebels, not only political, but sentimental, for she was married to a Federalist. I met her shortly afterward, and she was, indeed, a beautiful, elegant woman; and since João da Fonseca was a handsome, seductive man, they seemed fated to fall passionately in love, and so it was. Various other things happened, some graver than others, until one decisive incident brought about the couple's final separation.

They had been discussing this for some time, but, despite Maria Cora having sworn to the contrary, a reconciliation was still not impossible, again thanks to her aunt's intervention. She had suggested to her niece that she go and live for a few months in Rio or São Paulo. Then something very sad occurred. In a moment of madness, João da Fonseca threatened

Maria Cora with a whip. According to another version, he tried to strangle her. I prefer to believe the first version, and that the second was invented to cast a coarse, depressing light on João da Fonseca's violence. Maria Cora did not speak to her husband again. The separation was immediate, and she traveled to Rio de Janeiro with her aunt, having first, quite amicably, sorted out the couple's financial affairs. Besides, the aunt herself was very rich.

João da Fonseca and Prazeres went on to live a life full of adventures, which I will not go into here. Only one event impinges directly on my story. Some time after the separation, João da Fonseca had enlisted with the rebels. However strong his political passions, they would not have been enough to make him take up arms had Prazeres not issued a kind of challenge; that, at least, is what his friends say, although the matter remains obscure. According to their version, Prazeres, exasperated with their troops' repeated losses, told Fonseca that she was going to disguise herself as a man, don a soldier's uniform, and go and fight for the revolution, and she would have been perfectly capable of doing this too. Fonseca told her this was utter madness, and then she proposed that he should go in her stead; that would be a real proof of his love for her.

"Haven't I given you enough proof?"

"Yes, but that would be a far greater proof than all the rest, and would keep me bound to you until death."

"Are you not already bound to me until death?" he asked, laughing.

"No."

That may be what happened. Prazeres was, indeed, an impulsive, imperious woman and knew how to bind a man to her with bonds of steel. The Federalist, whom she abandoned for João da Fonseca, did everything he could to get her back, then moved east, where, it's said, he lives a wretched life, that his hair has turned gray and he has aged twenty years, and wants nothing more to do with women or politics. In the end, João da Fonseca gave in; she even begged him to let her go, too, and, if necessary, to fight alongside him; but he refused. The revolution would soon triumph, he said; once the government forces had been vanquished, he would return to the estate in Rio Grande, where she would wait for him.

"No," she said, "I'll wait for you in Porto Alegre."

Chapter IV

Just how long it took for me to fall in love is of no importance, but not very long. My love grew rapidly and vigorously and eventually became so all-consuming that I could not keep it to myself and, one night, I resolved to declare my love to her; however, her aunt, who could normally be relied on to doze off after about nine o'clock (she woke at four), did not fall asleep at all and, even if she had, I would probably not have said anything; I could not speak and, once out in the street, I felt as dizzy as I had when I fell in love for the very first time.

"Be careful not to fall, Senhor Correia," said her aunt when I went out onto the veranda, having said my goodbyes.

"Don't worry, I won't."

I had a bad night and slept for, at most, two hours, and then only fitfully. By five o'clock I was up and awake.

"I must put an end to this now!" I cried.

The truth is that, with me, Maria Cora was always kind and under-standing, but never anything more, but then that is precisely what made her so attractive. All the other loves in my life had been so easy. I had never met with any resistance, nor left with any regret, or only a little sadness, perhaps, a touch of nostalgia. This time I felt I was in an iron grip. Maria Cora was so full of life; beside her, it seemed as though the chairs themselves could walk and the figures on the carpet could move their eyes. Add to this a strong dose of tenderness and grace. The finishing touch was her aunt's evident fondness for her, which made of Maria Cora an angel. A banal comparison, I know, but I have no other.

I decided to take drastic action and to keep away from Engenho Velho, and I did so for many long days, for two or three weeks. I tried to distract myself and forget her, but to no avail. I began to experience her absence as one would that of a loved one; and yet still I resisted and did not go back. The longer the absence, though, the deeper my love, and so I decided that I would return one night, although I might not have done so had I not met Maria Cora in the same shop on Rua da Quitanda where I had gone with my stopped watch.

"Oh, so you come here too?" she said when she came into the shop.

"I do."

"I need to have my watch repaired. But why haven't you been back to see us?"

"Yes, why haven't you been back?" echoed her aunt.

"Business affairs," I murmured, "but I was thinking of coming this evening."

"No, don't come this evening, come tomorrow," said Maria Cora. "We're out tonight."

I seemed to read in those last words an invitation to declare my love, and in her first words some indication that she had missed me. And so the next day I went to Engenho Velho. Maria Cora welcomed me as warmly as ever. The poet was there, telling me in verse how the aunt had sighed for me. I again became a frequent visitor, and resolved to declare myself.

I mentioned earlier that she had probably understood or guessed my feelings, just as any other woman would. Now she must definitely have understood, and yet she did not drive me away. On the contrary, she seemed to enjoy the feeling of being deeply loved.

Shortly after that night, I wrote her a letter before going to Engenho Velho. She seemed slightly withdrawn; her aunt explained that she had received troubling news from Rio Grande. I did not connect this with her marriage, and tried to cheer her up. She, however, responded merely politely. On the veranda, before I left, I handed her the letter and was about to say, "Please read it," but my voice failed me. I could see that she was slightly embarrassed, and, to avoid saying what was best said in writing, I merely bowed and walked away through the garden. You can imagine the kind of night I spent, and the day that followed was, of course, the same, until evening came. Nevertheless, I did not immediately go back to her house; I decided to wait three or four days, not in the expectation that she would write to me, but to give her time to consider her response. I was sure her response would be a positive one, for, lately, she had treated me in a friendly, almost inviting manner.

I did not last the full four days; indeed, I barely managed three. On the evening of the third day I went back to Engenho Velho. I would not be lying if I said that I was trembling with emotion when I arrived. I found her at the piano, playing for the poet; her aunt, seated in her armchair, was deep in thought, and I was so giddy with excitement that I barely noticed her.

"Come in, Senhor Correia, but don't fall on top of me."

"Oh, I'm so sorry."

Maria Cora did not stop playing, but when she saw me, she said:

"Forgive me for not shaking your hand, but I'm acting as muse for this gentleman here."

Minutes later, she came over and shook my hand so warmly that I saw in that a response to my letter and was almost on the point of thanking her. A few minutes passed, fifteen or twenty. Then, saying that there was a book she wanted to ask me about, we both went over to where she had left it lying on top of the sheet music on the piano. She opened it, and, inside, was a piece of paper.

"When you were here the other night, you gave me this letter. Could you tell me what it says?"

"Can you not guess?"

"I might guess wrongly."

"No, you have guessed correctly."

"Yes, but, even though I'm separated from my husband, I'm still a married woman. You love me, don't you? Well, you may assume that I love you, too, but, as I say, I'm still a married woman."

Having said this, she returned the letter to me unopened. Had we been alone, I might have read it out to her, but the presence of the other guests stopped me. Besides, there was no need. Maria Cora's answer was definitive, or so it seemed to me. I took the letter and, before I put it away, asked:

"So you don't want to read it?"

"No."

"Not even to see what I said?"

"No."

"What if I were to go and fight your husband, kill him, and then come back?" I said, growing ever more frantic.

"Would you actually do such a thing?"

"Why not?"

"I don't believe anyone could ever love me that much," she concluded with a smile. "But, be careful, people are looking at us."

With that, she moved away and joined her aunt and the poet. I stood there for a few seconds with the book in my hand, as if I really were studying it, then I put it down and went and sat opposite them. They were talking about what was happening in Rio Grande, about the battles between Federalists and Legalists and their varying fates. What I felt then cannot be put into words, not, that is, by me, for I am no novelist. It was a kind of vertigo, a delirium, a horrible, lucid image, a battle followed by victory. I imagined myself on the battlefield, alongside other men, fighting the Federalists and finally killing João da Fonseca, before returning to Rio and marrying his widow. Maria Cora had contributed to this seductive thought. After her refusal to read my letter, she seemed to me more beautiful than ever, especially as she did not seem annoyed or offended, but treated me as affectionately as before, possibly even more so. I could have drawn from this a double and contradictory impression—either tacit acquiescence or complete indifference—but I saw only the first of these and left the house in a state of utter madness.

What I decided to do then really was the act of a madman. Maria Cora's words—"I don't believe anyone could ever love me that much"—were still ringing in my ears like a challenge. I thought about them all night and the following day, I went back to Engenho Velho. As soon as the opportunity arose to tell her of my resolve, I did so.

"I'm leaving everything I care about, including peace, with the sole aim of proving to you that I love you and want you solely and purely for myself. I am going off to fight."

Maria Cora looked utterly astonished. I understood then that she really did love me with a genuine passion, and that if she were widowed, she would not marry anyone else. I swore again that I was going off to the war in the South. Deeply moved, she held out her hand to me. This was pure romanticism. When I was a child, my parents believed that such actions were the only real proof of love, and my mother would tell me stories in verse of knights-errant who, out of love for their faith and for their lady, journeyed to the Holy Land to liberate Christ's tomb. Yes, pure romanticism.

Chapter V

I traveled south. The battles between Legalists and rebels were continuous and bloody, and this encouraged me. And yet, since no political passion prompted me to enter the fight, I must confess that, for a moment, I felt discouraged and hesitant. I wasn't afraid of death, you understand, but I nevertheless loved life, which is, perhaps, a synonymous state; whatever it was, it was not so overwhelming as to cause me to hesitate for very long. In the city of Rio Grande I met a friend, to whom I had written saying that I was going there for political reasons, although without specifying what those were. He wanted to know more.

"My reasons are, of course, secret," I responded, trying to smile.

"Fine, but there's one thing I should know, just one, because I have no idea of your views on the matter, since you've never told me. Whose side are you on: the Legalists' or the rebels'?"

"Oh, really! I would hardly have written to you if I wasn't on the side of the Legalists. I would have come here under cover."

"Have you some secret commission from the marshal?"

"No."

He could get nothing more out of me, but I had to tell him what my plans were, if not my motives. When he found out that my intention was to enlist with the volunteers fighting the rebels, he didn't believe me and perhaps suspected that I really had been charged with some secret plan. I said nothing that could have suggested such a thing, but he wasted no time in trying to dissuade me; he himself was a Legalist and spoke of the enemy with anger and loathing. Once he had recovered from his surprise, however, he accepted my decision, which he found all the nobler because it was not inspired by party politics. He said many fine, heroic words on the subject, words that would raise the spirits of anyone already eager for a fight. I was not such a one, or only for personal reasons, which had now grown more urgent. I had just received a letter from Maria Cora's aunt, sending me their news and her niece's best wishes, all expressed in very general terms, but imbued, I thought, with genuine affection.

I went to Porto Alegre, where I enlisted and set off to join the campaign. I said nothing about myself that might arouse any curiosity, but it was difficult to conceal my social status, where I came from, and my journey there in order to fight the rebels. A legend soon sprang up around me. I was an extremely wealthy republican, an enthusiast for the cause, ready to give my life for the republic a thousand times over—if I had that many lives—and certainly resolutely prepared to sacrifice the one life I had. I allowed these rumors to grow and off I went. When I asked in which of the rebel forces João da Fonseca could be found, someone interpreted this as a desire for some act of personal revenge; someone else thought I was a spy for the rebels hoping to enter into secret communication with Fonseca. Those who knew about his relationship with Prazeres imagined I was an old lover of hers wanting to exact revenge. All these suppositions died, leaving only a belief in my political fervor. The rumor that had me down as a spy was more problematic, but, fortunately, it was the product of two men's nighttime lucubrations and soon vanished.

I took with me a picture of Maria Cora, which she herself had given me one night shortly before my departure, complete with a charming little dedication. As I said before, this was pure romanticism; once I had taken that first step, the others followed of their own accord. Add to this my male pride, and you will understand how an ordinary, indifferent citizen of Rio could become a hardened soldier in the Rio Grande campaign.

I won't describe any battles, though, nor write about the revolution, which was of no interest to me, except for the opportunity it gave me, and for the odd blow I dealt it in my own small way. João da Fonseca was my rebel. After taking part in the Battle of Sarandi and Cochila Negra, I heard that he had been killed in some skirmish or other; later, I heard that he was fighting alongside Gumercindo, and had been taken prisoner and sent to Porto Alegre; but even this was not true. One day, I became separated from my regiment, along with two comrades, and we came across another Legalist regiment that was just setting off to defend Encruzilhada, which had been under attack by the Federalist forces; I introduced myself to the commander and joined his company. There I discovered that João da Fonseca was among those Federalists; the other men told me all about him, about his love affairs and how he was separated from his wife.

The idea of killing him in the hurly-burly of battle had something fantastical about it; I didn't even know if such duels were possible in battle, when one man's strength should be part of a single force obedient to one commander. It also often occurred to me that I was about to commit a personal crime, and, believe me, this was not something I took lightly. However, the thought of Maria Cora bestowed on me something like an encouraging blessing, absolving me of guilt. I threw myself into combat. I did not know João da Fonseca; apart from what others had told me, I could only remember a portrait I had seen of him in Engenho Velho; if he had not greatly changed, it was likely that I would recognize him in a crowd. But would such an encounter be possible? The battles I had already been involved in made me think that it would certainly not be easy.

It was neither easy nor brief. In the Battle of Encruzilhada, I think I bore myself with the necessary courage and discipline, and I should point out that I was becoming accustomed to life in this civil war. The hate-filled words I heard were very potent. Both sides fought with great ardor, and the passion I sensed in those on my own side began to infect me too. I had heard my name read out in a report of the day's fighting, and had received personal praise as well, praise which, then and now, I felt was well deserved. But let's get back to what really matters, which is to finish this tale.

In that battle, I felt rather like Stendhal's hero at the Battle of Waterloo, the difference being that it was a much smaller arena. For this reason—and also because I don't wish to linger over facile memories—I will say only that I did succeed in killing João da Fonseca in person. It's true, too, that I escaped being killed by him. I still bear the scar on my head from the wound he inflicted on me. The fight between us was short-lived. If it doesn't seem too much like something out of a novel, I would say that João da Fonseca understood my motives and foresaw the result.

After a few minutes of hand-to-hand combat in one corner of the town, João da Fonseca fell prostrate to the ground. He tried to and did fight on for a while; I gave him no opportunity to retaliate, as this, I reasoned, would lead to my own defeat, if "reason" is the right term to use, for I was not thinking rationally at all. I was blinded by the blood in which I had bathed him, and deafened by the clamor and tumult of battle. Amid the killing and screaming, our side quickly became masters of the field.

When I saw that João da Fonseca was well and truly dead, I returned briefly to the fray; my intoxicated state had somewhat diminished, and my primary motivation came back to me, as if it were the one and only. Maria Cora's face appeared before me like an approving, forgiving smile; it all happened very fast.

You have probably read about the three or four women who were captured too. One of them was Prazeres. When battle was done, Prazeres saw her lover's body, and her reaction filled me with a mixture of loathing and envy. She lay down on the ground and put her arms around him; the tears she shed, the words she spoke, made some of those present laugh; others, if not moved, were surprised. As I say, I was filled at first with both envy and loathing, but that dual feeling also disappeared, leaving not even surprise, and I, too, ended up laughing. After honoring her lover's death with her grief, Prazeres remained the Federalist she was; she had not put on a soldier's uniform, as she had said she would when she challenged João da

Fonseca, but she wanted to be taken prisoner along with the other rebels
and to remain with them.

Obviously, I didn't leave the government forces at once, I went on to
fight a few more battles, but eventually my prime reason for being there
prevailed, and I put down my weapons. During the time I was enlisted, I
wrote only two letters to Maria Cora, one shortly after taking up that new
life, the other after the Battle of Encruzilhada; in that last letter, I said nothing about her husband, nor about his death, nor even that I had seen him. I
announced only that the civil war was likely to end soon. In neither of those
letters did I make the slightest allusion to my feelings or to the motive for
my actions; nevertheless, for anyone who knew about either, the meaning
would have been clear. Maria Cora replied only to the first letter, serenely,
but not indifferently. It was clear—at least to me—that, although promising
nothing, she was grateful, or, if not grateful, admiring. Gratitude and admiration could lead to love.

I did not say—and I still don't know quite how to say it—that at Encruzilhada, after João da Fonseca had died, I attempted to cut off his head, but I
didn't really want to, and, in the end, I didn't. My object was quite different,
more romantic. Any genuine realists among you must forgive me, but there
was a touch of reality in this, too, and I acted in accordance with my state
of mind: instead, I cut off a lock of his hair, as the proof of his death that I
would take to his widow.

Chapter VI

When I returned to Rio de Janeiro, many months had passed since the Battle of Encruzilhada. However hard I tried to avoid all publicity and to disappear into the shadows, my name had appeared not only in official reports,
but also in telegrams and letters. I received various letters of congratulations
and inquiry. Please note that I did not return to Rio de Janeiro at once; I
preferred to stay in São Paulo and avoid any possible celebrations. One day,
when least expected, I took the train to Rio and went straight to the boardinghouse in Catete.

I didn't immediately seek out Maria Cora. It seemed best that she
should learn of my arrival from the newspapers. I had no one who could tell
her, and I couldn't bring myself to go to some editor's desk and announce

my return from Rio Grande; I wasn't a passenger newly disembarked, whose name would appear on the ship's list. Two days passed; on the third day, I opened a newspaper and saw my name. The article announced that I had come from São Paulo after being involved in the fighting in Rio Grande; it mentioned certain battles, and generally praised my conduct, and, finally, mentioned that I was once again living in the same boardinghouse in Catete. Since my landlord was the only person to whom I had spoken briefly about my experiences, he could have been the one who submitted these facts, although he denied this. I began to receive a few visitors. They all wanted to know everything, but I said very little.

Among the various visiting cards, I received two from Maria Cora and her aunt, who both sent words of welcome. Nothing more was needed; all that remained was for me to go and thank them, and I prepared to do so; however, on the very day I had decided to visit them in Engenho Velho, I was filled with a sense of foreboding . . . but why? How to explain my feelings of apprehension whenever I recalled Maria Cora's husband, who had died by my hand? The mere thought of what I would feel in her presence overwhelmed me. Given my main motive for enlisting, such reticence may seem hard to comprehend, but, to understand the unease that made me keep postponing the visit, you have only to consider that, even though I had been defending myself against her husband and had killed him in order not to be killed myself, he was still her husband. Finally, though, I plucked up courage and went to her house.

Maria Cora was dressed in mourning. She received me kindly, and both she and her aunt repeated their congratulations. We spoke about the civil war, about life in Rio Grande, and a little about politics, but nothing more. Not a word was said about João da Fonseca. When I left, I wondered if Maria Cora would now be disposed to marry me.

"I don't think she would refuse, although she certainly doesn't single me out for special attention. In fact, she seems rather less friendly than before. Can she have changed?"

Such were my vague thoughts, and I attributed her altered mood to widowhood, as was only natural. I continued to visit her, ready to allow the first stage of mourning to pass before formally asking for her hand in marriage. There was no need to make any new declaration; she knew how I felt. She continued to welcome me. She asked not a single question about her husband, nor did her aunt, and we spoke no more about the revolution. For my part, I reverted to the way things had been before and, not wishing to waste any time, I played the role of suitor to the full. One day, I asked if she was considering going back to Rio Grande.

"Not for the moment, no."

"But you will go?"

"Possibly, but I have no definite plans. It's merely a possibility."

After a brief silence, during which I eyed her questioningly, I finally asked if, before she left—assuming she did leave—she would change anything in her life.

"My life has already changed completely . . ."

She obviously hadn't understood me, or so I thought. I tried to explain myself more clearly and wrote her a letter in which I reminded her of that first letter of mine, which she had refused to open and in which I had asked for her hand. Two days later, I gave her this new letter, saying:

"I'm sure you won't refuse to read this one."

She did not refuse and took the letter. This happened as I was leaving, at the door to the parlor. I think I even saw in her face a slight hopeful flicker of excitement. She did not reply in writing, as I had hoped. Three days passed, and by then I was so anxious that I resolved to return to Engenho Velho. On the way there, I imagined all kinds of possible responses: that she would reject me, accept me, put me off, and, if not that second option, then I was prepared to make do with the third one. Alas, she had gone to spend a few days in Tijuca and was not at home. I left, feeling slightly annoyed. It seemed to me that she really didn't want to marry, but then wouldn't it be easier for her to say so or to write a letter telling me as much? This thought aroused new hopes in me.

I still remembered what she had said when she returned that first letter to me and I spoke of my love: "You may assume that I love you, too, but I am still a married woman." It was clear that she cared for me then, and there was no real reason now to believe the contrary, even though she had grown somewhat cool toward me. Lately, I had come to think that she did still love me, out of vanity, perhaps, or fondness or possibly gratitude too; or so it seemed to me. And yet she did not reply to my second letter, either. When she returned from Tijuca, she was less expansive, possibly sadder too. I was the one who had to raise the matter. Her answer: she was not, for the moment, ready to marry again.

"But will you marry one day?" I asked after a short silence.

"By then I'll be too old."

"So it won't be for years?"

"My husband might not be dead."

I was astonished by this remark.

"But you're dressed in deep mourning."

"I read and was told that he was dead, but it might not be true. I've seen other certain deaths later proven to be false."

"If you want absolute certainty," I said, "I can give it to you."

Maria Cora turned very pale. Certainty. Certainty about what? She wanted me to tell her everything—everything. The whole situation had become so painful to me that I hesitated no longer, and, having confessed that it had been my intention to tell her nothing and that I had told no one else, either, I promised to do so now, purely in obedience to her request. And I told her about the battle, in all its phases, the risks taken, the words spoken, and, finally, the death of João da Fonseca. She listened in a state of terrible anguish and distress. She nevertheless managed to master her emotions and ask:

"Do you swear that you're telling the truth?"

"Why would I lie? What I did is enough to prove my sincerity. Tomorrow I will bring you further proof if proof is needed."

I took her the lock of hair I had cut from the corpse's head. I also told her—and I admit that my object was to turn her against the memory of her late husband—I told her of Prazeres's utter despair and grief. I described her and her tears. Maria Cora listened to me with wide, wild eyes. She still felt jealous. When I showed her the lock of hair, she snatched it from me, kissed it, and wept and wept and wept. I felt it was best if I left—for good this time. Days later, I received a response to my letter; she would not marry me.

Her answer contained a word that is the sole reason for writing this story: "Please understand that I could not accept the hand of the man who, even out of loyalty, killed my husband." I compared this with that other word she said to me earlier, when I decided to go into battle, kill him and come back: "I don't believe anyone could ever love me that much." And that one word had taken me off to war. Maria Cora now lives as a recluse, paying for a mass to be said for her husband's soul once a year on the anniversary of the Battle of Encruzilhada. I never saw her again, and, rather less painfully, I never again forgot to wind my watch.

THE TALE OF THE CABRIOLET

"THE CABRIOLET'S HERE, sir," said the slave who had been dispatched to the mother church of São José to summon the priest to give the last rites to not one but two individuals.

Today's generation witnessed neither the arrival nor the departure of the cabriolet in Rio de Janeiro. Nor will they know about the days when the cabriolet and the tilbury filled the role of carriage, public and private. The cabriolet did not last very long. The tilbury, which predates both, looks likely to last as long as the city does. When the city is dead and gone and the archaeologists arrive, they will find a skeletal tilbury waiting for its usual customer, complete with the skeletons of horse and driver. They will be just as patient as they are today, however much it rains, and more melancholy than ever, even if the sun shines, because they will combine both present-day melancholy with that of the spectral past. The archaeologist will doubtless have some strange things to say about the three skeletons. The cabriolet, on the other hand, had no history, and left only the tale I'm about to tell you.

"Two?" cried the sacristan.

"Yes, sir, two: Senhora Anunciada and Senhor Pedrinho. Poor Senhor Pedrinho! And Senhora Anunciada, poor lady!" said the slave, moaning and groaning and pacing up and down, quite distraught.

Anyone reading this with a darkly skeptical soul will inevitably ask if the slave was genuinely upset, or if he simply wanted to pique the curiosity of the priest and the sacristan. I'm of the view that anything is possible in this world and the next. I believe he was genuinely upset, but then again I don't *not* believe that he was also eager to tell some terrible tale. However, neither the priest nor the sacristan asked him any questions.

Not that the sacristan wasn't curious. Indeed, he was more than curious. He knew the whole parish by heart; he knew the names of all the devout ladies, knew about their lives and those of their husbands and parents, their talents and resources, what they ate, drank, said, their clothes and their qualities, the dowries of the unmarried girls, the behavior of the married women, the sad longings of the widows. He poked his nose into everything, and, in between, helped at mass and so on. His name was João das Mercês, a man in his forties, thin, of medium height, and with a sparse, graying beard.

"Which Pedrinho and Anunciada does he mean?" he wondered, as he accompanied the priest.

He was burning to know, but the presence of the priest made any questions impossible. The priest walked to the door of the church so silently and piously that he felt obliged to be equally silent and pious. And off they went. The cabriolet was waiting for them; the driver doffed his hat, and the neighbors and a few passersby knelt down as priest and sacristan climbed into the vehicle and headed off down Rua da Misericórdia. The slave hurried back on foot.

Donkeys and people wander the streets, clouds wander the sky, if there are any clouds, and thoughts wander people's minds, if those minds have thoughts. The sacristan's mind was filled with various thoughts, all of them rather confused. He was not thinking about Our Holy Father, although the sacristan knew how He should be worshipped, nor about the holy water and the hyssop he was carrying; nor was he thinking about the lateness of the hour—a quarter past eight at night—and, besides, the sky was clear and the moon was coming up. The cabriolet itself—which was new in the town, and had replaced, in this case, the chaise—even that did not occupy the whole of João das Mercês's mind, or only the part that was preoccupied with Senhor Pedrinho and Senhora Anunciada.

"They must be young people," the sacristan was thinking, "staying as guests in someone's house, because there are no empty houses to be had near the sea, and the number he gave us is Comendador Brito's house. Relatives, perhaps? But I've never heard any mention of relatives. They could be friends or possibly mere acquaintances. But in that case why would they send a cabriolet? Even the slave is new to the house; he must belong to one of the two people who are dying, or to both."

Such were João das Mercês's thoughts, although he didn't have much time to think. The cabriolet stopped outside a two-story house, which was indeed the house of the comendador, José Martins de Brito. There were already a few people waiting outside, holding candles. The priest and the sacristan stepped out of the cabriolet and went up the stairs, accompanied by the comendador. On the landing above, his wife kissed the priest's ring. Grown-ups, children, slaves, a murmur of voices, dim light, and the two people who were dying, each waiting in their respective rooms at the back.

Everything happened as it always does on such occasions, according to rules and customs. Senhor Pedrinho was absolved and anointed, as was Senhora Anunciada, and the priest left the house to return to the church with the sacristan. The latter just had time to ask the comendador discreetly if the two were relatives of his. No, they weren't, said Brito; they were friends of his nephew, who lived in Campinas; a terrible story. João de Mercês's wide eyes drank in those three words and said, without actually speaking, that they would return to hear the rest—perhaps that same night. All this happened very quickly, because the priest was already going down the stairs, and he had to follow.

The fashion for the cabriolet was so short-lived that this one probably never took another priest to administer the last rites to anyone else. All that remained was this brief, insubstantial tale, a mere bagatelle that I'll have finished in no time. Not that its substance or lack of it mattered to the sacristan, for whom it was another welcome slice of life. He had to help the priest put away the Communion wafers, take off his surplice, and do various other things, before they could say good night and go their separate ways. When he was finally able to get away, he walked along by the shore as far as the comendador's house.

On the way, he reviewed the comendador's life, before and after he had received that title. He began with his business—which was, I think, that of ship's supplier—then moved on to his family, the parties he had given, the various parish, commercial, and electoral posts he had held, and it was only a step or two from that to sundry rumors and anecdotes. João das Mercês's vast memory stored away every fact and incident, however large or small, so vividly that they might have happened yesterday, and so completely that not even the people involved could have recounted them in such detail. He knew these things as he knew the Our Father, that is, without having to think about the words—indeed, he would pray as if he were eating or chewing the prayer, which emerged unthinking from his mouth. If the rule was to say three dozen Our Fathers on the trot, João das Mercês would do so without even counting. So it was with other people's lives; he loved knowing about them, finding out about them, and memorizing them so that he would never again forget them.

Everyone in the parish loved him, because he never meddled or gossiped. With him it was a case of art for art's sake. Often it wasn't even necessary to ask any questions. José would tell him about Antônio's life and Antônio about José's life. What he did was ratify or rectify one version with the other, then compare their two versions with Sancho's, then Sancho's version with Martinho's and vice versa, and so on and on. This is how he filled his empty hours, of which there were many. Occasionally, while at mass, he found himself thinking about some tale he had heard the previous evening, and the first time this happened, he asked God's forgiveness, but immediately canceled this request when he realized that he had not missed a single word or gesture of the holy sacrament, so consubstantiate were they with him. The tale he had briefly relived was like a swallow flitting across a landscape. The landscape remains the same, and the water, if there is water, murmurs the same song. This comparison was of his own invention and was more fitting than he imagined, because the swallow, even when it's flying, is part of the landscape, and the tale was part of him as a person; it was one of the ways in which he lived his life.

By the time he had reached his destination, he had told every rosary bead of the comendador's life, and he entered the house with his right foot first for luck. He had decided that, despite the sadness of the occasion, he would stay there for some time, and luck was on his side. Brito was in the front room, talking to his wife, when he was told that João das Mercês was asking after the two people who had received the last rites. His wife withdrew, and the sacristan entered, apologizing profusely and saying that he would not stay long. He had just been passing and wondered if they had already gone up into heaven or were still in this world. He was, naturally, interested in anything that affected the comendador.

"No, they haven't died, and may yet live, although I think it highly unlikely that she will survive," said Brito.

"They both seemed to be in a very bad way."

"Oh, yes, especially her, because she's the worst affected by the fever. They fell ill here, in our house, soon after they arrived from Campinas a few days ago."

"So they were already here?" asked the sacristan, astonished that he had known nothing of their arrival.

"Yes, they arrived nearly two weeks ago. They came with my nephew Carlos, and caught the fever here—"

Brito suddenly broke off, or so it seemed to the sacristan, who adopted the expression of someone eager to know more. Brito, however, sat for a moment biting his lip and staring at the wall, and did not notice the expectant look on the sacristan's face, and so both sat on in silence. Brito ended up walking the length of the room, and João das Mercês thought to himself that there was clearly more to this than a mere fever. He wondered, at first, if perhaps the doctors had made a wrong diagnosis or prescribed the wrong medicine; or if there was some other concealed illness, which Brito was calling a fever in order to cover up the truth. He kept his eyes fixed on the comendador as he paced up and down the room, treading very softly so as not to disturb anyone else in the house. From within came the occasional faint murmur of conversation, a call, an order, a door opening or closing. None of this would have been of any importance to those with their minds on other things, but our sacristan had but one thought, to find out what he did not already know. At the very least, some information about the patients' family, their social position, whether they were married or single, some page from their lives; anything was better than nothing, however removed it was from his own little parish.

"Ah!" cried Brito, stopping his pacing.

There seemed to be in him a great desire to recount something, the "terrible story" he had mentioned to the sacristan shortly before, but the sacristan did not dare ask him and the comendador, not daring to tell the sacristan, resumed his pacing.

João das Mercês sat down. He knew that, in the circumstances, the polite thing would be to leave, proffering a few kind, hopeful, comforting words, and then to return the following day. He, however, preferred to sit and wait, and saw no sign of disapproval on the other man's face; indeed, the comendador stopped pacing for a moment and stood before him, uttering a weary sigh.

"Yes, it's a very sad business," said João das Mercês. "And they're good people, too, I imagine."

"They were going to be married."

"What, to each other?"

Brito nodded in a melancholy way, but there was still no sign of the promised terrible story, for which the sacristan continued to wait. It occurred to him that this was the first time he had heard about the lives of people unknown to him. All he had seen of these people, shortly before, were their faces, but his curiosity was no less intense for that. They were going to be married. Perhaps that *was* the terrible story; to have fallen mortally ill on the eve of a new life, that was terrible indeed. About to be wed and about to die.

Someone came to summon the comendador, and he excused himself so hurriedly that the sacristan had no time to take his leave. The comendador disappeared for about fifty minutes, at the end of which time the sacristan heard something like muffled sobbing coming from the next room. The comendador returned shortly afterward.

"What was I saying just now? That she, at least, would die. Well, she's dead."

Brito said this unemotionally, almost indifferently. He had not known the dead woman very long. The sobbing the sacristan had heard came from Brito's nephew from Campinas and a relative of the dead woman who lived here in Mata-porcos. It took only an instant for the sacristan to imagine that the comendador's nephew must have been in love with the dying man's bride, but this idea proved short-lived, for the nephew had, after all, traveled to Rio with both of them. Perhaps he was to have been the best man. As was only natural and polite, he asked the name of the dead woman. However, either because he preferred not to say or because his thoughts were elsewhere—or perhaps for both those reasons—the comendador did not give her name, nor that of her fiancé.

"They were to be married . . ."

"May God receive her and keep her safe, and him, too, if he should die," said the sacristan sadly.

And that was enough to draw forth half of the secret that seemed so eager to leave the comendador's lips. When João das Mercês saw the look in his eyes, the gesture with which he beckoned him over to the window, and the promise he exacted from him, he swore on the souls of all his loved ones that he would listen and say nothing. He was not a man to divulge other people's confidences, especially those of honorable persons of high rank like the comendador, who, satisfied with these assurances, finally plucked up the courage to tell him the first half of the secret, which was that the engaged couple, who had been brought up together, had come to Rio in order to get married, when that same relative from Mata-porcos had given them some dreadful news . . .

"Which was?" João das Mercês prompted, sensing some hesitation on the part of the comendador.

"That they were brother and sister."

"What do you mean? Blood relatives?"

"Yes, they had the same mother, but different fathers. Their relative did not explain in detail, but she swore this was the truth, and for a day or more, they were both in a state of shock . . ."

João das Mercês was no less shocked, but he nonetheless determined not to leave without hearing the rest of the story. He heard ten o'clock strike and was prepared to hear the clock chime throughout the night and to watch over the corpse of one or both, as long as he could add this page to his other parish pages, even though these people were not from the parish.

"So was that when they fell ill with the fever?"

Brito clenched his jaw as if he would say nothing more. However, when he was once again summoned, he hurried off and returned half an hour later, with the news of the second death, news to which the sacristan had already been alerted by the sound of weeping, quieter this time, although not unexpected, since there was no one from whom it needed to be concealed.

"The brother, or bridegroom, has just passed away too. May God forgive them! I'll tell you the whole story now, my friend. They loved each other so much that, a few days after learning of the natural and canonical impediment to their marriage, they decided that, since they were only half-siblings, they would elope, and they fled in a cabriolet. The alarm was given, and the cabriolet was stopped on its way to Cidade Nova. They, however, were so distraught and angry at being captured that they both fell ill with the fever from which they have now died."

It is impossible to describe the sacristan's feelings when he heard this tale. He managed, with some difficulty, to keep it to himself for a while. He found out the names of the couple from the obituary in the newspaper, and supplemented the details the comendador had given him with others. In the end, without feeling he was being indiscreet, he divulged the story—without naming names—to a friend, who told it to another, who told it to another, and so on and so forth. More than that, he got it into his head that the cabriolet in which the couple had attempted to elope could well have been the same one that had carried him and the priest to offer them the last rites; he went to the coach house, chatted to an employee, and discovered that it was indeed the same one, which is why this story is called "the tale of the cabriolet."

ABOUT THE AUTHOR

Joaquim Maria Machado de Assis was born in 1839. His paternal grandparents were mulattoes and freed slaves. His father, also a mulatto, was a painter and decorator, his mother a washerwoman, a white Portuguese immigrant from the Azores. His mother died of tuberculosis when Machado was only ten and he lived with his father and stepmother until he was seventeen, thereafter earning his own living, first as an apprentice typographer and proofreader, and, only two years later, as a writer and editor on the *Correio Mercantil*, an important newspaper of the day. By the time he was twenty-one, he was already a well-known figure in intellectual circles. During all this time he read voraciously in numerous languages, and between the ages of fifteen and thirty he wrote prolifically: poetry, plays, librettos, short stories, and newspaper columns. In 1867 he was decorated by the Emperor with the Order of the Rose, and subsequently appointed to a position in the Ministry of Agriculture, Commerce, and Public Works, where he served for over thirty years, until just three months before his death. Fortunately, this job left him ample time to write: nine novels, nine plays, over two hundred stories, five collections of poems, and more than six hundred *crônicas*, or newspaper columns. In 1897, he was unanimously elected the first president of the newly established Brazilian Academy of Letters. He was fortunate, too, in his marriage to Carolina Augusta Xavier de Novais, to whom he was married for thirty-five years. Following her death in 1904, at the age of seventy, Machado fell into a deep depression, and published only one more novel and a collection of stories dedicated to her. On his death in 1908, he was given a state funeral, and to this day is considered Brazil's greatest writer.

ABOUT THE TRANSLATORS

MARGARET JULL COSTA has been a literary translator for over thirty years and has translated works by novelists such as Eça de Queiroz, José Saramago, Javier Marías, and Bernardo Atxaga, as well as poets such as Sophia de Mello Breyner Andresen and Ana Luísa Amaral. ROBIN PATTERSON has translated works by José Luandino Vieira and José Luís Peixoto. Their co-translation of the Brazilian novelist Lúcio Cardoso's *Chronicle of the Murdered House* won the 2017 Best Translated Book Award.